Book Two
The Trifecta: Resurrection

Thank you to all of those who supported my first book,
The Trifecta: Initiation.

Many thanks go to my parents, who provided detailed feedback
and supported me throughout the writing process.

I must also thank the talented artist, Noel Bradac, for designing
such a creative book cover.

I0680457

The Trifecta: Resurrection

1. The End?

"Captain, reroute all power to the forward cannon," Mr. Infinity commanded. He stood at the back of a room filled with a dozen computers facing toward a large, virtual screen. Infinity's metallic, black battle suit shone under the bright overhead lights, and his dark blue shades projected a menacing determination through the room.

"Sir, if I do that, our shields won't be able to repel their advancing forces in the northeast quadrant," the captain responded. He pointed to the projected map on the giant screen ahead of him and drew a red circle around the horde of opposing forces.

"Just reroute the power and I'll take care of the rest," Mr. Infinity insisted before pressing his right hand to the communication link on the side of his shades. "Malix, we need your team on the far northeast corner. It looks like Mr. Mental and Fireball are amassing their forces close to that quadrant. Take Gold Star with you to help hold them off. Buy us a few minutes while we focus our firepower on their advancing militia."

"No problem," Malix responded. "I've been wanting my crack at Fireball."

"Good, we'll need at least five minutes," Mr. Infinity instructed and then turned to the commanding officer who stood behind him. "Colonel, launch five more blasts from the cannon to clear some space. I'm heading out onto the battle field. You're in charge of our forces from here on out."

"Sir, do you think it wise to engage them in battle so soon?" the colonel asked. "We need your strategical expertise here."

"Omega is preparing to emerge from behind their lines, and our forces won't last long against him. After you clear out that area in the northwest, I will engage the remaining enemies in combat. When that happens, reroute our power to the shields on the northeast side and direct Gold Star to join me. Malix should remain to solidify our fortifications there. Do you understand?"

"Yes sir," the colonel responded in compliance.

"Good luck to you, gentlemen," Mr. Infinity called out to the room before zipping out through the door at the back.

Out on the battlefield, the sun shone down while Mr. Infinity zoomed across the dusty African plains, dirt flying behind him in thick clouds. A group of enemy soldiers stood in a field of tall, brown grass where they fired their black, high-powered rifles at Mr. Infinity as his body dashed in a straight line a few feet above the ground. But they could not calculate and calibrate their shots to synchronize with Mr. Infinity's increasing velocity, so the bullets only cut through the dust trailing behind him. After slowing to a stop, Mr. Infinity lowered his black boots down to the ground and formed a navy blue laser bubble around his body.

The bullets continued flying, but all dissolved before they could make contact with Mr. Infinity. Half a dozen silver hover copters the size of school busses hung a few hundred feet overhead. On their sides, they had two rotating turbines keeping them afloat in the sky where their powerful Gatling guns unleashed a flurry of bullets down onto Mr. Infinity. His shield repelled the first few metal projectiles, but within seconds, the endless stream overwhelmed his barrier. A blaze of light flashed across the field as the bullets pinned Mr. Infinity into the ground. Yet such an ordinary attack could not keep him down for long. After pressing his legs hard against the dirt, he launched himself like a spring up into the sky.

The hover-copters realigned their rotating chambers to aim them at Mr. Infinity, but before they could unload another barrage of bullets, he dashed through the air, both his fists leading the way as he tore through the nearest hover copter. After piercing the heavy exterior armor, the aircraft exploded into a ball of fire, and before the other five flying vehicles could react, Mr. Infinity launched a flurry of thin laser beams into the churning rotors, sending the copters crashing into the Earth.

While he observed the nosediving aircraft exploding on the battle field, Mr. Infinity hovered up in the sky with his teeth clenched in anger. After a few moments of allowing the hatred to well inside his chest, he lowered his body back toward the ground. But the second his boots touched the dirt, another group of enemy soldiers fired their advanced rifles at him. With each bullet that bounced off of his impenetrable exterior shell, Mr. Infinity only grew more enraged. His jaw shook with anger before he unleashed his fury onto the overmatched group of soldiers. Like a bolt of lightning, he flashed across the hundred foot gap that separated him from his enemies. Then as he stood next to one man, Mr. Infinity delivered a right punch that sent the soldier flying at least fifty feet.

And in an instant, the berserk hero bolted back and forth among the group of soldiers to hit each of them with powerful punches that surely would end their lives. After immobilizing all but one of the foot soldiers, Mr. Infinity froze his body just a foot in front of his final adversary. The man's jaw trembled with fear, and he tried to blurt out a plea for mercy, but no sound emerged from his lips. Mr. Infinity struck him with a right uppercut that was so swift the man could not see the attack until after the impressive force shattered his jaw, launching his body up into the air. But before he could travel more than a foot, Mr. Infinity reached up with his left hand and gripped the man by his neck to slam him back down into the ground.

With the most immediate group of soldiers neutralized, Mr. Infinity began strolling across the battlefield while dozens of smaller battles took place around him. As he walked forward, he turned his head left and right in search of Omega. "I know you're close," Mr. Infinity called out over the chaotic gunfire and explosions that raged around him. "Show yourself, brother."

"I'm right here," Omega sneered from a cleared out area one hundred feet to the left of Mr. Infinity. He hovered two feet above the ground, fully clad in his most advanced armor. A thick silver and black metal covered his legs, arms and torso. Over his head, he wore a tight, black helmet that covered the back of his skull and the side of his cheeks, but the front of his face could be seen through a clear plasma visor. His tele-lens, mechanical eye protruded from the right side of his face with a menacing red glow that blazed over the battlefield.

"This is where it all ends," Mr. Infinity shouted over the sounds of war.

"This is not the end," Omega replied with an overconfident tone in his deep voice. "Only one question remains. Have you finally mustered up the courage to kill me?"

"Whatever it takes to stop your madness."

"Is that what you think of me, brother? That I am mad?" Omega lowered his feet down to the ground and took a few methodical steps forward, closing the gap between him and Mr. Infinity. "I pity you brother, I truly do. You are blind to the tyranny that surrounds you. We were designed with a purpose, and you have lost your way."

Mr. Infinity said nothing at first. He stared down Omega with a gaze of anger that transformed into sorrow. "I am sorry, brother. In my quest to save mankind, I failed to save you."

Omega shook his head as he whispered to himself, "You are such a fool." Then he boomed his body forward in less than a millisecond to deliver a right and left jab to Mr Infinity's face. Each blow resonated a crashing noise like the echo of a collapsing building, which overshadowed all other sounds of the battle around them. Mr. Infinity shot into the ground and skidded to a stop after sliding fifty feet. Four

Trifecta soldiers came to his aid, running up alongside his body where they kneeled down to fire their assault rifles at Omega. One of the men wielded a grenade launcher, which he unloaded onto the evil overlord.

But such weapons were merely a nuisance to Omega who sped through the air, deflecting their attacks with a black, retractable shield attached to his left forearm. He froze his body between two of the soldiers and reached out to his sides, grabbing each of them by their armored vests. After smashing the two men together, he flung them one hundred feet in opposite directions. The third soldier turned his rifle toward Omega, but before he could pull the trigger, the villain slapped the weapon from his hands. Then after lifting up his right foot and tucking his knee up against his chest, Omega stamped his heavy, metal boot into the soldier's sternum, launching him across the ground. The man's bones snapped in dozens of places as he rolled and tumbled to a stop.

All of these actions took place in less than two seconds, but this distraction supplied Mr. Infinity with just enough time to push himself back up to his feet. Only one soldier remained, the one wielding a grenade launcher. He pointed the barrel at Omega, who chuckled as he turned his red, mechanical eye toward the soldier. Before the fool could pull his weapon's trigger, Omega unleashed a wide-spread beam from his eye, which incinerated the soldier into dust.

At that same moment, Mr. Infinity threw a right hook that crashed into the left side of Omega's helmet. He followed that with a left uppercut, but Omega lowered both of his wrists to block the attack. In retaliation, the villain spun his body 360 degrees with a roundhouse kick that caught Mr. Infinity in the side. Although he braced himself for the impact, Mr. Infinity still felt his body hurled to his right. As he rolled across the earth, he managed to plant his boots and left hand in the ground, allowing his body to skid to a stop.

Then Omega flew forward, his fists leading the way in an attempt to spear his brother to the ground. But Mr. Infinity was ready for this attack. Just as Omega neared impact, Mr. Infinity used all the force in his legs to drive his whole body up, delivering a double uppercut to his foe. Omega's body flung out of control as he soared straight up toward the sky. Taking to the air, Mr. Infinity shot up after him, grabbing hold of Omega's flailing body. The two adversaries gripped each other by the arms while they both continued their ascension toward outer space. As the two mega-humans approached the end of earth's atmosphere, they each struggled to take control of the other's body. The air grew thin, but Omega's helmet provided him with his own supply of oxygen, and Mr. Infinity's limitless power allowed his body to adapt.

"This is it," Omega shouted over the howling air that whisked by them. "Your rage has finally consumed you. I can see you are ready to do what is necessary." His mechanical eye began glowing red and then erupted into a two inch thick laser beam driven by incredible force. Although Mr. Infinity turned his head left in an attempt to dodge the blast, Omega still hit him square in the cheek. The strength of the beam forced him to release his grip on Omega's armor. As the continuous ray of energy emanating from Omega's eye pushed Mr. Infinity toward the ground, the overconfident villain smirked from high up in the sky. Though he hovered fifty miles above the earth's surface, his mechanical eye allowed him to zoom in on Mr. Infinity's body crashing into the earth, launching chunks of dirt and rock all over the battlefield.

As Mr. Infinity shook his head, his face turned red from the rage exploding inside him. After Omega hyper-boomed himself back down to ground level, he proceeded to gloat over his brother. "Come now, I still know you have far more left in the tank. Show me what you can *really do*."

Levitating his body out from the bottom of the crater, Mr. Infinity charged the power core deep within his chest. The limitless energy began buzzing as a white glow protruded from between his pectorals, and his eyes blazed with a white hot fury that would have intimidated any other foe.

But for Omega, this fell right into his plan. "Yes, unleash your fury," he cackled. "I want to see you release your full power."

"As you wish," Mr. Infinity growled before beaming his body through the air to crash into Omega. He pinned the overlord to the ground and smashed his face with four rapid punches that left a crack in his helmet. And while these blows did jostle Omega's senses, he quickly regained his composure to block Mr. Infinity's fifth strike. Then after pressing the bottom of his boots into Mr. Infinity's chest, Omega kicked both of his feet up to launch the hero through the air like a catapulted boulder.

Mr. Infinity flailed at first, but rather than hitting the ground hard, his advanced reflexes helped him land safely on his feet. However, Omega already began slicing through the air, wasting no time to retaliate with a right hook to his enemy's left cheek, followed by a short, powerful eye beam into his chest. The intense force of the laser pushed Mr. Infinity back, but he stayed on his feet to launch two concussive laser blasts from his right fist. Deploying the black, metal shield on his left wrist, Omega deflected both beams.

Still, this allowed Mr. Infinity time to leap through the air, landing with a hammering elbow to top of Omega's skull. He followed up this attack by gripping Omega's neck with his left hand. After cocking back his right fist, he clenched his gloved fist into a powerful weapon. Yet before he could throw a right hook, Omega activated one of his armor's defenses which surged 10,000 volts of electricity over his suit. This shocked Mr. Infinity with enough energy to force his hand open, breaking his grip on Omega's neck.

"Ha, this is what I've been waiting for," Omega chuckled, wiping away a stream of crimson blood that ran down his chin.

"What do you mean?" Mr. Infinity questioned as he tried to shrug off the blue electricity that still surged through his body.

Omega smiled, showing his menacing teeth like a terrifying tyrannosaur. "There is so much that you fail to realize. I truly am sorry that I could not liberate you from Auto's control . . . But fret not. You will still serve a great purpose in the civilization of this world."

Narrowing his eyes, Mr. Infinity shouted back, "Not if I kill you here!" He lifted both fists out in front of his chest and launched two successive, blue laser blasts. They combined into one powerful force heading toward Omega, who fired back with a single wide laser from his mechanical eye. The two beams collided with each other, causing energy to spew off in all directions. High-powered blasts of energy rained over the battlefield, killing hundreds of soldiers from each side. But the main beams pressed against each other, each one pushing the other back and forth like a tug-of-war rope.

As thoughts of Omega's reign crept into Mr. Infinity's mind, his rage only increased. His blazing eyes grew even more intense with a white, flashing light. After the reverberating ball of energy in his chest grew to the size of a basketball, he unleashed his Infinity beam toward Omega. This increase in power generated enough force to push back Omega's laser stream, but just before the Infinity beam collided with Omega's chest—he smiled.

Mr. Infinity's decision to unleash the Infinity beam from within his core had played right into Omega's hand. His smirk grew as he released the dark energy within his own chest, launching his notorious Omega blast. When the two endless forces of energy collided, they generated an incredible white and black explosion that boomed over the battlefield and beyond.

The black energy snaked in all directions, like a scattered bolt of lightning, while the white energy spread in an evenly distributed arcing ray of light. Yet both the dark and light energy destroyed everything in their path, and as if they had a mind of their own, they each targeted human civilizations. The omnipotent forces razed through villages, farms, towns, and major cities all over the globe.

As the booming explosion reached a climax, the incredible surge of energy shattered Mr. Infinity and Omega's bodies. The all-powerful villain's human eye widened as a realization dawned upon him—his demise was imminent. But then a confident smirk crept up the right side of his cheek and he called out a final message to his brother. "This is not the end!"

Then both mega-humans exploded into a burst of energy particles, effectively ending the booming force that had spread across the Earth. As the energy dissipated, Omega's final words echoed over the battlefield and through the plains of Africa.

"This is not the end, this is not the end, this is not the end..."

16 years later...

Just at that moment, Michael's eyes opened, and he jumped up from his sleep with an inhaling gasp, as if he was emerging from the depths of the ocean. The 16 year old boy sat in the back of a large armored jeep, his heavy breathing struggling to return to normal from the nightmare he just endured. As his heart rate returned to a normal pace, the enormous vehicle slowed to a halt, and the driver shifted the transmission into park.

"Mr. Infiniti, we have arrived," the driver announced over his right shoulder.

"Thank you," Michael responded while he reached down to pull the door's lever on his right. After stepping out of the car, he retrieved his blue and black shades from his suit pocket and placed them over his eyes to protect them from the bright hot sun rays bearing down from the blue sky. His black dress shoes sank into the primitive, dirt road beneath his feet, and he headed across the African field toward his childhood village.

With each step he took, a ghostly voice echoed the same five words over and over. Michael stopped and perked up his ears to focus on the faint speech. His eyes widened into a trancelike state as he discerned the words, "This is not the end." Then his jaw jabbered up and down like a robot as he responded with five words of his own. "This is just the beginning," he mumbled. After speaking these words once, Michael shook his head to free his mind, and the ominous dream faded from his memory.

2. Missing Bodies

Michael

August 20th

As Michael approached his former village, he noticed a distinct difference in the air quality. Back in Hero City, the air was pure, but every breath was like inhaling fake, disinfected oxygen. And although the air here among the trees and wildlife wasn't nearly as perfect, Michael felt at home with each deep breath he inhaled. His childhood village may not have been as sterile as Hero City, but he preferred such a primitive environment. The surroundings seemed so much more—real.

A tall, dark-skinned man greeted Michael. "Welcome back my friend," he smiled. The hot African sun glared off of his smooth, bald head as he reached forward to grab Michael's hand. "We are glad you finally received our message." Michael's chest swelled with joy to see a familiar face from his African village. His good friend was thin, wearing faded blue basketball shorts with a ragged, red Chicago Bulls T-shirt.

"It's good to see you, Sefu," Michael proclaimed, pulling his friend in closer for a hug. Then Sefu backed up to view how much his friend had grown over the past eight months while he was away in Hero City. "I really wish I was allowed to return here and visit more often, but the rules of the Trifecta forbid me from leaving. It took almost three months to get here after you sent your message. Now, what's all this about an emergency? Your message sounded urgent."

"It's your brother Alex," Sefu explained. "Or rather his grave." He bit his lip, possibly because he was unsure how to elaborate or because he felt uncomfortable sharing this sensitive information.

"What about my brother?" Michael inquired, leaning in closer to Sefu, which seemed to make him even more uncomfortable.

"Perhaps you should see for yourself," Sefu responded. He waved for Michael to follow him toward Alex's burial place, so they both hurried down the brown path toward the gravestone markers. Michael walked faster than his friend, taking the lead halfway to the graveyard. When he entered through the fence on the outskirts, he picked up his walk to a full sprint. Down under the shade of the tree that marked his family gravesite, Michael found a five foot deep hole where his brother's body once resided.

He dropped down next to the opening in the ground and examined the empty casket inside. The box was rudimentary, made from some scrap wood and a few rusty nails, but nevertheless, the coffin was empty.

"Where is he?" Michael screamed to his friend. "What happened to him?"

Sefu stood a few feet behind Michael but did not respond. His answer would surely sound crazy, and although he and Michael were friends, he had no way of knowing what kind of person Michael turned into since joining the Trifecta. Even Michael's physical features proved that he had changed. The teen stood nearly three inches taller and twice as muscular, but most noticeable was the way he carried himself. Less than a year ago, he walked with a hunch and always wore a smile, yet now he dressed in a dark pinstripe suit and covered his bright blue eyes with a pair of black and blue shades that created an intimidating aura.

"Sefu, tell me what happened to my brother." Without thinking, Michael stood up from the ground, and using both hands, he grabbed his friend by the collar of his shirt.

"I—I—" Sefu began, but he grew too frightened to answer Michael's question. His eyes trembled up close to the alien sunglasses that sat on Michael's large, smushed nose. But after glancing at his hands that held a vice grip on Sefu's shirt, Michael's senses returned as if he was waking from a trance. He realized how terrifying he appeared, so he immediately released his hold.

"I'm sorry, Sefu," Michael apologized, backing up a few feet as he gazed upon his trembling friend. "I don't know what came over me. Please, just tell me what happened to Alex."

Sefu gulped hard. "I'm not sure, Michael. None of us are. About three months ago, there was a terrible storm, and a bright lightning bolt engulfed the sky before striking this very sight. There was a terrible explosion that frightened all of our people into their houses until the storm ended."

After moving closer to the empty grave, Sefu stood on his toes to peer over the edge. "And when we came out of our homes to survey the damage, your brother's grave was empty. The wooden box was the only trace left behind."

Michael rubbed his chin, ruminating over Sefu's story. "And how long ago did you say this happened?"

"About three months ago. That was when I sent the first message," Sefu answered. "The storm was rather sudden. There was no rain, just a swarm of clouds and the single blast of lightning, but it was an odd blast. The bolt was bright at first, but then darkened the surrounding area in a black fog."

Placing his hands on his hips, Michael stared at the gaping hole in the ground. He suspected where that storm and flash of darkness emanated from, but he didn't want to believe his suspicion. The timing matched up with his battle against Mr. All-American—the same battle where he released the full energy in his chest, allowing part of that energy to escape.

Michael feared that the negative force in his chest might have found his brother, and this story only strengthened his supposition. He had refused to believe his brother absorbed the dark power, yet he had no choice but to admit the possibility now. After Michael inched over to the hole in the ground, he stared down at the deteriorating box that had been ripped open from the inside.

"Well hello there, Michael," a woman's voice chirped from behind the tree to his left. Michael's head jerked up to find the villainous Mastermind smiling at him. "Or should I call you Mr. Infiniti?" Her tone and arrogant smirk were meant to mock Michael, but he didn't find her amusing. Sefu stumbled backwards, a terrified expression in his bulging eyes, before he turned toward the graveyard exit and raced back to the safety of his home.

"Mastermind," Michael announced, clenching his jaw at the beautiful villain. He recognized her from the virtual images in his data book. She was gorgeous with flowing brown hair that extended a few inches below her shoulders. Although she was only 5 foot 4, her black high-heeled boots added three inches to her height. Her tan skin was especially dark in her face that was partially hidden behind a large pair of black and silver sunglasses. They held enormous square lenses and a frame that wrapped around the back of her head like a pair of goggles. Much like Michael's, she had a smushed nose, but hers was smaller and shorter than his.

She wore a sleek, tight-fitting black top without sleeves, which accented the white trim on the side of her abdomen and the silver M on the chest. Mastermind's bronze arms were bare, save for the black gloves she wore that ended just below her elbows. Each glove possessed a virtual screen that functioned as a remote control for her innumerable inventions. And to protect her waist, she wore a thick silver belt lined with dozens of hanging compartments. Below the belt, she donned black armored shorts that covered her legs just below the thigh. Then hanging over her back, a black cape flowed with metallic trim on the perimeter and the same shiny M imprinted on her back.

"I'm flattered you recognize me," the villain chuckled in a sarcastic tone, placing her fingers on her chest. "After all, you are the most notorious hero in the Trifecta."

"And you're one of the most nefarious villains," Michael responded, taking one step toward Mastermind, his courage undaunted by her surprise appearance. Yet she remained unfazed by his aggressive move forward, keeping her powerful grin focused on his hostile face.

"Don't get so angry just yet," Mastermind ordered. "That will come later. And please, call me Kate." The flirtatious femme fatale took one diabolical step toward her enemy.

"Back off!" Michael shouted, raising both his fists up in front of his face to create a boxer pose. Each knuckle began glowing with a blue radiance as they prepared to strike.

"No need for that," Mastermind smirked, holding her palms out in front of her. "I'm not here to fight; I'm here to admire my handiwork."

Michael scrunched his nose and furrowed his eyebrows together. "What are you talking about?" he asked, unamused by Mastermind's nonchalant approach.

"I mean I have what you're looking for," she elaborated. "Your brother's body is mine, and soon I will possess his soul, as well. If you want him back, you will have to defeat me in a game of wits. An impossible task, I assure you, but that doesn't mean we both can't have a little fun along the way. Hmm, hmm, hmm," she laughed through her closed lips, which succeeded in enraging Michael.

"Or I'll just end this right here and take back my brother by force if I have to!" he screamed at Mastermind, who kept her cool, collected smirk in the face of her enemy. Raising his right first, Michael aimed his glowing hand at her chest.

"Your brother is mine to control. You wouldn't want him anymore anyway." Mastermind crossed her arms over her chest, clearly unafraid of Mr. Infiniti's threat.

But having endured enough playful banter with this witch, Michael fired two blue energy blasts from his right fist. The beams hissed through the air, but both dissipated when they came within two feet of Mastermind's resting arms. She uncrossed them to raise her right hand, aiming a clenched fist at Michael's chest before lifting her left pointer finger to press a button attached to the keypad on her glove. After two battery-sized rockets emerged from the joint on her wrist, they launched toward Michael. The tips of the projectiles sizzled with an orb-shaped electric current.

Although Michael lifted his left arm, igniting a rectangular blue energy shield to block the attack, the mini-missiles phased right through the forcefield and collided with his chest. Upon impact, the projectiles generated an electrical explosion that surged through Michael's body, forcing him to his knees. He fell onto his right side and clutched at the birthmark on his chest, which burned and sizzled beneath his skin.

"Poor baby," Mastermind gloated with her large lower lip pouting forward. She stepped closer and crouched down next to Michael, bringing her lips within an inch of his left ear. "Your feeble mind is no match for mine. And that's why you won't win this battle or this war." The brilliant villain rose back up from the ground where Michael tried to regain control of the violent shaking in his body. His eyeballs widened, and his face turned white, the skin in his cheeks pulling taut.

"I've studied you Michael," Mastermind elaborated. "I know all of your strengths better than you do, but more importantly, I am aware of every weakness you possess— weaknesses to which you are completely oblivious." She turned her back to Michael, her cape blowing behind her in the wind as she completed her final thought before leaving him alone to convulse on the ground. "And I know your single greatest weakness. Your heart will betray you, as it does for all those who draw their strength from such an insignificant organ. Me, I rely on my brain, but you—you are a slave to your heart and emotions—which will inevitably lead to your downfall."

Mastermind pressed two virtual buttons on the control pad that was attached to her left wrist. The first released Michael from the electrical charge running rampant through his body, and the second ignited her flight mode. The enormous sunglasses sitting atop her small nose expanded over her head into a full black helmet before releasing two compartments below each lens that covered her mouth and cheeks. Before Michael fully recovered from the effects of her missile attack, Mastermind's boots lit a spark beneath her feet, launching her up toward the bright blue sky.

The radiant villain faded into a small dot and disappeared among the bright sun shining down on Michael's defeated body. He gazed skyward, unsure what these events signified, but he knew one thing for sure—he was in for rough year against yet another formidable villain.

An hour later . . .

"You did well," Mastermind spoke to Sefu from the entrance of his hut. She stood leaning up against the doorless entryway, her flight helmet hiding the pleased expression in her smirk.

Sefu's jaw trembled up and down like a jackhammer, but he could not move. "Please, I did as you asked, now leave me and my people alone," he begged, clasping his hands together.

"You did my friend, you did," Mastermind responded as her helmet broke apart into multiple pieces, each one retracting into another before they all fully receded into her massive sunglasses. Removing the shades from her face, she revealed her mud brown eyes as she slipped into the room. "You contacted Mr. Infiniti for me and lured him out to the graveyard, just as I instructed."

"Yes, so please, I beg you to leave us alone. I will forever hate myself for betraying my friend. I would rather be dead, but my people . . ." Sefu's lips froze as he took two steps backwards with Mastermind moving right up alongside him, placing her cheek next to his vibrating jaw. Although he tried to speak again, his lips were too frightened to utter a single syllable.

"Oh, don't worry, I will leave you alone forever as I promised," Mastermind whispered into Sefu's ear. She brushed her right glove over the top of his bald head. "But the first rule of executing an ingenious plan is to never leave any loose ends. So—I will leave you alone—but I'm afraid I can't leave you alive."

Mastermind backed away from Sefu, who began foaming at the mouth from the tiny virus chip she planted in his brain. He dropped to the wooden floor, and his eyes rolled back into his head while his eyelids fluttered like the flashing light of a dying computer screen. As the evil villain turned away from Sefu, she cackled under her breath.

Less than three hours later . . .

Mastermind returned to the dark computer room of her scientific laboratory. Her heels clicked at a rapid methodical tempo, like the second hand on an old stop watch, as she walked up to the long crescent-shaped console at the base of her projected computer screen. With her right forefinger, Mastermind pressed down on two large green buttons that manipulated the 3-dimensional screen just a foot in front of her face.

"Is it done?" a shadowed figure asked from the black corner of the room.

"I took care of the issue, as instructed," Mastermind responded. "A waste of time if you ask me, but—"

"You are not in charge here," the figure interrupted her with a deep, commanding voice. "And you would do well to remember that. Infiniti is formidable, and in time he could destroy us both, but our plan will neutralize his power. However, this plan will only work if we keep him in the dark about his brother's true location. Understood?"

Biting her tongue as she scrunched her face, Mastermind responded in a begrudging tone, "Yes, I understand."

"Good, then continue forward with your part of phase three, and I will take care of the rest," the shadow instructed, his voice growing deeper and more villainous. "Remember, *we* dictate how things move forward from here on out," he reminded Mastermind before vanishing back into the shadows, leaving the villainous genius alone in her computer room.

Turning her attention back to the keypad and monitor in front of her, Mastermind mumbled to herself with a smile, "Things change."

3. In Fear of Mastermind

Michael

August 24th

"Hero number five-zero-zero-zero, also known as Mr. Infiniti, you called a meeting before the High Elders. Please state your business at this time." Auto's voice echoed through the deliberating chamber of the three Elders. Scylla stood to his right, and on his left was the newest member of the Trifecta Council, Professor Eliki. They promoted her to the third seat only a month after the death of Octavian. This appointment didn't sit well with Michael, who was well aware that Eliki placed no faith in him, and she made every effort to undermine his development during his first year of training.

"High Elders," Michael began. "I come to you to report on my recent trip back to my village in Africa." Scylla and Auto leaned in over their glass podiums, showing clear interest in what Michael had to say.

"And what did you find?" Scylla asked. He kept a grim look in his cheeks and mouth, but the red sunglasses he wore hid his emotion, so Michael couldn't estimate how the Elder would react to this story.

"As you know, I received a distress call from one of my long-time friends within the village, and after many denied requests, you approved my trip back to investigate," Michael elaborated.

"We did," Auto nodded. His dark suit with black shirt created a faint, nearly invisible silhouette on the black walls, but his white shades with blue lenses gleamed throughout the room. "What did you discover?"

"My friend Sefu informed me that my brother's body disappeared from his grave," Michael explained, acquiring the attention of all three elders. Even Eliki leaned in over her advanced podium to hear every detail of Michael's story.

"How?" Auto inquired, his eyebrows and forehead scrunching into a concerned V-shape. "Who would have robbed his grave?"

"Sefu told me that there was an irregular storm that produced a single dark bolt of lightning over the gravesite. And when the people came out to investigate, the grave was empty. I checked the hole and found his coffin was ripped open."

"Was that all?" Auto asked with a sense of urgency in his voice. "Were there any other clues?"

"None that I could discover," Michael answered. All three of the Elders knew that Michael possessed keen detective skills, so if he couldn't find any other pieces of evidence, none were likely to exist. "But the biggest clue came from the villain who attacked me."

The trio of Elders froze before leaning forward with intrigue at this last statement.

"What villain?" Scylla clamored over the edge of his podium.

"Mastermind," Michael blurted, but before he could continue, each Elder exploded into a frenzy. They bantered back and forth without pausing, so Michael couldn't get a word in edgewise, but after about a minute, Auto returned order to the proceedings.

"Silence!" he screamed. His booming voice echoed across the walls of the circular pit that Michael stood in, prompting the other two Elders to cease speaking, so he could inquire further into Michael's encounter.

"Are you sure it was Mastermind?" he asked.

"Yes, I recognized her from the data books, but she also told me she was Mastermind before we fought." After Scylla and Eliki leaned in close to Auto, they both whispered something into his ear, and he nodded in agreement with them before continuing his inquiry.

"What did she want?" he asked of Michael.

"I don't think she wanted anything," Michael answered. He inhaled a deep breath as he stared up at the three leaders who gazed through their shades in disbelief. "She seemed more like she wanted to gloat because she had my brother's body, and she boasted that he was under *her* control."

"Was anyone else there?" Eliki interrupted.

"I don't know. I think she was alone, but somehow, she knew so much about me." Michael squinted his eyes, unhappy with himself that he held so few answers in such a frustrating situation.

"It must be as we suspected," Auto remarked to Scylla. "She's got to have an accomplice working with her. What happened next?"

Before he continued his story, Michael paused to wonder what the Elders knew about Mastermind that they weren't telling him. They seemed to be holding back some important piece of information, but he would have to wait until after he finished his story to ruminate on this mystery.

"She hit me with some kind of scrambler missile that immobilized me, and then she took off. It was all so random and—"

"Nothing Mastermind does is random," Eliki interrupted. "Every move she makes has been calculated carefully and well in advance. If you knew anything about her, you would know that." The Elder may as well have kicked dirt on Michael when she finished her sentence, but he had grown used to Eliki's backhanded comments, so he paid no attention to her sardonic tone.

"Indeed," Auto added in agreement. He rubbed his chin, signaling thought. "Why would she reveal herself?" he mumbled before sharing a concerned stare with Scylla. They knew something that Eliki and Michael remained unaware of, but Michael could only guess at what they were withholding.

Tilting his head back down on Michael, Auto asked, "Did she say anything else?"

Michael paused and rolled his eyes up to think if he'd forgotten anything. He snapped his fingers as he recalled her words while he lay paralyzed on the ground. "She told me that she's been studying me, analyzing all of my strengths and weaknesses."

Furrowing their eyebrows to a point, Auto and Scylla glanced at each other with distress in their cheeks. Michael knew neither Elder feared many people in this world, but Mastermind was in a league of her own. Her intelligence threatened even the greatest heroes, and if she knew Mr. Infiniti's weaknesses, she could be more dangerous than they thought.

"How could she have discovered him?" Scylla asked Auto. "We've kept his existence as secret as possible."

"Mr. All-American," he answered. "His treachery lives on, even after his death. He must have forwarded on information and other intelligence that she used to analyze his abilities."

"Then we have a problem," Eliki jumped in. "I suggest we put the Infiniti Initiative on hold for the time being until we can locate and capture Mastermind." Eliki made this suggestion without regard for Michael, who listened silently while looking up at the Elders.

"Out of the question!" Auto erupted. "The Infiniti 2.0 project is too important to be derailed by Mastermind."

"You underestimate her," Eliki suggested with a grave tone in her voice. "A terrible error to make. I, of all people, know that Kate's intellect should be feared. If she has intelligence on Mr. Infiniti, she will destroy him."

"Perhaps that is what she wants from us," Scylla suggested. He rubbed his fingers over his chin as he further contemplated his own remark. "Revealing herself in public is quite unlike Mastermind. Most of her moves are made from within her hidden lair. It is possible she made this move with hopes that we would terminate the Infiniti Initiative."

"Very possible," Auto nodded in agreement. All three Elders grew quiet while he rubbed his thumb over the graying goatee on his chin to help him consider all aspects of Michael's story before rendering a decision.

"She said she has your brother's body?" Auto inquired of Michael.

"Yeah, she told me—" Michael started to elaborate, but Auto cut him off by raising his hand.

"Then our next move is simple . . . We must take the fight to her and retrieve him."

"Suicide!" Eliki erupted, her face turning bright red. "Mastermind's base is well-hidden, and I guarantee you well-protected. Any offensive assault would surely end badly for us, and although Mr. All-American's plot to topple our best heroes failed, he still successfully depleted many of our best forces."

"Hmmmm," Auto reflected, both of his hands clutching the glass podium in front of him. Michael stared hard at him, trying to identify what the High Elder was thinking. Most villains knew their forces were weak after Mr. All-American killed so many heroes in addition to unleashing a devastating robot on the city. And this left the Trifecta vulnerable until they could recruit and develop more operatives. Still, Mastermind was surely aware that their defenses were weak, and yet she chose not to attack.

"Something larger is happening beyond our gaze," Auto announced. "Mastermind knows that Mr. All-American has slain most of our heroes, and she had Michael at her mercy, but she still chooses to hide in the shadows and play mind games."

"She's planning something we cannot yet see," Eliki jumped in. "But what is she plotting? Michael, did she say anything else that might help us uncover her intentions?"

Exhaling, Michael thought about this for a moment, analyzing every aspect of his encounter with Mastermind. Her comment about his heart worried him most, but he didn't trust

Eliki, or even Auto, with that information. He needed to think through her words before he revealed them to the Elders.

"No," Michael lied. "I don't think so."

"Then we must seek out Mastermind before she can complete her plan," Auto proclaimed. "She will have prepared for all contingencies, so we might as well take control of the situation and bring the fight to her. We'll commission our best operatives to begin searching immediately." The other two Elders' foreheads scrunched at the brow, their minds perturbed by his announcement, but they had to agree.

"That is unless there's something you're not telling us?" Auto asked Michael.

"No, there's nothing else," Michael lied again, for his keen observation skills had noticed something that Sefu neglected to realize. The coffin that contained Alex's body was pried open from the inside. Whether Mastermind really did have Michael's brother or not, Alex was almost certainly alive somewhere, and Michael feared that his resurrection might result in disastrous consequences.

4. Freedom

Michael

August 25th

"Have you deciphered all of the information within the data reel we obtained?" the dark, shadowed figure asked Mastermind from the entrance of her computer room. She sat at her master console, busy using an ion laser-cutter to manipulate the circuitry within a cube-shaped metal piece of technology. The cutter looked like a thick pen with a marble-sized energy ball at the pointed end, and every time Mastermind pressed a red button on the side, the ball of energy flashed a bright light across the room. While she continued working, she answered the shadow's question.

"Most of the information is ours, but there are still parts of the reel that I have been unable to interpret. The minds that designed the firewall did a brilliant job. Fret not though, for I have the first piece we need."

The shadow's eyes lit up in a green radiance when he heard this last piece of information. "How long before you can make ready the device?" he asked.

As the laser-cutter stopped sizzling, Mastermind rotated her chair 180 degrees to face the dark figure while she held the baseball-sized cube in her gloved hands. "I just finished the device now," she explained, prompting the shadow to inch forward from the dark entrance of her laboratory. But after he took one step, Mastermind tossed the cube at him, and he caught the smooth edges with the tips of his hidden fingers. "That will get you through the city's perimeter forcefield and beyond, but it will only work one time. Have you already prepared the invasion fleet for the extraction?" Mastermind questioned.

"We are ready to go," the shadow responded. "I shall lead the forces myself while you drop off the package." With that last statement, the shadow fled back through the doorway, disappearing into the blackness.

Mastermind turned her attention back to the computer screen. "Hmm hmm hmm," she chuckled to herself before tapping one of the virtual buttons on the touch screen of her console. The glowing projection screen above her flashed the words: "Extraction of information from data reel 100 percent completed."

"Soon the tables will turn," Mastermind smirked. "Very soon."

"Michael! Over here," Allison shouted from across the cafeteria. She stood on the tips of her toes while waving her hand like a searchlight to grab Michael's attention. As he strolled down the empty aisle between the tables, he hoped his friends might cheer him up and clear his mind.

"Hey, you can settle this debate for us," Archer proclaimed while Michael pulled out a chair and sat down. He forced the muscles in his face into a smile, hoping to disguise the heavy information that weighed on him. Sabrina and Max Force also sat at the table, each hero dressed in weekend casual clothes—a tight-fitting blue shirt with the Trifecta's three triangle logo on the chest and a pair of black pants covering the legs. Michael walked to the dining hall straight from his meeting with the Elders, so he hadn't changed out of his formal, pinstripe suit, yet the group of Blue team members were so captured in their conversation that none of them made mention of his clothes.

"And what debate might that be?" Michael asked.

"We're trying to decide which of the enforcers in the Four Faces of Evil was the most powerful," Archer explained, pushing himself up from the table. His tight, blue dri-fit shirt also had the Trifecta's three triangle logo inscribed on the chest. "I say it was Fireball because he could produce a flame hotter than the sun, but Sabrina and Allison disagree."

"We realize that Mr. Mental is more powerful," Sabrina interrupted. "Archer just doesn't appreciate the power of the human brain. Mr. Mental could command large armies against their will, and he could control some of the most powerful heroes in the Trifecta."

"But he wasn't powerful enough to control Fireball, which is why he would burn if the two came up against each other in battle."

"No, Mr. Mental could take control of an entire army and send them to destroy Fireball while he hid somewhere safe," Allison argued, her face growing red from excitement. With each exclaimed syllable, she threw her hands in front of her.

"You're all just going in circles," Max jumped in. He remained neutral in most of the spats between the three students. Their arguments always seemed to end up with Sabrina and Allison teaming up against Archer while Michael and Max tried to stay out of the middle.

"So what do you think Michael?" Archer asked, trying to calm his pounding chest. "Who was Omega's most powerful enforcer?"

"Light-bender," Michael answered without a moment's hesitation. This was a matter he gave much consideration to in the past when he was learning everything he could about Omega's origin and personality.

"Light-bender!" Archer yelled so loud that some of the nearby tables gave him even more annoyed glances than usual. The boy right behind him was tightening his grip on his fork in an attempt to curb his urge to stand up and tell the whole group to shut up. But the truth of the matter was most students, regardless of year, feared Michael, so they didn't dare upset him or his friends. Michael's victory over Mr. All-American solidified him as a threatening power, which made some heroes worry what would happen if he turned against them.

"How could you choose Light-bender?!" Archer shouted even louder. "He was the only one of the three enforcers who died in the Big Boom, not to mention his powers don't even register on the same scale as Fireball or Mr. Mental."

Although Michael was well aware of this, he read in the restricted archives that Omega made Light-bender his right-hand man, which is why he was the enforcer whom Omega trusted most with his diabolical plans. Mr. Mental's intellect was great, but Omega never fully trusted him with his plots. And no way would Omega have chosen a weak second in command, which led Michael to assume that Light-bender was far more powerful than most people realized.

"I just have a hunch that he was more powerful than you think," Michael responded. "And we don't know that he was killed in the Big Boom. We just know that he was never found, so he could be the only villain who escaped the blast. He can move at the speed of light, after all."

Crossing his arms over his chest, Michael rested his point, but his friends couldn't let the discussion go, just like every other debate they brought up. Michael found some of their arguments amusing, especially since he always avoided taking one side. Ignoring Michael's logic, Archer burst back in with Sabrina and Allison, ripping them to shreds over their claims and evidence.

Despite Michael's desire to observe the spectacle further, his stomach was growling like an angry wolf, so he excused himself for a moment and headed to the buffet table. He hadn't eaten or slept well since his battle with Mr. All-American. Something about that day changed the very fiber of his being, but he couldn't determine exactly how he was different.

After piling three protein pills and two half-inch slices of chicken onto his plate, Michael reached over a tray to scoop up some bio-enhanced mashed potatoes when a light whisper caught his attention. "Michael," the voice hissed into his ear like a slithering snake. Michael's head jumped up, searching the area for the origin of the voice. "Michael, you have grown." The teen whipped his head from left to right but couldn't find the source. "You have grown more than even I anticipated, but now is the time for more."

Then the voice faded away. Michael looked to the people sitting at the dining tables, searching for some prankster who was having a laugh at his expense. Yet nobody else seemed to notice the mysterious voice. Moving his eyes back and forth, Michael looked up to the rafters overhead, but Solar Flare interrupted his scan of the room.

"What are you looking at?" the bully jeered, sticking his face a few inches from Michael's.

He found a twisted pleasure in constantly badgering Michael, especially since the great Mr. Infiniti triumphed over Mr. All-American. Meanwhile, this pompous classmate's ill-devised quips grew on Michael's nerves more and more each day. "None of your business," Michael snapped back. "Now get out of my face," he commanded.

Milton took a step backward, surprised by Michael's aggravated reaction. After almost a year of crafting insults designed to dig under Michael's skin, Milton finally saw the first sign that his attempts were working. But after Michael lashed out at him, Milton's face turned pale, even more surprised to find that he didn't like the beast he had unleashed.

Refocusing his glower, Milton attempted to respond to Michael's outburst, but before he could, an alarm sounded over the PA system. "Alert, prison break attempt in progress. All first and second-year students, return to your dormitories immediately. All other heroes report to the detention cells for battle. Alert . . ." And then the message repeated.

Michael looked up to the speaker hanging from the corner of the ceiling as the announcement blared in Melvin's monotone voice. Turning from the table, Michael sprinted toward the main entrance while dozens of other heroes scrambled for the back exit. Archer and crew watched Michael dash toward danger and started to follow, but Professor Hawk intervened and corralled all of them to head back to the dorms.

In the meantime, Michael burst through the main doors before his boots skidded to a stop on the street. He pulled his shades from the inside pocket of his suit coat and placed them over his eyes to help in assessing the situation. "Melvin, pull up a map of the penitentiary building and give the best known path for travel," Michael ordered.

A virtual, 3-dimensional model, showing an overhead view of the city, projected before his eyes with a blinking light that indicated the point of attack on the Cell Tower. The map inked a red line, marking the quickest way for Michael to take flight and reach the breach of the city's jail. Without a moment's hesitation, he pushed his feet off the ground and launched through the air. As he zoomed over the city streets, his suit coat and tie flapped in the wind like a waving flag. With no time to return to his dorm to pick up his combat clothes, Michael's current threads would have to suffice for this battle.

In less than a minute, he arrived at the building's outer wall and observed a gaping hole in the east side of the stone exterior. A few dozen feet to the right of the hole, a helicopter was sitting with the blades still rotating in anticipation of the escaping prisoners. Dozens of soldiers, carrying high-powered rifles, surrounded the chopper. The men were protected by a purple laser that projected over their heads in a design to shield the helicopter against any form of attack. After surveying the situation, Michael landed on the street next to a group of roughly 30 heroes who stood outside the jail's perimeter walls while Eliki devised a plan for foiling this escape attempt.

"Mr. Fleming, this is not a mission that calls for second-year students!" Eliki shouted to Michael as he jogged into the middle of the group. "Go back to your dormitory, immediately!" she ordered.

"No way, you need—" Michael began to protest.

"We don't need anything from you here," Eliki interrupted. "As one of the High Elders, I am ordering you to return to your room or face expulsion." Michael felt like a child scolded by his mother as Eliki pointed back in the direction of the dorm buildings, emphasizing her authority over him. He scrunched his nose and tightened his eyebrows at her, but ultimately, Michael knew his place, so he acquiesced to her command.

Eliki began shouting orders to her troops while Michael floated his body up into the air and sauntered his way back toward his room. He was in much less of a hurry to retreat back toward the dorms than he was to arrive at the jail. But before he traveled three blocks, a voice whispered to him over the earpiece in his shades.

"Stop!" Michael heard. "Go back and apprehend the villains. You must prevent them from escaping."

Michael turned his head, searching the area for the entity that controlled this voice. "Who are you?" Michael asked. For nearly a year he was haunted by this ominous stalker, and yet he had no clue who was guiding him.

"Go back!" the voice commanded again.

"Not unless you tell me who you are," Michael yelled up to the sky. He twisted his head from left to right but received no answer. Before he could demand the voice respond, a loud explosion erupted from the jail, and a short, horrible screeching squeal pulsed through the air with a shrieking wail designed to overwhelm and immobilize the minds of Eliki's forces.

Michael's sunglasses flashed a warning that read, "Professor Eliki and her accompanying forces immobilized by temporary paralysis. No other members in pursuit." He realized he had to go back, even if that meant disobeying a direct order from Eliki.

Smoke rose from the penitentiary building, and Michael's sunglasses zoomed in to observe the group of heroes lying unconscious on the ground. All of the Trifecta's immediate forces were down except for him, and Michael felt there was something extraordinarily dangerous about this jail break, like someone of supreme significance was trying to escape. He would either have to chance going in alone or risk leaving the city vulnerable to an irreversible attack.

"Hurry!" the mysterious voice commanded. Although Michael disliked taking orders from this unknown source, he had no choice but to obey, so he dashed through the air toward the Cell Tower's breached hole.

The paralyzing wail dissipated, allowing Michael to approach the getaway copter. A group of eight soldiers, dressed in black SWAT suits and large, glaring helmets, met Michael with resistance as he landed next to the helicopter's protective bubble. Each man aimed and fired his heavy assault rifle at Mr. Infiniti, attempting to rip right through him with an overwhelming number of bullets.

But Michael had other plans. He lifted his left forearm in front of his body to form a rectangular, blue energy shield that blocked the incoming attack. Each bullet dissolved against the blue light like an ice cube against a raging fire. All eight soldiers held the trigger down on their guns until they emptied the clips. The last bullet fired and disintegrated against Michael's energy shield, leaving the soldiers open to attack.

Mr. Infiniti's black dress shoes pushed off the ground, and he hovered in the air with his hands pulled up against his chest, elbows pointed to the sides. Then he flung his hands out in front of him and over his head into a Y-shape, like a gymnast landing a full dismount, releasing eight blasts of blue light from his open palms. The energy cut through the air, knocking over the defenseless soldiers like plastic army men. They each hit the ground with a thud, their minds unconscious from the stunning blow, which allowed Michael to lower his feet down toward the crumbling hole in the wall without opposition.

As he hovered down, Michael used his shades to analyze the powerful properties of the purple, protective shield over the copter. He could have tried to disable the vehicle, but he had no time to test his powers against the advanced technology. So instead he chose to rush into the building to stop the attacking soldiers before they could liberate too many captive villains.

Dashing down toward the hole, Michael plunged through the entrance. On the other side, he entered a long hallway lined with heavy cell doors. Each one was labeled with a number and a different name over the door's frame. But none of these cells appeared damaged in the least, nor could Michael find any sign of escape in this section, so he began sprinting down the hallway as fast as he could. When he arrived at a T-intersection he turned right, but his face froze in shock as he viewed two notorious villains heading straight for him.

Five minutes earlier . . .

"This is it," the dark shadow proclaimed. His identity remained shielded by the black cloak he draped himself in and the ominous shroud of darkness that consumed his entire body.

"The portal that traps Fireball and Mr. Mental," a soldier dressed in a black and white suit of armor, murmured with a smile. His head was shielded by a thick, metal helmet that extended six inches in front of his face where the long snout came to a sharp point. He carried a long silver axe in his left hand while he placed his right hand close to the red energy field that shielded the metal doorway in front of him.

The two villains stood in the center of the Cell Tower. They prepared to enter a gateway at the end of a long hallway that was lined with a dozen other doors. But this particular doorway was different from all of the others. The red energy glowing on the surface emanated a radiation unlike any force the soldier had ever encountered. "A marvel of science. How do you plan to breach the portal's gateway?" he asked.

The shadow lifted up the box he received from Mastermind and answered, "With this." After placing the cube up against the glowing door, a black energy beam escaped from a penny-sized cannon on the front.

The soldier backed away from the dark energy that began sucking all the life force from the room, but the shadow stood fearless. Within 10 seconds the box tore open a hole in the energy field to reveal a solid metal doorway. Mastermind had succeeded in doing what nobody else could. She breached the vortex that trapped Fireball and Mr. Mental, two of the most dangerous villains ever, in another dimension.

Even if the two super criminals did discover a way to escape their cleverly designed prison cells, they would have found themselves trapped within this alternate dimension with nothing but food, water, and a few maintenance bots. Travel through the portal was so dangerous that the Elders only used this prison as a last resort for predators as powerful as the Four Faces of Evil.

"Incredible," the soldier blurted, his mouth hanging wide open. "I never fathomed a device could breach the portal designed by the Trifecta scientists."

"Exactly why you are but a soldier in our army, Titanon," the shadow replied. "You lack vision and imagination." The box emitted a last bit of dark energy, and the man lowered the cube back down within the shroud of darkness around him. "Now open the door," he ordered.

Titanon rested his axe against the wall so he could place both of his black gloves up against the door before vibrating his hands from left to right as if they were experiencing a violent seizure. The door shook as well until the entire metal structure collapsed from the welded hinges—hinges that the Trifecta never intended to work again after the Elders had sealed the entryway shut. A darkness loomed from within the other dimension, causing Titanon to back away from the entrance, but the shadowed figure passed through without hesitation.

"Come along, Titanon," he ordered. "Our time is limited." After he entered the room, a light beamed through the hallway, leading Titanon to follow his commander. On the other side of the portal, they traveled down another gray hallway just like the ones in the main jail. At the far end, stood three ten foot tall doors, two of which were labeled Fireball and Mr. Mental. The shadow hovered forward without pausing, but Titanon crept behind, his chin shaking as he searched for any sign of a trap.

The pair of villains reached the two labeled doorways, and the shadow pointed to the left one, followed by the right. Titanon rushed forward to place his gloves against the left door that jailed Fireball, and his hands vibrated again until he pushed over the heavy piece of metal in front of him. Initially, the inside was dark, but then a bright glow illuminated the room, revealing a spherical glass tank filled with water. In the center of the tank, Fireball floated like an astronaut in space, but his dazed eyes widened when he recognized the shadow who had arrived to liberate him.

Titanon started moving forward, but the shadow blocked him with his left hand. "The other door," he reminded his soldier. After backing up, Titanon curved around his leader to break down the door that imprisoned Mr. Mental. Once the gate had fallen, the shadow signaled for Titanon to help Fireball out of the glass case while he entered the dark room to rescue Mr. Mental.

Upon his entry, the small prison cell lit up to reveal Mr. Mental who sat hunched over in a metal chair. The immobilized villain was dressed in a tight, black T-shirt and similarly tight shorts that reached down to his knees. On his head, a silver helmet sizzled with an electric current. "You've served your last day," the shadow announced to the captured criminal. Mr. Mental attempted to lift his head, but the helmet scrambled his brainwaves, preventing him from thinking even enough to move his forehead from side to side. He was like a sick boy with a strong case of the flu, yet he still mustered enough strength to smirk at the sight of his savior.

The shadow sidled up to the incapacitated villain who fought to lift his head. His lips moved slightly like a wiggling worm, but he failed to utter a single syllable. "Rest easy," the shadow instructed, placing his clouded hands over the shackles that pinned Mr. Mental's wrists against the arm rests. A loud reverberating buzz hummed through the room for a second, and when the cloaked man removed his hands, the restraints were broken. The brain wave disruptor was next, but simply removing the helmet could do irreparable damage to Mr. Mental's mind, so the shadowed man pulled out the metal cube one last time. Placing the box up against the helmet, he watched as the cranial restraint cracked in half before falling to the concrete floor.

"Free!" Mr. Mental coughed as if he was gasping for air after nearly drowning. "Thank you."

"Don't thank me yet," the shadow suggested, throwing a pair of red shades and a small data drive on the floor. "I can't be found here, so you and Fireball are on your own getting back to the escape copter. Your powers will take considerable time to fully return, but the drive attached to those shades has all the information you will need. Outside, a boom copter will take you to the necessary destination. Titanon will assist in your escape. Understand?"

Mr. Mental kneeled on the floor with his right fist propped against the cement while he nodded his head in confirmation. The brain wave disruptor helmet sapped all of his strength, so he would need ample time to fully recover, which would only make his escape that much more difficult. When he looked back up from the floor, the shadow had disappeared, and Titanon was helping Fireball into the room.

"We've got to get out of here," he instructed, easing Fireball down to the floor for a moment. "The Trifecta's forces are only momentarily incapacitated. Hurry, you must rise." Fireball pushed himself up from the floor and stood firm in his spot, staring down on Mr. Mental with his hand extended to help up his comrade.

The mental giant's legs were weak, yet somehow he found his bearings, took hold of Fireball's palm, and lifted himself from the ground. Titanon glanced over his left shoulder to check for Trifecta troops who could barge through the door at any moment. "Please, we must go now!" he insisted.

"Fret not, weakling," Mr. Mental jeered. "My mind is recovering, and I can sense only one other entity entering the building. Fireball and I will take care of him."

As Fireball snapped his fingers, he ignited a red flame in each of his palms. He opened his fingers and then made a fist three successive times, like he was revving an engine, the flame burning higher with each release. "Yes, I feel my powers returning, still not at full force, but I think we can handle whatever lackey they've dispatched."

"Then let's get going," Mr. Mental suggested. The two villains led the way back down the hall toward the portal's opening. On the other side, they found dozens of Titanon's soldiers waiting to escort them to the boom copter. As they walked, Mr. Mental placed the shades over his eyes to scan the information on the data drive. He felt a rush of knowledge returning to his mind, including the best plan for escaping the prison and city before the Trifecta could stop them.

They drew closer to the building's opening, but Mr. Mental's eyes flashed yellow as he sensed Mr. Infiniti approaching. Pausing for a moment, he raised his hands to stop the rest of the group before announcing, "Someone's coming."

"No problem. We'll barbecue him," Fireball smirked, fueling the flames in his palms as his powers continued recovering.

This was the moment when Michael turned the corner to find the two powerful enemies staring him down like a pair of lions licking their chops before devouring their meal. Titanon stood behind them, cowering at the sight of Mr. Infiniti while his loyal soldiers surrounded him to form a human shield of protection.

"Stop right there!" Michael ordered, wishing he had some backup to help fight against these two jackals. Mr. Mental and Fireball looked at Michael like he was a small child whose antics annoyed them, and they both chuckled a bit before Fireball responded.

"Apparently you don't know who we are," he laughed. "You must be new here. I am Fireball and this is Mr. Mental. We are the most powerful villains on this planet, capable of crushing any hero who opposes us. So what should we call you when we're laughing about your death later today?" Fireball asked, ending his query with a mocking cackle. His overconfident smile showed his amusement with the single hero sent to oppose him and Mr. Mental.

"Hmmm," Mr. Mental grinned, staring in wonder at the hero standing before him. "I know who you are—Mr. Infiniti." His grin grew as he analyzed Michael's mind and cross-checked his identity with the information he downloaded from the data drive in his shades.

"It's not possible," Fireball doubted, taking one step toward Michael before freezing in his place. There were only two beings on the planet whom he feared, and the original Mr. Infinity was one of them. "He was destroyed in the Big Boom. It can't be him."

"I've read his mind," Mr. Mental explained. "This being is different, but it seems he is a new version of the hero we once battled."

Taking a step backward, Fireball suggested, "Let's find another way. Let the soldiers fight him while we escape."

"Ha," Mr. Mental laughed in a calm tone while rubbing his palms together like a praying mantis. "No, I think I'll go right out the front."

"Are you crazy?" Fireball gnashed his teeth at Mr. Mental, grabbing and pulling his arm the opposite way down the hall. "Come on brother. We are still weak with little chance of winning this battle. We should retreat while we can."

Mr. Mental unhooked his arm from Fireball's grip and walked toward Michael like a confident conqueror. "Upon reading your mind, I confirmed that you have many of the same traits as the Mr. Infinity that we knew, but I also realize your mind is young and far more feeble than your predecessor." As Mr. Mental strode forward, Michael tried to engage him in battle but found he could not move.

Mr. Mental leaned in just an inch from Michael's ear to whisper, "I can control you." Michael felt his arm trembling as his palm reached forward to shake hands with his foe. "Ha," Mr. Mental chortled. "How delightful. I always dreamed of commanding Mr. Infinity's mind. I guess this is the next best thing."

"Are you sure you can maintain the control over him?" Fireball questioned.

"No doubt," Mr. Mental answered, nodding his head, a huge grin pulling on his cheeks. "Michael here will lead our exit party, and he'll make sure none of his friends get in our way. Just think how they'll regret sending him to oppose us when he leads our escape."

After turning toward the blown hole in the outer wall, Michael led the group of villains toward their ride. Mr. Mental sent him out first to make sure the coast was clear. The purple energy shield still protected the copter, but many of the incapacitated heroes regained consciousness and stood ready to fight. At least 100 new heroes joined them, all led by Eliki who lifted her body above the group surrounding the bubble that shielded the copter. Her face transformed to both shock and anger at the sight of Michael emerging from the building's opening, but her jaw dropped another inch when she observed Mr. Mental and Fireball following behind him.

"Freeze!" Eliki screamed down to them. Mr. Mental glanced up at her and smiled, fully aware that despite being on Eliki's home turf, he had the advantage in this battle. Mr. Infiniti's powers remained under his control, and Eliki couldn't risk harming the Trifecta's greatest weapon.

"Go," he commanded Michael, forcing his puppet up in the air to confront Eliki. While Mr. Infiniti engaged the Trifecta heroes in battle, Mr. Mental jogged toward the boom copter with Titanon following right behind him. But Fireball disagreed with their decision to run.

"Why retreat now?" he asked. "We have control of *their* most powerful weapon in the heart of *their* city. We should take advantage of this now."

"There is more to this game than you know, brother. We must regroup with our other forces. This spat is only a blip on the radar of our Master's ultimate plan. Get in the chopper, so we can escape this place before the Elders send more reinforcements." Fireball disliked retreating while in a position of advantage, but he understood he had no choice but to follow Mr. Mental's directions. He pouted, stomping his feet as he marched over to the helicopter and hopped in. The remaining ten soldiers followed right behind him while Mr. Mental wiped clean the minds of those soldiers they were leaving behind.

As he sat down to rest in the belly of their escape vehicle, Mr. Mental spoke, "Trust me brother, we will soon have the victory we've desired for so long." And Fireball believed him, for the glare in Mr. Mental's eyes and the tone in his voice seemed so sure that this time things would be different. Something on that data drive gave Mr. Mental the confidence that the world would be theirs. But Fireball could not know how right his brother was.

5. Nightmares Never End

Michael

August 30th

"Who do you think you are?" a bright computer screen asked.

Michael stood in front of an enormous, wall-sized console, the screen's glaring light shining down on his sunglasses. The entire rest of the room was dark, like an endless void that surrounded Mr. Infiniti. He glanced down to analyze his gloved hands, wondering how he ended up in his battle suit. "Where are we?" Michael asked.

"Who do you think you are?" the computer repeated, his lifeless tone echoing across the darkness and back to Michael's ears. As he widened his eyes behind his shades, Michael's mind recognized this voice as the one that guided and commanded him through his previous year of training.

"Who are you?" Michael asked.

"No!" the computer echoed back, the light flashing brighter than before. "Who do you think *you* are?"

Michael didn't understand the question, but this was the third time the computer asked, so he attempted an answer. "I'm Michael Fleming, a boy—"

"No!" the computer interrupted. "That is not who you are. Who are you, *really*?"

This question further confused Michael. Something about the ominous computer didn't add up. Over the past year, the mysterious voice pushed him forward, but Michael never took enough time to question where that voice was guiding him. So Michael decided to approach this query with the response he thought the computer wanted. "My name is Mr. Infiniti."

"Yes," the computer's voice echoed through the blackness, light flashing with each syllable he uttered. "You must embrace your new identity if you are going to become truly limitless."

"What do you mean?" Michael inquired.

"For Mr. Infiniti to grow, Michael must die," the computer explained.

After taking one step backward, Michael dropped his jaw. This statement shocked him yet filled in many of the missing pieces to the puzzle—pieces he couldn't seem to uncover before. All this time, he followed the directions from this mysterious entity while failing to question the path he was following, but now he knew. The computer was replacing him for some diabolical reason. "Is that what you've been doing this past year?" Michael asked. "Trying to erase who I am?"

"Yes," the computer responded. "And the process is moving closer to completion. Your power will change the world. And once you unlock all of your potential, you will release an omnipotent force that you cannot yet comprehend. You have been my pawn, and very soon you will realize your destiny. Ahahaha." The computer screen flashed in and out as the monotone voice cackled.

Michael squinted his eyes and opened his mouth, unsure how to interpret this assertion. "I'm not your pawn!" he screamed at the computer, attempting to reach out and attack the radiant screen that continued cackling. But the rectangular light faded away like a car driving off into the distance, which left Michael in a state of darkness.

After what seemed like ages, the black, surrounding cloud finally dissipated, and Michael discovered he was lying in a bed, his entire body covered by sweat. "You're okay," a familiar voice assured him. "It was all just a dream." Molly stood next to the hovering hospital bed, squeezing Michael's right wrist in her hand to help free him from his nightmare. Her white teeth gleamed, and her calming blue eyes brought Michael back to reality. He sat in an advanced care room with two visitor chairs, a virtual television screen on the far wall, and a hanging blue light that beamed down over his forehead.

"What happened?" Michael asked, patting down his chest to make sure he wasn't still dreaming. A tight pair of blue Trifecta pajamas stuck to his skin from the moisture of his perspiration.

"You've been here almost five days," Molly explained. "Mr. Mental's mind control has long-lasting poisonous effects on his victims' minds. Most people usually take 5-15 days to recover from his mental venom. It's actually astounding that you recuperated so quickly."

"So that was Mr. Mental," Michael murmured. His chest pumped in and out, trying to regain a regular breathing pattern after enduring such a horrible nightmare. "I thought I recognized him. Then Fireball escaped with him?"

Molly closed her eyes and nodded her head. "I'm afraid so. Both were never supposed to see the light of day again, and now we're faced with the greatest world-wide threat in years."

Michael sighed, closing his eyes for a second. He felt partially responsible for their escape. Not only did he fail to apprehend them, but he actually helped them. "How did they break out of their prison?"

"Titanon, a tricky scientist, was with them when they left, but all of our camera and defense systems within the tower were disabled. We believe Mastermind was behind the breakout. Titanon is a brilliant inventor, but he's not capable of devising such a well-crafted plan. Plus, last year Mastermind stole a piece of technology and top secret information, which we believe allowed her forces to penetrate the dimensional barrier that had Mr. Mental and Fireball trapped."

"Did I hurt anyone?" Michael asked, a panicked squeak in his inquiry.

"No, Eliki stopped you before you could do any real damage. She's okay, but I wouldn't expect any high praise from her any time soon."

Great, Michael thought. Eliki already disliked him before, and now that she was on the High Elder Council, she seemed to like him even less. He figured almost killing her wouldn't help that relationship.

For at least a minute, Michael said nothing until Molly broke the silence. "What were you dreaming about before you woke up?" she inquired.

Scrunching his eyes to think back to his nightmare, Michael had to work hard to recall the events. The details were faint, but he did remember the computer and the last words spoken to him. Night terrors were now a regular occurrence for Michael, but this one stood out to him. He knew the ominous computer was important, as if all of the mysteries surrounding the voice would be answered if he could dissect and interpret the meaning of this one dream.

"I don't fully remember," Michael answered, afraid to reveal any details until he analyzed the significance. "But I do know that it was a nightmare."

Molly exhaled her disappointment through her nostrils. She must have noticed that Michael was wary of divulging any information to her, which had to be disconcerting after she came clean with him last year. "Well if you remember anything, let me know," she requested, trying to keep her voice in a positive tone. "Classes are starting back up soon, so I'll be seeing more of you, right?"

Michael's face blushed, and his eyes glanced down at his chest. "Yeah," he responded with a slightly boyish giggle in his answer.

"Well I should get going," Molly sighed. "I have to assist the new history professor with his preparation for the first day." Michael released a long breath, disappointed that Molly was leaving him so soon. "Besides, there's someone else here to see you."

"Who?" Michael asked, leaning up in his bed.

"You'll see," Molly smiled, turning toward the recovery room's door. She pushed open the entryway and Stone stepped in. A dark scowl formed in his dark blue eyes and stern chin. Molly shot him a conspicuous glare before exiting the room, leaving the two men alone.

"It's been a while," Stone grumbled. This was true. Although Stone remained Michael's mentor for one more year, the two hadn't had a one-on-one conversation since they both faced Mr. All-American and stared death in the eye. Michael hoped that experience would bring him closer to his mentor, but Stone only seemed to grow more distant.

"Yeah, I tried to get in touch with you a few times," Michael began, but he didn't know how to finish his sentence. Stone purposely avoided any contact with Michael, yet the young teen didn't dare point this out to his icy mentor.

"I know, but I've been out of the city for the past few weeks on business," Stone explained, removing his hands from behind his back. "That's why I wasn't here for the jail break." Michael wondered what Stone was up to out in the world. The Trifecta kept first and second-year trainees hidden away in their little bubble of a community, so Michael could only speculate what their members did outside of Hero City.

"Michael, I have some questions to ask of you," Stone announced, his deep graveled voice echoing through the room. He dropped his stern frown and still eyebrows for a concerned gaze in his eyes, which now turned completely black like those of a shark. Michael never saw him show any emotion before. *Perhaps our confrontation with Mr. All-American did strengthen our relationship*, he considered. However, even after all of his triumphs and growth, Michael still felt immense intimidation in the presence of Stone.

"What happened between you and Mastermind in that African field?" Stone asked. Michael's forehead scrunched together into a puzzled expression. Nobody knew about his encounter with Mastermind except for the Elders. Which begged the question—*how did Stone know?*

"What do you mean?" Michael replied, trying to play dumb with a calm tone. But Stone wasn't buying his coy routine, and he wasn't one to beat around the bush.

"You know exactly what I mean," he grunted. "Your brother's body is missing, a fact that worries and intrigues me." Leaning in over the bed, Stone placed his snorting nose just three inches from Michael's face. "So tell me exactly what happened out there."

Stone's proximity to Michael elevated his intimidation, causing more reluctance in Michael to divulge any crucial information. Worried that he might reveal something he kept hidden from the Elders, Michael rolled his eyes up in an attempt to search his extensive memory. While Stone exhaled another snort, like a bull preparing to charge a matador, his patience grew thin, so Michael started from the beginning, describing every detail that he remembered having given to the Elders.

As Michael explained his confrontation with Mastermind, Stone's countenance remained rock solid, hiding his thoughts and opinions. About five minutes into the story, Stone did finally ease back from Michael's personal space, and he eventually rested his heavy body in one of the room's two wooden chairs, which creaked from his weight. After almost 10 minutes of explanation, Michael finished his story with the pain he felt while Mastermind flew off into the distance.

Stone stayed silent, staring straight ahead through Michael. The young hero wondered what his mentor was thinking, but he didn't dare interrupt the brute's thought process. For at least two minutes, the two sat noiseless before Stone asked, "She's been studying you?"

"Yeah, that's what she said." Michael took a deep gulp, worried what Stone's next question would be.

"And this is all you told the Elders?" Stone stared into Michael's blue eyes, glaring straight into his soul. As Michael nodded in response, he felt uneasy about lying to both the

Elders and his mentor. "So you didn't mention what you noticed about the coffin, then?"

At this statement, Michael's eyes sprang open like a revealing curtain as he realized Stone already knew what he had omitted from his story. *But how?* Michael pondered. His mind raced for an appropriate response; however, he came up empty. Sitting in his frozen state, Stone knew he had forced Michael's mind into a panic.

"There's no use playing games with me," the brute interrupted Michael's thought. "I examined the gravesite myself, and I know that you kept something from the Elders—something that they didn't notice—but I'm willing to bet that you did."

"It was pried open from inside," Michael admitted, glancing down to the ground on the right side of his bed. "The coffin, I mean."

Nodding in confirmation, Stone agreed with his assessment. "The indentation marks on the inside of the coffin door revealed this, a minute clue that any other mind would overlook." Michael was surprised that Stone noticed such a detail that all others had missed. Perhaps he was more intelligent than he let on . . . Or perhaps he was working with someone else. Either way, Michael needed to proceed with caution. Mastermind found her research on Michael from somewhere, and despite their new levels of trust, Michael wasn't ready to rule out Stone just yet. As much as he wanted to fully trust his mentor, he still held a small shred of doubt and mistrust in the back of his mind.

After Stone's arms pushed his body up from his seat, he moved to the side of Michael's bed. "Take this," he instructed, handing Michael a round quarter-sized piece of metal technology. "A gift from one of my colleagues. It's a beacon you can use to contact me. If you press your thumb against the top, it will directly connect you to me, bypassing Melvin's watchful eye."

As Michael rubbed his fingers around the edges of the circular disk, he asked, "Why would you want to avoid Melvin?"

Stone leaned in two inches closer to Michael, scrunching his statue-like forehead as he analyzed Michael's face. "Unfortunately, I can't give you all of the answers. There are some things that you have to learn for yourself." The powerful giant exhaled, huffing through his nose. "But you can find comfort knowing that you have friends who will be watching over you. Should you need our help, press the button on the disk for instant contact with me."

Looking down to the silvery device in his hands, Michael wondered who Stone's accomplices were. But when he glanced back up from his thought, Stone had disappeared. For a giant bruiser, he moved with slippery stealth.

While rubbing his forefinger back and forth around the edge of the button, Michael realized whatever his feelings were toward Stone, this small gesture created a stronger bond of trust with his mentor. And Michael's impending battle with Mastermind made allies a necessity for him as he prepared to weather the coming storm. Still, one question did concern Michael—*how did Stone notice such a tiny detail in Alex's coffin?* This was a mystery he would need to uncover if he was going to find his brother's missing body and outwit Mastermind.

6. Homecoming

Mr. Mental

September 1st

"Welcome back to the the Four Faces," Mastermind announced as she walked in from an electronic sliding doorway. Mr. Mental and Fireball sat next to each other on the opposite side of a 25-foot wide circular, glass table. Titanon rested in his own black chair near the door, and while Mastermind stopped next to her lackey, she did not take the open seat next to him.

Both Mr. Mental and Fireball squinted at her with investigative eyes. After six days in a recuperation chamber, they each changed into their formal business suits, the first change of clothes since their incarceration 16 years earlier. Fireball wore a dark black suit with a goldenrod colored tie hanging over a white collared shirt. But Mr. Mental's threads were slightly more elaborate as he donned a black suit with white pinstripes and a dark red tie over a black dress shirt with matching red pinstripes.

"I wasn't aware we had a new member," Mr. Mental commented. His right cheek tensed, forming a superior smirk while he talked.

"So you still don't want me in your little club," Mastermind laughed. "Well forget the fact that it was my efforts which saved you from that dismal prison where you were caged for the last 16 years. You *should* be in my debt, but that is superseded by the orders of your Master."

Mr. Mental and Fireball both sat up, widening their eyes when they heard her say this. "He has spoken to you?" Fireball inquired.

Now Mastermind formed a smirk of her own. "I thought that might interest you. Our shadowy associate and I have been working without rest for the past six years to resurrect him from his grave—and now we are closer than ever."

Fireball's wide eyes looked to Mr. Mental for answers while the super genius placed his forefinger and thumb against his chin, his mind searching through his thoughts. Among the two of them, Mr. Mental provided the brains and Fireball supplied the brawn. "So he put *you* in charge, then?" Mr. Mental questioned in a skeptical tone.

"In a manner of speaking, yes," Mastermind responded. She placed the palms of her black gloves on the table and leaned in toward the two villains. "Is that surprising to you?"

Mr. Mental snickered under his breath. "Not at all. I just wanted all of the facts before analyzing the situation. I'm sure a mind of near-equal intelligence would understand that." This last statement was an obvious jab at Mastermind, but she didn't bite.

"Clearly," she smiled at him. "Titanon here can show you to your quarters when you are ready. In your rooms, you will find the data files to bring you up to date on our future plan. With your added abilities, our organization will be formidable, but the Trifecta still poses a threat. We must work together to achieve our ultimate goal." After finishing her last statement, Mastermind turned back toward the sliding door, her dark cape flinging through the air. Titanon followed right behind her like a loyal servant. After the door closed, he stood by the entrance and waited for the two villains to follow him. Lifting his left hand, he motioned for Fireball and Mr. Mental to proceed with him, but they ignored his gesture.

Instead, Fireball leaned in close to Mr. Mental to whisper something into his ear. "Are you really going to let this scab call the shots?"

"Fear not, brother. She only thinks she is in charge. Do you really think our Master would relinquish control to let her lead the way?"

"But how can you be so sure that—"

Mr. Mental held up his hand and extended his palm. "I am always sure. Do not doubt my analysis. Remember the data drive that I downloaded into my shades during our escape?"

"Yes."

"Well that drive gave me innumerable pieces of information that showed me the future. Our Master's plan will bring all of our desires to fruition, but Kate shall not be a part of that conquest."

"Then what's our next move?" Fireball asked.

"In order to get what we want most, we follow her orders—for now." Mr. Mental grinned, a yellow glow of confidence blazing from deep within his irises. After pushing back his chair, he removed a pair of red shades with a single, wide lens from his jacket pocket. After flipping the intimidating sunglasses over his eyes, he headed toward the sliding door. Fireball walked behind, his scrunched forehead still slightly confused, but questioning Mr. Mental was senseless. He had no choice but to place his trust in the hands of his brother.

Meanwhile, a multitude of data projected through the lens on Mr. Mental's shades, his brain scanning through all of the information. "Hmmm hmmm hmm," he chuckled to himself. "Mr. Infiniti will never see it coming."

7. Power

Michael

September 6th

A week passed after Michael woke from his coma, and the first day of classes finally arrived. He grew eager to start year two of his training after he already developed so much in just half a year. But what haunted him was he actually agreed with the computer in his dream—he needed to grow more. His encounters with Mastermind and Mr. Mental revealed how vulnerable he actually was, pulling him back to reality. Embracing his identity as Mr. Infiniti might be the only way to expand his powers—but he wasn't quite ready to let go of his past.

"Welcome back to Combat and Weaponry class," Professor Malix announced to the lecture hall of 30 students. They all sat in their seats, anxious to discover what they would learn in year two. Archer and Allison sat to the right of Michael in the middle of the third row, but Sabrina arrived extra early to reserve herself a spot up front. Per Professor Malix's instructions, all students came prepared for battle, each boy or girl dressed in armored gear. Michael's blue and white battle suit felt heavy, his cape sticking between his seat and the golden, armored shorts that covered his thick upper legs. Archer's right arm held his helmet up against his ribcage, but Allison already placed the blue headdress over her hair, and she activated the two yellow, retractible goggle lenses down over her eyes.

"Now that you've completed your first year, I believe we're ready for a new challenge," Malix proclaimed. "I'd like to introduce the latest development from our technology department." He double-tapped the screen on his control book, which activated a sliding door behind him, revealing a human-shaped robot. "These are the new enforcers of justice. With Mr. Mental on the loose, the Elders figured this was the best time to reveal and begin testing our new line of robots. Robo-one, activate! Authorization code zero-zero-two-eight."

The robot's blank white eyes lit up with a yellow glow, and his shoulders sprang upright. Even though his exterior was comprised of a hyper-dense metal, the flexible white hue gave the appearance of human flesh. The torso was angled to form a V with broad shoulders that narrowed down to a thin waist. Although the legs were thick, their surface curved like the muscles of a human. Yet the face appeared as the most shockingly human feature of this automaton. While the eyes glowed yellow, they also had pupils and irises. Two metal ears protruded a few inches below the top of the skull, and a long pointed nose stuck out from between his circular, rotating eyes. As he spoke to his creator, his mechanical jaw jabbered up and down. "Greetings Professor Malix, how may I be of service?"

"Robo-one, say hello to our class of students," Malix instructed.

The robot raised his right hand, showing his five realistic fingers. "Greetings students, I am here to assist in your education." The movements of the robotic limbs and face were incredibly life-like, far different than any of the other rudimentary mechanical men that the Trifecta already used for practice.

"Some of you have bested our virtual drones, but these robots are designed to analyze your strengths and weaknesses and then exploit them. This will force you to adapt by enhancing your best abilities while also learning to overcome your deficiencies." The students looked on with a glistening awe in the whites of their eyes. "Now, who would like to test Robo-one on the battlefield first?" Malix looked out to the group of students with an eager smile, but nobody seemed anxious to jump at the chance to have their butts whooped by a mindless robot. "Anybody?" Malix asked, raising his eyebrows in hopes that someone might volunteer.

Allison elbowed Michael in the ribs with her left arm, but his confidence was shaken after Mr. Mental tossed him around like a puppet. Perhaps Michael allowed his ego to swell too far after defeating Mr. All-American. In any case, Mr. Mental's intellect effectively humbled the great Mr. Infiniti.

"I'll take him," Solar Flare announced, raising his right hand up above his shoulder. Although he showed less confidence since the rise of Mr. Infiniti, he remained determined to show up Michael any chance he had. And with Michael's reluctance to step forward, Milton couldn't pass up this chance to prove himself on day one of his second year.

"Excellent," Professor Malix muttered, only half sincere in his statement. Although Solar Flare was powerful, and he would make a suitable test subject in this experiment, he wasn't Mr. Infiniti. "Then let's go," Malix instructed as he headed for the back exit that led to one of the smaller virtual combat rooms. The robot followed right behind the professor, his yellow glowing eyes flashing in anticipation of imminent battle.

As the students filed down the hall in one large pack, each whispered his or her excitement and anticipation for the skirmish between Solar Flare and Robo-one. Milton's small posse surrounded him like a human shield, keeping the other students out of his way. Metal Man pushed open the door for him, and they all followed behind their leader into the training room. Then Solar Flare cruised forward like a boxer entering an crowd-filled arena.

Some of the most prominent heroes, including Stone and a few of the other professors, were standing in the observation platform that hovered over the virtual battlefield like skybox seats in a football stadium. They gazed down upon Mr. Infiniti, but they must have noticed he was not the intended fighter. Michael's eyes looked up, his shades magnifying in on

Stone, who was standing alone. This disappointed Michael because he hoped to spot Stone with his accomplice.

Stone glared down with a scowl to show his disappointment, as did most of the spectators when they saw Solar Flare was set to fight, rather than Mr. Infiniti. Michael recognized Eliki a few yards to the left of Stone, but he couldn't discern if Auto or Scylla were there to observe. The Elders rarely ever supervised classes. Typically only professors or scientists doing research and analysis occupied the observation platform, but today the room was mostly filled from window to window. Michael deduced that they hoped for this skirmish to do more than just test the new robotics system. They wanted to see how the robots would stand up against someone of Mr. Infiniti's power and magnitude. No wonder why Malix seemed so disappointed when Milton volunteered over him.

The virtual battlefield's adaptive molecules transformed into a small city block with half a dozen 2-3 story buildings and one intersection, but the rest of the area faded into a plain white background—the default setting for when the simulator wasn't in use. Malix instructed the other students to head up to a nearby brick building and take notes while he talked with Solar Flare to prepare him for battle against Robo-one. After pushing himself off the ground, Michael hovered up to the top of the three story building while most of the other students, who were non-fliers, entered through the ground floor, making their way up the virtual stairway to watch from the roof.

As Michael focused his gaze on Solar Flare, he intensified his hearing while zooming in with his shades. "Remember my instructions. Are you ready?" Malix inquired of the cocky second-year student. Solar Flare nodded back without a word, a glowing confidence hovering over his body.

"Okay, then here we go," Professor Malix grinned before instructing the robot to initiate his battle circuits. "Robo-one, activate combat skills level two and engage Mr. Krueger in battle," he ordered and then retreated to the roof of the virtual building where his students waited for him.

"Acknowledged," the robot responded as his docile eyes transformed into a menacing red and yellow that shone like the blazing flames of the sun. After Solar Flare snapped the fingers of his right hand, igniting a teardrop-sized flame, he extended his arm and pointed his palm skyward to expand the fire to the size of a baseball. The robot stood still, his glowing eyes analyzing his opponent.

Like a warrior preparing to charge his opponent, Solar Flare cried across the battlefield, "Let's go!" He pulled the fireball behind his head and heaved his whole body forward like a pitcher whipping a fastball. The flaming projectile burned through the air and burst into an impressive explosion when the flame crashed into Robo-one's chest. Solar Flare twisted his right palm, as if he was turning a dial, to manipulate the growing flame that surrounded the robotic prototype.

"Ha, this is your new secret weapon?" Milton laughed, lifting both of his hands over his head to expand the fire into a flaming storm that swirled around Robo-one like a red and yellow tornado. "Pathetic."

But much to his chagrin, the tides of this battle changed with the wind that began swirling alongside the spiraling stream of fire. Solar Flare's pupils widened upon seeing the robot stroll out of the flaming wall without so much as a scratch in the metalloid exterior.

"As I said, Robo-one is designed to analyze and exploit your strengths and weaknesses," Professor Malix shouted over the crackling flames. "His vacuum-powered center is one of the dozens of features engineered for a variety of purposes." All of Solar Flare's firepower was useless against a strong gust of wind. His abilities depended on the movement of air, and with Robo-one in control of the oxygen surrounding him, he could easily repel the fiery attacks.

Solar Flare's eyebrows tightened, growing worried for only a second, but then he transformed his cheeks into a determined glower. Tensing his fingers, he collected more oxygen from the surrounding area, building the dense ball of fire that surrounded Robo-one. As Solar Flare's eyes winced, his head shook from the strain of maintaining so many heavy embers, yet his efforts paid off. As the flames grew, the robot's whirlwind defense started to break from the overpowering heat.

While emitting a blazing red flame, Solar Flare's eyes propelled his rage and power. After opening his palms wide, he pulled both hands back to his pectorals before launching them forward like a slingshot. This last-ditch effort blasted one enormous ball of fire through the wind barrier, knocking Robo-one off his feet. Before his mechanical arms could push himself back up from the ground, Solar Flare landed on top of him, punching the white robotic face with a blazing right fist. He grabbed Robo-one's left shoulder to pin him down against the virtual street while he beat the dazed robot into a senseless stupor.

Professor Malix leaned in closer to the action, intrigued by Solar Flare's surprising resistance. Having personally helped in designing the combat program that ran Robo-one's defenses, he looked surprised to find Solar Flare could possibly win this bout.

With one more intense punch, Solar Flare smashed in the metal exterior of Robo-one's thin face, shattering the reinforced glass in his left eye. The mechanized gears in the robot's joints stopped moving, and his body fell limp.

"That's enough," Professor Malix called out to Solar Flare, but the red rage in Milton's heart took control. He dropped his fist two more times, smashing a deeper dent into Robo-one's dome-shaped skull. "I said that's enough," Professor Malix called again, jogging out to restrain Solar Flare before he could permanently destroy their precious prototype.

Every student's wide eyes stared in awe at the impressive power Solar Flare displayed. Malix gripped his arm, pulling him off of Robo-one, whose face sizzled with white and blue sparks like a flickering firework. Michael was particularly shocked by Milton's increase in strength. Although he established himself as one of the best heroes in their class, Milton never wielded such incredible physical and pyro-kinetic power before.

Turning to the awestruck group of students who stood atop the adjacent building, Solar Flare pointed his right hand to the crushed robot. "Rule number one of battle," he cried across the street. "Never underestimate your opponent. This is the best the Trifecta can muster, yet their fancy weapon can't even go one round against my power." Solar Flare glared at Malix, who was leaning over his defeated drone. Then Milton shifted his gaze back to Michael's bewildered face. "You all underestimate me!" Solar Flare shouted. After he turned his back and began walking toward the battlefield exit, he muttered under his breath, "That's your biggest mistake."

As Michael watched Solar Flare strut his way down the virtual street, he could have sworn that something was different about his rival. A new, strange aura surrounded him, and while Michael couldn't pinpoint exactly what was different, he intended to find out.

8. Recruitment

Mr. Mental

September 12th

Deep in the recesses of Mastermind's lair, she sat at the base of her enormous computer monitor, rocking back and forth in her chair as her eyes scanned and analyzed a dozen split screens displaying the schematics for a new weapon. As the gears turned in her mind, a message popped up at the bottom of the main monitor:

The robot failed in combat. His advanced adaptation design worked, but his assailant overpowered him. Solar Flare defeated the prototype. We may have overlooked his strength in our bid to recruit him. Mr. Infiniti did not fight.

As she read this, Mr. Mental approached her from behind, his silent steps providing the stealth he needed to catch a glance at the message before Mastermind closed the report from her source.

"My dear Kate, you have been busy at work during our exile, haven't you?" he commented.

Mastermind powered down the screen, dimming the light behind her as she swiveled her chair around to face Mr. Mental. "Well someone had to do something while you slumbered," she sneered.

Widening his eyes, Mr. Mental clenched his teeth as he growled, "Let me assure you, there was nothing pleasurable about that 'slumber.' Now let's get down to business."

"Yes, I figured it wouldn't be long before you came asking me for help." Mastermind leaned back in her black chair, spreading her fingers against each other in front of her chest. "So what is it that you need?"

Mr. Mental rolled out a malleable piece of metal on the table to his left. He pressed a button that projected virtual schematics for four different pieces of technology. "These are the items that I require if you want me to uphold my part of our bargain."

Mastermind perused the items' descriptions, scrutinizing every possible reason Mr. Mental might want such seemingly useless pieces of technology. Individually, each item held insignificant capabilities, but thanks to the data drive Mr. Mental received during his escape, he knew what all four pieces could do when combined. His design would augment the technological powers of any technopath, and just as he anticipated, Mastermind could not predict what he planned to do with such a device.

"Very well," she affirmed, nodding her head up and down. "I will order Titanon to begin searching for these items, and he will procure them by November. In the meantime, I have work for you to do. Head to the meeting room in five minutes. I'll be along shortly." She swirled around in her chair and returned to the work on her computer.

"As you wish," Mr. Mental responded. While he exited Mastermind's computer room, a smirk slipped up his right cheek. His confidence swelled, having now confirmed his belief that Mastermind remained oblivious to the coming force that would destroy her.

Just over five minutes later, Mastermind strolled in through the glass sliding door to her meeting hall where Fireball and Mr. Mental sat waiting for her. "Gentlemen, now that you've had some time to recover, I trust you've caught up on the information I laid out for you in the data files," she smiled, standing behind the enormous glass table in the center of the room. Titanon remained behind her left shoulder, his gaze fixed straight ahead like a soldier at attention.

"Indeed we have," Mr. Mental answered.

"Then I take it you understand that many things have changed since your incarceration?" Mastermind questioned. Her smug eyes stared down past her lifted nose with a sense of supremacy. Both villains valued knowledge above all else, and Mastermind finally had an edge on the once superior Mr. Mental.

"The more things change, the more they stay the same," Mr. Mental commented, unfazed by Mastermind's egotistic tone. "How much of the data reel have you deciphered?" he inquired, though he was certain he already knew the answer.

"I am still working," she lied, her brown eyes scrutinizing Mr. Mental's naked, red irises as if she was attempting to see through his exterior and into his soul.

"I could help you," Mr. Mental offered, making a deliberate effort not to give away his true thoughts or intentions.

"Thanks, but no thanks. My mind is more than capable of deciphering the full data reel."

"Of that I have no doubt," Mr. Mental smiled. "Tell me Kate, is there something you're not sharing with us?"

"Why whatever do you mean?" she replied coyly, placing her hands on her hips. Fireball sat between the two mental giants, his eyes bouncing back and forth like a ping pong ball as they played a mind game he couldn't comprehend. Mr. Mental grew more and more suspicious of Mastermind's true motives, and she seemed well aware of this. Still, both villains appeared perfectly confident that they could outwit the other. Only time would tell which mind would come out on top.

"The time has come for you to get to work," Mastermind announced, tapping her finger twice on the glass table in front of her.

"And what kind of work would you have us do?" Fireball asked in an insolent tone, showing how annoyed he was to have to follow such an inferior super human.

"Recruiting," Mastermind answered. She placed her fingertips on the table's surface and rotated her wrist counterclockwise. "The Trifecta has rebuilt its forces over the past 16 years, but they've exhausted all of their resources. We, on the other hand, still have many allies hiding in the shadows, waiting for the resurgence of the Four Faces. I need you to hunt them down and renew their allegiance to us."

"So who did you have in mind?" Mr. Mental inquired, squinting down on her with a scrutinizing stare.

"I have composed a list," Mastermind explained, placing her palm flat against the glass table before sliding her hand to her right, projecting the data from the clear surface into a virtual 3-dimensional screen that displayed a list with three individuals. Each superhuman's name was accompanied by a holographic mugshot. "These are the three particular super humans I want you to search for. Their last known locations can be found in this data book." Mastermind reached out with her left hand and tossed a wallet-sized plastic book to Mr. Mental.

After cradling the data book in his hands, Mr. Mental pressed his right thumb to the pad on the black screen. A line of white light moved up and down, scanning his thumb print identity. "Access granted," the tiny speakers spoke aloud while Mr. Mental rested the mechanical reader in his palm. The words on the screen were nearly invisible, but the data book projected the print into a larger virtual screen, making the text much easier to read. The villain's devious eyes skimmed through the information, his mind scrutinizing every bit of data. Fireball sat next to his compatriot, waiting for his assessment of the situation while Mastermind grinned from the other side of the table with a smug air of supremacy.

"Is this a joke?" Mr. Mental questioned. But Mastermind only chuckled under her breath, seeming to have already anticipated he would object to this task. "The first two I understand. They can be reasoned with, but the third—you can't expect us to recruit him." Fireball glanced up at the virtual picture projection. He undoubtedly knew which recruit Mr. Mental objected to, and both villains had to realize such a mission was tantamount to suicide.

"His participation in our plan is absolutely necessary to the success of our next step," Mastermind explained as she used her foot to slide her chair out of the way before leaning forward with her palms resting on the table. "You of all people should realize that."

Mr. Mental exhaled through his nose. "Very well then. We'll pick him up last." He crossed his arms over his chest. "And what will you be doing in the meantime?"

"Working," Mastermind answered, turning away from Mr. Mental and Fireball to exit through the automatic sliding doors behind her. Her cape fluttered over her back as her boots clapped against the floor at a rapid pace. Mr. Mental focused his gaze on her swaying brown hair while he tried to analyze the devious witch's true motives. Although he began piecing together parts of her end-game, too many variables remained unaccounted for. Yet this recruitment mission brought him a little closer to the final picture.

"Come Fireball," Mr. Mental ordered. "We've got some reinforcements to track down." He led the way through the hall toward the armory where they could pick up their weapons and suits for battle. The dark room was enormous, larger than most houses, with mechanized walls that rose 50 feet from the industrial, reinforced concrete floors. Some of the most advanced weaponry known to man covered every inch of these walls, and Mr. Mental pointed toward the back right corner where his and Fireball's suits waited for them.

As Mr. Mental inhaled a deep breath through his nose, he approached the control pad on the back wall and activated a group of hovering mechanical shelves. They rotated left by five feet and then zoomed down 20 feet to floor level, allowing Fireball and Mr. Mental to gather their gear. Each villain reached out, pulled his battle suit from the wall and began dressing for his first mission in over 16 years.

Although Fireball stood a few inches taller than Mr. Mental, he was also slightly thinner with short, reddish-blond hair and a narrow face that was spotted with a few freckles. He wore a black jumpsuit, armored with thick padding, like a race car driver's. The trim on the outside of his pants was black with a red glowing line running down the center. A small yellow tri-point flame was printed on the center of his chest, and over his head he wore a tight mechanical helmet that protected his mind from extraneous attacks. The helmet also held two red lenses that emitted a hot crimson flame. These embers rose eight inches up above his head, like a pair of horns, before they dissipated into the air.

Mr. Mental had dark, messy brown hair, tight cheeks that led down to a pointed chin, and dark red eyes that occasionally changed color with his mood. He was average height, around 5 foot 9, with a medium build in his chest and shoulders. The super genius geared up in far more complex equipment than Fireball's, specifically his suit, which was his own design. Most of the equipment was made from silver chrome that glared under the overhead light. His mechanized boots gave him flight capabilities and a walloping kick, while his knees were covered in a padding outlined by a thick, metal spike. And on his quads, Mr. Mental protected himself in a shiny black, armored plating. He also utilized a silver belt with dozens of hanging compartments to hold hundreds of advanced weapons. Most of the devices were Mr. Mental's creations, but some of them implemented designs from Omega, the foremost expert in advanced weaponry.

The silver chest plate on Mr. Mental's torso was comprised of the rarest metal on earth, and the shiny armor protecting his arms was also mechanized to provide him with extraordinary strength. At full power, he could lift a mammoth tank over his head. However, this was an advantage that Mr. Mental rarely utilized as he allowed the minions under his mind control to perform most of his dirty work. Over his armor, he donned a long black overcoat with a glowing red light that lined the outer-edges.

But the most advanced piece of technology had to be the round, red goggles pulled over his eyes. Much like Michael's, they could analyze his surroundings, but even more astounding—Mr. Mental's goggles linked directly into his brain, amplifying the power of the built-in computerized database.

"Who are we recruiting first?" Fireball asked as he lowered his helmet over his head, the burning eyes searing through the air in an intimidating fashion.

"Who do you think?" Mr. Mental replied, raising his eyebrows at his brother.

"The Magician?"

Mr. Mental closed his eyes and nodded his head. "The Magician." Both villains knew that persuading The Magician to rejoin their ranks would be difficult. They hadn't left him on the best of terms before the Big Boom, but they understood that he would make a formidable ally in their campaign against the Trifecta.

"Well then let's go," Fireball chuckled in an eager tone. "I've missed his optimistic demeanor over these past 16 years." Both villains strolled down the hallway while Mr. Mental pulled his gloves down over his hands. They entered Mastermind's hangar, loaded with two dozen different transport vehicles. This room eclipsed the size of the armory with a ceiling that extended 100 feet above their heads and a cement floor that spanned the area of a football field.

Pointing his right hand to the M-shaped jet plane in the center, Mr. Mental instructed, "We'll take that one." He led the way under the belly of the house-sized aircraft and pressed his thumb against the data book that Mastermind gave to him. A high-pitched hydraulic hiss screamed through the air as the compartment cracked open directly beneath the jet, lowering a ramp down to the concrete hangar floor.

"This is Mastermind's personal airplane," Fireball deduced aloud.

"Exactly," Mr. Mental smiled. "I like the M-shape, and if we sustain some damage, I won't be too broken up." He led the way up the ramp and into the heart of the mechanical beast where the interior of the jet contained four compartments; the largest of the two included the main deck and the cockpit. The two villains stepped into the main deck, which had four round tables, each surrounded by ten swivel chairs bolted to the floor of the compartment. Two luminescent 120-inch projectable screens lined the walls on each side of the room, and three enormous, circular lights were arranged in an equilateral triangle along the ceiling.

Fireball followed a few feet behind Mr. Mental's black overcoat as he advanced his way toward the cockpit. Stopping at the thick steel door that protected the airplane's brain, Mr. Mental pressed his palm against the scanning panel to the right of the entrance. The scanner's light swept from top to bottom, analyzing Mr. Mental's palm print. After confirming his identity, the lock clicked, and the door slid from right to left, exposing the ten chairs and control systems in the cockpit.

"Ahhhh, beautiful," Mr. Mental proclaimed, his eyes analyzing every aspect of the room. "I love all of the toys!" he exclaimed, his eyes lighting up like a child's on Christmas. Hurrying toward the left pilot chair, he dropped down into the plush seat and gripped the circular navigation wheel with his hands.

Fireball was more cool and collected, strolling up behind his brother to sit in the chair on the right. "Have you learned all of the controls?" he asked.

Like a chaotic pinball, Mr. Mental's eyes bounced back and forth from buttons to lights to levers. "I've got the gist of it," he responded, pressing the green ignition touch screen in the center of the eight foot wide dashboard. The round dome-shaped turbines installed beneath the four corners of the M-shaped ship began rotating clockwise, lifting the air craft off the ground. Mr. Mental's arms held steady, keeping the jet hovering 20 feet above the cement while the hangar roof split apart, creating an exit for the advanced transport vehicle to soar up into the sky.

Fireball pressed the card-sized touch pad controls on his right armrest, launching a pair of black belt straps over his right and left shoulder. They connected and clicked together at the center of his chest. While clutching the armrests on his side, he closed his eyes and took a few deep breaths. Mr. Mental laughed at Fireball's fright, well aware that mechanical flight was unnerving to his comrade, despite the exhilaration he found while using his own pyrokinetic powers to soar through the air.

"Fear not, brother. I have the navigation controls well in hand," Mr. Mental assured Fireball as he pulled up on the steering yoke. The transport's turbines pushed them up above the hangar's roof and over the building. Once the jet cleared the hangar doors, Mr. Mental flipped up a plastic lid on the control board and slid his right forefinger across a blue screen, igniting the rear thrusters to launch them forward like a slingshot. Fireball's back pressed against the chair as they blasted across the sky, heading for their first target—The Magician.

9. Fliers Fall

Michael

September 12th

"Welcome back to Air and Water class," Professor Hawk announced, the sharp ends of his metallic wings pointing toward the ceiling of the lecture hall. "I trust that Professor Dolph kept you plenty busy last week. I'm delighted to congratulate you on surviving year one, which also means you are entitled to some technological upgrades—namely this one." Professor Hawk pointed to the shiny metal backpack that sat on a table next to him. The silver casing was thin and lightweight but strong like a plate of armor. Along the front, two thick nylon straps extended from the shoulders down to a rectangular bottom that radiated a blinking yellow light.

"As I'm sure you all know, this is our newest version of the Trifecta's anti-gravity pack," Professor Hawk explained as he ran his fingers up and down the left strap of the pack. "You are actually quite lucky because our science department worked on this over the summer, and they just revealed their improved flight pack. The navigation system and maneuverability of this device is superior to anything else out there, which will give you many advantages against the threats that are looming over us."

All of the students sat in their seats, clad from head to toe in their battle armor. They each realized Professor Hawk was referring to the recently escaped Fireball and Mr. Mental. Their breakout occurred only two weeks earlier, leaving the entire city on edge. Nobody had seen Auto or Scylla since the attack, which could only mean they were tirelessly working to prepare for an impending strike by Mastermind. Michael wondered what the Elders were planning, or better yet, how they were preparing. Even with Mr. Mental and Fireball, Mastermind didn't have the forces to initiate an all-out assault on Hero City—at least not a successful assault.

"Those of you who don't have flight capabilities will learn to use the flight pack," Hawk explained. "They aren't required when you're out on real missions, but you never know when you might need one." Allison nodded in agreement. After a year of Air and Water class, all students realized the strategic and combative advantages of flight, especially those without this power. Many of the fliers took this for granted, unaware of just how precious their flight power was. Even Michael made this mistake from time to time. He almost forgot what his life was like before he could fly just a few short months ago.

Professor Hawk walked down the aisle with a thin, cylindrical clicker in his hand. He pressed a red button toward the top, activating the yellow light at the bottom of the flight pack, which levitated the buoyant metal two feet above the table. "I've updated your data books with the schematics and other information for successfully operating this model," Professor Hawk informed. "You have 30 minutes to skim through the text and meet me out in the courtyard for our first flight lesson."

About ten of the students smiled at the opportunity to utilize such cutting edge technology. Archer was actually salivating in anticipation of his first-ever flying experience. But others looked worried. One hero two seats in front of Michael took a heavy gulp, possibly while he contemplated plummeting through the air due to a lack of preparation. Springing a challenge like this was not out of the ordinary for some professors, but Hawk almost never dropped something this important in their laps with only 30 minutes of preparation time. Michael wondered if the Elders were anxious to get their members trained quickly before Mastermind could strike.

The professors all remained on edge, and some of the well-known heroes, whom Michael only saw on rare occasions, were constantly present in the streets. Since the breakout, the best heroes like Stone rarely left the city. Michael hoped to ask him for some answers, but his mentor had no time over the past few days for a meeting. Every day, Michael considered requesting a second conference with Stone, but he and Malix always seemed to be hard at work with Eliki in the city's War Room, a place where Michael had never been. Very few students were allowed entrance, and no first or second-year had ever set foot inside.

But Michael heard stories. Supposedly, the main room contained a 3-dimensional hologram of the earth that was hooked into the satellites surrounding the planet. From this advanced map, the Elders and other high-ranking heroes could use Melvin (Master Efficiency Link Via Internal Network) to monitor major criminal activity across the globe while also plotting out varying strategical approaches to any battle.

Professor Hawk exited the lecture room, leaving the students to sit in their chairs while they read through the data and schematics for the flight pack. Although he wouldn't need one of the packs, Michael analyzed the information in his data book. In the first five minutes, he breezed through the general controls, but then he shifted his attention to the engineering and thermodynamics behind the new design.

The light-weight metal was quite rare, but the small proton-accelerated reactor was the aspect that caught Michael's attention. Somehow, the Trifecta scientists constructed a revolutionary way to harness enormous outputs of energy that could change the world, but they were only using the power source for something as trivial as a jet pack. *Why not modify this reactor design to evenly distribute energy across the globe?* Michael wondered.

Archer pinched Michael's cape and yanked on the blue trim, interrupting his thought. "Yo, I don't get how the left and right stabilizers work," he commented, scratching the top of his buzzed head. "Did you figure it out yet?"

"You just rotate the dial in your palm clockwise to increase the thrust and counter-clockwise to decrease it," Michael explained, pointing to the diagram on the data book. He pressed his right forefinger against the touch screen and swiveled the small ring in the picture, which changed the energy force emitting from the palm plate. "That way you can increase the thrust in one hand while decreasing it in the other. It's designed that way to allow for maneuverability around tight corners."

"Whoa, thanks for the lecture, brainiac," Archer joked. Michael would have taken offense to this nickname, responding with a witty quip of his own, but his focus remained on the technical data in the manual. His brain could absorb and analyze text like an advanced computer, an ability that he continued to develop since beginning his training in Hero City. While his power was unlike any of the other students, his brain made him even more unique. Only a few of his peers, including Sabrina, could maintain pace with Mr. Infiniti's mind.

While Archer played with the control manual some more, Michael further analyzed the power source of the flight packs. But even he had trouble comprehending the physics of the containment field that harnessed and amplified the energy condensed within the power core. He discovered a cross between thermodynamics and advanced mechanics working together to achieve something nobody had ever imagined. Yet what Michael found odd was that the Trifecta made no mention of this breakthrough discovery. There were so many possibilities that could have benefitted the world, but for some reason, they chose to keep this a secret.

"Come on." Archer interrupted Michael from deep thought by tapping his right shoulder. "We have to head out to the courtyard to test out the flight packs. We'll see how the brainiac does in combat today," he chuckled.

"Oh yeah," Michael muttered, shaking his head from his daydreaming state while once again ignoring Archer's insult. "Let's go." Placing the riddle of this new power containment field in the back of his head, Michael resolved to come back to the issue at a later time.

Archer and Allison hurried toward the open courtyard a few blocks behind the Hall of Heroes. This area wasn't nearly as advanced as the indoor practice arenas or the virtual training city, but the open area would prove sufficient for basic flight education. Michael and Sabrina followed a few yards behind their friends, and both glanced at each other with a smile, showing their amusement at Allison's and Archer's eagerness to fly.

Solar Flare strode his way forward with his buddies Metal Man and Nexon on his left and Manfrin on his right. As he glanced over at Michael, he chuckled a bit with a smug confidence in his curled right lip.

"I wonder what he's so happy about?" Michael commented to Sabrina as he flipped his head toward Milton. Sabrina glanced in his direction, squinting her eyes while she analyzed his jubilant demeanor.

"I'm not sure," Sabrina responded to Michael. "Logically, he should find this class session boring since he already knows how to fly." Michael nodded his head without saying a word. Ever since Solar Flare crushed Robo-one, Michael couldn't stop wondering where he found this new excess power.

But before Michael could further analyze Solar Flare's increased strength, he found he had reached the middle of the outdoor courtyard. Allison and Archer strapped the flight packs to their backs, clicking the metal buckle across their chests to securely fasten the metal levitator against their bodies. Max Force stepped up behind them with his specially enlarged flight pack already hooked over his shoulders.

"You guys ready for this?" he asked, a bright smile beaming in eager enthusiasm.

"I guess we'll find out in just a second," Archer answered. Although he showed an anxious ambition to fly,

Michael guessed his roommate was still a little nervous about the potential fall he might suffer. And Michael didn't blame any of his teammates for such feelings. He still remembered the day he first learned to fly and the fear he felt when Solar Flare dropped him a few thousand feet.

"I trust that you all reviewed the directions for operating your flight packs," Professor Hawk called out as the remaining students shuffled into the courtyard. "And some of you may be a bit nervous, but fret not. We won't be flying too high on our first outing."

Archer released a sigh of relief at hearing this, but Allison pouted her lips in disappointment. She always had a reckless abandon that Michael found intriguing. He set his own flight pack down on the ground, as did the other fliers before pushing their way toward the middle of the courtyard. But as Michael strolled toward the center, he noticed Solar Flare holding back with his right pointer finger pressed against the comm. link receiver on the side of his helmet.

Leaning his head forward with his right ear pointed out like a radar dish, Michael focused his hearing with all his strength to overhear Solar Flare replying, "I'll handle it. No problem." Unfortunately, Michael only caught the very end of Milton's conversation, and he had to wonder, *Who was Solar Flare receiving orders from?*

But before Michael could contemplate this mystery, Professor Hawk interrupted his thought. "Although you won't be focusing on high altitude flight just yet, we will be testing your maneuverability skills at a height of no greater than 40 feet," he announced. "That means do not fly higher than the dorm buildings behind us. In the meantime, my natural fliers, come see me while your teammates prepare themselves."

Michael and the six other flying heroes headed over to Professor Hawk to receive a briefing on their mission. After handing each of them a small laser pistol with a red handle and white barrel, he instructed them to test their teammates' flying abilities and then moved on to explain the rules for his non-fliers.

"Now in order to master your flight packs, you will navigate your way through the obstacle course I've laid out," Professor Hawk announced. He lifted his left wrist and pressed two buttons on his metal armband, which activated two dozen red, green, and blue floating lights. Each looked like a glowing lantern, hovering in the air at different heights from 10-40 feet above the courtyard. "Your objective is to touch at least five of the lights that correlate with your team color."

"No problem," Metal Man boasted, crossing his arms over his chest. "This'll be easy."

"Not so fast Mr. Owen," Professor Hawk interrupted. "The challenge is to make contact with five lights before your flying teammates can shoot you down."

"What!?" Archer blurted, his eyes widening in shock at hearing he could potentially fall 40 feet.

Professor Hawk lifted both of his hands out in front of him to calmly reassure his students. "No need to worry. Let me explain further. Your flying classmates possess a blaster pistol, and I instructed them to shoot down members of the opposing teams while protecting their own teammates. If they blast the sensor on the top of your flight pack, the anti-gravity controls will disengage, allowing the pack's auto-pilot to gently set you back down on the ground. The blaster pistols are slow and take time to re-charge, so focus on changing directions to avoid their fire. Now let's ignite those anti-gravity packs."

Archer and a few other students let out a sigh of relief before pressing the red button on the top of the left strap of their pack, which activated their flight capabilities. He and the other students hovered only three feet off of the ground, awaiting the professor's instructions to begin their task.

Michael held the red and white pistol in his right hand, squeezing the handle in his palm with his trigger finger resting on the side. "Go!" Professor Hawk yelled, initiating a panicked scattering of students through the air, like a swarm of bees escaping from an exploding hive. Pushing his feet off the ground, Michael jetted toward Metal Man while Solar Flare engaged Allison. As Michael followed after Metal Man, he used the advanced targeting system in his shades to lock onto his prey. Aiming the tip of his pistol at Metal Man's flight pack, Michael pulled the trigger, generating a flash of blue light that collided with the side of his pack, just missing the control sensor on top.

Realizing he had a tail, Metal Man swerved left, making contact with the first floating green light. Michael bit his lip, wishing he could use his laser fists in this trial. He wasn't accustomed to using guns, so hitting his target with his laser pistol proved more difficult than anticipated.

In a change of strategy, Michael scoped out the most adjacent green light, which Metal Man would most likely head for next. As the green team member dashed through the air, Michael anticipated his flight path before firing a single laser shot just a few feet ahead of his prey. This time Metal Man's sensor fell right in the path of the flashing beam of light, disengaging his anti-gravity controls. Michael smirked when he saw Metal Man's panicked face as he plunged twenty feet before his pack kicked in to slow his pace, dropping him on the ground with a light thud.

"On to the next one," Michael commented, but his attention shifted to Allison, who was maneuvering her way up and down through the air like a jumping dolphin as Solar Flare chased after her. He hovered through the air on a platform of swirling orange flames with a white fire emanating from his eyes. Rather than zoom after Nexon, Michael chose to cut Solar Flare off before he could shoot down Allison's flight pack.

As Allison rocketed straight up toward the highest blue light, Solar Flare pulled her directly into his sights. While he squeezed the trigger, he smirked, gazing on at the projected green light beaming through the courtyard. But Michael soared into the path, freezing his body in mid-air to absorb the laser into the infinity symbol on his chest. The collision sizzled in a crackling green light, like a short-circuiting wire, as Michael hovered in the air, his arms extended out to his side at a 45 degree angle. He observed Solar Flare's face, expecting his overconfident smirk to fade, but instead he grew a full-blown smile.

Then Michael's vision started blurring, and he felt a dizzy spell in his head while his chest turned numb. After shaking his head to regain his senses, Michael noticed he was inching back toward the ground, so he focused his energy to keep his body afloat. However, to his dismay, he started falling faster, and within seconds, gravity had taken full control over him. As he plummeted back toward the ground of the courtyard, Michael braced himself for his imminent crash.

When he smashed into the ground, his body forced a crater into the earth, launching chunks of dirt through the air in a faint cloud. Professor Hawk double-tapped a red button on his left wrist, initiating a piercing ring over the students' headsets, which directed them to cease their flight and return to the ground. After rushing over to Michael's side, Hawk shook the fallen student's right shoulder to check for signs of life.

Michael's eyes remained closed, but his chest was moving in and out, indicating he still had breath left in him. With a few more nudges from Professor Hawk, Michael roused from his incapacitated state.

"What happened?" Professor Hawk questioned, his breathing rapid and panicked out of fear that his class might have killed Auto's prodigy.

The world was spinning around Michael as he placed his right hand on his head. "I'm not sure," he answered, blinking his eyes a few times to regain his sight. "I absorbed a shot from Milton's laser pistol—and I felt fine for a moment—but then something happened to my head, and my chest went numb. The next thing I knew—I was falling."

"Are you okay?" Hawk inquired, a grave look of concern in his gaping mouth. The rest of the class grouped around behind him, many of them stuck in disbelief at seeing Michael fail. All except for Milton, who curled his lips into a smug, overconfident sneer, as if he planned Michael's fall.

"Yeah, I'm okay," Michael answered, brushing the dirt off of his pants and shoulders. "I can already feel everything healing."

"But that fall shouldn't have even hurt you," Archer commented. A few other students nodded in agreement, clearly confused by Michael's fallibility.

"In any case, we'll get you down to the medical building just to be sure everything is okay," Professor Hawk instructed. "For everyone else, class is dismissed."

As Archer and Sabrina helped Michael up from the ground, the rest of the students meandered back toward the Hall of Heroes where they would await their next class. "Are you sure you're okay?" Allison asked Michael.

The bruised hero rubbed a bump on his forehead, which wasn't healing as quickly as usual. He felt his damaged muscles working their way back to 100 percent, but something still didn't feel right. Michael hadn't experienced such difficulty controlling his powers for months, so he worried something was wrong. Yet because he didn't want to alarm his friends, he pretended everything was okay.

"Yeah, I"m fine," Michael fibbed. But then he noticed Solar Flare touching the side of his helmet again, and through the clear part of his visor, Michael could have sworn that Milton's lips mouthed the words, "It's done."

10. Magical Mending

Mr. Mental

September 12th

After arriving at the coordinates provided by Mastermind, Mr. Mental and Fireball stepped down from the jet's metal ramp and headed north. The moon and stars slightly illuminated their dark and depressing destination—a medieval English castle that was crumbling from years of abandonment. Although time had broken the large stone bricks into several pieces, Mr. Mental knew what waited within the walls. He and his brother headed for the dilapidated building before stopping ten feet in front of the fortress's outer entrance. A tall, stone gate protected the castle's perimeter, but this was just a decoy. Mr. Mental's red goggle lenses displayed three arrows attached to a few flashing paragraphs of information, which helped him detect a powerful energy aura that surrounded the stone walls.

"Is he in there?" Fireball asked of Mr. Mental.

"No doubt," he answered, nodding his head. "I can see the magical trail oozing from the cracks in this rundown building. It appears that Mastermind's information was accurate."

After Fireball took two careless steps toward the gate, Mr. Mental grabbed his shoulder. "Not yet," he explained, his head moving from right to left to survey the area. "The invisible shield that surrounds this castle is designed to repel intruders. We must approach with caution or risk death." Fireball nodded in agreement. Essentially, he merely accompanied Mr. Mental to provide brawn should they run into trouble.

The super genius crept up closer to the stone wall of the perimeter where he noticed a high-heeled boot print pressed into the earth below his feet. The track showed markings similar to Mastermind's boots, which cautioned Mr. Mental that she may have sent him into a trap. He crouched down to scoop up a pile of dirt from the right side of the imprint. While each piece of earth sifted through his hands, Mr. Mental's goggles analyzed the make-up of the soil, picking apart any oddities in the molecular structure.

"What are you doing?" Fireball asked. He leaned forward, still wary of imminent traps that The Magician might have laid out to threaten intruders.

"Just gathering clues," Mr. Mental responded, a calm, nonchalant tone in his steady voice. After moving his hand two inches from his face, he rubbed a pile of dirt between his thumb and forefinger, smearing the dark soil into his black gloves. "Come, let's go in."

"Are you certain?" Fireball asked, immediately realizing the stupidity of his question.

"Aren't I always?" Mr. Mental sneered while strolling forward through the open gateway and into the empty courtyard that separated the castle from the perimeter walls. "We mustn't stay long. Death lives here."

Realizing Mr. Mental was right, as usual, Fireball kept his helmet's visors on alert for any signs of a trap. The courtyard had the dark, eerie feel of a cemetery. Clouds darkened the night sky overhead, but even more abnormal was the earth below their feet, which was hardened and dead like an old clay tennis court. Mr. Mental's heavy metal boots thumped against the ground, echoing through the entire courtyard. Although he could have easily avoided this by activating his suit's stealth technology, he appeared unconcerned with The Magician knowing they were on his doorstep.

The tail of Mr. Mental's black overcoat fluttered behind him from his hurried pace. Normally, he moved with slow methodical steps, just like his mind, but here he was evidently concerned with something that pushed him forward. He approached the wooden double doors that protected the outside of the castle. They were 14 feet tall and combined to create a strong arch that would bar any normal thief from intruding. But for two superior criminals, this barrier posed no problem.

Mr. Mental pointed to the door without speaking a word, directing Fireball to go to work. The flamethrower snapped his right fingers, sparking a flame around his hand. But before he could fling the fire forward, the earth began rumbling beneath his feet.

Fireball looked down to his boots and then up at the shaking castle. He turned his head from left to right, a smile growing behind the visor of his helmet. "Finally some action," he uttered to himself. Behind the two villains, the hard earth started to split open like the shell of a cracking pistachio. Both Mr. Mental and Fireball turned to face the impending danger that emerged out of the dead dirt. From the breach in the ground, a thin white hand surfaced, placing a bony palm flat against the earth before pulling the body up above the opening in the courtyard.

Shock widened Fireball's flaming eyes, pulling his cheeks taut. To his surprise, the hand wasn't just skinny, but rather the thin, white fingers, arms, legs, and skull were all dead. A decayed skeleton stood 100 feet in front of the evil duo, his empty eye sockets targeting the two intruders.

Mr. Mental didn't look surprised. His examination of the soil gave him hints that there was a magical force living deep beneath the Earth's surface.

"This is all The Magician could muster," Fireball cackled in a high pitch like an amused child. "A single skinny skeleton. I expected more from him."

"Don't underestimate him," Mr. Mental warned. "You and I both know, things aren't always what they seem with The Magician." Fireball nodded, allowing Mr. Mental to step back while he launched a burning stream of yellow flame toward the wobbling skeleton. After pyro-kinetically swirling the fire around the bony body, Fireball pushed one large flaming burst from his chest, which he anticipated would knock the skeleton into the next century.

"The Magician must be slipping," Fireball smiled back at Mr. Mental as he cut off the fiery stream, confident that he bested the simplistic castle defenses. But to his dismay, the skeleton emerged from the whirling fire, his bones charred like an overcooked steak, but still moving just fine. In fact, he looked to be moving faster with a slightly longer stride. The fire that scorched across the courtyard died down, revealing at least a dozen more skeletons pulling themselves out from their graves deep within the ground. They all gravitated toward Fireball like a slow, swarm of hungry zombies, their legs wobbling at first, the way a newborn deer's would when first learning to walk. But as they drew closer, their strength increased, a determination in their eyeless sockets glowing bright red.

"Perhaps not," Mr. Mental replied, smirking at the originality of this deadly ambush. Even in the face of death, Mr. Mental still appreciated the genius behind a good trap.

"Can you make mental contact?" Fireball asked.

"With a skeleton?" Mr. Mental raised his eyebrows. "And how would I do that?" He took a few steps back up against the wall of the castle, using his goggles and mind to analyze their situation. At least 40 skeletons had emerged now, and the leader moved within 15 feet of them.

"So what do we do?" Fireball inquired. Despite their desperate situation, he remained calm and utterly confident that Mr. Mental would devise a plan.

"Turn up the heat!" Mr. Mental ordered. "Bone burns at 1600 degrees Fahrenheit, so cremate these walking nightmares."

Fireball licked his lips before igniting another flame in his right palm. His eyes burned deep with an overpowering rage that fueled the flames within. Extending both of his arms, he clapped them together, creating one boulder-sized fireball between his palms. The first skeleton crouched down, preparing to leap toward the two villains. But before the pile of bones could ascend into the air, Fireball unleashed his volatile fire like a flamethrower. When he released the fireball into a stream, the flame transformed from a hot, red glow to a searing white flame that tore through the body of each skeleton.

The scorching fire sliced through the bone like a samurai sword through whipped cream. One skeleton had his torso severed at the spine, separating his upper body from his legs. Yet both halves continued moving, the two arms dragging the top half forward while the bottom half hopped without direction.

"Ahahaha," Fireball cackled like a madman as he expanded the white flame into a 15 foot wide cylinder that engulfed the remaining skeleton bones. The burning bodies released a ghostly howl, as if they could actually feel the pain, but Fireball was relentless. He scoured the rest of the yard with his white fire until nothing remained but piles of smoking ash.

"Well done," Mr. Mental commented. "But this was only the first of his defenses."

"Do I detect fear?" Fireball mocked. No member of the Four Faces was permitted to display genuine fear. This proved to be one of their greatest strengths—and also their fatal weakness.

"Not at all," Mr. Mental laughed. "I'm just warning you. Be prepared for whatever awaits us inside these castle walls."

"I'm ready for anything," Fireball boasted. "I believe I proved that just a moment ago. Now, let's see about burning down that entrance." He turned to the large double doors behind him, reigniting the flames in his hands to incinerate the doorway that stood between them and the inside of the medieval castle.

Mr. Mental grabbed Fireball's arm, directing his fist down toward the ground. "Wait just a minute, brother." Fireball's eyes glanced through his helmet at Mr. Mental while the blazing fire in his pupils subsided. "There's no need to destroy the entryway."

"Well then how do you suggest we get in?" Fireball asked, a confused squint forming in his fiery eyes.

"By pushing the door open," Mr. Mental explained. "I would be willing to bet it's not locked."

"And what makes you so sure?" Fireball inquired.

"Think about it. How many intruders could have survived that horde of undead skeletons? Therefore, there is no need for him to lock the door. Besides, we have a more pressing defense to worry about."

"And what might that be?"

"If my deductions are correct, which they always are, the magic that brought those skeletons to life is a temporal void, meaning time is all out of whack here. I'd estimate we're aging at about ten times the average rate, and the pace will only continue climbing exponentially. If we don't escape the castle grounds soon, we'll whither away to nothing."

The flaming visors on Fireball's helmet widened, showing his surprise before he responded. "Then let's get moving."

Mr. Mental's armor helped him push open the right side of the heavy door. The wooden bottom scraped against the stone bricks in the floor, and the hinges creaked like 70 year old bones. Inside the castle, Mr. Mental rotated his goggles in a 160 degree arc, surveying the enormous main entrance. The room was one long hall measuring at least 300 feet long with a ceiling 50 feet overhead that curved into an arch. Dozens of stone pillars lined the walls on each side with massive medieval silver suits of armor standing next to them.

Realizing they had no time to gawk, the two villains picked up their pace, keeping their legs relatively straight as they moved them back and forth like the blades on a pair of electric scissors. The echo of their footsteps bounced off of the crumbling stone walls that seemed to cry in a ghostly tone as Mr. Mental and Fireball passed them. While Fireball kept his eyes peeled for any conceivable traps, Mr. Mental seemed unconcerned with the possibility of an attack. His glowing, red goggles gazed straightforward, cheeks fully calm.

A creaking screech sounded on their right, startling Fireball so much that he lit his right fist, preparing to launch a stream of fire in the direction of the disturbance. He pointed the light at the closest pillar, but only found empty space. "I don't like this," Fireball whispered. "Why aren't we running into any opposition?"

"We will," Mr. Mental replied, little concern in his steady tone. "But not yet."

"Leave!" a snake-like voice hissed through the hall. "Get out!" Fireball stopped in his tracks, turning his head from side to side, using his helmet to search for the source of this mysterious voice. However, Mr. Mental didn't break stride. His eyes glanced up at the ceiling, and his right lip curled into a smirk that nearly reached his goggles.

"Why don't you show yourself, Phillip?" Mr. Mental called out. "I know you're here."

Just then, like magic, a tall, thin man materialized from the wall on the far side of the hall. He wore a long black cloak over his shoulders with a hood that shielded his face.

"You always were quite the know-it-all," the cloaked figure jeered at Mr. Mental. "But this time, you don't know what's good for you. Leave me be, or I will destroy you both."

Fireball took offense to this last remark, expanding the flame around his right fist while pushing his way around Mr. Mental's right shoulder. "It's been a long time, so maybe you forgot how things worked before," he shouted down the hallway. "You belong to us. If anyone is going to leave this place destroyed, make no mistake, it will be you."

Mr. Mental lifted his left hand to hold back his comrade. "We are not here to fight you," he shouted to the cloaked man. "We merely wish to talk."

"Hahahaha," the ominous figure cackled in a low voice, lifting his arms out from within the safety of the dark cloak, so he could pull back the hood that covered his head. Fireball leaned his helmet forward, shocked to see that The Magician hadn't aged over the past 16 years. The sorcerer's round face and flat forehead didn't show a single wrinkle. Similarly, the curly brown hair on his head still maintained the same youthful chestnut color.

"He hasn't aged a day," Fireball blurted out loud.

"Indeed, you are looking quite good," Mr. Mental called down to The Magician, although he wasn't surprised by his youthful appearance. "Using a temporal interference sphere to feed on the life force surrounding you. Quite ingenious, even if it does pose a severe danger to your own health."

"You're looking rather spry yourselves," The Magician shouted back. "How, pray tell, did you manage to keep your good looks?"

"16 years trapped in the void of another dimension," Mr. Mental explained, contempt in his angry tone. Both he and Fireball remained eternally irate regarding their incarceration in that cruel penitentiary—a fact that fueled their motivation to exact revenge on the Trifecta.

"What are you doing here?" The Magician inquired, a hint of distrust in his voice as he cut right down to business.

"We've come to recruit you back into our ranks," Mr. Mental smiled, fully aware how The Magician would respond.

"Join *YOU!*" he screamed at the two of them. "Perhaps your stay in that form of purgatory clouded your memory. Maybe you've forgotten what you did to my wife!"

"We realize that Omega's actions created a difficult situation for you, but—" Mr. Mental began explaining.

"Don't EVER speak his name in my presence!" The Magician roared. "He sacrificed my wife for his own purposes—and now I have no purpose in living."

"Untrue," Mr. Mental interrupted. "If you really believed that, why create this temporal time distortion? No, you and I both know you were waiting—waiting for us." He grinned at this egotistic statement.

The Magician shook his head and closed his eyes in an attempt to resist Mr. Mental's logic. "Can you take control of his mind?" Fireball whispered to his partner while both of them watched The Magician with still eyes.

"No," Mr. Mental responded through the right side of his mouth. "He's grown stronger since we last fought with him. His magical powers protect him from my mind control, but no need to worry. There are other ways to persuade." Mr. Mental's ability to twist the minds of others extended beyond his power to literally control brains. He possessed extensive knowledge of how the mind works, and he knew his manipulative words could have an equally potent effect on his prey.

"You don't know what I was waiting for," The Magician grunted through his clenched teeth. He stepped back closer to the wall behind him, an indication that Mr. Mental's words were working.

"Look at yourself," Mr. Mental barked, his clenched jaw forging an aggressive attitude in their conversation. "The Great Magician hiding in the deep shadowed walls of an old run-down castle. You and I both know that you are destined for far greater things than this. I can tell that your power has grown since that fateful day. Come back with us, and we will help you obtain what you desire most."

The Magician placed his hands on his head, scrunching his eyes together while shaking his head back and forth. "No, I promised myself I wouldn't return to my old ways. That life only brought me torment. I lost the only thing that really mattered to me."

In a terrible rage, The Magician's eyes blazed with a bright red light that spiraled around in a clockwise motion. He lifted his hands in the air, forging the same red light around his open hands as he called out, "Mendontu." Mr. Mental and Fireball turned to view the dozen suits of armor that lined the walls as they rustled to life, freeing their legs from the stone platforms beneath their sturdy, metal boots. Each sentinel wielded a different weapon and a shield marked with the same symbol of a red lion with a long, fiery tail and ferocious claws. Mr. Mental backed away from them, inching closer to The Magician, who who grasped his head between his hands as he muttered something to himself.

"What should we do?" Fireball asked of his comrade as he ignited a red flame around each of his hands.

"Hold them off for a moment while I finish convincing our friend here," Mr. Mental ordered. "And Fireball," he elaborated, pausing to turn back toward his comrade. "Have fun."

Fireball smirked at this comment before engaging the mystical guardians in battle. The closest suit of armor wielded a long, shining sword, which he lifted over his right shoulder before swinging the blade down across his body, nearly slicing Fireball in half. But before the sharp sword landed, the villain dodged to his right. He tucked into a ball, rolled across the brick floor and then sprang up with a flame ignited and ready in his right hand. After sliding to a stop, Fireball cocked back his right arm and hurled a wicked fastball at his assailant. While swirling through the air, the ball of fire melted through the suit's armored chest, leaving the magical monster incapacitated. But this was only the first of a dozen foes, so Fireball wasted no time in engaging his next enemy while releasing an enthusiastic cackle.

As Fireball enjoyed his maniacal attack on the medieval suits of armor, Mr. Mental slinked closer to The Magician, whose scattered mind was escaping him. He jolted his body up and down while both palms squeezed his temples, his fingers digging into the top of his skull. "My head, get out of my head," he screamed.

"I'm not in your head," Mr. Mental spoke. "Your magically mangled mind is playing tricks on you, just as I know it has for some time now. Join us and I can ease your pain."

"No, I've seen your true intentions," The Magician cried. "I won't help you like last time." An inferno of fire raged behind Mr. Mental, and loud clangs of metal echoed through the hall as Fireball continued his merciless attack on the militia of armored guards.

"You know you don't have a choice," Mr. Mental hissed, sure that he almost had his target convinced. "I know what you want most, and you can't fulfill your destiny while hiding out here. You need us far more than we need you."

"But my wife—" The Magician started.

"That's all in the past," Mr. Mental interrupted. The logic of his words took hold of The Magician's mind, needing only to throw in the final dagger. "There's nothing you can do about that now but move on and progress forward. Become the legend you used to dream about."

The Magician's eyes glowed white at this last statement. He never wanted money or power, but fame was another story, and Mr. Mental preyed on this weakness, fully aware that The Magician's mind was so scattered he wouldn't be able to resist his basest desire. "Very well then," the magical wizard responded before snapping his fingers to deactivate the few remaining suits of armor—which disappointed Fireball who was having endless fun.

"I'll join your new regime, but under one condition," The Magician elaborated before pausing for a response.

"And what might that be?" Mr. Mental inquired, raising a suspicious left eyebrow.

"I want full technological access this time." The Magician spoke these words in a commanding, matter-of-fact, tone—almost as if he had prepared this request before Mr. Mental and Fireball even arrived.

Behind his goggles, Mr. Mental squinted his eyes into a suspicious glare, and he became more convinced that someone, possibly Mastermind, had already reached out to The Magician. "Now why would a super human powered by magic need access to our technology?" Mr. Mental asked.

"Your headband and goggles enhance your powers, and as I'm sure you've already guessed, I found a way to develop my own magical gifts," The Magician explained. "But I need a few pieces of your tech. to finish my magical development and achieve the clairvoyance necessary to revive my fallen love."

Although Mr. Mental disliked compromise, he found this request intriguing. "Very well then," he agreed. "We will give you access if that is all you require to rejoin our ranks."

"That's all I want," The Magician responded, a dead tone in his raspy voice.

Mr. Mental reached into a compartment on his belt and underhand tossed a small data chip to The Magician. "Meet us at these coordinates at noon two months from today," he instructed. "We have more recruiting to do, and we will require your assistance with our final target." The Magician nodded before turning to disappear into the shadows of the wall from whence he came.

"Come on, let's get out of here," Fireball entreated, yanking on his brother's arm. While Mr. Mental squinted his gaze toward the black cloud surrounding the wall, his mind analyzed The Magician's mystifying words. "Do you want to whither away to nothing?" Fireball pleaded, nearly ripping Mr. Mental's arm out of his shoulder.

"Come, we're leaving," Mr. Mental proclaimed. He turned and strode back down the hall toward the main entrance. The large double doors burst open when he approached, revealing the charred and blackened graveyard. Oddly, green pieces of grass already began sprouting from beneath the dead soil. Mr. Mental stopped to examine the dirt one more time, but Fireball wasn't willing to wait with him. He rushed ahead, nearly breaking out into a sprint to escape the effects of the time dilation bubble.

However, Mr. Mental realized a few extra seconds would make little difference, so he knelt down and rubbed the gritty earth through his fingers again. There was some clue within the soil that he missed on their way in. He felt sure the key to The Magician's perplexing request lay somewhere within the soil; he just needed to discover the right door. After gritting the soil through is fingers for about 30 seconds, Mr. Mental dropped a sample into a test tube the size of a pinky. When he returned to Mastermind's lair, he could further analyze the magical phenomenon under a more accurate microscope.

"Are you coming?" Fireball shouted from outside the courtyard walls. Mr. Mental stood up from his crouch, reaching down to hook the soil sample into a compartment on the side of his belt. He paced forward, his immense brain computing the data available to him.

As Mr. Mental exited the courtyard's gate, Fireball asked, "Why would The Magician need your technology to enhance his powers?"

"He doesn't," Mr. Mental responded, keeping his gaze focused straight ahead on their transport vehicle. "He was lying to me." The master genius searched through his incredible brain for a more elaborate response, but he couldn't find one. "Now I have two months to figure out why."

11. What Dreams May Come

Michael

November 13th

"Are you coming to class?" Archer asked of Michael. He held open the door to their room as he waited for an answer.

Michael sat hunched over on the bed, his head pounding from a horrible headache. Ever since his fall in Air and Water class, he had been experiencing short bursts of severe pain in his skull as if his brain was going to explode. With each brain attack, Michael lost focus and control of his powers. And when he woke up this morning, his head felt the most potent effects yet. As he rubbed his temples, he answered Archer, "No, I'm going to stay here. Maybe if this headache goes away, I'll continue searching through the files about Mastermind. Hopefully, I can find some information to help find my brother."

A week earlier, Stone had dropped off a few classified files, but all of the data was encrypted for use by technopaths. And although Michael did show moments where he wielded technopathic gifts, his powers hadn't developed enough to effectively decode the information. In six days of work, he only managed to decipher the first three pages of what appeared to be a 1,000 page document.

"Suit yourself," Archer responded. "If you're feeling better, meet Max and me at the dining hall for lunch." He released the door, which slammed shut, leaving Michael alone to fight the horrible pain in his head. Reaching over to his desk, he grabbed the only photo he had of him with his brother. After lying back down on the bed, Michael pulled the picture close up to his eyes and wondered where his brother was. Then within a few moments, the pounding in his brain relaxed, and Michael's eyes closed, leading him off into a dream.

"Hmmm, hmmm, hmm," an amused woman's voice echoed from behind Michael. Dressed in his advanced battle suit, he turned around to face his newest nightmare. Mastermind stood with her thick thighs spread apart, her hands resting on her hips while her elbows pointed straight out to the side. She stared down with a smug grin that enraged Michael.

"You, why do you keep haunting me?" Michael cried.

Lowering her hands to her side, the villain took two steps forward. "Because I can," she replied in a mocking tone. "I've proven once before, and I will prove again and again that you are weak. I am the superior being here, no matter what the Elders believe. And I will prove that to the world. Very soon, you and your brother will be my slaves."

These last words pried Michael's eyes wide open. "You have Alex?" he shouted. Mastermind nodded back without a word. "He would never work for you!"

"Hmmm, hmm, hmm," Mastermind chuckled again. "He has already begun." She pulled a quarter-sized piece of metal from one of the compartments on the right side of her belt and pressed her gloved thumb against the surface. A virtual image popped up from the device, generating a miniature hologram of Michael's brother.

But Alex was dressed in a wardrobe designed for war. A thick, black metal armor plate protected his upper-torso. The pieces of metal on his shoulders extended out a few inches to the left and right of his body like the armor of a samurai suit. His biceps were protected by a hybrid padding, leading down to a pair of strong metal gauntlets covering his forearms and fists. The forearms appeared especially thick because they carried hundreds of technological advancements. Two metal boots reached up from his feet to his knees, and a thick metal shell coated his upper legs and lower abdomen.

But the most shocking aspect of this image was the dark face of his brother. He never looked so cold, so—angry. Alex's dark, black sunglasses shielded the emotion from his eyes, but the scrunched nerves in his taut face showed his hatred.

"Your brother works for me now, just as you will, soon enough."

"You liar!" Michael gritted his teeth, taking two steps toward his enemy.

"I don't need to lie," Mastermind responded, remaining calm in her arrogant stance. "The truth is my ally, something that your brother has kept hidden from you all of your life." Michael froze in his place, raising his left eyebrow at her last statement. "Don't tell me you haven't figured it out by now. You know that your brother is just like you. And that is the truth that will grant me sovereignty over both of you, making me invincible."

"We'll never work for you!" Michael shouted, clenching his gloved fists in anger as he took a step forward.

"Ha, it's already begun."

Michael had heard enough, so he launched two rapid laser beams from his right fist. But Mastermind deflected them with a shield she projected from her mechanical gloves. She retaliated by firing a single coaster-sized disk from an opening just above her left wrist. The circular piece of metal spun through the air, expanding in surface area with each clockwise rotation. By the time the disk reached Mr. Infiniti, the metal had grown ten times into a wall that could have crushed him. Instead, the malleable metal wrapped around his body, trapping him in a squeezing sheet of metal like a cocoon.

"Ahhhhhh," Michael screamed from inside the constricting shield as the walls crushed his arms, torso and legs.

"As you can see, you don't stand a chance against me," Mastermind gloated. "I've anticipated every move either of you could possibly make. My intelligence is superior to all."

"There's more to life than intelligence," Michael grunted through this tightening trap. "Imagination is more important." Pushing his arms away from his body, Michael snapped a few pieces of the metal that were squeezing him. His right hand sliced through the casing, exposing his whole forearm from the elbow down.

"Imagination is for the weak. It only creates possibilities. My knowledge gives me the power to make such possibilities a reality." Mastermind reached down to her left wrist to press a red button at the base of her metal glove, which activated an electric shock throughout the metal trap she designed. "I told you before, I've studied you, and I have anticipated every move you can possibly make. My technology will enslave you, *Michael*."

Those words widened Michael's eyes, reminding him of his dream from months earlier. He needed to abandon his identity as Michael if he wished to defeat Mastermind. While diving deep into the power of his core, Michael searched for the limitless strength of Mr. Infiniti. He opened the door in his chest that unleashed enough raw energy to snap through the entire constricting cocoon. Thousands of metal shards flung through the air, catching Mastermind off guard.

She pressed another button on the front left side of her belt, which generated a bubble-shaped energy barrier around her body. Each metal shard dissolved into dust upon contact with her shield, forming a dark cloud of dust in the air, which created the same dreary atmosphere as a stormy day. To clear the air, Mastermind lifted her right fist and remotely ignited a powerful fan. But as soon as the metal dust particles dissipated, her eyes jumped open at the sight of Mr. Infiniti's enraged fist crashing down on her.

"Anticipate this!" he shrieked, smashing his clenched fist into Mastermind's cheek. Her body spun through the air before smacking against the ground. Two of her bones cracked, but Mr. Infiniti wasn't sure which ones had broken. As he pinned down her right shoulder with his left hand, he pulled back his right fist to deliver another punishing blow. However, before he could smash her face again, Mastermind disappeared into thin air like an evaporating apparition.

"What the?" Mr. Infiniti mumbled, whipping his head left and right in confusion. He hopped to his feet, wary of a sneak attack by Mastermind. Yet before he could analyze the situation, the world around him transformed into blackness for a few seconds before a giant computer screen appeared in front of his eyes. The bright white luminescence shone down on Mr. Infiniti as a monotone voice spoke to him.

"The real Mr. Infiniti still waits to be unleashed," the screen echoed, the light flashing in and out while Michael stared up at this mysterious entity. "When will you learn that there is so much more to you?"

"There is more to me than Mr. Infiniti," Michael sneered back at the mocking computer. "That's what you don't seem to understand."

"Until you embrace Infiniti, you will never prevail in battle with Mastermind. She possesses special qualities that you do not, but Mr. Infiniti can defeat her."

"I am special too. I don't need to abandon who I am to stop her."

"And how has that strategy panned out for you thus far?" the computer questioned. Michael furrowed his brow at the truth in this statement. Perhaps he was inadequate for battle with super beings like Mastermind or Mr. All-American. After all, he only beat Mr. All-American because he unleashed the infinite power within his core. Yet even after considering this machine's logic, he still refused to believe that he needed to relinquish his identity as Michael, the humble boy from Africa.

"What if I refuse?" Michael inquired of the computer screen.

"Then you will fail." The blinding light from the screen flashed in and out as the essence within the computer dissipated back into darkness.

"You must learn to command technology the way she does. Only Mr. Infiniti has the *imagination* to battle Mastermind's technological expertise. Embrace him, or she will destroy you along with your loved ones—and your brother will fall under her control."

The light glimmered in and out again, until the computer screen's presence dissolved, leaving Michael alone in his perplexed state. "Alex," Michael muttered to himself. "Where are you?"

When the light returned, Michael jolted up from his sleep and found a robot standing over him with a thick needle jammed into the skin of his forearm.

12. New Frontier

Mr. Mental

November 13th

"Welcome back to the world," Mr. Mental announced, pointing his right hand toward hundreds of buildings clustered together along the skyline of New York City while the bright afternoon sun beat down over the skyscrapers. He and Fireball stood at the base of the Brooklyn bridge with a black two-seated convertible waiting behind them. They'd left their hover transport farther out in the country to avoid drawing attention, and now they needed only to follow the long line of cars moving over the bridge toward the heart of the city. Most of the cars were archaic, the majority still surviving from the early 21st century, but Mr. Mental noticed a number of the more advanced turbo-mobiles zooming into the city. These automobiles were the latest craze among the more wealthy members of New York because they came equipped with a hover function that allowed them to travel up to 15 feet above the ground.

"Ah, what a grand sight," Fireball commented, amazed by the tall skyscrapers, some which he recognized, while others were brand new, built to replace the towers destroyed in the Big Boom. Mr. Mental's extensive reading informed him that this was one of the few cities the Trifecta had fully resurrected since that devastating explosion. Chicago managed to miss most of the fallout, but Los Angeles still lay in ruin from hundreds of toppled buildings and torn up streets.

"It's not quite what we remember, is it?" Mr. Mental remarked. Both he and Fireball were natives of New York, and during their time in the Four Faces, they recruited most of their muscle from the streets of Manhattan. In fact, Mr. Mental still held a hidden apartment in one of the high rises downtown, a location he hoped to visit at a later date.

In their last recruiting mission, both villains wore their battle armor, but in an attempt to blend in among the people of New York, they dressed in their fancy executive suits. Mr. Mental's black suit was coated with thin, white pinstripes, accented by a black dress shirt with red pin stripes and a bright white tie that stood out among the dark background. Sticking up from his left coat pocket was a white handkerchief folded into a triangular point. He wore a black fedora hat that concealed his thin, technological headband, which he designed to amplify his mental powers ten times over. Then a pair of red sunglasses with a single, wide, polarized lens sat atop Mr. Mental's nose.

Each leader in the Four Faces of Evil fashioned his own executive suit like this one, increasing their organization's intimidating reputation when they first rose to power.

"I think she looks more magnificent than ever," Fireball marveled. "The greatest pain during our exile was missing such grand sights as this. Are you certain we'll find our next recruit here?"

Mr. Mental nodded. "She resides in the heart of the city. The information I pulled from her file indicates that she has replaced us as the new Kingpin of the underworld in this town. Recruiting her will grant us many of the resources that Mastermind's feeble brain didn't think to acquire."

Fireball stared up at the closest building, his eyes wide with determination. Mr. Mental knew this trip to New York was just what his comrade needed to remind him of their purpose— to rule such incredible cities as this. "Do you know which building is hers?" Fireball asked.

Mr. Mental chuckled before responding. "Take your pick." Lifting his arms wide into a Y formation, he elaborated, "She owns just about every inch of this town, including somewhere around 70 percent of the buildings. Luckily, I can scan the minds of the drones who walk these streets to find out which ones work for her." The psychic villain closed his eyes to calm himself while his mind scanned across four city blocks on the other side of the bridge. In only 30 seconds, he delved deep into the unconscious part of over 4,000 brains before coming out of his meditative state.

Fireball assumed Mr. Mental succeeded. "Found one? So where are we going?"

"I didn't find one," Mr. Mental sighed. Fireball's mouth drooped, bewildered at the thought of Mr. Mental's brain power failing. "I found thousands."

"What!?" Fireball blurted.

Mr. Mental nodded, his eyes closed as he reluctantly answered, "I told you she owns the city, but her control is not limited to the buildings. Just about one in four of the citizens pledges allegiance to her. She has 4 generals, 15 lieutenants, and 40 commanders leading a total of nearly half a million forces." Fireball opened his mouth but his lips fell speechless. Although finding this new Kingpin of crime proved easy, reaching her would be another story.

"This is even better than I thought," Mr. Mental smiled.

Turning toward Mr. Mental, Fireball raised one eyebrow higher than the other. "What do you mean?"

"We want to recruit her for her talents, but even more so for her resources. The more resources she has at her disposal the better for us. And even more interesting, one of her generals is currently relaxing in that building there." Mr. Mental lifted his left arm skyward, pointing to the towering skyscraper on the other side of the bridge. Both villains used their shades to zoom in on the rectangular building's exterior, which was covered by thousands of reflective square windows that reached up 50 stories to a smaller penthouse on the top where Mr. Mental's index finger pointed.

"Come, we'll drive in to get a closer look, and then I'll evaluate the best approach to infiltrate the building," Mr.

Mental commanded. Both he and Fireball hopped over the side of the convertible that waited behind them. Fireball took the driver's side so Mr. Mental could think while they drove into the heart of the city. As if possessed by a race car driver, he zoomed around the other cars, weaving in and out of traffic like a madman with a time limit.

When they exited the bridge, Mr. Mental pointed toward a good spot to park their car off on a side street. After making their way two blocks down to a large street filled with people swarming in all directions, Mr. Mental directed Fireball into a secluded alleyway where they wouldn't be seen.

The two villains exited the car, using the doors this time, and Mr. Mental pressed a button on the inside cuff of his dress shirt, activating a system of defenses to protect the expensive coupe from prowling punks. Angling his head upward, he pointed his right hand toward the opposite side of the street where their targeted tower waited. "Think you can get us up there?" he asked Fireball, who took a deep breath to refocus his fiery glare upon the building's penthouse that stood 50 stories above the street.

"No problem," Fireball scoffed in a cocky, sneering tone. He snapped his left fingers, setting his hand ablaze in a red flame. "Grab on," he commanded, extending his right hand out to his comrade. Mr. Mental gripped Fireball's wrist, and the two villains took off. Fireball's left hand shot out an intensely hot burst of fire toward the ground, which propelled the two upward like a rocket ship taking the initial, blazing launch from the ground. They soared up over the streets, above the roofs of the shorter buildings, toward the peak of their intended target.

Mr. Mental's armor gave him the capability of flight, but in his regular suit, he became grounded, leaving him no choice but to depend on Fireball's flying capabilities. The acceleration that Fireball accomplished gave both super villains a rush before he eased their feet back down onto the roof where they stood just 5 feet from the penthouse windows.

As Mr. Mental's eyes lit up in a yellow glow that illuminated through his shades, he announced, "He's in the center room. The whole exterior is rigged to set off an alarm that will alert the entire building of our presence."

"Right," Fireball smiled with an anticipatory grin that reached to his ears. He took two methodical steps closer to the window and pulled back his left hand, which was still blazing with a reddish orange flame. After giving a confirming glance to Mr. Mental, Fireball threw his left hand forward, launching a 3 foot thick streaming fire that melted the glass window. He worked his open palm counterclockwise in a circle to tear open a hole that would work as their entrance into the general's lair.

"The silent alarm has been sounded," Mr. Mental announced. "Dozens of soldiers will swarm the penthouse in seconds."

"Terrific," Fireball grinned, licking his upper lip like a predator preparing to devour his prey. "Let's go greet them."

Mr. Mental shook his head. "You hold them off any way you see necessary. I'm going to visit the general." He strode forward in a calm, unhurried pace, the powerful wind blowing his suit jacket around like a cape. Fireball rushed ahead, leaping through the steaming hole in the wall like an excited burglar through a broken store window. His face lit up as bright as an electric billboard while his anxious legs propelled him forward.

As Fireball sprinted toward the elevator on his right, Mr. Mental stepped over the melted puddle of glass and headed toward the center room. He reached down to grab the doorknob but found the entrance was locked. Placing his right hand in his suit pocket, he pulled out a phone sized remote control before waving the device over the electronic door panel, initiating a click that deactivated the lock.

Fireball's maniacal laugh echoed from down the hall, accompanied by dozens of horrifying shrieks. As Mr. Mental stepped through the door, he found a slim figure sitting in a black, leather chair that stood behind a clear, glass desk. A black, metal pistol rested in his right hand, which was pointed straight at Mr. Mental's head.

"You picked the wrong building to rob," the man jeered from behind his simplistic weapon. Mr. Mental hummed a little laugh through his closed lips, yet still the general's hands remained calm, unwavering in the face of a superior being. But Mr. Mental knew the fool's hubris would soon subside.

"Noooooo!" a horrid voice shrieked from the stair entrance. More soldiers ran into Fireball's burning flames to be cooked alive like a heard of cattle.

"Your weapon is not necessary; you may put it away," Mr. Mental instructed. Instead of heeding his warning, the general squeezed the trigger twice, firing two bullets straight toward Mr. Mental's head. The first projectile reflected back over the general's shoulder, shattering the glass window behind him, while the second deflected to the left and pierced the dark wood paneling in the wall. The villainous genius smirked, fully aware that guns were no use against the magnetic field created by the buckle on his belt.

"Mr. Jackson," Mr. Mental laughed. "Nothing you can do will pose even the faintest threat to me, so I'm telling you now to put down your weapon." Against his own will, Jackson's arm shook toward the desk where he dropped the pistol. He fought Mr. Mental's control, but his efforts were futile. A feeble mind like his had no chance to defy a man of such immense brainpower.

Mr. Mental strode closer to the general's desk, placed his palms flat against the glass surface, and leaned in close to the trembling Mr. Jackson. "Now, you have something that I want," Mr. Mental hissed, an insidious smile creeping up his cheeks. "I require your assistance—and you're going to be happy to oblige."

Jackson nodded his head up and down, his eyes frozen, mouth half agape. Mr. Mental took full control over the general's will, and he tapped into every conscious and subconscious thought stored within his shallow mind. "Let's go," Mr. Mental ordered, turning his shoulder on the general to head back through the office door. Like a mindless zombie, Jackson followed his master, leaving his gun on the desk. Before stepping through the door, he stopped to place his right palm up against a green screen on the wall. A light flashed, scanning his palm print identity, which caused a compartment tray to pop down like a mailbox door. Inside the open tray sat a single plastic identification card—the very piece of technology that Mr. Mental needed to gain entrance to the stronghold of his next recruit.

Mr. Mental sidled up behind Fireball, who was laughing at the path of fire he forged down the staircase. Across the hall, the elevator's doors were spread wide open with the cable burned through. The wire held small remnants of red fire smoldering at the point of separation, like the burned down wick of a candle. The soldiers inside the elevator box had been crushed in the fall when Fireball cut the wire with a searing hot flame.

"Done having fun, brother?" Mr. Mental asked as Fireball launched two short streams of fire down the burning staircase. Red flames roared through the pathway, feeding upon the walls and ceiling.

"I could do this all day," Fireball answered over his left shoulder without bothering to look back. "Did you obtain what you needed?" Jackson walked up behind Mr. Mental with his keycard in hand.

"Our new ally here will gain us entrance to the fortress," Mr. Mental answered. "Now if you would please remove the flames below, we may exit this place and move forward."

Fireball sighed. "If you insist." Extending his arms straight out from his body, palms pointed down, Fireball's hands acted like a powerful vacuum, sucking the flames back up to his fingertips. The flames returned to him from the walls, stairs and ceiling, leaving a path of blackened ash in front of the two villains. Mr. Mental stepped around Fireball, leading their way down the staircase.

While Fireball would have liked to forge their way forward with a relentless flamethrower, Mr. Mental took a more subtle approach. Using his incredible scanning powers, he swept each floor below for the minds of any opposition. Such weak-minded fools would fall to his control without any effort. After striding down ten steps, he had to leap over a few charred skeletons. Fireball must have barbecued at least 30 soldiers.

Walking the entire 50 stories was impractical, but Mr. Mental knew they would find a main elevator after they passed the top two floors. Fireball had only destroyed the express penthouse elevator, keeping the regular elevators functional for their escape.

Mr. Mental led his two followers to the elevator doors and pressed the down button when his ears detected the clapping sound of two boots running toward them. From down the hall a soldier cried, "Halt or I'll fire!"

As Mr. Mental waved his hand in front of his chest, his shades radiated a yellow light, indicating he had seized control of the grunt's mind. After the soldier lowered his rifle, he strode over to the elevator, his face frozen like a lifeless mannequin.

The elevator doors parted, allowing the four men to stride in. Jackson pressed the button for the ground floor, and the elevator transported the occupants down toward the lobby. Overhead, the generator hummed, dropping the elevator three stories before the compartment slammed to a halt. The lights in the elevator ceiling died, trapping the four men in darkness.

"The attendant in the lobby has manually stopped the elevator," Mr. Jackson explained as he pointed to the corner of the ceiling. "The camera up there will keep them notified of any move we make."

Fireball and Mr. Mental both smirked at each other, fully aware that no simple trap could contain them. Mr.

Mental's eyes lit up behind his shades as he focused his mental gaze on the attendant responsible for causing their standstill. At least 30 foot-soldiers waited for them in the lobby, their guns pointed at the elevator entrance. Still, finding the correct mind took less than five seconds for Mr. Mental. "He's mine," the villain assured his comrade, forcing the attendant to reactivate the elevator's motor. Both the lights and engine sprang back to life, propelling the villains down toward the ground floor.

Three of the soldiers in the lobby rushed over directly in front the elevator entrance, pointing their black, high-powered assault rifles at the door as they watched the dropping digital numbers above the entrance. The 8 inch screen read 40, ten seconds later 20, then 10, and as the numbers dropped closer to 0, the soldiers grew more nervous. 9,8,7. Guns shook up and down, metal pieces rattling like a penny bouncing on a kitchen counter. 6,5,4. Legs vibrated from side to side, knees clicking off of each other, jaws trembling up and down. 3,2,1. As the doors slid open, each man's jittering forefinger bounced off of the front of his trigger.

Empty.

The large group of soldiers turned their heads to each other with their foreheads scrunched in confusion. The elevator compartment appeared completely vacant. One man was instructed to check, so he inched his way into the elevator doors, his gun barrel leading the way. His head peeked into the small box but found nothing.

Mr. Mental smiled, as he and his three followers walked right through the enormous, cube-shaped lobby. They remained invisible to the swarm of men whose perplexed eyes searched in all directions. "Where are they?" one of the men called out, his voice echoing through the silent entrance hall.

Their eyes could see Fireball and Mr. Mental, but their brains failed to comprehend what they observed. This was just one of the many clever tricks Mr. Mental could utilize against his enemies. He led Fireball and Jackson through the lobby of vexed soldiers before stopping at the building's main entrance.

When Mr. Mental's hand gripped the metal handle to the glass doorway, he analyzed the group of police officers positioned on the streets outside the building. Undoubtedly, most of them were on the payroll of New York's current Crime Lord.

Fireball reached out to grip the wrist of Mr. Mental's suit jacket, and he looked up at his comrade with a long face, like a child begging for permission to misbehave. Mr. Mental understood his brother wanted to handle this obstacle with force, but if they killed all of those police officers, the Kingpin would know they were coming for her. Instead, he preferred she presume that they disappeared with money as their only objective.

"No," Mr. Mental instructed, shaking his head from left to right, to which Fireball clenched his jaw together, exhaling deeply through his teeth. But his pouting was useless, and he knew better than to quarrel with the decisions of his brilliant partner. Pushing the door open, Mr. Mental shielded his group from the minds of the hundred police officers that filled the streets.

The group picked up their pace, particularly because Mr. Mental grew increasingly more anxious to complete their mission, so he and Fireball could return to Mastermind's lair. He didn't trust her, and although he had a pair of eyes watching her, the devious witch would still find a way to carry out her self-serving plot.

"Why are we still bringing these drones with us?" Fireball inquired, pointing back to the two men walking behind them. "What use could these insignificant soldiers serve?"

Mr. Mental did not turn his head or break his gait, but he did answer, "In chess, the pawns often serve the greatest purpose. And these two plus a few more will be invaluable in our infiltration of this new Kingpin's headquarters." Lighting his eyes into a bright yellow glow, Mr. Mental pointed both fingers forward like two pistols. Twenty-two of the police officers standing on the outskirts of the perimeter broke from their ranks, now under Mr. Mental's control. They jogged behind him like a group of faithful soldiers following their drill sergeant.

"We must head north toward the center of the city," Mr. Mental explained to Fireball.

"If she doesn't join us, we could be making another powerful enemy. Are you certain she will band together to help our cause?" Fireball asked.

"You should already know the answer to that question—" Mr. Mental laughed in response while leading his small militia down the middle of the street. Having obtained all of the necessary tools, he'd grown confident they would fulfill their mission within the hour, moving one step closer to the resurrection of the Four Faces.

"—I am always certain," he sneered.

13. The Chase

Michael

November 13th

Michael stared at the intruding robot who glared back at him like a raccoon caught in a car's headlights. The automaton's circular orange eyes rotated back and forth while Michael sat on his bed, sucking in rapid breaths with a bewildered look of shock in his taut cheeks. For a moment, he believed he had to be stuck in a dream. However, he felt a sharp pain in his right arm where the robot had stuck him with the needle, which dawned a realization for him—this was no dream.

"What are you doing here?" Michael questioned. But the robot did not answer. Instead, he stood up and rotated his head toward Michael, almost as if he was somehow *surprised* that Michael had risen from his slumber. "Robot, I asked you a question. What are you doing here?" Michael's tone grew more commanding, but this did not elicit a verbal response from the intruder. Instead, after stumbling back one step, the robot turned and dashed out through the door.

In only a few seconds, Michael shook off his bewildered stare and hurried out the door to chase after the thief. After entering the hallway, he viewed the robot's mechanical limbs pumping as fast as they could. When the robot reached the end of the hallway, he turned left without slowing his speed, so Michael sprinted after him. Although Michael tried activating his enhanced speed, he found his muscles refused to comply, which forced him to work harder than ever just to reach a normal sprint.

After turning the corner, Michael observed the robot waiting by the elevator where his mechanical head rotated to catch sight of Michael. But before Michael could start down the hallway, the robot took off sprinting again in the opposite direction. This would lead to a dead end, so Michael grew confident that he could trap and confront the mysterious drone.

Except when the automaton reached the end of the hall, he leaped through the tall, reinforced window. Shards of glass showered the sidewalk four floors below while Michael chased toward the opening. He leapt out through the window and tried to hover his way down to street level, but once again, his powers refused to cooperate, and he hit the ground almost at full force.

"Aghhh," Michael cried in pain as his knees cracked. Something was truly wrong. Even without his flight powers, his strength should have protected him from the impact of the crash. Somehow the robot must have stolen his abilities. because although Michael could feel his powers working, they were functioning at minimum strength, almost like a car that's running on fumes. His legs took the brunt of the damage from the fall, and while his healing powers fell faint, Michael rallied just enough strength to stand up. As he scanned his surroundings, he noticed that the entire street was eerily empty, save for the robot moving fast toward the south end of the city.

Despite the burning agony running through his legs, Michael mustered enough strength to chase after the robot. At first, he couldn't move at full speed, but as he found a rhythm in his stride, his strength began to return. In an attempt to quicken his approach, he took a hopeful attempt at leaping up into the air to fly, but luck seemed to remain with the robot in this chase as Michael fell back to the ground. Reaching up to the earpiece on his shades, he called to Melvin for help.

"Melvin, there is a rogue robot running down Alpha Street. Shut it down," he ordered—No reply. "Melvin, answer me!"—Still, the central computer system gave no response. "Mastermind," Michael mumbled. *She must have found a way to interfere with my communication link*, he thought before picking up his run to a full sprint, extending his stride while pumping his arms in a circle like the chugging wheels of a train.

When Michael turned right at the next intersection, another hero almost ran him over with a small motor-bike. After skidding to a stop, the man jumped off of his bike and started yelling in a scolding tone, but Michael ignored every word, choosing instead to hop on the motor-bike and take off.

"Hey, where do you think you're going?" the man shouted as Michael zoomed off down the street in hot pursuit of the robot, who was no longer running. The mechanical thief had activated a pair of motorized skates beneath his feet, allowing him to travel up to 40 miles per hour. Although Michael rarely borrowed Archer's motor-bike, he'd grown rather adept at using the vehicle.

Turning the throttle, Michael accelerated down the street. As he chased after the robot, he passed a few other Trifecta members who glared at him with confused eyes. And Michael didn't blame them because he felt just as confused by this perplexing situation. *Why would a Trifecta robot infiltrate my room to drain my powers?* he wondered. But that quandary would have to wait until later. At the moment, he needed to keep his mind focused on catching this robot.

As he turned left at another street, Michael's eyes widened upon seeing the robot had stopped less than one hundred feet away. His mechanical fist pointed toward Michael before launching two battery-sized rockets from the top of his wrist. Normally, Michael's advanced reflexes would have saved him, but with his powers drained, he moved too slowly to dodge this attack. Each rocket hit the pavement directly in front of him, which launched his motor-bike up toward the sky and hurled his body through the air. Michael's head spun, disorienting him until he landed on the ground with a thud.

When he pushed himself back to his feet, his eyes caught sight of the robot zipping away down the street. A brief feeling of fear that the thief would escape overtook Michael, but then he regained his senses to analyze his options. Looking down at the bike he borrowed, Michael realized the explosion from the rockets had wrecked his only chance of catching the robot. A bent front tire and a snapped axel made driving the vehicle impossible, but then Michael also wondered if the robot purposely tried not to harm him. After all, only the bike had taken serious damage, and if those two missiles succeeded in a direct hit on Michael, his powers weren't there to save him. In any case, with the motor-bike trashed, Michael prepared to sprint after the robot, although he realized he had no chance of catching his prey on foot.

But just then, a stroke of luck fell his way when Archer pulled up alongside him with his own mini-bike. "What's going on?" he asked. "I saw you hauling down the street like a madman."

"That robot did something to me; he drained my powers somehow," Michael explained, pointing his right hand down the street. "I've gotta chase after him."

"Well then hop on," Archer suggested, angling his head toward the empty spot on the back of his bike seat.

"I'll travel faster without you," Michael responded while pushing Archer off of his own motor-bike. "Contact Molly and ask her to help you follow behind me."

With that last statement, Michael turned the throttle and took off. After heading down the next street, he caught a faint glimpse of the robot speeding around a corner five blocks away. Fortunately, Archer's bike was much faster than the one Michael borrowed before, so he started closing the gap on his quarry. As Michael turned down the next street, he angled his body close to the ground to maintain his intense speed. Just three blocks away, the metal drone continued retreating away from Michael as he wondered just where this robot was going.

But before Michael could close any more ground, the relatively empty street started to fill with people. The last class period had just let out, prompting hundreds of heroes, scientists and professors to hustle to their next class or appointment. Navigating through the traffic of each body proved difficult for Michael, but he still managed to keep his eyes on the retreating robot.

Off in the distance, Michael caught sight of the drone turning down a narrow alley, so he weaved his way through the dozens of bodies that stood in his way. A few of the heroes yelled at him as he narrowly avoided crashing into them. Then after swerving around the corner of the alley, Michael found the robot standing idle, and his rotating, robotic eyes turned toward the young hero.

"Freeze!" Michael commanded, although he realized this would likely do nothing to stop the robot from whatever he was planning. And sure enough, the automaton's belly popped open and dropped down like a draw bridge before his chest spewed out half a dozen explosive spikes. The robot stared at Michael and then looked down at the explosives in his way, almost as if he wanted to warn Michael against the danger. One fact grew more clear for Michael—this robot wanted to escape without hurting him. But this clue only created more mystery for Michael.

After rotating his body back around, the robot's wheels squealed, and he zoomed off toward the opening at the other end of the alley. Analyzing the dangerous situation, Michael determined the best strategy to continue his pursuit, so he backed up Archer's motor-bike and revved the engine a few times. After burning the rubber of the tires against the pavement, he built up as much speed as he could, heading straight toward the trap. Then, just before his front tire would have triggered the deadly explosives, he popped the bike up against the alley wall and turned the throttle as hard as he could. The bike jerked forward while Michael's momentum kept him up against the wall just long enough to clear the explosive spikes.

As the tires hit the ground, Michael released a breath of relief but then looked up, remembering that he needed to continue his chase. The robot had just reached the opening of the alley where he turned left onto Hero Way. *No more fooling around*, Michael thought as he rushed across the alley. When he exited onto the street, he noticed that at least 50 maintenance bots stood among a few dozen heroes who still lingered outside the city buildings. And although he might have been paranoid, Michael felt as if every robotic eye was fixed on him.

Three blocks down, he located the robot running on foot now, possibly to help blend in as he attempted his escape. Although Michael's motor-bike zoomed forward, as he tried to maneuver his way through the vehicle and pedestrian traffic, more and more robots emerged from buildings to block his way. One even came close to jumping in front of him with enough force to knock him off of his seat. However, he swerved left just in time, nearly causing his bike to slip out from underneath him. Despite the hundreds of pedestrians and robots on the street, Michael kept his eyes locked on his target.

After squeezing between two maintenance robots, he accelerated forward. The robot turned his head left and his glowing eyes rotated back and forth. Whoever was controlling him must have been amazed that Michael could keep up without his powers.

At this point, Michael reached his full speed, and within seconds, he would have narrowed the gap that separated him from his prey. As he accelerated within 5 feet of the robot, he leaned forward on the motor-bike, preparing to tackle the automaton to the ground.

But right when Michael angled his body forward with his feet ready to spring ahead, the robot turned and shot two spikes from the top of his left wrist. Both projectiles pierced the front tire, popping the rubber, which flipped the bike out from underneath Michael. The chassis rolled forward with an intense force that crashed into and knocked over the robot.

Michael realized that some of his powers must have started to return because as he tumbled and skidded across the sidewalk, he felt his advanced skin protecting him from certain death. The impact still hurt, but not nearly as much as if he had no defensive powers. His flailing body finally came to an abrupt stop when the back of his head smacked against the sidewalk. Unfortunately, Michael's protective shell hadn't strengthened enough to protect him from this. His eyesight started to fade, and he felt woozy like he was going to pass out from the blunt trauma to his skull.

Yet just before Michael drifted off into a slumber, the robot walked up to stand over him. Although Michael could have been hallucinating, he swore the mechanical menace was smirking down on him as he spoke to the injured hero.

"Your powers are growing," the robot's voice box announced in a muffled and distorted tone. "But you are no match for Mastermind . . . Not yet." After those last two words, the robot turned his shoulder and started walking up the stairs to the Trifecta Headquarters. Michael fought to pry his eyes open as he observed the retreating robot. He moved his legs in an attempt to stand but then felt his muscles go limp, and his head fell back against the cement, redirecting his gaze straight up into the blue, cloudless sky.

Up overhead, Michael's last image was of Molly flying down to rescue him. A smile crept up the side of his right cheek until he realized she was not coming to his aid. And then, blackness overtook him.

14. Assimilation

Mr. Mental

November 13th

"This is it, our target's stronghold" Mr. Mental proclaimed, his head tilted back as he stared up toward the sun. He and Fireball stood tall at the bottom of a gray, 80-story building designed like a modern pyramid. The base was magnificent, covering more than a square city block, but as the building rose, the surface area divided in half—except for the top, which was crowned by a 150 foot wide rotating cylinder shaped like a wheel. This circular floor, which covered the highest stories, looked like a hat. But unlike General Jackson's building, these top floors were mostly empty, only used on rare occasions. The leader of this new crime syndicate protected herself in the deepest depths of the building's tenth floor, possibly the most fortified place in all of New York City.

A specially designed metal, which interfered with Mr. Mental's psychic abilities, shielded the lower walls. That was why he had so much trouble locating her exact position within the city. At the base of the building, eight cylindrical, revolving doors lined the outer-walls where Fireball, Mr. Mental and his small army prepared to enter.

"So what do we need these lackeys for?" Fireball asked, pointing back toward the police force waiting behind them.

"You'll see," Mr. Mental smiled. He pointed his right finger toward the entrance, and the swarm of police foot soldiers rushed forward into the building like a stream of water breaking through a cement dam. They flooded the enormous lobby, an octagonal room with 50 foot high ceilings, where they headed straight for the main elevators and stairs. A small group of five security guards burst out from behind their desks, drawing pistols from the holsters on their right hips. But before they could fire the first shot, Mr. Mental commandeered their minds as well, assimilating them into his forces. The elevators dinged, and the group of soldiers piled into the compartments while a line of a few dozen other men hustled up the main stairway on the right side of the lobby.

Mr. Mental, Fireball, and Jackson remained calm outside the building, waiting for the lobby to clear. "That should do an adequate job of distracting our quarry," Mr. Mental explained. With his head, he pointed to the general standing on his right. "Using the help of our new friend here, we can head in, undetected until it's too late."

"What are we going to do when we find her?" Fireball asked.

"All I need is a face-to-face meeting," Mr. Mental answered, his countenance stone serious. "That will get us what we want. Now let's go. We must move quickly while her vision is distracted."

Mr. Mental followed behind Jackson, who ran ahead to the elevator on the far left side of the hall. The general pressed his right palm flat against a book-sized panel that sat on the wall next to the elevator. A single line of light flashed up and down the panel, scanning Jackson's identity before opening the elevator doors. Mr. Mental and Fireball stepped inside the elevator, followed by their mindless drone. He pulled his keycard out of his pocket before slipping the I.D. into a slot on his right. A few seconds before the elevator took off, Mr. Mental scanned the rooms above to confirm that their target remained distracted by the infiltrating police officers. The doors slid back together, and Jackson instructed the elevator to head for floor number ten.

"Voice code acknowledged," the automatic computer announced over the speakers in the ceiling as the elevator zoomed up the shaft. Mr. Mental and Fireball stood next to each other with Jackson at the front of the compartment. Fireball glanced over to his comrade with a playful grin. He wasn't the brains of the Four Faces, but he could still appreciate the brilliance of his teammate's plan.

In under five seconds, the elevator reached floor ten, a bell dinged, and the doors separated for the villains to exit. Jackson led the way out into a 100 foot long hall that ended at a purple door with an intricate crown logo over the archway.

"The throne room," Mr. Mental laughed upon seeing the crown above the entrance. "Excessive egotism is a trait I like to see in my fellow conquerors." He broke from his momentary thought, refocusing his attention on his mission. "Lead the way," Mr. Mental commanded of his drone.

Jackson's legs flew back and forth as he headed toward the entryway. The sensors over the entrance detected his approach, automatically sliding the door up into the ceiling, allowing a bright light to shine through the entrance and into the hallway. Despite Jackson's unquestioning loyalty to his new master, his eyes widened in fear, realizing he was walking to his doom. Mr. Mental and Fireball followed him through the doorway into a marvelous, purple room. The ceilings stood at least 20 feet high, and every metallic wall was covered in a royal purple paint that gleamed like a recently waxed car.

At the far end of the enormous chamber, in the center of the wall, the Kingpin rested in a hovering mauve throne. She wore a large rounded pair of black shades with purple lenses hiding a secret she held in her left eye while her long, black hair rested over her shoulder.

"My dear Jackson," she called from across the room while she sat as still as a statue with her fingers resting on the smooth armrests. "Your betrayal deeply saddens me. I always liked you, but now I'll have to end your life."

"Oh, don't blame him," Mr. Mental laughed as he strode past Jackson, tapping his slave on the shoulder. "I'm the one responsible." He focused his gaze upon his target as she sat in her chair that hovered up and down a few inches due to the advanced magnetic force that she had built into the bottom of the seat.

"You must be new in town," the woman cackled. "Nobody comes into my fortress and threatens me. Nobody." Her hovering chair inched forward, the anti-gravity device pushing her farther up from the floor.

Fireball leaned in close to Mr. Mental to whisper in his ear, "Can you take control of her mind?"

Mr. Mental tilted his head back to his right and shook his forehead a bit from left to right. "Her mind is strong. With enough effort, I could take control, but that would severely decrease her superhuman abilities. I was correct in assuming that she is in fact one of us. Besides, mind control isn't necessary here. As I said, I need only a few words to sway her into our employ."

"I don't know how you turned my general against me," the woman sneered while her hover throne propelled closer to her enemies. "But I must applaud your guts, though foolish they may be, to infiltrate my own throne room." She paused her approach about 15 feet from Mr. Mental before pressing a black button at the front of her right armrest. Two thin cylindrical cannons popped out of the wall, one from the left and the other on the right. A second later, two more pistol-sized guns emerged from each side of the chair's head.

"So tell me, who might you be?" she asked, leaning forward in her chair with an insane grin in her mouth and tight cheeks.

Mr. Mental smirked back as he answered, "They call me Mr. Mental, and this is my associate, Fireball." The villain used his right thumb to point back to his partner in crime, fully aware of the weight that their names carried. After dropping her jaw for a second, the woman eased back down into the plush seat of her throne.

"And I know who you are, Sharp Shot," Mr. Mental smiled.

"Impossible," Sharp Shot muttered to herself, her face frozen in shock. She tried moving her arms but couldn't find the strength.

"The first rule of becoming a supreme conqueror and overlord," Mr. Mental replied. "Nothing is impossible."

Tilting her head up and to the right, Sharp Shot shook herself out of her daze. "You may or may not be Mr. Mental, but either way, as I said before, nobody comes into my throne room and threatens me." The pistols on each side of her chair made a whirring noise, like a blender, as the barrels rotated, pointing their laser sights on Mr. Mental's chest. The two red dots hovered over his black shirt and white tie, but his cheeks remained tranquil, unfazed by her threat.

Fireball, on the other hand, wasn't so calm in the face of her attempt at intimidation. He pushed his way forward, forming a blazing flame around his right fist, but Mr. Mental clamped him by the left shoulder with a lobster-like grip. In the middle of his step, Fireball felt his body yank back like a fish on a reel. Only Mr. Mental could get away with such a bold move. Any other human would have found himself incinerated for placing hands on the powerful villain.

"We are not here to fight you," Mr. Mental explained. "We come to help you." Lifting his right hand, he pushed back the cuff covering his left wrist, exposing a metal control pad that protected most of his forearm. Using his index finger, Mr. Mental pushed two buttons on the touch screen of the remote, which projected a 5 foot wide virtual image between him and Sharp Shot.

The blue screen revealed a detailed, glowing map of Hero City. "Your empire is strong, but theirs is growing fast. The Trifecta is developing a new weapon that will cripple your control over this city."

"I do not fear them," Sharp Shot boasted, lifting her right lip to show her teeth as she talked. "I built my empire into the greatest crime syndicate across the globe because I refused to let them bully me into being frightened. That is the source of my strength."

The screen that separated the two villains flipped from a vertical to a horizontal layout with the 3-dimensional buildings standing perpendicular to the floor. Fireball stood back, aware that Mr. Mental's powers of persuasion were about to work.

"Deep within the heart of the city, there is a storm brewing," Mr. Mental explained. A bright blue infinity symbol and another dark red omega symbol blinked outside the virtual version of the Trifecta Headquarters. "And from that storm will come the greatest war of all time. One that will eclipse the campaigns and skirmishes of 16 years ago."

Sharp Shot squinted her right eye at the blinking emblem. She was young during the previous war between Omega and Infinity, but she still recognized their symbols. "I don't fear either of them," she lied while struggling to keep her lip perfectly still.

"If that was true, then you would be a fool," Mr. Mental laughed. "But my mind sees past your hardened exterior. Your thoughts betray you."

After taking one deep breath, Sharp Shot dropped down from her hover chair, drawing a silver pistol from her right hip. Both of her hands gripped the purple handle, helping her aim the barrel at Mr. Mental's head.

"Your weapons don't frighten me," Mr. Mental sneered, crossing his arms over his chest. "And while I realize you don't have the same respect that we do for the power the Trifecta wields, I believe there is another factor that will motivate you to join us."

"Then you would be mistaken," Sharp Shot scoffed at Mr. Mental. "I have no interest in joining your cause; now get out of my throne room before I blow both of your heads off." While finishing her last sentence, she jerked her pistol forward, determined not to give in to Mr. Mental's manipulative words.

But the mental giant remained calm, his lips frozen, shades staring straight forward as he uncrossed his arms and turned his body back toward the exit. After taking three steps, he called back, "If that's the way you want it." Fireball's left eyebrow raised, and he jerked his head forward, confused why Mr. Mental would give up so easily. Sharp Shot holstered her weapon on her hip and circled back toward her hover chair. "But you should know they're training a new Blue Archer," Mr. Mental uttered from the right corner of his mouth while continuing his calculated retreat.

Sharp Shot whirred around, her dark hair swirling through the air like a violent tornado. "What did you say?" Her nostrils flared, face red with fury.

A big smile crept up Mr. Mental's cheeks, but he didn't turn to face her while answering her question. "They're training a new Blue Archer. Does that grab your interest?"

After Sharp Shot strode up to Mr. Mental, she grabbed him by the right shoulder, and he turned to face her, revealing his arrogant smirk. "If you're lying to me—" she began threatening; however, Mr. Mental lifted his right arm to brush off her grip on his shoulder, freezing her thought in mid-sentence.

"I'm not lying, but I am fully aware of your animosity toward the original Blue Archer. This is why you will join us." Mr. Mental stated this with a mater-of-fact tone as if there could be no argument.

Sharp Shot stared at Mr. Mental with an angry scowl in her soft, round cheeks and short, pressed nose. "The original Blue Archer went into retirement shortly after he did this to me," she explained as she removed her purple shades, revealing the damage done to her left eye. Although the stunning purple iris in her right eye lit up the room, this beauty was overshadowed by the circular telescope that sat in place of her left eye. The purple glass bulged out from her face, like a telephoto lens that emitted a mild purple glow. Below the glass scope, Sharp Shot's skin showed a white scar that ran almost two inches across her left cheek.

"How did you know?" Sharp Shot asked as she huffed an angry breath of steam through her nostrils.

Mr. Mental tapped his forehead with his right pointer finger and answered, "Nothing hides from this mind. I know you hold great contempt for the Archer who slung his arrow through your eye. And I know that you want revenge against him. We can help you there. To get to him, you'll need to breach the protective shield of Hero City, but that's not the hard part. If you want the new Blue Archer, you'll have to go through his best friend—Mr. Infiniti. Are you prepared to do that?" As he finished his question, Mr. Mental leaned in closer toward Sharp Shot, who glared back with a purple fire in her right eye.

Exhaling a deep sigh, she asked in a compliant tone, "What do you want from me?"

Mr. Mental formed a grinch-like grin. "All in due time," he answered. "All in due time." The super genius turned back toward the exit, and Fireball sidled up next to him.

"Well done," he whispered to his brother.

But Mr. Mental gazed straight ahead, unwilling or unable to break his gait. There was one last task weighing on his mind. "Two down, but number three will be the true challenge," he reminded his brother.

"Mr. Mental!" Sharp Shot shouted to him from her hover chair. He paused but didn't turn his head. "I will join you, but I have one condition."

"Yes, the Blue Archer is yours to kill," Mr. Mental responded while keeping his back to Sharp Shot.

Her mechanical eye rotated 180 degrees as she squinted the other half of her face into a look of surprise. "How did you know I was going to ask that?"

Mr. Mental tapped his right hand against his forehead again and called back without turning to face Sharp Shot. "Nothing hides from this mind." Fireball snickered under his breath, always amazed by the power his comrade wielded—but Mr. Mental was not joking.

"Nothing hides from this mind," Mr. Mental mumbled under his breath. "Not even you, Mastermind." Beneath his shades, he narrowed his eyes, the rest of his face stone serious while he pulled down on the flexible brim of his fedora.

15. That Which Does Not Kill Me

Michael

November 13th

"Michael, are you okay?" Allison asked.

Darkness cleared as Michael's eyes opened to view Archer and Sabrina standing a few feet behind a leaning Allison. She crouched over Michael's body with her cute, pointed nose just a few inches from his. Turning his head, Michael observed his surroundings and realized he somehow ended up back in his dorm room. After sitting up on his bed, he reached back to feel for a bump behind his head; however, his body appeared to have healed all of the damage he sustained while chasing after the thieving robot.

"Yeah, I think I'm okay," Michael answered as he blinked his eyes clear of the haze that clouded his vision. "But how did I get back here?"

"I can answer that," Archer chimed in. Reaching down to his helmet, which rested in his left arm, he pressed a button on the side of the blue visor, launching a projected video screen in mid-air. The projection displayed a map of the Trifecta's city with a blinking light just outside the Headquarters. "We followed the tracking device on my bike to find you passed out on the sidewalk. And by the way, thanks a lot for trashing my ride."

"Yeah, sorry about that," Michael coughed while rubbing his eyes. "Couldn't be helped."

"Well my dad is gonna flip when I tell him that I need a new one," Archer huffed, although he didn't seem too broken up—most likely because his father was loaded from the rewards he received during his time as one of the Trifecta's elite heroes. "What were you doing out there?"

This question fully revived Michael from his daze and even ignited a fiery rage in his eyes. He gritted his teeth as he responded, "That robot stole my blood and drained my powers." Michael turned his head to his friends, his nostrils flaring with anger.

All three of his compatriots raised their eyebrows into an inquisitive expression. "What robot?" Archer asked.

"The one that I was chasing when I borrowed your motor-bike. Somehow, he sedated me while he drew blood from my arm, and I think he planned to finish without me ever realizing what he stole. But I woke up before he could escape. It was weird—"

Michael paused for a moment and stared straight forward to think about that moment when he woke up. "What was weird?" Sabrina asked, breaking the awkward silence in the room.

After shaking his head from side to side, Michael responded, "The robot. He reacted as if he was surprised—like he had human emotions. When I caught him draining my blood, he panicked and almost showed—" Then Michael stopped again to consider what he was going to say next. He knew how he wanted to describe the robot's reaction, but he also realized his observation made no sense.

"Showed what?" Allison shouted, imploring Michael to finish his thought. So he answered her with the one word that best characterized the robot.

"Fear."

Michael's three friends now scrunched their eyebrows into confused expressions. "How could he show fear?" Archer asked. "No Trifecta robot is designed with emotional capabilities."

"I know," Michael responded. "And yet—he was afraid. I know it sounds crazy, but it's true. Could these new robots be even more advanced than the Trifecta knows?"

"Not likely," Sabrina interjected. "I met with Dr. Andruin, the lead scientist on the project, to discuss their new developments. He showed me the schematics, and not only are these new robots designed without an emotional chip, but they have a specific program installed to prevent them from fully understanding emotions."

"And yet, I know what I saw," Michael reiterated. "That robot, his eyes lit up and rotated into a wider angle. He was startled by my waking." Michael's tone grew in confidence as he became more sure that he was right.

"I think we're missing the big picture here," Archer jumped in. He intensified his concerned glare onto Michael's heavy eyes. "Why would a robot steal your blood?"

"And even more alarming, why did that drain your powers?" Allison added.

"All good questions," Michael nodded, his gaze glued to the wall straight ahead. "It's possible this was a plan devised by Mastermind. She may have been testing out a new weapon designed to sap my abilities. Or maybe she's trying to obtain more data to study me, giving her an even greater advantage the next time we meet."

"Do you remember anything else before the head injury knocked you out?" Sabrina questioned.

"I remember there was something," Michael began. "Someone showed up, and I thought they were there to help me, but I can't remember who it was. My head was spinning out of control . . . Were you the first ones to find me when I was unconscious?"

Archer nodded. "The whole street was deserted when we arrived. It was actually kind of eerie." He looked at Michael and bit his lip like he had something else that he was holding back from his friend.

Michael noticed his roommate's hesitance. "What else was there?" he demanded in a commanding tone, quite uncharacteristic of his kind nature.

"When we found you, you were mumbling something, kind of babbling on, but we didn't understand what you meant."

"What was I saying?"

"It was mostly incoherent babble, but you blurted the word traitor, and then told us no hospitals," Archer elaborated. "That's when we brought you back here."

"You were out for almost an hour," Allison added. "We started to worry that you weren't going to wake up, so we called in for help."

"What?!" Michael jumped up from his bed, nearly pushing Allison over as he landed on the tile floor.

"Don't be mad," Sabrina implored with her hands out in front of her in an attempt to calm Michael.

"Who did you call?" Michael's eyes widened in panic.

"We asked Melvin to patch us through to one of the Elders, but he said they were busy, so he contacted Stone instead," Allison explained. All three of Michael's friends looked at him with shaking eyes for fear of how he would react to this news.

But to their surprise, Michael exhaled a sigh of relief. Although he would have preferred they not contact anyone, he trusted Stone enough to keep this situation a secret. The last thing Michael wanted was the Elders grilling him for more information about his seemingly impossible encounter with *their* robot. Still, he wanted to sort through the story before divulging all of the details to Stone, so he began rerunning every event through his head.

Michael's friends remained silent for a moment while he thought, but then a knock at the door interrupted their solitude. Archer gulped hard and looked to Michael as if he was seeking his roommate's permission to answer the door, so Michael gave him a solemn nod and prepared to answer the inevitable, forthcoming interrogation.

Archer turned the knob and pulled open the door, revealing Stone's towering figure and cold, expressionless face.

Michael licked his upper lip and looked up at his mentor, whose broad, ox-like shoulders were covered by his navy blue suit jacket. The other three students stood motionless, each of them petrified into silence.

Without stepping into the room, Stone's gravelly voice instructed, "Mr. Fleming, follow me for the answers you seek."

16. Blood

Mr. Mental

November 15th

"Did you procure the blood sample necessary to move forward with our research?" Mr. Mental asked. He stood in a dark storage room with his glowing, red shades covering his eyes. The overhead light illuminated the immediate area around him, but the rest of the room remained clouded in darkness. Then in a startling instant, the room began glowing green as the mysterious shadow's eyes lit up at the other end of the room. Close to 20 feet separated the two figures who, for over a month, had been using this secret storage room to plot behind Mastermind's back.

"We obtained it, just as predicted," the shadow responded before tossing a vial of blood across the room. The glass, cylindrical container floated through the darkness, but Mr. Mental had no trouble catching the blood without dropping the fragile vial. "Do you have the tools to augment his blood?"

"Yes, I should have no problem, despite that witch's refusal to let us see the data reel you helped her steal," Mr. Mental griped. "At least she came through and obtained the pieces of technology necessary to refurbish the weapon."

"Good, then get right to work," the shadow instructed. "We'll need your data to finish preparing the weapon as soon as possible."

"Mastermind is keeping us busy with recruiting, but I'll put a rush on my experiments. You should have the data within the month. Everything else is falling into place. When we invade their city, the Elders will pay for their insolent resistance."

"Indeed," the cloaked figure grunted. "Just make sure you keep pushing Mr. Infiniti to prepare him for that moment. Should he fail that day, all will be lost."

"No need to worry," Mr. Mental smiled. "When the time comes, Mr. Infiniti will execute our plan."

17. And the Plot Thickens

Michael

November 13th

"Follow me for the answers you seek," Stone had grumbled. And with those concise words, he left down the dorm hallway. Michael's confusion kept his feet cemented to the ground at first, but then he snapped out of his daze and hurried out the door to follow his mentor. He hustled down the corridor and turned left, but racing after Stone reminded him too much of his recent chase to catch the robot. In fact, when he turned the next corner, he suffered a flashback, his mind envisioning the drone crashing through the window at the end of the hall. Michael's legs lost strength and his breathing grew heavy while his eyesight blurred for a moment before he regained his composure.

But what alarmed Michael most was the sight when he lifted his head. The shattered window at the end of the hall showed no signs of damage, and like a beacon of light, the sun shone through the flawless glass plating. However, Michael had no time to contemplate this peculiar obscurity; he needed to catch up to Stone before the elevator doors sealed shut.

Just as the panels started to close in on each other, Michael slipped through into the compartment. Stone remained still, his broad shoulders pointed straight toward the door without revealing where he was leading them. When the elevator dinged and the doors parted, he strolled out of the dorms and onto the street.

Michael couldn't stand Stone's silent treatment any longer, so he blurted, "Where are we going?" Still Stone said nothing, keeping his eyes focused straight ahead. "What did Archer tell you? I mean, I assume you didn't take a break from hunting Mastermind just for a friendly chat."

Stone kept walking without saying a word, his gaze fixed on the streets ahead as he headed toward the south side of the city. They walked about five blocks before coming to a stop in front of a small stone castle of European design. The brown building rose four stories high with a three level turret on each side. Both cylindrical towers had conical roofs like a sorcerer's hat, and erected between these turrets stood a semi-circle of stairs that provided two pathways up to the castle's only entrance.

This building had caught Michael's attention on many occasions, but he never knew what purpose the castle served. After following Stone up the stairs to the large, arched double doors, he tilted his head back to gaze at the emblem over the entrance—a white circle surrounded by a blue glowing symbol.

"Here were are," Stone announced, placing his right palm up against the keypad scanner to the right side of the door. The light blazed from the bottom to the top of the rectangular box, analyzing Stone's identity before the heavy doors swung open. Both heroes stepped into the building's foyer, a relatively small room with a short ceiling that nearly grazed the top of Stone's smooth bald head, which led Michael to believe this wasn't Stone's house.

"Where are we?" Michael asked.

"Somewhere safe and hidden from prying eyes and ears," Stone explained. "I don't want anyone eavesdropping on our conversation. Now tell me about your dream," he instructed Michael, who tilted his head in confusion. They had stopped in this small room without exploring any other part of the castle, leading Michael to wonder if Stone was hiding something deeper within these walls.

The giant leaned in closer before unleashing his heavy breath onto Michael's face. "I don't have much time, so I'll get straight to the point. I know you've been experiencing terrible nightmares, and in order to help you, I need a description of the events that transpire each time."

Michael's heart beat faster, surprised to discover that Stone was already aware of his night terrors, and he worried even more what Stone already knew of his recent encounter with the robot. So much mystery surrounded this visit from Stone, which made Michael's answers somewhat risky, but still he felt compelled to tell the truth.

And in fact, he had wanted to reveal the details to someone other than Archer for some time, so he began explaining. "I'm not sure where it begins, but at some point I always end up battling Mastermind. She and I start with heated words, which eventually leads to a difficult struggle. In my earlier dreams, she always crushed me with varying pieces of technology, just like she did when we met in Africa. But lately, I've been able to fight back."

As Stone rubbed his right hand against the stubble on his chin, Michael could see his mind was analyzing the significance of these events. "And what has happened when you fight back?" Stone asked.

Without hesitation, Michael answered, "I'm starting to win." Scrunching his forehead, he evaluated whether he should tell Stone about the computer screen. Not even Archer knew about that part of his dream—mostly because Michael feared the computer's logic was correct in assessing and proclaiming a necessity to abandon his past in order to embrace Mr. Infiniti's future. He couldn't hold this secret any longer, so he decided to divulge the last part of his dream.

"I usually get Mastermind right where I want her, and then she disappears into thin air."

"Hmmmm, and that's where your dream ends?" Stone inquired, a rhetorical tone in his voice, almost as if he knew Michael still held out the final event.

While taking a deep breath, Michael's nerves ran up and down his skin and his hands shook as he responded, "No." Stone inched forward a bit more in anticipation of what

Michael would say next. "After she disappears, an enormous computer screen forms in front of me."

Stone's eyes widened while his loud breathing nearly halted. Michael noticed the unusual body language from a man who normally showed little emotion. "What did the computer do?" he asked of Michael.

"Every time it just talks to me." Michael bit his lip, immediately regretting his decision to mention the computer. Stone's heightened interest told Michael that his mentor was already privy to some information that he wasn't sharing. In some way, Michael felt that Stone only asked questions to which he suspected the answers.

"What does the computer say?" Stone asked, narrowing his gaze into Michael's blue irises.

He bit his lip harder before responding, so hard that he thought he might tear right through his skin. After taking a deep breath, Michael replied, "The conversation is never the same, but each time, the computer gives me the same message." Stone continued leaning in even closer, inching his nose less than a foot away from Michael's. "It tells me that I need to abandon my identity as Michael and embrace the Mr. Infiniti persona."

Upon hearing this, Stone backed off of Michael's personal space and placed his right hand on his chin. "Hmmmmm," he hummed to himself, his eyes frozen in deep thought. Michael wondered what he was thinking, but his own thoughts remained fixed on the bizarre events of his dream.

After a few moments of silence, Stone came to a decision and broke from his meditative state. "I think it's time you met with my partner," he announced, turning his head back down upon Michael's shocked face.

"Who?" the confused teen asked. This was a riddle that kept Michael's mind busy for the past two months. He knew Stone had a partner, yet nobody in the entire Trifecta organization worked well with him.

"You'll see," Stone grunted as he opened the door on his right and headed out of the room. "Follow me." Michael cocked his head to the side and squinted, wary of a possible trap. Although Stone had garnered most of Michael's trust, the suspicious teen grew more cautious every day he spent in Hero City. Yet he was desperate for answers, so he walked behind his mentor, anxious to discover this mysterious ally.

While following Stone's brisk pace down a narrow hallway, Michael observed the ancient armaments hanging as decorations over a dozen doors on the surrounding walls. An array of 40 different shields, swords, and other elaborate medieval weapons lined the corridor, but Michael was surprised to see a staff mounted over the door at the end of the hall. While Stone placed his palm against the panel next to this main entrance, Michael squinted to examine the staff closer, and he identified the A symbol melded to the top. This was the same staff that the Trifecta displayed in the center of the Hall of Heroes. Michael pulled his shades from inside his suit coat in order to acquire a magnified view with schematic details of the weapon, but before he could activate them over his eyes, the armored door slid open, and Stone pulled Michael in with him.

"Mr. Fleming," a familiar voice exclaimed from within the next room. Professor Malix stood in front of over a dozen 55-inch holographic computer screens all positioned against the wall behind him. At the base of these screens, a long line of control buttons, switches, and levers blinked different colors across the room. Despite the lack of even one window, the room was well-lit by ten circular lights installed directly in the ceiling.

Michael's head jumped back in disbelief. "Professor Malix?" his voice echoed through the room. "*You're* Stone's ally?"

"Ha, are you surprised?" Malix smiled, crossing his arms over his chest.

"Well yeah, I mean everyone knows that you two don't get along, so I guess you were the last person I expected to find here."

"Good," Stone grunted. "The feud between the professor and myself is a facade designed to hide our allegiance. You're a bright kid, so if we fooled you, most others will be as well."

Michael smiled at this rare compliment from his mentor. "That's why the two of you were talking last year before Mr. All-American killed Professor Enzo. I should have guessed." He took his right palm and lightly slapped his forehead upon realizing his oversight.

"Indeed," Malix nodded. "But don't assume that our enemies were so easily fooled. Mastermind and Mr. Mental are beyond genius, and they may have seen through the false face of our contempt for each other. However, I don't have to tell you of their intelligence, do I Mr. Infiniti?"

Michael nodded in response. "Does Auto know?" he asked.

Stone and Malix glanced at each other before Stone tipped his head to his partner. "You might as well tell him," he instructed.

"Michael," Malix began explaining. "Auto has been the leader of the Trifecta for many years now. He is one of the most powerful beings on this planet, and he wields the greatest authority over the people of Earth." Professor Malix paused for a moment as if he was unsure how to relay the second half of his thoughts.

"Don't beat around the bush," Stone interrupted. "We suspect Auto isn't all he appears."

"What?" Michael huffed, shaking his head while waving his hands back and forth in disbelief. "No way. He's been supporting me since my first day here."

"Power corrupts," Malix elaborated in a flat, factual tone. "I've known Auto for a long time, and the one thing I know for certain about him is he covets his strength and control above everything else. He tried to hide away his lust for power, but I can see through his fake smile. You view Auto as a benign leader who cares only for your development as a hero, but he has an ulterior motive that he's kept hidden from you."

Michael's eyes narrowed, unsure if he wanted to ask the question that jumped to the forefront of his mind. But he'd come too far to wimp out now. "And what motive might that be?"

"You are his chance for redemption in the eyes of the people," Malix explained. "The world was in turmoil, and we desperately needed salvation from the evil warlord who was terrorizing Earth's people. So they appointed Auto to the position of Head Elder with his promise to rid the world of evil. To accomplish this, he instituted the Infinity and Omega projects, which would create his two champions of peace. And when they eradicated the evil force for good, we did experience a brief moment of peace, what some would even call a utopia. Yet times of tranquility never seem to last long. Omega's betrayal of the Trifecta made things worse than ever, and the people blamed Auto."

"They also blamed him for the Big Boom, which is why he's kept the details of that day a secret," Stone added. "For the past 16 years, people around the world have called for his impeachment from the Trifecta Council, some even for his imprisonment."

"That's the true reason why he needs you," Malix elaborated. "Auto hopes that your rising power will restore humanity's faith in him."

"Then why are you worried about him?" Michael inquired. "Don't we all want what he does—peace for Earth?"

"On the surface, it seems that is what he wants, but like I said, Auto isn't all that he appears," Stone snorted through his large nostrils before grabbing a pen-shaped remote from the glass table on his left. Turning his body toward the computer screens behind him, he squeezed the remote in his palm, which expanded the picture on one of the holographic screens into a single, large image spread across the entire back wall.

The enlarged screen showed a picture of Auto handing off a briefcase to a shadow-covered figure. "This is when we first became suspicious of Auto," Professor Malix announced. "Both Stone and I believe that the Trifecta's discovery of you was no accident, which prompted us to take a closer look at the surveillance cameras I hid around the city. This one shows Auto making a deal with someone we can't identify."

"So what?" Michael defended his friend. He refused to believe that Auto was anything but virtuous, despite the slight sliver of doubt he held in his heart.

"This video image was captured the day before the hunter attacked you and your brother," Malix explained. "We think it was a payoff. He hired that hunter to attack you so Fortune-teller could find you in the jungle. It was all a set-up from the beginning."

"No, Auto has looked out for me—he's my friend—he–he wouldn't have had my brother killed. He wouldn't do anything to hurt me." Michael remained in denial, refusing to believe another word from Malix or Stone's mouths, but then Malix reminded Michael of a fact that shattered his blanket of ignorance.

"No, he wouldn't do anything to harm you? Then why did he order Molly, the girl for whom you hold such strong feelings, to spy on you?" These hurtful words froze Michael in his place. His cheeks grew white, and his jaw dropped. Malix and Stone both stood back, aware that their logic would kick in shortly.

After close to thirty seconds of silence, Michael's blank stare narrowed into an infuriated scowl, like a snarling wolf, as he snapped his teeth at Malix. "How did you know about that?"

"She told Professor Aldridge, who was our third member until his untimely demise. He was her confidant, although she never guessed that her mentor used her confiding words against her. We tried to prevent his death, but Mr. All-American was clever, somehow always one step ahead of us."

"An uncommon ability for a hero whose fame was built on strength and a pretty face," Stone added, a hint of jealous contempt in his tone. Despite Mr. All-American's betrayal and death, Stone still seemed to hold a personal grudge against him.

"Exactly," Malix agreed. "It's likely that he was working for another, which is why, as you know, someone killed him. They didn't want any loose ends."

"So you think it was Auto?" Michael asked. All of this information felt overwhelming like his perception of the world had been flipped upside down.

"No," Malix responded. "In all my time here with the Trifecta, Auto has constantly avoided engaging in battle. He tends to let his minions do his work, so the question begs, who is in his employ and is also powerful enough to blow a hole through Mr. All-American's chest?"

Resting his left hand on his chin, Michael pondered this query, but he couldn't think of anyone. He shrugged his shoulders with a stumped look in his eyes. "I have no idea. Who?"

"A good question," Malix proclaimed. "But neither of us had a clue either. That is until now."

"What do you mean?" Michael asked.

"Your dream," Malix elaborated.

"What about it?"

"I'm sure you are aware by now that Stone and I know of your haunting nightmare encounters with Mastermind." Michael nodded to confirm this. "Mmmmm hmmmm," Malix hummed, planning out his next few words carefully. "These were no mere nightmares. They are the key clue to our theory. And considering the timing of when they started—"

"You think Mastermind is working with Auto," Michael interjected before Malix could continue his explanation.

The professor smirked and complimented Michael. "You are quite the detective."

"But why would they work together? They have virtually opposite goals for the world."

"As we said before, Auto isn't all that he appears. I fear that something insidious is at work here, and your nightmares are the key to unlocking the mystery. "

"What do you mean?" Michael questioned.

"There is more to this game than we can see on the surface, but I believe the computer screen in your dream is a manifestation of Auto—which would fit with his agenda because he also wants you to embrace Mr. Infiniti. However, I grew most suspicious today when you were attacked by one of the new Trifecta robots."

Michael froze, and his breathing increased. "How did you know about that?" he inquired.

Malix smirked before responding, "We've both been keeping an eye on you ever since your battle with Mr. All-American. That's how we knew about your brother's coffin and your incessant nightmares that have ensued since. It's nothing personal really. So much of this plot revolves around you that we want to make sure we have all of the clues to make informed decisions."

Although Michael wanted to be mad, he understood their concern, and he didn't blame them for keeping track of him. However, he did wonder *how* they were watching him. But before he could contemplate this any further, Malix continued with his explanation.

"Your encounter today with the Trifecta robot was disturbing. That's why we decided to bring you in."

"Why?" Michael asked.

Stone remained silent for this part of the conversation, allowing Malix to elaborate for the both of them. "Because we want to know why you were chasing that robot. What did he do to you?"

"He drained my blood, which temporarily sapped my powers," Michael explained. "But I—"

Before he could finish his second sentence, Malix cut him off. "I see. So that's how you ended up unconscious on the ground. We were both perplexed when we heard this."

"I don't understand!" Michael blurted to interrupt the professor. "Why is all of this happening."

Malix looked to Stone, who gave him a single nod to go ahead and reveal the last bit of information. "We believe, whatever Mastermind has planned, it's big. She gathered intel on you all of last year, but she still knows that you are a threat, and she'll do anything necessary to neutralize your power . . . Still, that's only the beginning of our worries," Malix explained.

Michael inhaled a deep breath through his nose and swallowed a heavy gulp of saliva before asking, "What do you mean? What else does she have up her sleeve?"

"She's begun recruiting," Malix elaborated. "She was undoubtedly behind the breakout, but more disconcerting, Mr. Mental has begun contacting some of the most powerful super humans on the planet."

"I've identified two of their major targets for recruitment." After plopping down in a computer chair, Malix rolled himself across the floor and twirled around to the control panel opposite Stone and Michael. After double-tapping his right hand against the touch screen, two holographic images projected down from the lights overhead. While hovering a few feet from Michael's face, the two profile pictures expanded into a pair of 3-dimensional heads that rotated in horizontal circles like a carousel.

"Sharp Shot will undoubtedly be one of their first stops," Malix speculated. "Mastermind's eye has focused on her over the past few years, and she has many of the skills and resources they will need to build up their organization."

"Who's the second?" Michael asked, squinting his eyes to focus on the other profile.

"That is The Magician," Malix explained. "He is a former member of The Four Faces and one of their greatest enforcers. Very powerful and very mysterious. After the Big Boom, he disappeared from the world."

"Maybe he was destroyed then," Michael suggested.

Malix shook his head. "No, Stone and I have been watching his former residence in England, and there has been significant activity in recent days. Plus, before his demise, Professor Aldridge said that The Magician would be one of the most crucial pieces to our salvation in the coming war. Unfortunately, Mastermind wiped most of his profile from our database when she stormed our city last year, and only Professor Aldridge had in-depth knowledge of The Magician's true identity and abilities."

"So what do you know about him?" Michael asked.

After Malix pressed a button on his wrist and slid a lever down on the computer console, the 3-dimensional images of Sharp Shot and The Magician dissipated back into the ceiling and transferred to the computer screens. "All of the important information is on this," Malix answered, handing Michael a silver data drive. "DO NOT upload the information to the general data files. Stone and I suspect that someone is monitoring Melvin's program right now, so we've avoided entering any of our plans onto the Trifecta mainframe. We advise you to keep all of your sensitive information on your personal hard drive as well."

Michael nodded without saying a word.

"In any case, that will be all for today. And in the meantime, don't discuss this with anybody, not even your friends. Auto's contacts reach far beyond his headquarters. He has prying ears everywhere in this city."

Before turning toward the door, Michael nodded in agreement, although he wasn't sure who he would even trust with such dangerous information. Archer and Allison came to mind first, but then he decided against burdening them with more of his own problems. For now, he would have to face this journey alone.

"Oh and Michael," Malix called to him before the door closed.

Michael turned back to face the professor. "Yeah?"

"There's something you should know about Blue Moon." Michael's eyes expanded, afraid of what Malix might say next. "Shortly before his demise, Professor Aldridge informed me that she refused to continue spying on you. She told Auto that she couldn't bear to betray your confidence any longer. I thought you might like to know." Malix nodded his head in an affirming way that made Michael feel he could trust his new ally. The professor was one of Michael's favorite teachers, yet now he felt an even deeper connection, although a gut instinct told Michael that Malix and Stone still held back some crucial piece of information.

18. Rage

Mr. Mental

January 17th

Having successfully recruited The Magician and Sharp Shot, Mr. Mental knew he had one last super human to collect. He and Fireball both realized this would be the most difficult and dangerous mission of the three, which is why they put off this trip for as along as possible. Their former teammate left their employ on bad terms, and he possessed fearsome power. The first two recruits were but children compared to him.

So to provide some extra insurance on this mission, Mr. Mental chose to bring Sharp Shot and The Magician along with him and Fireball. Although Mr. Mental dressed in his business attire, the other three chose to wear their battle suits. For Sharp Shot, her scientists had forged a powerful suit made of a tight, purple metallic material that hugged her skin. The rare substance could repel bullets and stop fire while the light-weight design still allowed her to utilize her advanced agility in battle. Hanging from a holster on each of her hips, two silver pistols glared under the moonlight.

Meanwhile, The Magician draped himself in the same black cloak he wore back in his castle, but he added a pair of dark boots on his feet and a black, armored vest over his torso. Given his magical talents, he had little need for advanced armor like Sharp Shot's. His sorcery would be his shield in the event of danger. And while Fireball also geared up in his helmet and battle armor, Mr. Mental donned the same dark pinstripe suit from his trek through New York City—with the exception of one item—a dark, cotton vest beneath his jacket, both of which hugged up against his slim figure. Just as before, his black fedora hid the powerful headband that amplified his powers.

The Magician's dark cloak covered most of his body, but he pulled the hood back to reveal his face as their group approached the intended target.

"Are you sure about this one?" Fireball asked Mr. Mental. His right hand gripped his teammate by the bicep.

Mr. Mental turned his head to his brother and his eyes glanced down at the meathooks wrapped around his own arm. After releasing his grip, Fireball threw his hands an inch above his shoulders to show his apologies for doubting the brains of their group. "How many times must I remind you that I am always sure?" Mr. Mental responded, a sneering scowl glaring from his scrunched nostril and lip. "We will sway him."

"He is bound to still hold contempt for all of us," The Magician chimed in.

"After what we did to him, I wouldn't blame him for holding a grudge," Mr. Mental commented. "But you know he has even greater disdain for Mr. Infinity." Mr. Mental grinned, rolling his eyes back to The Magician. "And therein lies the key to persuading both sides of his erratic personality." The Magician nodded back with a slightly nervous smile. He remained fully aware what the brute could do because he and Mr. Mental had teamed up to create this monster.

"If you say so," Fireball chuckled, always amused by Mr. Mental's confidence.

"I have seen Mastermind's ultimate plan, and the final stage will require some serious muscle, which is why we need Jonathan's special skills." Turning his head from left to right, Mr. Mental's shades scanned the area while displaying a few bits of information about the barren graveyard ahead of them. Having used the data provided by Mastermind, he tracked down his former experiment's whereabouts to this burial ground in the middle of a tiny German town. A few barren, leafless trees were spread out across the graveyard, but otherwise, the vast area was only filled with thousands of identical gravestones.

Although Fireball, The Magician, and Sharp Shot's company was designed to provide backup, Mr. Mental remained confident that his words would be more than enough to accomplish his goal.

The four villains gazed through the bars of the graveyard's gateway. A few clouds drifted through the sky, temporarily cloaking the bright moon overhead. Mr. Mental jerked his head forward, signaling Fireball to burn through the 10 foot tall metal gate. In most cases, Fireball relished any opportunity to use his powers for destruction, but here his muscles remained tense and constantly on edge. After snapping his right fingers, he launched a small ball of red flames from his palm, which seared through the lock on the entrance.

"Come," Mr. Mental instructed his fellow villains before sliding past the broken gate. Using the new anti-gravity metal in the soles of his dress shoes, he hovered his way across the single, dirt path that passed by thousands of graves. Sharp Shot examined the few headstones directly to her right, and her eyes widened. Each tombstone had the same inscription scratched into the stonework: "Here lies Jonathan Breck, a man forever damned to both life and death."

"The gravestones," Sharp Shot began to ask, but Mr. Mental cut her off.

"Shhhhh," he hissed over his shoulder. "Absolute silence is imperative at this point. I want my voice to be the first he hears."

Fireball and The Magician looked to their left and right, glancing over their shoulders while Mr. Mental pressed forward without hesitation. The clouds ahead drifted to the left, revealing the bright light of the full moon. A single beam shone down upon a tall, slender man standing in the distance at the top of a hill. His back was turned to the approaching hostiles, but his long pointy ears detected the slight squish from each light footstep.

"Jonathan Breck," Mr. Mental shouted across the graveyard.

The thin man pried his eyes wide open before turning to glance over his left shoulder. He recognized this voice, one that haunted him in so many dreams. "Mr. Mental," he barked in an enraged voice. "What are you doing here?"

"Jonathan," Mr. Mental called back. "We need to talk." Breck squinted his eyes, intensifying his gaze upon Mr. Mental and company. His red pupils bounced from right to left, surveying the group of villains.

"I see you've brought Fireball and The Magician with you, but I don't recognize your third minion," he growled across the graveyard.

"Minion!" Sharp Shot grunted, pushing her way past Mr. Mental. "I'll show you who's a minion here." She pulled the pistol from her right hip holster, but Mr. Mental stopped her before she could aim ahead.

"No Sharp Shot," he commanded, paralyzing her mind to prevent her from engaging her quarry. Against her will, she re-holstered the pistol and stood up straight at attention.

"Good girl," Mr. Mental smiled. He hovered past her and then lowered his dress shoes down to the ground. Closing the gap between him and Breck, he moved only a few slow steps at a time. The Magician and Fireball followed his lead, all three fully aware what would happen if Breck grew hostile. "As I said, we need to talk," Mr. Mental called in the calmest voice he could generate.

"It's been a long time," Breck growled back. "But I still remember what talking means to you. Talk is your form of manipulation." The thin stickman placed his right fist in his left palm and cracked his knuckles. "Now leave me be before I grow angry." Breck turned his back on the villains and strode off toward the far end of the graveyard. As he walked, his thin shoulders bobbed up and down like the front legs of a wolf.

"Is this your life now?" Mr. Mental yelled, elevating his voice, which unnerved his team members.

"Brother, what are you doing?" Fireball hissed, keeping his eyes focused on the tall, lanky Breck, who whipped his head back around. "You're going to transform him," Fireball warned.

"Exactly," Mr. Mental smiled, fully sure of himself.

"What did you say?!" Breck roared like a bestial creature. Over one hundred feet separated him from the group of villains, but Fireball and The Magician both backed away while they focused to keep their breathing calm. "You want to know about my life!" Breck barked. His hands expanded to the size of a catcher's mitt, his fingers doubling in length while his nails grew to sharp points that glistened under the moonlight.

"You ruined my life," Breck growled, his voice growing deeper and more menacing while his body expanded. The long, thin limbs blew up like balloons, and his eyes turned blood red. "You made me into this monster!" he howled. His nose elongated, face growing thinner while two horns emerged from his forehead, and his teeth sharpened into powerful daggers. Heavy patches of brown fur emerged from beneath his skin, and his torso transformed into a thick bone plating that covered both his chest and back before extending down over his arms like a suit of armor. At his elbows, two thick spikes emerged like a pair of sharp swords.

"You made me into The Wolfman!" Breck snarled, his entire body now fully transformed into a towering beast that stood nearly 9 feet tall. He crossed his arms over his face and then flung them to his sides. The razor sharp finger nails gleamed in the moonlight as The Wolfman sauntered toward Mr. Mental, a prowling glare in his crimson eyes.

"What are you thinking?" The Magician cried, his eyes bulging in the face of The Wolfman. Fireball took two steps backward but held his ground while Mr. Mental released Sharp Shot from his mind control, allowing her to rush to his side.

"Let me shoot him," she pleaded, clenching her teeth as she leaned in close to her leader.

"Your weapons would have no effect against him," Mr. Mental warned. "He is my ultimate creation." The Wolfman picked up his stride, leaning down on all four limbs to bound up and down toward his prey. With three quick rotations of his arms and legs, the fearsome monster closed the 70 foot gap between him and Mr. Mental.

"Owwwwoooooo!" he howled, leaping in the air before bringing his yellow nails slashing down on Mr. Mental's motionless body. The Magician had entered into a full retreat with Fireball ready to follow. Despite Mr. Mental's warning, Sharp Shot pulled both pistols from her hips and aimed their thin barrels at The Wolfman.

The animal's right paw slashed across his body, but the dagger-like nails bounced off of Mr. Mental's energy shield. He walked without fear for a reason. His brilliant mind always planned ahead, which prepared him for encounters such as this. He had spent the last three months devising a plan to reclaim his greatest experiment, and now The Wolfman would put his strategy to the test.

"How do you like my new shield?" he gloated. "I adjusted it just for you. A mixture of both science and magic," Mr. Mental elaborated. "Your achilles heel. You are a creature of my own making, a masterpiece. And while the magic and science running through your veins makes you impervious to each individually, combining the two forces brings you back down to the realm of mortality."

"We will see," The Wolfman roared, enormous splatters of drool flying from his snout and fangs. He flung his right paw up in the air and slashed down with all of his strength. Though Mr. Mental's shield deflected the sharp, swiping claws, the force did push both him and his shield back three feet. Then two more swift swipes knocked him back a few more feet. Widening his eyes, he grew worried, but not fearful. Pressing a button on his belt, he adjusted the frequency of the repellant force that generated his shield.

"That won't stop me!" the monster growled even louder, peeling back the droopy lips of his long snout to show his fearsome, keen teeth. But before he could deliver another slash at Mr. Mental, Sharp Shot came to his aid, firing three consecutive shots that tore through The Wolfman's bone plating. The first bullet pierced his left bicep, and the other two hit his abdomen.

"Then maybe that'll stop you," Sharp Shot jeered. She held her pistols out away from her body, each one aimed at The Wolfman's oversized chest, an easy target to hit.

"Sharp Shot, stand down!" Mr. Mental called back over his shoulder, realizing her deviation from his plan could prove troublesome. With any of his other prized experiments, he would have worried about Sharp Shot doing damage, but with The Wolfman, he knew she could only succeed in further enraging his bestial side.

"You insolent worm," The Wolfman screamed, his deep intimidating voice echoing through the graveyard. "Owwwooooooo," he cried to the moon with his snout pointed skyward. All three of the bullets that sank through his muscles popped back out like the buds of sprouting plants. Each metal slug hit the soft ground, and The Wolfman flashed his head back down toward Sharp Shot. His gleaming red eyes squinted together, focusing on his prey as he growled.

"I'm warning you," Sharp Shot squeaked out. "Those were just warning shots. Come any closer to either of us, and the next one goes through your skull." Despite the trembling in her hands, Mr. Mental knew Sharp Shot's perfect aim couldn't be altered by her fear.

The Wolfman laughed in a deep growl that sounded like two rocks scraping together. "You must be new," he sneered through a wide grin while his long red tongue rubbed over his razor sharp teeth. "Let me introduce myself!" he cried before charging toward Sharp Shot. Lowering his torso closer to the ground, he bounded his way forward with his arms and legs pushing off the soft dirt, leaving behind deep foot and handprints in the ground.

As Sharp Shot fired two more rounds from each pistol, a pinging sound echoed through the air before each bullet sliced straight through The Wolfman's skull. One of the bullets pierced his fearsome right eye, and the other three formed an equilateral triangle in his forehead, stopping him clean in his tracks. As The Wolfman let loose a crying howl that could have moved the moon, Sharp Shot formed an arrogant smirk in her right cheek.

"Hi," she gloated, her shoulders bouncing up and down as she laughed. "Nice to meet you." Rolling her eyes over toward Mr. Mental, Sharp Shot bragged to him, "You see, I don't know what you were so worried about."

But she would soon find out. The Wolfman let out two more yelping howls as he shook his head from left to right. His red eye re-formed, and he intensified his fiery glare on Sharp Shot. Each of the four bullets fell from his forehead, bouncing only once off of the soft, dirty ground.

Sharp Shot's eyes sank, and her jaw dropped, lips trembling up and down like a mounting earthquake. "Impossible," she mumbled. "How?" The Wolfman clenched his growing fists, the sound of his cracking knuckles ringing through the air.

"Jonathan," Mr. Mental hollered in an attempt to grab The Wolfman's attention. But his efforts were useless. Once The Wolfman's rage reached a certain point, his tunnel vision took over, and at this specific moment, his eyes locked onto the woman who just deposited four bullets into his skull. With his snarling snout leading the way, he took two sharp bounds and launched himself 15 feet above the ground. The moon glistened off of the monster's tan horns and the bone plating that covered his forearms as they reached high over his head. As he crashed down toward Sharp Shot, she dove to her left, firing one shot from each of her pistols while she rolled over the dirt.

Mr. Mental recognized her skill was formidable but not nearly sufficient to survive more than a few moments against such a dangerous foe. While Sharp Shot kneeled on the ground, she fired three more shots at her target's right arm and abdomen. Yet her advanced bullets could no longer pierce his strengthening shell, and the more she attacked him, the more savage The Wolfman became. As he fixed his gaze upon her, Sharp Shot's pistols sparked out a few more bullets. These shots pierced his skull but had less effect in slowing him down, so she began running while she fired her next few shots.

Jonathan, hear me now. Mr. Mental pried his way into The Wolfman's mind, hoping he could gain enough control to calm the beast from his enraged animosity. Sharp Shot unloaded an entire clip of ammo from each of her pistols, but the bullets were no more than a nuisance at this point. *You must listen to me*, Mr. Mental spoke into The Wolfman's thoughts. In his infuriated state, The Wolfman's mind was almost uncontrollable. Even the monster himself held limited command over his decisions, so Mr. Mental had to focus all of his power into reaching the subconscious man that lay within the beast. If he could calm him for a moment, he could bring The Wolfman close enough to his human form to reason with both the beast and the man. This was his plan from the start until Sharp Shot deviated from her role.

Unfortunately, she continued making Mr. Mental's objective more difficult. Each bullet she fired, only poked the devil, maddening his irrational side. Both Fireball and The Magician understood this, so they intervened to help their leader. Neither one was foolish enough to take on The Wolfman, but they held no qualms with restraining Sharp Shot. She reloaded her clip in less than a second and planned to unload the entire round again. But she only launched two bullets before The Magician used his levitation abilities to rip the guns from her hand while Fireball formed a fiery shield to melt the bullets before they could puncture The Wolfman's blazing eyes.

Sharp Shot reached out for her guns as they flew from her fingertips, but she fell flat on her face. Glancing up from the dirt below her cheek, she squinted her eyes into a bewildered stare. However, her gaze took a quick turn from confused to scared when she turned her head to the ravenous monster on her left.

But Sharp Shot received some help, and some luck, in the form of Mr. Mental. He succeeded in seizing a weak hold over The Wolfman's conscious mind, causing the ferocious beast to lose his focus and motivation to rip Sharp Shot limb from limb. The monster wrapped his fingers all the way around each side of his head as if they were palming a basketball. His shoulders flung back and forth, then left to right as he tried to shake the presence of Mr. Mental from his mind. "Get ouuuut!" he howled, his snout pointing toward the bright moon. The sharp nails on his fingers dug into his skull, an ill-advised way to literally tear the thoughts out from his head.

Listen to me, Mr. Mental commanded through his thoughts. *We didn't come here to fight. Bring back Jonathan so he and I can talk.* Mr. Mental kept his right fingers pressed softly against the right side of his headband, but his cheeks and nose winced from the struggle to maintain contact with the beast's erratic mind. Just five seconds of infiltrating his conscious brain proved exhausting, but Mr. Mental pressed on to make contact with The Wolfman's human side.

"Get ouuuut!" the hairy brute erupted again like a volcano, throwing his arms in the air as his torso writhed in all directions. Mr. Mental's efforts began wearing on The Wolfman. His mind caught a vision of Jonathan Breck while the beast's exterior shrank back down from his oversized demon form. As the horns in his head reverted into his skull, the bone plating and shaggy fur covering his arms and torso retreated back beneath his skin.

Sharp Shot and Fireball watched the shrinking monster as he transformed back into a tall, lanky man. Fireball smirked while Sharp Shot's eyes and mouth pried open at the astounding sight before her. As The Wolfman's enormous chest collapsed to half the size, his hectic breathing returned to a normal rate. Mr. Mental approached Jonathan Breck, whose bare chest and arms were pressed against the cold earth. While taking long, slow breaths, his human mind regained consciousness.

"Now let's all just stay calm here," Mr. Mental warned, flipping his eyes between each of his team members.

"I didn't think you could control his mind," Fireball blurted, his eyes fixed on Breck's recovering body.

"The Magician's help," Mr. Mental explained. "With the mixture of his magic and my technology, I can influence— not control—the beast. I was only able to calm his enraged state, but his chaotic brain waves make him impossible for me to command."

"You've only stunned my animal side," Breck announced, turning himself off of his stomach and onto his back. "But he will be back soon."

"Well then we'd better get to talking," Mr. Mental smiled while adjusting the black gloves on his hands.

"I may be more docile than my alter-ego, but I have nothing to say to you," Breck barked, his gruff voice deepening back toward his bestial form.

Mr. Mental stepped right up to Breck, confident that the monster would remain in hibernation for at least a few more minutes. Gazing down on Breck's frail body, Mr. Mental raised both eyebrows and grinned through his teeth, "I think both of your personalities will be interested in what I have to say. That's why I wanted to speak to each of you at the same time."

"We hate you!" The Wolfman snapped back, clenching his teeth as he tightened his cheeks and forehead.

"A fact that I am well aware of." Mr. Mental crouched down over Breck's body, extending a hand to help him up. "But you hate *him* even more." As The Wolfman's brown eyes turned blood red again, he tightened his forehead.

"What do you mean, *him*?" His voice grew deeper, like a ferocious lion fighting to protect her cubs.

"The Trifecta," Mr. Mental elaborated. "They're training a new Infiniti."

This statement stirred a blazing fire in The Wolfman's red eyes as his whole body shook like a tremor from the rage mounting inside of him. "What did you say?"

"I said they're training a new Mr. Infiniti," Mr. Mental repeated. He smiled and gloated, "I thought that might pique your interest." The Wolfman's right hand doubled in size, taking hold of Mr. Mental's right forearm, so he could help him up from the ground.

Now the roles reversed. Breck stood on his feet, his muscles expanding again while he towered over Mr. Mental's insignificant body. "I thought Infinity was destroyed?" he snarled.

"Power like that can't be extinguished in one try. You of all people should realize that. I know that you hate what we did to you, but you hate *him* even more."

"I've waited for years to get my revenge for what he did." Talking about Mr. Infiniti angered Breck, increasing his monstrous size. He towered over Mr. Mental, having nearly reached his maximum height of 9 feet. The brown fur started to grow from his forearms and cheeks like the short, sprouting grass of a golf green while his chest expanded and closed with long, deep breaths. Mr. Mental didn't need to access The Wolfman's mind to recognize that he was contemplating his decision.

Halfway between his human and beast form, he let out a long snort to render his verdict. "I will join you," he began. "But I want my shot at this new Mr. Infiniti. He is mine to destroy. Got it?"

"I believe that we can arrange something along those lines," Mr. Mental smiled, lifting his eyebrows an inch above his eyes. "Welcome back to The Four Faces." He reached out with his right hand, and Breck took hold with his enormous paw. "We've got a great deal of work to do over the coming months."

While Mr. Mental chuckled, his shoulders bounced up and down. As he shook The Wolfman's hand, a gleaming yellow light radiated from behind his red shades, signaling his assurance that he now possessed the last piece necessary for the final phase of the resurrection.

19. Upgrade

Michael

January 18th

"Michael, how are you feeling?" Auto asked while he moved up behind his young friend, placing his right palm on Michael's shoulder. The cuff of his pinstripe suit pressed up against Michael's back, startling him from a deep state of contemplation. Both heroes stood in the main atrium to the Rec. Center, only a few feet from the base of the large fountain with Madeline Price, the founder of the Green team, in the center. Michael wore a new white suit with a black vest underneath his coat and a golden tie that was accented by thin, royal blue stripes.

"Just fine," Michael answered, turning to view Auto's expressionless face. This was a lie, but he wasn't completely sure how to describe what he was feeling. His fluctuating powers left him more vexed than ever, and after his conversation with Stone two months earlier, he wasn't sure how far he could trust the Trifecta Leader. Since then, every conversation he'd had with Auto felt uneasy, and Michael now noticed a fake sincerity in his voice.

Auto looked into Michael's glassy eyes, indicating the young teen was far from fine. Something had changed within Michael from the year before, something even he himself couldn't comprehend. "You haven't seemed fine these past few months," Auto suggested to Michael. His voice seemed calm and soothing, but Malix and Stone did say Auto isn't always what he seems. "What's bothering you, my boy?"

Michael considered the answer to this question. He thought about his problems almost every day; in fact, since his arrival in Hero City, that's all he ever seemed to have—problems. The two most prevalent ones of late being his brother's missing body and his lack of control over his abilities. But he couldn't pinpoint the exact source of these problems. Somehow, deep down in his gut, he just knew Mastermind hadn't manufactured the fluctuations in his powers.

Dozens of factors influenced the changes manifesting inside of him, yet some part of his subconscious knew someone else was behind this metamorphosis. Nothing in his life seemed to happen by accident, which constantly worried him that he really was a pawn in someone's game. And after speaking with Stone and Malix, he began wondering if Auto was the chess master.

"I'm still just having trouble adjusting to this life," Michael replied, which was neither completely true nor false. Michael needed at least another year to adapt to all of the subtle nuances that came with living and training in Hero City.

As Auto closed his eyes, he nodded, "I understand. This is a difficult world to navigate, but that's why I'm here to give you guidance." He scrunched his eyes, intensifying his gaze upon Mr. Infiniti's heavy shoulders. "Is Mr. Mental still weighing on your mind?"

Michael lowered his head, placing his stare on the tiles beneath his feet. "I feel more foolish than anything," he pouted. "I let Mr. Mental get the best of me, and he escaped because I underestimated him."

Auto moved closer to place his right palm on Michael's shoulder. "Mr. Mental's powers are incredibly formidable. It's amazing that your young mind even survived such a focused attack by him. Are you still feeling the residual effects of his control?" Michael suspected this was the question that plagued most of the Trifecta members. But honestly, he wasn't sure how much command Mr. Mental still held. Perhaps he was responsible for Michael's loss of control.

Closing his eyes, Michael shook his head a few inches from left to right. "I don't think he has any control over me, but—" Michael wanted to say he couldn't be sure; however, he thought better of announcing this to Auto.

"But what?" the Elder inquired, leaning forward on his toes to reach a few inches closer to Michael. There was an eager glistening in his eye like he already knew what Michael suspected. His nightmares were getting worse; in fact, they haunted him almost every time he closed his eyes.

"Nothing," Michael mumbled through his lips. He rotated his head to his right and took two steps away from Auto.

The Elder narrowed his gaze in disbelief before easing the tension with a smile. "If you say so." However, Michael could see Auto suspected he was withholding an important piece of information. Yet the most disconcerting feeling for Michael was a gut intuition that somehow Auto already knew what was wrong, and this meeting was merely an opportunity to confirm his suspicions.

"I have something for you," Auto announced to his young protégé. Michael looked up, his eyes examining Auto's face as the Elder reached inside his suit jacket. He slipped his right hand into his coat pocket and pulled out a thin, gold card. "This is for you." Auto extended his hand forward, inviting Michael to take the card from him.

Though Michael hesitated for a moment, he eventually clamped the card between his thumb and forefinger. Flipping over the thin piece of durable metal, he pulled the front side up to his eyes. The text on the front projected into a virtual screen that read, "He Is Ready," with the bottom signed by Auto.

Michael squinted at the virtual image, his eyes scrutinizing the three words that didn't make any sense. "What does this mean?" he questioned.

"Take this card to your suit designer," Auto instructed. "At my request, he has been preparing a newly designed piece of technology for you. But I ordered him to wait until you were ready. Now is the time. Go see him, and use your new tool wisely." A smile crept up Auto's cheek while his head drooped down and his eyebrows rose up his forehead.

As Michael examined the card further, he flipped the thin, laminated metal between his fingers. When he looked up, he found Auto had disappeared. "I'm ready," Michael mumbled to himself, not quite sure what that meant just yet. But he would soon find out.

Choosing to skip yet another lunch, Michael zipped straight to the Hall of Heroes where Jacque was waiting for him. Immediately after Michael stepped through the main entrance, the tailor called to him from the hall on his left. "Mr. Infiniti!" he shouted, tapping his left foot up and down like a methodical machine. "I've been expecting you for quite a while now."

Michael opened his mouth to respond, trying to inform Jacque that he raced over after receiving the card from Auto, but the frantic designer interrupted him by storming over to Michael's side. "I've been preparing this for you since the day we first met. Ahaha." Jacque rolled his eyes up toward his brain as he grew a smile. "Can you believe that was a year ago? How the time does fly."

"Yeah, Auto told me to give you this," Michael explained, extending his hand with the card between his middle and forefinger. "He said I should—"

But once again, Jacque's impatience interrupted Michael in mid-sentence. "Forget about that," he jittered, holding his palms together while tapping his fingers against each other. "Come with me." He reached out and snatched Michael by the arm, dragging him as if he was a doll.

After pushing through the double doors to his workroom, Jacque tossed Michael into a mechanized barbershop style chair. The bewildered teen gazed at his tailor who was sliding a heavy chest from underneath a long, metal table. After bending down on his right knee, Jacque removed a pinkie-sized silver key from his shirt pocket. Placing the key into the lock on the chest, he lifted the round lid and froze, staring with an awestruck twinkle in his eyes. His breathing slowed to a calm, uncharacteristic state.

Turning from the box, Jacque faced Michael with a shiny blue piece of metal resting in both hands like a newborn puppy. "Do you know what this is?" Jacque inquired. Michael squinted his eyes and leaned forward in his seat to examine the cylindrical piece of technology. The metal was shaped with an angle that kept one end wider than the other, like a traffic cone.

Michael shook his head. "I'm not sure. It looks like—"

"It is a power band," Jacque explained before Michael could finish his thought. "Hold out your left wrist," he ordered. Michael's left brow rose as he looked at his tailor with bewildered eyes. "Hold out your left wrist," Jacque repeated more sternly this time.

This time, Michael did what he was told and extended his left arm out parallel to the floor beneath him. After Jacque unhooked the arm band's metal latch, he placed one half against the underside of Michael's forearm. Lifting the other half over the top of Michael's wrist, he snapped the latch back into place. A coaster-sized screen, illuminated with a blue light, sat on top of Michael's forearm while a low humming charge resonated through the room.

Scrunching his forehead, Michael jumped back in his seat at the startling motion. "What's going on?" he cried.

"The arm band's recognition circuits are activating, just as I thought they would," Jacque smiled. Michael struggled to breath while the circuits flowed through him, tingling every nerve and muscle in his body. Then he experienced an intense burning in his birthmark with a pressure that he hadn't felt since his encounter with Mastermind.

"What do you mean?" Michael struggled to blurt out because of the discomfort he was experiencing.

"This armband was originally designed by Mr. Infinity, himself. Only he could activate the energy particles inside, but I had a hunch that you would possess the same strength and willpower to re-boot the circuitry."

The intense tingling and burning subsided, but Michael still felt a rush of energy flowing through him. "Wow," he muttered, pulling his wrist closer to his face. "What does it do?"

"Among other things, it will amplify your power, hopefully stabilizing the extreme fluctuations you've been experiencing," Jacque explained, reaching his left hand out to press his finger against the touch screen. The dim blue light sprang to life. "Press your right thumb against the pad." He leaned forward, a sparkling twinkle radiating from the center of each of his eyes.

Michael placed his thumb against the pad, which increased the whirring hum that continued buzzing around the room. The luminescent blue light radiated around Michael's body, blinding both him and Jacque. When they opened their eyes, they found a virtual hologram of a blank face projecting from the wristband.

"I have been successfully uploaded," the arm band proclaimed to Michael, who recognized the familiar voice as Melvin's.

"As I suspected," Jacque smiled. "Activation of the arm band's advanced circuitry caused them to automatically download Melvin's A.I. into the hard drive." The tall tailor bowed down, leaning in closer to examine the screen on Michael's new weapon.

"All systems are operational," Melvin announced while the blue light in the wristband flashed in and out with each syllable spoken. "I await your orders."

"With Auto's guidance, I've designed and updated the tech. within the wristband," Jacque explained. Michael's eyes were glued to the glowing screen as documents full of text flashed in front of him. His immense intellect absorbed the knowledge, instantly preparing him to properly harness and operate the potential within his new weapon. "The A.I. will give you even more tactical options than your sunglasses can, but more importantly, I upgraded the weaponry with designs to combat the specific technology utilized by Mastermind."

This name caused Michael's head to jump up from the screen. "What do you mean?"

"I mean that mini-missile that she used to momentarily paralyze you would be useless now," Jacque elaborated, turning his shoulder toward the table behind him to pick up a pistol the size of a flashlight. Pointing the black firearm at Michael, he pulled the trigger twice, launching two small projectile missiles. Time slowed for a moment, allowing Michael's eyes and brain to analyze the incoming attack. The electro-shock tips crackled with blue electricity, and Michael realized they were the same mini-missiles that Mastermind used against him back on the plains of Africa.

But Mr. Infiniti's instincts kicked in as he lifted his left wrist to block the projectiles. The sizzling heads bounced off of a blue laser shield erected from the wristband. Although Michael's own power formed the shield, the band adjusted the strength and frequency of the barrier to withstand and repel the scientific circuitry designed by Mastermind.

"Awesome," Michael blurted, turning his wrist back and forth to examine the incredible design of his new sidekick.

"That's just the tip of the iceberg," Jacque explained. "Mastermind may know your greatest weaknesses, but with this new weapon, you will be able to stand against her."

Michael extended his left arm and pointed his extended fingers toward Jacque's computer screen. The wall-sized monitor sprang to life with the controls under Michael's command. "It's generating some sort of new technopathic communication powers," his voice murmured, shocked by this new discovery. "I can almost hear the computer's thoughts."

"The wrist band has tele-communicative circuits that will allow you to make contact with virtually any other piece of artificial intelligence. Omega himself designed the rare microchip that makes this possible, and only he and Mr. Infinity were given the privilege of wielding such an incredible power.

"The band is synced with Melvin's presence in your shades, which will help you fully comprehend the foreign computer programs you encounter. Among other things, this will make you even more dangerous against opponents who rely on advanced technology—Mastermind in particular."

"How long have you been working on this?" Michael asked.

"I began my work on your initiation day, but I focused all of my efforts on this project immediately after your run-in with Mastermind. Ah, but I have yet to show you the personal touch that I added."

Jacque reached out his right arm to press a tiny button the size of a grain of rice that stuck out a millimeter from the side of the touch screen. The instant he pushed his thumb to the activation switch, the screen sprang to life, radiating a surprising luminescence that blinded him for a moment.

"Place any one of your fingers against the touch screen," Jacque instructed. Michael looked at him like a confused child, afraid what would happen if he followed Jacque's orders. Still, he acquiesced, pressing his right pointer finger firmly against the sensitive surface. In a flash of light, Michael's sunglasses projected a 3-dimensional image of himself. His head jumped back an inch in surprise, which told Jacque the program worked.

"You should see a virtual version of yourself, yes?" Jacque asked.

Michael nodded his head but said nothing.

"Gooood," Jacque elongated his response, expressing his pleasure in the success of his newest design. "I've uploaded several wardrobes, so you can instruct Melvin to give you different options for your attire, and the armband will comply."

"What do you mean?" Michael asked, turning his head left to Jacque's grinning face.

"I'll show you. Choose your battle suit," Jacque directed.

Using his mental connection with Melvin, Michael selected his battle suit, transforming the miniature, virtual version of himself that was standing before his eyes. The dark designer suit that was covering the 3-dimensional figure reshaped into a new version of Mr. Infiniti's battle suit.

"Has the model version changed before your eyes?" Jacque asked, anticipating Michael's response.

"Yeah," he answered, his voice squeaking from surprise.

"Excellent." Jacque's smiling countenance made Michael wonder what personal stake he had in this invention. In this moment, his eyes glared with something different—something almost sinister. "Now activate your new attire," he ordered.

As if he was moving a muscle, Michael's mind instinctively told his sunglasses to activate the wardrobe that rotated before his eyes. His shades remotely communicated with the wristband, which activated a low humming noise like a truck sitting idle with the engine running. Millions of tiny fibers flowed from beneath the edges of the wristband, the whole bunch crawling like microscopic spiders all over Michael's skin.

The glove on his left hand was the first piece to formulate before his eyes. Michael's bare fist was protected in the glove's energy shield as the spidery fibers scurried across his left arm, covering his bicep and shoulder in blue padding, topped by metal plating. In less than two seconds, the fibers formed over his chest, down his torso and then covered his right arm. The heavy padding and armor forged the infinity symbol in his chest plate, and the word Infiniti on top of both shoulders.

Michael's legs were the only part of his body not yet covered. His golden belt with compartments formulated first and then the outer-metal plating ran across his quads, finishing with his heavy, white boots tipped by the shiny, blue steel toes. The last piece to form was Michael's white cape with a blue border, which hung from his shoulders.

Jacque marveled before the success of his creation while Michael moved his right hand over the wristband, amazed by the instantaneous transformation of his clothing. The virtual screen in front of Mr. Infiniti's eyes displayed dozens of text boxes that scrolled information from the top to bottom of his shades. Three main text documents attached to three different arrows that pointed to a virtual image of his gloves, belt, and body armor.

The text box that connected to Michael's gloves had the most interesting information. Among other new powers, Mr. Infiniti's gloves generated an energy output ten times more powerful than ever before. He sensed that his laser fists could blow through almost any solid object.

While the aesthetic design of Michael's battle suit was mostly identical to his previous one, he did still notice a few differences. His black gloves were the first, most noticeable change, but the new gold belt around his waist gave a certain magnanimous glow. Not to mention the frame of his shades, now turned gold, held a single, royal blue lens that spanned over both eyes and part of his face.

"The nanites packed within your wristband give you the ability to change wardrobe in mere seconds," Jacque explained. "With Auto's help, I programmed in eight different dress suits along with your basic and this new, advanced battle suit."

"Wow," Michael muttered as his eyes scanned and analyzed dozens of different functions added to his battle suit. Jacque and Auto had affixed hundreds of new gadgets to

Michael's belt, including a stealth activator that caught Michael's attention.

"How does the cloaking device work?" Michael inquired.

"Aha, you have a good eye for quality," Jacque proclaimed. "That is one of the most valuable and rare upgrades designed by Auto. The nanite technology grants your clothes the ability to bend the light around you, which essentially allows you to turn invisible."

Michael pressed his right forefinger against the touch screen on his armband and then slid his hand forward, which activated the stealth function in his battle suit. Before Michael's eyes, his arms and gloves grew as clear as a glass window. "Incredible," Michael muttered, waving his left hand from left to right in front of his face. As he moved his limb, his arm remained clear, but became slightly visible, like a shaking glass of water.

"As you can see, the invisibility is only 100 percent effective when you remain perfectly motionless," Jacque explained. "As soon as you move, the light-bending chips in your suit can't keep up with the motion of your limbs. However, this new application to your suit will allow you to remain undetected if you stay still."

"Awesome," Michael exhaled.

"And that's just the beginning," Jacque elaborated. "It will take some time for you to analyze all of the different functions and applications that the wristband provides. Read through the manual that has been uploaded to your shades, and work on mastering the added power you now wield."

Michael nodded in agreement. The Trifecta's standard supply of gadgets were easy for him to comprehend and master, but this armband's complexity extended far beyond any other piece of technology he experienced or even read about before. Auto must have commissioned every single Trifecta scientist to work on this project. Yet one question lingered at the forefront of Michael's mind.

"Why now?" he inquired of Jacque, staring into his tailor's eyes.

Jacque waited a moment before answering, leading Michael to question if he would reveal the truth. Because this was the first sign of deception Michael had seen in his friend, he grew wary of this powerful gift.

"Let's just say the return of Mastermind made this necessary," Jacque explicated.

Michael accepted this explanation, but he detected a hint of duplicity in Jacque's answer. Never before had he questioned Jacque's motives, but Stone and Malix's enlightening information left Michael suspicious of everyone, even his closest allies.

After a few seconds of transparent thought, Michael broke free of his trance and excused himself from Jacque's work room. "Thank you for your help, but I should be getting to my next class," he lied, fully aware that he had nearly an hour to spare.

"Of course," Jacque smiled, accepting his gratitude. "Let me know if you have any questions."

"I will," Michael gulped as he turned toward the exit behind him. He pushed open the swinging double doors and headed back toward the streets of the city.

Jacque exhaled, falling into his barber-style chair.

The enormous computer screen in front of him sprang to life, projecting the image of a shadowed figure, cloaked in a shroud of darkness with glowing green eyes at the head. "Did he take the bait?" the shadow asked. Jacque leapt up from his seat, frightened by the first sound of the figure's voice.

As he responded, his jaw chattered up and down like a talking puppet. "I did just as you instructed. I installed the modifications exactly to your specifications."

"Excellent," the shadow laughed. "You've done your job well, but if you reveal even a shred of your work to anyone, we will find you."

Jacque nodded as he replied, "I understand. I won't tell a soul."

"Good, see that you don't, or we will know. And remember, when Mastermind begins her attack, that piece of technology will save his life." The screen died, and the shining light turned black, leaving Jacque alone to sit in his misery. He held an old, metal belt buckle in his hands and rubbed his forefingers around the smooth edge. The center displayed the blue infinity symbol from the very first suit he designed for Mr. Infinity.

"May I be forgiven," he whispered to himself.

20. New Alliances

Mr. Mental

January 30th

"Have you finished all of the preparations for Mr. Infiniti's battle?" Mr. Mental inquired. He sat at his desk in the small office that Mastermind provided for him. A virtual computer screen radiated the only light in the entire room, save for a hidden figure's glowing green eyes in the back corner of the office.

"Everything is all set," the ominous shadow responded. "We've given him his new weapon, along with ample time to master the controls, and the necessary battle programs are uploaded and ready for his two trial runs tomorrow and next month. If he succeeds in tomorrow's test, I suggest we move up his final trial. Once he has harnessed the full power of his new weapon, we need only for our operative to lead him to the necessary spot next to the Picasso Sculpture. Are you sure you can still make connection with Mr. Infiniti's mind to resurrect the necessary memory?"

"I am always sure," Mr. Mental grinned. "Our connection is faint, but once he's outside of their city, making contact with his mind won't pose a problem. Just so long as his body is ready. This will prove a large step forward in his evolution while leaving just enough time for him to fester over the inevitable nightmares that are bound to ensue. The final day is approaching quickly. We have little room for error at this point."

"Indeed. Will all of the other pieces be ready?" the shadow asked.

Mr. Mental swiveled his chair counterclockwise to face his ally's silhouetted body. "We have recruited our last member, but I still need more time to analyze the potential outcomes of every move the Trifecta and Mastermind might make. We must be ready for all scenarios if we are to foil Mastermind's hidden agenda. Are you sure she doesn't know we are aware of her plan?"

"I'm fairly certain. I only caught a glimpse of her notes after she decoded the data reel that she stole from the Trifecta. If we knew where she hid the reel, we could get a better idea, but for now, you have all of the variables I can provide."

"No worries," Mr. Mental assured. "The information you interpreted from her computer screen does fit with my assumptions, and I am thoroughly preparing for any deviations she might throw our way. Just monitor his practice run tomorrow, and then make sure his final test goes as we planned. We can't afford for any slip-ups there." As he finished this sentence, Mr. Mental turned his chair back toward the glistening screen of his computer.

"I'll take care of it," the shadow hissed while the automatic door slid open on Mr. Mental's left side, flooding the room with light—yet only Mr. Mental remained. The shadow had disappeared in the same mysterious fashion as he always did.

Before the super genius could return to his work, he knew he had one piece of business to discuss with Fireball, so he scanned the building for his comrade's brainwaves before proceeding down toward Mastermind's meeting room. As he strolled through the dark metallic hallways, Sharp Shot sidled up alongside him, hoping to get closer to the man she pegged as the brains of their entire operation. And while Mr. Mental could read right through her thoughts, he was happy to have a new protégé whom he could mould into his own obedient killer.

"Where are you going?" Sharp Shot asked, turning her artificial eye toward Mr. Mental while he kept his gaze directed straight ahead.

"I must visit with my brother to give him a job," Mr. Mental answered. "We have much to do and very little time."

Sharp Shot exhaled a deep breath like a disappointed child. Mr. Mental scanned her outer-most thoughts to find her true motive. "I wish you would entrust me with some of these jobs. I could contribute so much to your plan if you'd just let me in on the details." She pouted her lip to appear hurt, but Mr. Mental could not be so easily manipulated.

"Ha," he chuckled. "You aren't as good as you think at pretending to be the wounded damsel who feels neglected." He stopped his gait just before entering through the sliding doors to Mastermind's meeting room. After turning his body toward Sharp Shot, he lifted his right hand to remove his shades, revealing the dim, yellow glow in his irises. "I can see through you like a glass sculpture."

Sharp Shot released her eager puppy dog eyes into an angry squint. "You know, some people can be too smart for their own good," she sneered.

"Hmmm, hmm, hmm," Mr. Mental laughed again through closed lips. "I'll admit, you do fascinate me. Your ambition can take you far, but only with the proper guidance. Stick close to me and we'll see just how much of your potential you can reach." With that last statement, he stepped to his left, activating the sliding doors. Fireball sat waiting at the other side of the table, a disgruntled frown on his face.

"You kept me waiting," he growled through his teeth. "You know I hate to wait."

Before the doors closed behind Mr. Mental, Sharp Shot slipped in right behind him. "So sorry, my brother," Mr. Mental responded in a calm but insincere tone, unconcerned that he had kept Fireball waiting. "It couldn't be helped. But I do have your responsibilities ready and outlined for you." Mr. Mental reached into the inside pocket of his coat and retrieved a small data drive, which he tossed over to Fireball. "Read through the directions and fully analyze the blueprint on there," Mr. Mental ordered. "Your role will be integral after the infiltration."

"Whatever you say, brother," Fireball agreed, dropping his petulant demeanor. He lifted himself from his seat and walked around the table to where Mr. Mental and Sharp Shot were standing. "I will get started on this right away," he assured his compatriot as they shook each other's hands.

"Thank you, brother," Mr. Mental smiled. "We know you will come through, as always."

Fireball released his firm grip on Mr. Mental's hand and exited the room, the glass sliding doors automatically closing behind him, which left just Sharp Shot and Mr. Mental alone.

"Why are you so devoted to each other?" Sharp Shot asked after she watched Fireball strut down to the end of the hallway. "You and Fireball, I mean."

Mr. Mental froze at this question, his eyes glassed over in thought. After taking a single, deep breath, he turned to her, his face sullen. "I wasn't always like this, you know?" he responded. His cheeks sank behind the gloom that shrouded his face.

"What do you mean?" Sharp Shot inquired, leaning a bit closer to Mr. Mental, his last comment having piqued her interest.

"I mean I wasn't always an evil genius hellbent on revenge and destruction," he elaborated, his cold face still blank as a white board. "I used to be a petty thief, just trying to survive by using my gift. Sure, I could interpret and influence the thoughts of the weak-minded, which made it easy for me to pickpocket them or trick them into doing what I wanted, but I never stole more than I thought others could bear to lose. I was nothing compared to what I am now." Mr. Mental paused, turning his gaze to his right, as if divulging this information was difficult for him.

"Then one day, I got nabbed by one of the Trifecta's low-level operatives. He caught me tricking a man into believing that his watch was cursed. When I picked up the watch from the garbage, their soldier was there to slap a pair of handcuffs on me. I tried to run, but I should have known that escape from their controlling clutches was impossible."

"What did they do with you?" Sharp Shot asked, her ears glued to the surprise and suspense of Mr. Mental's story.

"Humph, from this point on, it might be easier for me to show you," Mr. Mental suggested. He reached out with his right hand and placed his open palm next to Sharp Shot's left temple, but she jumped back an inch out of reflex.

"That is, if it's okay with you?" Mr. Mental requested.

Sharp Shot nodded for him to go ahead, so he pressed his right hand flat against her left temporal lobe, transferring one of his most important memories to her. They both stood as by-standers in this memory with Mr. Mental's own voice narrating the experience.

I was sitting in the back of their prisoner transport vehicle, my hands cuffed and resting on my knees. Next to me sat another criminal whose body rocked back and forth on the bench seating that lined both sides of the transport. The engine roared, and the truck took off, heading back toward the original Trifecta Penitentiary. There, we would face dire penalties for our crimes.

"What did they nab you for?" the other man asked Mr. Mental.

I examined him a bit closer before answering. He had a gruff beard and wild, wide eyes that popped from his sockets. "I've stolen things from people, conned them out of their possessions," Mr. Mental responded to the man.

"Serious charges," he muttered, shaking his head from side to side. "You'll be lucky to avoid harsh judgment from the trial council."

I was young at this point, unaware of the severe and secret laws the Trifecta managed to impart on the world. Like most naive people around the globe, I had no idea what horrible punishments lay ahead.

"What kind of serious judgment?" Mr. Mental asked.

"If you're lucky, life in their prison camps," the man answered.

"And if I'm not so lucky?" Mr. Mental's eyes widened, afraid of the answer.

"Death," the man muttered in a matter-of-fact tone. "That's where I'm headed, the death chamber, part of their zero tolerance crime policy."

The present day Mr. Mental inhaled deeply and then exhaled a dozen wavering breaths of fear. He gulped hard before elaborating for Sharp Shot. *I wanted to ask more questions, but my mind was weak then, unable to analyze and evaluate situations the way that I can now. So I sat in silence, contemplating my imminent end at the hand of the ruthless Trifecta. I couldn't imagine what horrible demise they had planned for me. But that was the moment that changed my life forever.*

A loud pop echoed through the transport truck, and both prisoners were thrown from their seats as the entire vehicle dropped before the rims of the wheels began screeching across the street. The vehicle slid sideways and then slowly tumbled over onto the right side, throwing Mr. Mental and the other prisoner even further inside the holding section.

After the truck slid to a stop, Mr. Mental heard a loud hissing noise, like a blowtorch, as the door on the back of the vehicle melted into a puddle like ice cream under a heating lamp. The liquid metal cooled on the side of the overturned transport, leaving a wide hole in the back for a new figure to enter. Sharp Shot recognized this man as a young Fireball, wearing a tight, outdated suit of spandex with a red mask wrapped around his head and over his eyes. This was the common old-school super villain ensemble, what all super humans wore before the institution of the battle suit concept.

Mr. Mental lay on his side, his hands still cuffed as he stared up at the magnificent man who had flames flowing around his gloves. *This was my first glimpse of the man who would become my brother and ally, and looking back now, I realize I had never seen such a marvelous sight.*

"Gentlemen, let me help you with those," Fireball offered as he torched a flame through the binding chain on each of their cuffs. After taking two steps forward, he reached down to help Mr. Mental stand up. "Patrick Jordan," he spoke.

"How do you know my name?" Mr. Mental asked, taking two steps back toward the wall of the overturned transport. He squinted at Fireball with a distrustful scowl while the other man hustled through the hole at the back of the vehicle and scurried away.

"My partner and I have been watching you for some time now," Fireball answered. "We've been searching for you."

"Searching for me? Why?" Mr. Mental inquired with a hint of both confusion and panic in his voice. "What do you want from me?"

"We've been looking to recruit one final member to help lead our new organization."

I was confused. Here I knew so much about Fireball—everyone around the world did—and yet I couldn't understand what use someone of his power would have with a small fry like myself. Still, he had caught my curiosity, so I bit on his bait.

"What kind of organization?" Mr. Mental asked.

"Come with me, and I'll show you," Fireball smiled, extending his hand in a gesture of friendship. "We only have 1.2 minutes before Trifecta reinforcements arrive, and they will wield greater firepower. We can't talk here." Fireball reached forward for Mr. Mental to grab his hand.

This was not yet the turning point for me. I knew of Fireball's capabilities along with his motives. And although I feared deception by his kind, I was in such a dire situation that I had no choice but to accept his help. So I went with him.

After Mr. Mental gripped Fireball's wrist, they took off. Fireball blasted his way out of the hole in the car, carrying Mr. Mental with him.

At this point, Mr. Mental fast-forwarded ahead to the back alley of a warehouse where Fireball slowed to a stop. After setting Mr. Mental on the grimy pavement, he landed himself. Sirens blared through the city while police hover-copters swarmed the skies overhead with their search lights shining down on the streets. Fireball stepped up to a large, metal docking door in the side of the alley's brick wall exterior, and the entrance automatically lifted for him to enter.

"Come, we can hide here while we wait for their forces to settle," he instructed of Mr. Mental, who looked at him with suspicious eyes.

I was intrigued by this villain's interest in me, but I approached with caution. For some reason, I couldn't read his mind, which unnerved me. Still, I had no choice but to follow him into his shelter from the hundreds of Trifecta eyes that were searching for me.

After Mr. Mental stepped into the warehouse, the metal door slammed shut behind him, and the lights died. Sharp Shot jumped at this startling change in mood. "What's happening?" she cried.

Not to worry. No harm can come to you here. These are only memories.

Then a new voice echoed through the pitch black room. "He has fear," the man's ominous voice proclaimed.

"Just a small amount," Fireball's voice responded. Mr. Mental did not move. He seemed to be searching for the mind of the second man but could not find him. Fireball elaborated, "I know he lacks significant strength now, but I can see his potential. When all is said and done, his power will rival even our own. Trust me."

"Very well then," the other voice agreed. "Let's just hope you are right." And with that last sentence, a pair of green eyes radiated from across the room, flickering three times before the lights returned. In an instant, dozens of hanging fixtures illuminated the warehouse without making a single sound, the way most large lights do when warming up.

Fireball stepped up a few feet from Mr. Mental with a friendly smile. "My partner just worries too much," he explained. "He and I both believe in you, and we want you on our team. I've been searching for someone with your particular skill set for some time."

Mr. Mental fixed his eyes on Fireball while trying to discern his true motives. "And if I say no?" he questioned.

"Then you are free to go about your mundane life of petty theft, worrying that any day might be the one when the Trifecta captures and sends you off to their death camps. Or you can join our growing organization with the promise of greatness. We've scoured the globe, looking for a final member to lead our forces, and I want that person to be you."

I felt conflicted. In all the time since I discovered my powers to read and influence minds, I never once considered taking up a battle with others. I had been shy and in many ways ashamed of my powers. When facing bullies, I turned the other cheek. While others stepped on me to advance their own lives, I told myself that using my powers against them would only bring me trouble.

"Why me?" Mr. Mental asked, tilting his chin up, allowing him to look down his nose upon the arrogant smirk of Fireball.

"I believe in you," he answered. "As does my brother. The Trifecta is squeezing in on people like us."

"Criminals," Mr. Mental interrupted, a tone of disapproval in his voice.

"No," Fireball shook his head. "People with a different point of view than their own. The Elders have nearly snuffed out the last remnants of free will in this world. That is why we are forming a resistance. Their oppression has pushed us to the point of desperation, so we must shove back. People will hate you for leading us in their liberation, but every story needs a great villain—and we need someone of your supreme intelligence to help guide our forces as we attempt to take back the autonomy the Trifecta stole from this world."

I was even more intrigued after hearing these words. My mind felt a sense of liberation, as if a thick layer of brainwashing simply melted away, revealing a truth that I could not see before.

"How can you possibly amass enough strength to defeat Omega and Mr. Infinity?" Mr. Mental questioned. "They wield ungodly power. They are invincible."

Fireball waved his hand out in front of his body and closed his eyes for a moment. "You needn't worry about them. Omega shares our views of the Trifecta, and in time the world will see that Mr. Infinity is no match for his brother's supreme strength and intelligence. We are extending this generous offer to you for the next 24 hours. You can contact us using this." Fireball extended his hand and slapped a wallet-sized device in Mr. Mental's palm. He stepped back, and Mr. Mental almost jumped when he saw his new ally fading into darkness. "24 hours," Fireball called out as he dissolved into the shadows. "We'll be waiting."

That was where the memory ended as Mr. Mental brought Sharp Shot back to real time.

"So I'm guessing you took him up on his offer," Sharp Shot commented, blinking her eyes to shake off the residual effects of Mr. Mental's connection with her.

"This was the turning point of my life," Mr. Mental nodded. "And I owe Fireball for that. He saved my life that day. Not just from that truck that was carrying me to my doom; he saved me from an enslaved existence. I was blind, just as the rest of the world is, but that day he opened my eyes. So I did accept their offer, and I've never looked back. Without their help, I could never have developed my power. That is why I am so devoted to my brethren. We may not be related by blood, but we are tied together by our cause. I suggest you devote such loyalty to us as well."

Sharp Shot smiled at Mr. Mental with a twinkle in her real eye. "So that's the real reason why you showed me this," she laughed. "To gain my allegiance."

"I believe in you the same way that they believed in me," Mr. Mental responded, a sincere nonchalance in his tone. "If I have your trust, I can help you increase your powers ten times over, just as mine did."

Sharp Shot curled her lips and wiped her tongue over her top teeth. "You don't need to worry," she chuckled. "I know that Mastermind will try to collect me, but I believe in you just as you have placed your faith in me. You have my allegiance." She reached out to shake Mr. Mental's hand, and he grew certain that she would be the perfect protégé as his plan moved forward.

"No!" Michael screamed out, leaping up in his bed during the middle of the night. His new armband buzzed on his wrist, and he felt a swelling in the birthmark on his chest.

"What happened?" Archer called over to his roommate. "Another nightmare?"

"Yeah, but it was different this time," Michael responded through his heavy breathing. "It was so bizarre. I dreamed that I was watching Mr. Mental and Fireball on the day that they first met." As a river of sweat dripped down Michael's cheeks, his wide eyes scanned his body and the room to regain some sense of awareness. He unhooked the armband from his wrist, and his heart rate began to slow.

Archer stared at his roommate, wiping his eyes with his hands. As Michael patted down his arms and chest, Archer blurted the only response he could think of. "That is crazy. Tell me about it." So Michael went into as much detail as he could remember, describing the same vision Mr. Mental just showed to Sharp Shot.

21. Technopath

Michael

January 31st

After Michael finished describing his nightmare to Archer, he couldn't fall back asleep. Instead, he sat on his bed, contemplating his difficult situation. Despite all of his exhaustive searches to find his brother, he hadn't discovered any evidence to help him uncover Mastermind's evil plot. And she hadn't made any appearances since he last saw her at the end of the summer.

When dawn broke, Michael snapped on his new wristband to activate his battle suit for a day of training. Just as before, the tiny nanites crawled over his body, draping him in some of the most advanced armor on the planet. After waiting for Archer to change into his battle suit, Michael led him out of the dorms and toward the battle simulation building.

All professors cancelled classes in advance for this day in order to allow the senior Trifecta members to confer with each other. So Michael and Archer scheduled a session in the Trifecta's high-tech, virtual training city. Now that he fully read the manual and ran a few minor trials with his new wristband, Michael wanted to test out his developing technopathic skills to prepare for his next meeting with Mastermind. He figured if he couldn't outsmart her, he might need his brute strength to force some answers out of her.

Plus Michael felt he needed the practice since the armband was just now stabilizing the fluctuation in his powers. The fall in Air and Water class was only the beginning of a chain reaction that led to at least a dozen more events where his powers failed him.

He considered contacting Stone for more advice, but he and most of the other high-profile heroes were either out of the city trying to track down Mastermind's lair, or they were working to fortify the city's defenses. Eliki and Auto had already fixed the glitch in the shield, so Mastermind couldn't force her way through again. Meanwhile, Professor Malix had become so busy that he cancelled four class sessions in two weeks, so he could direct Melvin in their manhunt. But even the Trifecta supercomputer failed to find her.

When the two teens reached the practice building, they met up with Molly, who was waiting for them in the main entrance. Because Michael and Archer were still only second-year students, they needed an advanced student or a professor to monitor their session in the virtual training city. And when Michael requested that Molly be the one to observe them, she could not have seemed happier to oblige.

"Hey, are you guys ready?" Molly asked as they approached her, a beaming smile reaching up to the blush on her rosy cheeks.

Michael nodded as he inhaled a deep breath, but Archer answered in his loud, obnoxious voice, "Is that a serious question. Haven't you learned by now that I'm always ready?"

"I don't know, is *that* a serious question?" Molly joked in a sarcastic tone, attempting to deflate Archer's overconfident ego. "Well, I'm glad you're already suited up so we can head straight to the teleporter," she added before turning her back to lead them deeper into the building.

"Awesome," Archer grinned. "Say Molly, how about I make you a deal. If I outscore Michael in this simulation, then you agree to go out on a date with me. How about it?"

"Sure," Molly responded without hesitation. Michael shifted his head toward her, and his heart jumped for fear that she actually intended to go on a date with Archer. However, she put his mind at ease by elaborating, "That's how confident I am that Michael will crush you in this training simulation." She winked at Michael as she finished saying this, and then she led the two teens toward the teleportation platforms.

After arriving at the teleporters, Michael and Archer stood on the beaming platforms while Molly took her place in the observation room. She stood among hundreds of virtual, video screens that would monitor their progress.

Before sending them on, Molly gave the two tens one last instruction to survive the simulation that Michael had chosen. "Remember your training, and use your imagination to defeat the logic of your enemy."

Michael nodded up to her and then called out, "Do it."

Molly pressed a red hovering button, which activated the transporter, sending Michael and Archer to the virtual city. They had reserved their 30 minute training window almost a week in advance, and during those 6 days, Michael only grew more anxious to test out his new wristband.

Once the teleporter finished ripping the two boys from the Trifecta building, transporting them to the virtual city, Archer pulled his right glove over his hand and sealed his motor-cycle helmet over his head. Michael observed the surrounding fake city's buildings as they morphed, growing and shrinking like the moving waves of an ocean's tide. Even after dozens of visits, this virtual world still amazed Michael every time he teleported here for battle training.

After sifting through his nightmares and all of the data he could find on Mastermind, Michael knew which simulation he wanted to engage. Touching his right finger to his shades, he requested, "Molly, prepare training exercise 412."

"It's already uploaded and ready to go," she responded via the communication link in Michael's shades. "Melvin will help me in monitoring your progress."

As Molly ended this sentence, Melvin announced over Michael and Archer's headsets. "Begin environment simulation for training 4-1-2, difficulty level eight." The cement ground beneath Michael's feet transformed into soft green grass and moist, squishy dirt. Hundreds of buildings vanished, replaced by trees that sprouted from the ground to tower hundreds of feet over the two heroes.

"You ready?" Michael asked Archer, who nodded in response as he activated the musical sound system in his helmet. He blasted a blaring rock song, which Michael's shades displayed in text, identifying this music as Radiation's song "Bone Crusher." Then Archer's determined grimace disappeared when his blue helmet visor flipped down over his face.

As Michael bobbed his head back and forth, Molly initiated the training protocol. "Melvin, activate the simulation," she ordered.

Observing the enormous trees, Archer attempted to ease the tension of this dangerous situation by making a joke over his communication link. "A jungle, you should feel right at home," he laughed.

"I grew up in the plains of Africa where the plants were nothing like this. We're in a South American rain forest. Much different from your typical African jungle."

"Whatever, trees are trees," Archer shrugged, his voice barely recognizable over the music seeping through his helmet. "I don't see a difference."

"Cut the chitchat," Molly commanded. "You should be on your toes at this point."

Michael had already planned to ignore Archer's ignorant comment. They could be attacked at any moment, so he didn't have time to explain the differences between the thousand varying types of trees that existed in the world. Aware of what they would face in these jungles, Michael agreed with Molly that they needed to stay alert.

"What kind of enemies did you have her activate?" Archer asked while his helmet moved from left to right, his viewport scanning the surroundings.

"One of Mastermind's inventions. Her personal enforcers that she sends out to do her dirty work. You'll see."

And Archer would see in just a second as the crackling of falling trees echoed through the fake forest. Dozens of thick vines rustled back and forth from the impending machines drawing closer. Archer glanced over to Michael, his frantic head turning back and forth, showing fear at the powerful movements of the approaching enemies. Trees toppled over, yet the advancing robots resonated no sound or vibration through the ground.

But because Michael had done his homework on Mastermind, he knew what was coming. She already studied him, so he returned the favor, analyzing every last detail available to him through the Trifecta's database. Melvin was particularly helpful in picking out the most imperative aspects to focus on. He showed Michael the source of her technopathic strength, but the new wristband directly prompted Michael to devise a plan. And this session would test his new theory.

Archer lifted his left arm, holding the front end of his bow straight out in front of his torso. He had the string pulled back with two arrows resting on the small ledge above the grip, each projectile prepared to launch at any moment. The rustling grew closer, and a few vines ripped from the trees just twenty feet off in the distance.

"Here they come," Michael announced as a dozen squid-like robots crashed through the nearest clearing, their mechanical tentacles clinging to the thick trunks of the surrounding trees. Each robot had one circular eye that glowed a menacing red, which glared across the final twenty feet that separated them from the two heroes. Archer gasped for only a second before regaining his composure.

The two lead robots blasted a powerful thin laser from the center of their red eyes, and the projectile sliced through two trees, sending them crashing down to the ground. Each beam flashed toward Michael and Archer, so they scrambled to split the robots' focus.

While Michael took flight, leaping ten feet in the air to his left, Archer dove to his right before rolling across the ground. He sprang back up into a kneeling crouch, aimed his two arrows and fired them toward the closest attacking drone. The evil eye of the robot rotated, cutting the first arrow in half, but the second traveled too swiftly. Immediately after the arrow's tip collided with the robot's metal exterior shell, an orb of yellow fire exploded, yet the robot still emerged with only slight signs of damage.

"Your typical, explosive arrows will have little effect on these robots," Molly explained to Archer. "You'll have to think outside the box if you want to take them down."

A reverberating hum buzzed through the forest as eight more of the squid robots charged their laser eyes. Michael already knew that their hard shells were almost impervious, but their weakness lay in their tentacles. The flexible design allowed the long limbs to wrap around objects and squeeze them like a vice, but this also made them vulnerable to attack. Four robots focused their continuous laser stream on Archer, who tumbled across the ground and hopped back up like a gymnast. After yanking three arrows from his quiver, he set them against the string of his bow and fired a single barrage through the air.

"Then let's see how they do against these," Archer replied to Molly.

Two of the robots paused their laser stream so their extended legs could push them out of harm's way. However, the third arrow stuck right up against the side of one of the robots and emitted a loud charging noise before surging an electrical shock through the drone's systems. The powerful blast of electricity fried the robot's central brain, causing the heavy body and limbs to collapse to the jungle floor with a thud louder than a collapsing elephant.

"Not bad, but I wouldn't count on that working every time," Molly jeered back.

Meanwhile, Michael had his hands full with six of the other robots who all focused their mechanical gaze on him. While three followed his movements with their unstoppable red laser stream, the other three fired short powerful blasts that exploded upon impact. Michael weaved through the air in and out of the laser streams like a jet plane maneuvering through a tight, weaving canyon. As he pulled up hard, he aimed his sunglasses at the droids below him.

After a quick analysis of each drone's location, he threw his arms out and up into a Y-formation. As Michael's hands flung across his body, he released multiple laser flashes that ripped through the air. The first few sliced off two of the four robotic arms belonging to the closest robot, while five other blue beams lacerated three legs from one robot and two from another. These automatons collapsed to the ground but still fought to pull themselves back up.

"Not bad, you found and exploited their greatest weakness," Molly commented. "But trust me, they will adapt."

As she spoke, the remaining bots stopped firing their incessant laser beams, pausing only for a moment to observe the damage done to their fellow drones. They glared down on their fallen brethren and then back at Mr Infiniti. Their eyes blazed in a bright red light, either out of fear or anger, which did not surprise Michael. He had read that Mastermind's squid-drones were powered with semi-simulated emotions, supplying him with an added advantage.

After regrouping with their capable comrades, the few functional robots abandoned their attacks on Archer to focus all of their attention on Michael. Two of the original twelve robots could not revive themselves, while another pair of the active drones crawled forward on only two functional legs.

Archer flipped up his helmet visor, and he called out to the drones, "Hey, I took down just as many of you as he did. Get back here you cowards." Although he and Michael both dismantled one of the squid-drones, the remaining enemies still identified Michael as the greater threat.

Among them, a pair of lead robots squatted down before springing up from the ground like two pouncing monkeys. Michael lifted his left fist and blasted the first robot back to the ground, but the second reached him, wrapping all four powerful tentacles around his body. The top two and bottom two tentacles locked onto each other, crushing Michael's torso. His battle suit's padding and armor gave him some protection, but that would only save him for so long. In a few seconds, the drone's binding arms would squeeze his guts out of his body like ketchup from a bottle.

"Aggghhh," Michael cried, his nose pointed toward the sky as he writhed in pain. But after taking one deep breath, he clenched his fists and broke free of the robot's clutches, snapping three of the tentacles like a rope pulled too taut. The squid-bot's body dropped to the ground with an earth-shattering thud, yet the others wasted no time in their attack. Two of them refocused their energy on Archer to keep him from helping his friend while the other robots worked together to bring down Michael.

Before he could analyze their attacking formation, three more squid-bots pounced up on top of him, dragging him down to the ground. Seven robots dog-piled on top of Michael, pinning him against the green grass. Though he struggled to break free from their grip, as soon as he threw one tentacle off of his arm or leg, two more took hold.

"Brawn won't do you much good here because you can't outmuscle that many robots," Molly advised. "You're going to need to find a different strategy."

Michael agreed, so he struggled to reach a button on his wristband. After psychically activating the device, the energy dug deep into Mr. Infiniti's core, helping him to unleash his power and imagination. An unstoppable force revived from within, surging through his arms and legs, but just as Molly had told him, he would not use brute force in his retaliation.

This was the situation he hoped for, the chance to use his imagination, coupled with his new wristband, to attack the artificial intelligence of Mastermind's technology.

Dozens of tentacles slashed and pounded at Mr. Infiniti's arms and torso, but he calmed himself as his mind, assisted by his armband, navigated through the air and into the core consciousness of each squid-bot. The movement of his mind was like flying a dozen spirits that infiltrated the exterior of the drones' bodies as only a ghost could. Their shells were nearly impenetrable against physical attacks, and their technological minds proved invulnerable to psychic beings like Mr. Mental, but Michael's hunch that he could make a technopathic connection with them turned out to be true.

Each robot continued to pummel Mr. Infiniti, completely unaware that he was seconds away from defeating every single one at once. In one swift thought, he pulled the plug on all seven attacking robots, deactivating their core consciousness. Their glowing, red eyes blinked once before dying into a black abyss as their legs collapsed, dropping their heavy bodies on top of Mr. Infiniti. His excess energy faded, but he still had plenty of strength to push his way out from underneath the pile of robots as if he was a mountain climber crawling out from under an avalanche.

Archer had landed another electrifying arrow on one of his robots, but the second one had fallen to the ground at the same time as all of the others. He walked over to Michael and grabbed his friend's hand to help him back up on his feet. While Michael brushed the dirt off of his arms and legs, Archer tapped one of the robots with his right toe, just to make sure the drone was actually dead.

"What did you do?" he asked, knocking over the robot's circular body to reveal the blank eye.

"I shut them all down," Michael replied, trying to catch his breath while his healing powers went to work. Dozens of cuts and bruises still covered his body, but they closed and shrank as quickly as they had formed. An even greater marvel came from Michael's battle suit, which automatically repaired all of the damage in less than a second.

"Not bad," Molly complimented Michael's ingenuity.

Archer looked back down to the lifeless drone beneath his boot and inquired, "I can see that you shut them down, but how'd you do it?"

"A new power," Michael explained. "Mastermind's strength is her technology, so I thought this simulation might help me unlock the ability to make contact with the artificial intelligence that drives her machines. Not only did I make contact, but I was able to pull the plug as if I was turning off a light switch."

"Awesome," Archer blurted. "Guess that means I won't be getting my date with Molly though."

"Thank goodness," Molly added with a sigh of relief. "And that was very awesome. Not even the original Mr. Infinity had that level of control over his technopathic abilities. Most impressive."

"Yeah, I figured it would work," Michael smiled. "But I needed the right situation, the right pain to give me enough motivation and drive to unlock such an ability. The next time I come up against Mastermind, she won't best me."

"What makes you so sure you'll see her again?" Archer asked, turning his attention away from the defeated drones. Flipping up his visor, he gazed on Michael's determined scowl.

"Call it a hunch," Michael answered, his sunglasses focused straight ahead. "She and I will meet again, and this time, she will answer for her crimes."

Archer noticed Michael's tightly squeezed fists and furrowed brow. "What did she do to you?" he inquired, even though he knew this was a sore subject for his friend. However, over the past few months, he'd become more curious than cautious in his questioning of Michael.

"She took something from me," Michael explained. "And I intend to get it back." With those last words, Michael trudged off the battlefield, killing the simulated jungle around him. He headed toward the teleporter, so Molly could beam him back and analyze his performance.

While Michael strode away, Archer remained frozen in his boots, attempting, but unable to move forward with his roommate. As he observed Michael's methodical movements, he understood there was something changed in his friend. A different aura surrounded him—the aura of Infiniti.

And from the shadows, a dark figure smirked as his eyes gazed upon that same aura. Before vanishing into the darkness, the shadow spoke to himself. "Just another step forward in your evolution—but your next trial will be the real test——Mr. Infiniti."

22. Ghosts and Memories

Mr. Mental

February 2nd

Jonathan Breck sat in a chair around the large round table at the center of Mastermind's meeting room. His long torso leaned over a virtual notebook, which projected 3-dimensional images of just one man—Mr. Infinity. As if he was turning the page of a book, Breck flipped his right pointer finger across the images. Each time, he activated a new 3-dimensional screen shot of Mr. Infinity in action.

The bright overhead light shone down on Sharp Shot, who sat at the other side of the table where she observed Breck from the corner of her eye. She was too nervous to turn her head for fear that she might draw attention from the dormant beast sleeping within Breck's deceivingly harmless human exterior. "He makes me nervous," she whispered to Mr. Mental, who resided in the chair right next to her. "Are you sure we should trust him?"

Mr. Mental paused from the virtual document he was reading, and his chest chuckled without making a noise. "There are few souls in this world who I know better than him," he answered. "His hatred for the original Mr. Infinity will drive him forward, and in his fully enraged state, he is nearly unstoppable. He'll do his job well."

Sharp Shot glanced back over at Breck's infuriated glare. "What did Mr. Infinity do to incite such animosity in The Wolfman?" she asked.

"He broke his spine in half," Mr. Mental responded, turning his attention back to his electronic data book. Sharp Shot's eyes widened and her jaw dropped, but she seemed more surprised by Mr. Mental's nonchalance. He returned to his work, analyzing the technical documents before him, yet still Sharp Shot wasn't satisfied with this blunt answer. So she decided to dig for more information.

"And he survived?"

Again, Mr. Mental broke his gaze from the electronic book in his hands and turned back to Sharp Shot with a sigh. "Come with me," he ordered, gripping Sharp Shot's muscular bicep to drag her out of the room. He pulled her behind him until the two villains stood on the other side of the sliding doors. As soon as the glass panels sealed shut, Mr. Mental began conversing while Breck paused his obsession with Mr. Infinity to turn his pointed nose just a couple degrees toward the super genius. He peered from the corner of his left eye for a few seconds and smiled before returning to his festering hatred of Mr. Infinity.

"Why'd you bring me out here?" Sharp Shot inquired, ripping her arm free from Mr. Mental's clamping grip.

Even in his human form, Jonathan's hearing is superhuman, Mr. Mental spoke his thoughts directly into Sharp Shot's mind. She jumped back two feet, startled at first by Mr. Mental's voice speaking right into her head. Most people required at least a dozen experiences with this form of communication before they fully adjusted to the phenomenon.

Relax, Mr. Mental impressed another thought into her brain. *Remember I can communicate with your mind directly. Now as for your questions about Jonathan . . .*

Yeah, why did you bring us out here to talk about him if we could have silently communicated through your telepathy? Sharp Shot's mind asked.

I couldn't risk you blurting out something that I didn't want him to hear, Mr. Mental explained. *I'm sure Jonathan knows we are talking about him, but at least the soundproof glass will prevent him from detecting the specific details.*

Sharp Shot glanced back through the transparent doorway to look upon Breck, who was snarling at each image of Mr. Infinity. *How could*—she started asking again before Mr. Mental cut her off.

I know you were too young to remember him, but at the peak of his strength, Mr. Infinity of old was more powerful than all of us combined. And that power gave him certain privileges that no other member of the Trifecta was authorized. He could kill at his own discretion.

But their code—Sharp Shot tried to butt in with an erratic thought.

Mr. Mental closed his eyes, shook his head, and waved his left hand to stop her mind in mid-sentence. *The Elders permitted Mr. Infinity to break the code as he saw fit. And in a heated battle with The Wolfman, he grew so enraged that he literally ripped the beast in half at the waist.*

I saw his regenerative capabilities in the graveyard, but I still find it difficult to believe that he could survive such a gruesome injury.

His healing abilities kept him alive long enough for The Magician and I to perform reconstructive surgery. You see, I created The Wolfman with my most ingenious research, but science only goes so far against magic.

Magic? Sharp Shot lifted her left eyebrow while fluttering her right eyelid up and down. *Mr. Infinity was powered by magic?*

He drew his strength from many different sources, the two primary ones being science and magic. So we took this opportunity to strengthen The Wolfman's power.

How so? Sharp Shot's forehead scrunched more as her confusion and curiosity grew.

The Magician and I worked together to fuse both magic and science into one brilliant experiment. Using my chemicals and The Magician's most potent potion, we merged the monster's spine back together, resurrecting him from the grave. However, this was not enough.

What do you mean?

Omega wanted an enforcer who could go toe-to-toe with any member of the Trifecta, including Mr. Infinity. So The Magician helped him draw upon an unspeakable evil from deep within the darkest part of Death's realm. Our Master forced a powerful demon into the soul of The Wolfman, making him immortal among the world of men.

Then why does he hate you?

Mr. Mental took in a deep breath and closed his eyes before letting his chest deflate from a powerful sigh. *Let me show you.*

The telepathic villain touched his right hand to Sharp Shot's forehead, imposing a sequence of intense memories into her mind. He flipped through dozens of images from the horrifying procedure of fusing The Wolfman's spine back together, but he ended by focusing on one specific memory. Both Mr. Mental and Sharp Shot stood in the background, observing the scene as if they were watching a movie.

Slightly younger versions of Mr. Mental and The Magician stood before a metal laboratory table. Two alloy bindings kept Jonathan Breck's hands strapped down to the platform's shiny surface. The restraints rattled like ghostly chains while Breck's arms writhed in pain.

"Is it done?" a voice questioned from the shadows behind Sharp Shot. She turned to observe the source of the inquiry. Stepping forward from the darkness was the most fearsome and devious force on the planet—Omega.

"My Lord," Mr. Mental gasped, startled by his unexpected presence.

"Have you completed the task as I instructed?" Omega repeated, a lifeless tone in his speech, his mechanical red eye dimly glowing in the dark room.

Both The Magician and Mr. Mental stepped to the side, revealing The Wolfman's shaking body. His legs were melding back into his torso like two liquid pieces of metal.

"We followed your instructions exactly," Mr. Mental explained. "The healing process has begun, and the new mixture is running through his system."

"Excellent," Omega smiled. "Then it's time for me to add the finishing touch." Mr. Mental's eyes flashed over to The Magician, searching for any sign that his comrade was aware of Omega's intentions, but the sorcerer's trembling chin showed he was just as surprised by their Master's arrival.

"We didn't anticipate any additions to our mixture," Mr. Mental's voice quaked. "Any new variables could have— unanticipated side effects."

"Oh, I'm counting on that," Omega chuckled in a confident tone that showed he knew what he was doing. After removing a finger-sized vial from the left compartment on his belt, he twisted a two-inch long needle onto the open end.

The Wolfman's writhing began to settle, his arms now flopping with less energy, like a fish who's been out of water for several minutes. Omega gripped the subject's wrist with his left palm while lowering the needle with his right. The green chemical mixture bubbled inside the vial as the god-like overlord pressed the needle through Jonathan Breck's thick hide. After squeezing the red button on the end of the vial, the green liquid rushed into The Wolfman's veins. He howled from the pain that surged through his body as Omega's special concoction infused a new life force into the beast's essence.

"He's radiating an incredible dark magic," The Magician commented, taking two steps backward.

"And his brain waves are literally leaping from his forehead. What did you do to him?" Mr. Mental inquired.

"I just evened the playing field," Omega smirked, taking two large steps backward. The Magician and Mr. Mental observed his actions, so they both backed up as well. Jonathan Breck's body began pulsating and expanding like an inflatable raft being pumped up a few gasps of air at a time. His shoulders expanded like a sponge absorbing water, and his chest doubled in size in less than five seconds. With incredible strength, his pulsating muscles ripped free of the restraints that held down his arms, and he leapt up from the metal operating table. Two brownish tan, bone-like plates sprouted from beneath the skin on his torso and arms while his blazing red eyes narrowed in on Omega.

Breck was gone, and a new Wolfman towered in his place. "What did you do to me?" he roared, tightening his enormous fists. His long, sharp nails dug into the skin of his palms, and his teeth scraped against each other as a shooting pain rushed through his head. Squeezing his skull between his humongous hands, The Wolfman felt two sharp points pressing through the skin and fur that protected his forehead. A pair of intimidating horns sprouted from his head like a crown, anointing him the King of Demons. Bending his knees to a 45 degree angle, he squatted down, preparing to pounce on and thrash Omega.

In a show of amusement, Omega's shoulders bounced up and down while he chuckled. "I made some improvements."

"Improve this!" The Wolfman cried, leaping forward. Both The Magician and Mr. Mental stood frozen in their place, too shocked to interfere. The Wolfman lifted his right arm and began swiping down across his body, but before he could make contact with Omega, his brain sent him into an agonizing pain that paralyzed his muscles, collapsing his body to the ground like a fallen puppet.

While The Wolfman thrashed on the ground in a fit of agony, Omega stepped up over his body. Mr. mental detected the sound of millions of voices echoing through The Wolfman's head. "You see, that's your problem," Omega gloated, gazing down on his test subject. "You always fail to think things through." The powerful overlord placed his right foot on the monster's neck, decreasing the internal pain he was causing. The millions of crying souls that rushed through The Wolfman's brain started to die down.

"This is where you belong, beneath my heel." Omega gnashed his teeth, the rage in his right, mechanical eye blazing inches above his head. "I've tolerated your insolence long enough, but no longer." He rubbed his boot into The Wolfman's face, as if he was snuffing out a cigarette, before finally releasing the beast from his stomping foot.

"Get up," Omega commanded through a sneer. Despite the rage in The Wolfman's heart and his desire to tear Omega limb from limb, he obeyed. His gigantic hands pressed off of the floor, and he stood straight up like an obedient soldier. "That's right," Omega smirked, narrowing his eyes on his new creation.

"He's giving off ineffable amounts of dark magic like nothing I've ever felt," The Magician commented. "How did you do this?"

"The serum I injected into his veins was a gift from a demon of the underworld, mixed with a few of my own personal touches," Omega explained. "While Jonathan still maintains some autonomy over the bestial side of his duplicitous personality, there are millions of dead souls trapped in there with him. And every single one is under my control." Omega turned to Mr. Mental and smiled. "It also makes him immune to mind control, and virtually immortal in the realm of men."

Mr. Mental squinted his eyes and tightened his forehead to test Omega's theory. He focused all of his power into penetrating The Wolfman's head, but he found himself swimming in a sea of minds, all different with varying hopes and dreams. Sharp Shot had remained motionless for this entire scene, her mind captivated by the intriguing turn of events, but now she felt the strain that was placed on the young Mr. Mental's brain.

"Our Wolfman here is now the ultimate soldier, an unstoppable berserker who can't be reasoned with, killed, or controlled," Omega delighted. "At least, not by anybody but me. This is truly how the world should be the foolish drones my puppets, and I the puppet master."

The Magician and Mr. Mental both winced at the thought of this for fear that Omega would group them in with those puppets. Still, they didn't dare cross his path. Each of them possessed immense powers, making them capable of a bout with any super human on the planet, with the exception of two—Omega and Mr. Infinity.

Omega turned to Mr. Mental. "Soon my friend, soon." He slapped his right palm down on Mr. Mental's left shoulder. "I will be that puppet master." Nodding his head, Omega stepped past his enforcer, leaving him and The Magician alone with the menacing monster. Before pushing open the doorway, Omega paused for a moment. "The battle is approaching," he declared. "Prepare our troops for the final assault, and let The Wolfman lead the way."

As Omega disappeared through the doorway, Sharp Shot found the room around her fading up and down like water rippling in the wake of a dropped stone. After a moment, the wavy air grew calm, and she discovered Mr. Mental had returned them back to the hallway in present day.

"Wow," were the only words Sharp Shot could express. That was the most and least she could say about the scene she just witnessed.

"You can see why The Wolfman detests us," Mr. Mental remarked aloud. "He blames myself and The Magician for the initial pain of the rebirth, but his true hatred lies with the two mega-humans who caused the most damage. Mr. Infinity for his callous decision to rip The Wolfman in half—and Omega for impressing the demon into his body."

Sharp Shot cocked her head to the right, unsure of Mr. Mental's true motives in their plan. "If The Wolfman can't be controlled, you wouldn't have recruited him. What's your end game here?" she inquired, sharpening her tight gaze on Mr. Mental's eyes.

But he only smiled, turning his shoulder on her as he headed down the hallway, away from the glass door. A second before turning right toward the next corridor, he made one last comment for Sharp Shot to contemplate. "Think back to the memory. You saw for yourself, The Wolfman can be controlled." Mr. Mental zoomed his shades in to observe Jonathan Breck, who was snarling at a 3-dimensional image of Omega. The mental giant chuckled before mumbling to himself, "All of the pieces are falling into place. The battle is approaching."

23. A Test of Courage, Wisdom, and Character

Michael

February 10th

"Welcome to the last class of first semester," Professor Malix called out. He stood at the front of a lecture hall filled with every second-year student, each dressed in his or her best business suit. "As you know, this is your last session of Basic Combat and Weaponry before you move on to the advanced level in second semester. I have been impressed with the growth that so many of you have showed over the past year and a half." He glanced over at Solar Flare, who had reclaimed much of the respect he lost the previous year when Mr. Infiniti stole his thunder. While Mr. Infiniti's powers fluctuated up and down, Solar Flare's steadily accelerated at an astounding rate. Even some of the most powerful fourth and fifth-year students couldn't compete with him.

"Today's class will test all of the skills you've learned thus far and will pit each of you against each other," Malix announced. "Let me elaborate on your mission." The professor picked up a glass, card-sized remote and tapped two buttons on the touch screen, which projected a 3-dimensional version of the Trifecta's training city. "This is the largest virtual city we have in our archives, designed to mimic Chicago, Illinois in its condition before the Big Boom. We will teleport each of you to a different spot in the city."

As Malix disclosed this information, a blinking light with each student's emblem appeared in a different part of the city map. Michael used his shades to zoom in on his blue infinity symbol that was blinking on the north side of the city, and he noticed that Max Force and Nexon would land adjacent to him. Then he searched out Archer's symbol, which was on the west side near the river. Allison would also begin a few blocks from there right next to Solar Flare.

"Each of you will receive 100 tag darts," Malix continued. "Your objective is to stick one of these darts in each of your peers before they can tag you. If someone sticks you with a dart, I will immediately beam you back out of the battlefield. If I deem that you are in danger of sustaining irreparable damage, I will immediately beam you back. And if you run out of your 100 darts, I will immediately beam you back. There are no other rules. Any questions?"

Sabrina's hand shot up, not much of a surprise to the rest of the class.

"Yes, Ms. Nixer," Professor Malix smiled.

"Will there be other obstacles in the city?" she asked— a wise question that had also crossed Michael's mind.

"Each of your professors, along with myself, have equipped this simulation to test every area of your training thus far. You won't know what they are ahead of time, but if you remember your training, you should be able to disarm these obstacles without a problem."

Michael found this form of a final assessment intriguing, but he worried more about how he would fare against his classmates. At his best, he could defeat all of them without breaking a sweat, but if his powers faded while he was on the battlefield, he wouldn't last more than a few minutes. His best hope was that his new wristband would give him the boost he needed to maintain his highest level of performance. In only a few weeks of practice, he had mastered many of the functions and stabilized his more chaotic powers. But the trial with Mastermind's drones was the most reassuring test. *I can only hope that trend will continue here,* Michael thought.

Yet before Michael could swim too deep into his worries, Professor Malix interrupted his thought. "While I monitor each of your statuses, Melvin and one of the Elders will observe your performance. They will each analyze your current strengths and weaknesses, which will help them decide how they will form your classes for second semester and your teams for the following school year. These will be your permanent teams when you engage in your first field missions next school year." Most of the students turned white at this announcement, realizing their entire heroic future could hinge on how well they performed in this battle.

"Now go suit up for battle and report to the teleport station within 15 minutes for transference to the virtual city," Malix instructed. "Good luck to you all. I'm sure you'll all perform brilliantly."

After taking a hard gulp, Michael stood up from his desk. All of the students filed out of the room while he hung back for as long as he could. After all of his peers had vacated the room, he pressed the tiny button on the side of his armband, activating his newest battle suit. This would be the premier of Mr. Infiniti's fresh new look. While observing the virtual version displayed on his shades, Michael thought the darker colors and advanced armor technology made him look older and even a bit more intimidating, which prompted him to wonder if that was Jacque's intent.

After the fabrics fully transformed over Michael's body, he began jogging out of the room, but he was surprised by a visitor.

"Where are you headed off to so fast?" Molly asked from just around the corner. Her sweet, harmonious voice helped calm Michael's nerves as he turned to face her bright smile and blue eyes before answering.

"They're sending us out for a battle in the virtual city," Michael explained.

"I know that," Molly laughed. "The question was rhetorical. I just wanted to check in with you before you head out to take the test that will determine your fate." She kept a light-hearted tone to ease the mood as she said this.

Michael blushed, embarrassed by his stupid response, but he couldn't find the right words to respond, so Molly broke the silence. "I wanted to wish you luck before you go out there. I've rigorously studied every super human who ever walked this earth, and I can honestly say that you are special."

These reassuring words of confidence erected a smile from Michael. "Thanks Molly. I'll do my best out there."

"I'm sure you will," she grinned. "Just remember all that you've learned here. Calm yourself when the battle starts. The first students to fail are the ones who panic in the beginning minutes, so keep your cool, analyze your surroundings, and devise a plan."

"Got it," Michael nodded before jogging down the hall and away from Molly.

"Michael," Molly shouted to him just before he turned around the hall corner. He stopped to look back at her and was surprised that her normally cheerful face was replaced with one of concern. "Just remember, the Elders believe in you—I believe in you—but you must believe in yourself."

Michael nodded again without saying a word, his mind too distracted by what he could have sworn was a vexing look of distress in Molly's eyes and cheeks. As he headed down the hall toward the building's teleportation room, he considered the possibility that this test was more important for him than anyone else.

Just over ten minutes later, all of the students stood in the teleportation room, ready for Malix to beam them into the virtual city. "I have uploaded the drop zone coordinates into each of your visors," he explained. "You will all hit the grid at the same time. Then it's up to you to survive for as long as you can. Good luck."

With those final words, the reverberating sound of the teleportation scanner initiated, and in less than a second, every student found him or herself standing alone in the city. Michael discovered he landed among dozens of tall buildings, but the largest skyscrapers stood over ten blocks south of his location. He determined this was the direction he should head in order to use one of the rooftops as a perch while avoiding the attention of others. After pushing himself off of the ground, he began zooming up through the air, but before he could ascend even 40 feet, a powerful blow crashed into his back, plunging his body into the fake cement below. Dozens of pieces of street splashed in all directions.

The heels of Nexon's boots pressed into Michael's spine as he reached down to tag Michael with a dart. Despite the disorientation caused by the crash, Michael maintained enough of his senses to reach back over his shoulder and stop his foe from sticking the dark into his neck. Nexon struggled to thrust his fist downward, but his strength proved to be no match for Mr. Infiniti. In one swift motion, like a baseball outfielder gunning down a runner, Michael flipped Nexon forward with an overhand toss.

The Green team member wailed as his body flung out of control until he smashed right through the storefront window of a three-story building. Unfortunately, he leapt back up on his feet before Michael could escape up into the air. In any case, this was a good chance for him to tag his first enemy, mostly because Nexon would be easier to defeat than some of the other Green team members, specifically Solar Flare.

Nexon hopped up on the broken windowsill and perched his body like a monkey on a branch. After crouching down on the edge of the store window, he used the full force of his legs to pounce toward Michael with another dart gripped in his right hand.

Don't panic, Michael thought. He closed his eyes to calm his mind, slowing time as he had in so many other pressured situations, which allowed him to devise a plan. Nexon pulled his right fist back before jamming his hand down in a stabbing motion with the needle of his dart leading the way. Yet before Nexon could land his attack, Michael opened his eyes and fell to his back, using both legs to kick his attacker behind him. As Nexon flailed his arms again, he crashed into the brick exterior of yet another building. And after his limp body fell to the ground, a heavy pile of bricks collapsed on top of him.

However, this wasn't enough to stop Nexon. He burst out from under the substantial number of bricks, throwing his arms up and then to his sides like an angry monster emerging from the ocean. "It will take more than that to stop me," his voice roared.

Michael knew better than to engage in banter with his enemy, especially since quite a few more students lurked through the city with eyes gunning for him. His best bet was to quickly defeat Nexon before returning to his original plan of heading for the taller skyscrapers. Nexon charged toward Michael, who dug his feet into the ground, bracing himself like a bullfighter. Once the brute rushed within ten feet of Michael, he leapt off of the street in an attempt to spear Michael down against the pavement.

But just as Nexon's boots left the ground, he let out a yelp because Max Force intervened, tackling Nexon's body from the side before hurling him against the pavement. Nexon smacked the side of his head on the road, leaving him disoriented enough for Max to tag him with a dart. The instant the toxin transferred from the dart to his blood stream, his body warped back up through the teleportation satellite and then returned to the transference room in Hero City.

After Nexon's body vaporized away, Max Force turned his head toward Michael, who prepared for battle with his Blue teammate and friend. But Max's fear showed in his petrified face as he took a hard gulp. Michael moved two steps forward, prompting Max to flee down the street. He sprinted north, which was opposite of the direction Michael hoped to go, so he let his friend go for the moment.

After taking to the air, Michael soared up 50 feet before zooming toward the skyscrapers in the south. At this height, he could grab a bird's-eye view of the action down on the streets.

However, he didn't dare hover for too long out of fear that an excellent marksman like Archer might spot him. Instead, he headed toward the large antennae on top of a tall tower, which his shades identified as the Hancock Building. Once he reached the roof, Michael found a good perch at the southwest corner and activated the cloaking device built into his wristband ,rendering him invisible to the naked eye.

Using the magnifiers in his sunglasses, Michael scanned the action below to identify four different battles going down. The closest was between Archer and Manfrin, in which Archer looked close to a victory, but more interesting were the dozen red rockets launching toward them. Undoubtedly one of the many obstacles designed by Melvin. Michael hoped to analyze what type of rockets they were, but then out of nowhere, Sabrina whooshed by right in front of his face.

She flew so close to Michael that she nearly crashed right into him. Quickly turning his head right like a bird, Michael's shades locked onto her while she descended toward Metal Man, who was sprinting away from a chasing robotic lion. As Sabrina descended, she tucked her arms against her body, accelerating to her maximum velocity. Michael zoomed in on her fingertips, noticing her hand already had a dart ready to tag Metal Man.

Realizing both of these heroes were two of the most powerful on the battlefield, Michael chose to pursue Sabrina in an attempt to take them out before more of his classmates arrived. He felt guilty targeting his friend, but Sabrina's sharp mind made her a dangerous opponent, and he knew her cold and calculating character would prevent her from hesitating to take him out.

Unfortunately for Sabrina, Metal Man saw her coming, so as her approach reached within 10 feet of him, he paused to activate his metallic skin. When Sabrina collided with Metal Man, she bounced right off of his hardened shell while also pushing him back a few feet. Although her left shoulder and ribs sustained a heavy blow that knocked the wind out of her, she still curved her trajectory just enough to minimize the damage.

Metal Man should have released his metallic exterior to provide his muscles with more flexible movement, but he had to worry about the mechanical lion who still stalked him. The 1500 pound robotic beast pounced forward and tackled Metal Man to the street. If not for the teen's super sturdy skin, his collision with the ground would have resulted in serious injury.

While these events unfolded, Michael dashed down through the air, his arms tucked back against his sides to reduce wind resistance. At the same time, he tilted his head up, allowing his shades to analyze the terrain and his targets. As he approached, the mechanical lion turned her head up toward Michael, easing her weight off of Metal Man.

Then as Michael thrust his hands out in front of his chest, he fired two blue laser blasts that sliced through the robot's feline head and shoulders, generating a powerful explosion that shook the surrounding buildings.

Sabrina rolled to the side, avoiding the immediate inferno, but the force of the blast still propelled her into a barrel roll across the street pavement. Metal Man wasn't so lucky as the hottest flames superheated his metallic skin, which cooked his body inside. Although the fire dissipated, he had no choice but to release his hard shell, leaving him vulnerable against Mr. Infiniti.

As Michael approached the ground, he flipped his legs forward so he could land feet first on the pavement. He then sprinted over to pick up Metal Man before he could recover from the chaos of the explosion. Lifting the Green team member over his head like a barbell, Michael hurled him forward in a javelin thrower's motion. Metal Man soared through the air before landing on the street where he skidded to a painful stop.

While Michael watched Metal Man's flight, he received a proximity warning across the screen of his shades, which read: BEWARE! IMMINENT ATTACK FROM BEHIND!

Spinning his body around, Michael observed Sabrina's right hand over her head, striking at a downward angle with a dart clutched in her palm like a knife. If not for his advanced reflexes, Michael would have fallen right there. But as Sabrina's attack drew closer, he flung his right arm up to grab her wrist, using his momentum to flip her around so that he was facing her back while twisting her harm behind her.

"I'm sorry about this," Michael sighed in a regretful tone as he used his free left hand to pull a dart from his belt before sticking the needle into Sabrina's neck. The serum infiltrated her blood stream, transporting her back to Hero City. Michael hoped that his first tag wouldn't have to be against one of his close friends, but Sabrina's incredible intelligence made her a serious threat, and as he saw just seconds earlier, she wouldn't hesitate to eliminate him.

Accessing the visual display on his shades, Michael viewed a grid showing a picture of the dozen students who already fell in the battle. As he checked through the faces, noticing Sabrina's was the latest added to the list, he took note that Solar Flare and Archer were both still active.

Meanwhile, Metal Man lifted himself from the street and brushed off some of the debris stuck to his arms and legs. By observing Metal Man's fatigued body language, Michael could tell that he sustained substantial injuries. Yet he still had enough energy left in the tank to turn his head left, refocusing his attention on Michael.

"You're mine," he scoffed with an angry determination in his squinting eyes. As he dashed forward, Michael's eyes darted in all directions to analyze the best way to defeat his enemy. Metal Man threw one dart toward Michael, who flicked his left hand forward, deflecting the projectile with his laser shield. And although that was a simple move for Michael, he realized Metal Man's attack was a desperate attempt to distract him while the Green team bruiser leapt forward with another dart ready.

Michael smirked as Metal Man's feet pushed off the ground, falling right into the hero's plan. Just before his angry peer stabbed down with the dart, Michael fell on his back and kicked up in the air, propelling Metal Man straight up above the surrounding rooftops. After shooting up four stories, Metal Man plummeted back toward the ground, leaving only one chance for survival. He had to change into his metallic form, so he closed his eyes and transformed his skin back into a hard shiny alloy that would protect his body from the impending crash, just as Michael had anticipated.

Once Metal Man's back hit the ground, cracking a small crater in the cement, Michael knew he had only moments to exact the final part of his plan. After taking hold of Metal Man's left wrist, Michael used his freeze beam to supercool the metal shell into a brittle icicle, and then he smashed the crystalized casing. Flipping a dart up from his belt, Michael stabbed the point into Metal Man's arm, a feat he could not have accomplished without icing and then breaking through his armored skin.

As Michael accessed the defeated list again, he watched Metal Man's profile picture pop up along with two others, including Allison. This disheartened Michael, but then he thought better someone else defeat her rather than him.

Archer still remained, but more disconcerting was the thought of facing Solar Flare. Michael didn't fear him, but he certainly respected the significant power his nemesis learned to wield. Returning to his original plan, Michael took to the air again, heading for a different building this time. He eyed Trump Tower, which was closer to the river and would give him a central location for scouting out his best opportunities to tag other competitors.

But after ascending 300 feet in the air, Michael hit a snag, feeling his flight powers dying. "No, not now," he cried out. Just as his powers had done on multiple occasions in the past, they began fading from him. His body plunged down head first, like a professional diver, and he realized within two seconds that reengaging his powers was folly. He would hit the ground in mere moments, which meant he had one choice.

Having studied his new weapon, Michael devised a backup plan for such emergencies. After single tapping a button on his wristband, he called out the single word, "Activate." Another one of Jacque's new designs forced Michael's cape into a stiff glider that allowed him to float on the zephyrs blowing through the windy city streets.

Although Michael's cape curved his trajectory from a 90 degree plummet to a 45 degree glide, his extreme velocity would eventually end in a painful crash, possibly against the side of one of the buildings. So extending his hands to his sides, Michael gripped the edge of his cape and used what little strength he had to guide himself into a trajectory running parallel to North Rush Street. This would eventually lead him to the river where he could soften his landing.

Thanks to Michael's quick thinking, his long gliding trip slowed his speed enough that he just narrowly reached the Chicago River where he then let his body drop 20 feet into the cold, murky water, a much better ulterior to crashing against the street—especially with the chance of Solar Flare lurking nearby. Michael figured his fire-based enemy wouldn't prowl too close to the city's larger sources of water, so the river provided the best landing sight.

After swimming his way up to the surface of the river, he began breaststroking toward the closest shore on the south side. Once he reached the cement shoreline, he found a low point where he could pull himself out of the water. As he stood on the cement sidewalk that followed along next to the river, the water ran right off of his battle gear; yet a soggy suit became the least of his worries. Somewhere out in the city, Solar Flare was undoubtedly searching for Michael, who was stuck at ground level with no super powers. He considered hiding, but then he realized cowardice certainly wouldn't help his ranking at the end of this battle.

After determining the best plan of attack, or rather survival, Michael began accessing the list of students who still remained on the battlefield. Solar Flare's arrogant smirk stood out at the top of the list, followed by Michael's profile and then only three other students. Archer, Max Force, and a Red team member named Reflex still continued to fight.

Michael ran up a stone ramp along Wacker Drive and then sprinted toward the cover of an awning over the entrance to a tower on Michigan Avenue. Even that short dash left him winded, a sign that his powers had completely vanished. His best hope was that they return soon before Solar Flare could find him.

But then Michael realized something. This was his chance—a chance to prove to everyone else, but more importantly to himself, that his powers did not define him. When conferring with Mr. Infinity's journal during the previous year, the legendary hero imparted one piece of wisdom that explained his greatness . . . Imagination is everything—more important than anything else. At this moment, Michael knew he could rely on this idea to lead him to victory.

Although he stood without his powers, he wasn't powerless. He just needed to imagine a new strategy. Using the mental link with his shades, he activated a virtual overhead map of the city.

"Melvin, can you show me the location of the remaining students?" Michael asked, hoping to devise a new strategy using the tools that remained available to him.

"Negative," Melvin responded. "By order of Professor Malix, all students are barred from accessing that information." Michael grimaced. He knew that they weren't supposed to have access to the radar map, but he hoped there might be a loophole to help him locate Solar Flare.

"Okay then, can you give me in infrared view of the city?" Michael inquired.

"Affirmative, bringing up infrared view of the map," Mevlin confirmed.

"Yes," Michael cheered to himself, pumping his fist as the first part of his plan came into view. As long as Solar Flare had his flames ignited, the infrared map would show his location. The other three students wouldn't appear unless if Michael zoomed in close to their position. But Michael wasn't as concerned about surviving an encounter with any of them.

"Zoom out and move to the hottest moving object," Michael ordered. The map expanded before navigating north to Old Town where Michael first began this battle, likely because Solar Flare headed there to look for him. That gave Michael some time to devise a plan for setting a trap. After noticing Solar Flare zipping back south down Clark Street, Michael figured he had about 2-5 minutes before his enemy would arrive.

Unfortunately, the ground began shaking as Max Force trudged by the adjacent intersection with a determined scowl in his eyes. His battle suit looked tattered with a few rips around his shoulders and left bicep. As he lumbered along like an angry rhinoceros, he surely would have seen Michael if not for the cloaking device that camouflaged him against the building's exterior wall. Even if Michael could defeat Max, that would prevent him from preparing to battle Solar Flare, so after watching Max run by, Michael exhaled a brief breath of relief.

But that relief was short-lived when an explosive arrow hit the building a few feet above Michael, causing dozens of bricks to rain down on him. The heavy stones piled on Michael's back, burying him like snow from an avalanche. If not for the advanced armor on Michael's legs and torso, he would have been squashed like a bug, but instead he ended up pinned against the ground.

"You can come on out, Michael," Archer shouted from 100 feet away. He kept an arrow aimed forward with his bow string pulled back to his shoulder. "I know that explosion won't keep you down for long, so let's go."

What Archer didn't realize was that Michael couldn't lift the bricks off of his back, and in a short time they might even kill him. "Do you give up?" Professor Malix asked through Michael's sunglasses. "I can teleport you out right now."

"No, I won't give up," Michael grimaced through the bricks surrounding his jaw. In a leap of faith, he calmed his mind and slowed his breathing for a moment. His wristband activated a whirring noise while the birthmark on his chest started burning as if someone was stabbing him with a hot knife. After a moment of serenity, Michael's senses cleared and he burst out from underneath the pile of bricks. However, that short surge of energy left him winded, giving Archer the upper hand.

He launched a barrage of four arrows, each designed with a different function. The first exploded in a flash of light to blind Michael, and the three seconds of intense luminescence might have worked if not for the advanced screen in Michael's sunglasses. However, even with this protection, the flash damaged Michael's eyes enough to make him start seeing white spots.

The second arrow stuck into the building's exterior before emitting a horrendous screech that brought Michael to his knees while he clasped his ears. A millisecond later, the third arrow stopped dead in the brick exterior and then exploded into a ball of fire purposed for bringing down more bricks on Michael's kneeling body. And the final arrow spiraled through the air before separating into four equal pieces that created a strong, metallic net to pin the bricks down over Michael. This time he couldn't escape. Without his super strength, he had no chance of breaking free from this trap.

But in this moment of desperation, Michael felt his wristband give him another boost to reignite his powers, flooding energy through his whole body. His eyes burned behind his shades as he blasted his way out from under Archer's trap. Stone bricks exploded straight up toward the sky like an erupting volcano with Michael emerging directly behind them. As he hovered in the air, he extended his jaw forward, showing his lower teeth like an angry pit bull before attacking an intruder.

Archer drew two more arrows from over his right shoulder and fired both at the same time. They hurled through the air but only for a second before Michael disintegrated them with a dark blue laser blast from his left fist. He then darted down and crashed into Archer, bulldozing him into the street. Although Archer's helmet protected the back of his skull from splitting in half, his armor wasn't thick enough to shield his shoulders from cracking against the cement.

And while Michael's rage tempted him to inflict more damage, his senses returned, reminding him that Archer was his best friend. So instead of continuing his assault, he pulled a dart from his belt and inserted the tip into Archer's neck, instantly teleporting him away.

Immense power swelled through Michael's upper body, increasing his breathing from the adrenaline rush he felt. This form of energy exuded a different kind of power unlike anything he had experienced before. While the dynamic force in his chest seemed mostly familiar, this new strength significantly altered his emotions. He could almost taste the difference in this new energy—like the difference between vanilla and chocolate ice cream. Both were cold and had the same texture, but they each created a distinct and different flavor. This was the new Mr. Infiniti.

After standing back up from his crouched position, Mr. Infiniti accessed the list of remaining students. Only one still stood—Solar Flare. Re-engaging the infrared detector on the map of Chicago, Mr. Infiniti found that his enemy was fast-approaching from the North. Despite his accelerated fluctuation of strength, he returned to his original plan to surprise attack Solar Flare.

Jetting himself up through the air, Mr. Infiniti landed atop the building closest to the river on the corner of State Street and Wacker Drive. Solar Flare flew 30 feet above the pavement, now close enough that Mr. Infiniti could zoom in on his helmet. The visor was flipped down, so Mr. Infiniti couldn't see his face, but he could have sworn Solar Flare's tongue was sticking out a quarter inch between his lips, a typical assertion of his confidence.

Clinging to the edge of the rooftop where his head and torso hung over like a gargoyle, Mr. Infiniti activated the cloaking device on his wristband. Solar Flare drew closer, and once he flew within pouncing range, all Mr. Infiniti needed to do was tackle his enemy into the river below. Despite Solar Flare's successful expansion of his own powers, he still had one fatal weakness—water.

This was the moment. Mr. Infiniti extended his legs off of the gray stone roof, shooting himself forward like a bullet. The sudden movement automatically uncloaked him, revealing his attack to Solar Flare, who seemed *too* prepared. Before Mr. Infiniti could travel 40 feet, Solar Flare hurled both fists forward, blasting his enemy with a double stream of fire. The incredible force from the flames launched Mr. Infiniti backward into the building behind him where he crashed through the outside window and two more interior walls before sliding to a stop on the tile floor of an office.

Impossible, Michael thought. *There's no way he could have reacted that quickly—unless he knew I was coming.* Such a turn of events was both surprising and confounding to him, but he had no time to analyze the situation as Solar Flare's flames came bursting through a dozen other windows that surrounded the building. Flames ran rampant through the floor, each individual ember searching for Mr. Infiniti while Solar Flare hovered safely outside the building. He could see through the eyes of his raging fire, so he had no need to enter.

"Come on out," Solar Flare called in an inviting tone. "I want to see your face when they teleport your sorry butt back to the city." He laughed at this joke, but Mr. Infiniti wasn't there to fool around. With this new sensational power surging through his body, his rage determined to shut Milton's big mouth once and for all.

"Here I come," he mumbled to himself as he exploded out from the building. Solar Flare was ready with another burst of flames, but this time, Mr. Infiniti retaliated with an ice beam from his right hand, which led his flying attack. The blue laser sliced right through Solar Flare's hot flames like a knife through pudding. With the fiery attack disarmed, Mr. Infiniti achieved the freedom to increase his velocity until he reached Solar Flare's helmet. Driven by a blinding rage, he punched the armored cheek with an uppercut that packed enough force to launch Solar Flare 200 feet up through the air.

The wallop from this blow nearly knocked Solar Flare unconscious, which would have ended this duel. But to Mr. Infiniti's dismay, his enemy retained just enough of his senses to ignite a propelling flame that cushioned his fall. He landed on his shoulder against the cement of the street below where he rolled to a stop at the corner of State and Washington Street. Before Solar Flare could rise from his fall, Mr. Infiniti landed on top of him, grabbed his left shoulder and bashed his helmet with three swift punches. The final blow splintered a spider web crack across Solar Flare's visor.

Mr. Infiniti cocked his fist back to deliver another punch, but before he landed the fourth strike, Solar Flare received some fortunate help. A two ton drone mimicking the physique of a gorilla tackled Mr. Infiniti to the ground, releasing Solar Flare from his hold. The sudden jolt caught Mr. Infiniti off guard, allowing the gorilla to pin his arms against the street.

This compromising position loaned Solar Flare an opportunity to burn his foe's trapped body. However, before he could act, Mr. Infiniti's rage remedied the situation for him. His eyes burned in a slightly dark flame as he threw his torso forward, blasting a white laser from the symbol on his chest.

His birthmark sizzled, creating a beam that seared right through the robotic gorilla's body before exploding to deactivate the entire system.

Solar Flare and Mr. Infiniti each stood up from the ground at the same exact moment. Mr. Infiniti kicked the remaining pieces of the robot to the side, leaving just the two super humans to face off against each other. They both stared down their opponent like two gunslingers in an old-fashioned western duel. Because of the cracks spread across Solar Flare's visor, he deactivated his helmet function, causing the advanced head case to split down the middle before ejecting behind him.

"You can't win," Solar Flare barked across the 100 feet that separated him from Mr. Infiniti. His eyes emitted a powerful white flame that rose to a triangular point like a blowtorch. "I've upgraded my powers to a magnitude you can't even comprehend." As he threw his right hand forward, he angled his palm up with all five fingers blazing forth an intense flame that expanded into a whirlwind of fire, surrounding Mr. Infiniti in a supernova.

This display of power was incredible. The profound heat simulated standing on the surface of the sun. Most of Mr. Infiniti's advanced armor burned away, but his thick skin proved capable of holding off the raging flames, if only for a moment. In one quick motion, Mr. Infiniti dashed left and out of the encompassing fire that circled around him like a whirlpool. This gave him a few seconds to breathe before Solar Flare noticed his movement and pyrokinetically navigated the flames toward his enemy.

"There's no escape this time," Solar Flare boasted over the hissing noise of the firestorm he wielded. Just before the roaring flames re-engulfed Mr. Infiniti's body, he felt his powers fading again, so he refocused his mind, strengthening his skin to withstand the oncoming heat that now surrounded him for a second time. Although he tried to escape, his legs would not move. They collapsed his body to one knee while he held himself up with his right fist. All of the air dissipated away, leaving Michael to suffocate if the flames didn't finish him first.

Malix could not ask him to give in because his communication link had burned into oblivion. By all rights he should have just beamed Michael back out of the battlefield after taking so much damage, but he couldn't have known Michael's powers were fading. And deep down, Michael sensed that Malix wanted him to win this battle.

No, not this way, Michael thought. *I can't lose like this.* Then, just as his hope was dissipating, he received some help from a familiar source.

"You can still win," the mysterious voice hissed to him. "Use the armband. Access the core of your power source to reboot your energy. Only by releasing your full force will you be able to defeat him."

Michael once again wanted to question this person's identity, but time grew limited. In a matter of moments, the flames would burn his body to ashes. So, like a good pawn, he followed the instructions, using the wristband to look deep into the core of his power. Just as he had done on previous occasions, he had to mentally navigate his mind through his body to find the glowing power source at the center of his chest.

Yet to Michael's surprise, the core looked and felt different—almost in a state of change. Parts of the normally bright, glowing orb had turned black, and these dark patches emanated a deep freeze colder than the arctic tundra. Something seemed wrong, but before Michael could determine what was changing, the blackness lashed out and gripped his arms like the tentacles of an octopus. He sensed the energy fusing through his body, giving him a surge that made him feel stronger than he had in months. Even in his most extreme bursts of power, he never experienced such raw energy, as if he had full control of the sun.

"Ahahahaha," Solar Flare cackled in a maniacal tone that enraged Mr. Infiniti. Using the new power at his fingertips, he formed a black, protective bubble around his body, preventing any more flames from reaching him. Solar Flare was so busy relishing in his apparent victory that he failed to notice Mr. Infiniti emerging from the whirlwind of flames.

After breaking through the surface of Solar Flare's attack, Mr. Infiniti released his shield, revealing his nearly naked body, several parts of his skin charred like an overcooked steak. But in a flash of light, he healed every burn on his skin, and after accessing the console on his wristband, he activated a new battle suit that emerged to clothe him. The only missing piece was his shades, which had disintegrated, revealing his glowing eyes. Yet while they normally radiated a bright white or blue light, instead an irradiated, dark flame emerged from his pupils.

Solar Flare stopped laughing when he noticed an unscathed Mr. Infiniti prowling toward him. "No, that's not possible—that's not fair," he pouted with a tone of disbelief. "How could you have survived such intense heat?"

Mr. Infiniti inched forward one methodical step at a time, like a proud tiger moving in to devour his injured prey. His shoulders hunched over a bit with his head popping forward, a stern glower in his black eyes and determined chin. "With me, anything is possible," he sneered in response to Solar Flare before unleashing the burning, black radiation from his eyes, which tore through Solar Flare's armor in less than a second. Now he felt the same searing pain that Michael had endured just moments earlier.

"Agghhhhh!" Solar Flare cried in pain up toward the sky. After only five seconds, the agony ceased, replaced by a flash of light as Mr. Infiniti dashed through the air to smash one powerful right hook into Solar Flare's unprotected face, launching him 100 yards through a whole building and onto the cement of a courtyard on the other side of Washington Street. Before Solar Flare could even open his eyes, Mr. Infiniti sped through the air and lifted him off the ground.

With his left fist, Mr. Infiniti held Solar Flare two feet above the pavement and cocked back his fist for another strike to the face. "There's no dart waiting for you in my belt," Mr. Infiniti growled through a snarling sneer. "I've had enough of your opposition, so our conflict ends here." Mr. Infiniti fired a quick jab that Milton could only hear before the solid concrete knuckles cracked his cheek bone with enough force to launch him another 100 yards, but Mr. Infiniti yanked him back with his left arm.

"What are you doing?" Malix shouted through a loud speaker in a nearby building. With Mr. Infiniti's shades destroyed, Malix couldn't make direct contact with him through the comm. link, but he could access one of the thousands of P.A. systems placed around the city. "You're going to kill him."

"Good, he doesn't deserve to live," Mr. Infiniti scoffed back at the professor. The dark energy that he unleashed from his chest had taken control of his mind, clouding his judgment. He pulled back his right hand and delivered two more swift jabs to Solar Flare's face, which swelled into a purple bump that made him almost unrecognizable. Forming another black energy flame around his eyes, Mr. Infiniti prepared to vaporize Milton forever.

"Don't do it!" Molly called over the intercom. "Michael, this isn't you. I know you're not a killer." Molly's words snapped Michael out of his enraged condition, pulling him back to reality and back to his true persona. The burning energy in his eyes dissipated, returning his irises to their beautiful blue state.

Blinking his eyes free of what felt like a dream, Mr. Infiniti looked to his right and noticed a towering metal sculpture that looked like a dragon staring down on him. Then his vision began blurring, and he grew so dizzy that his body swayed from left to right like he was going to pass out. A flash of fire formed all around the sculpture with Omega hovering over the head, his jaw laughing maniacally without making a sound. Then the evil overlord bellowed four mysterious words: "You must ready yourself."

But just as quickly as this ominous vision materialized, Michael felt his senses return, and the flames disappeared, leaving no burn marks or any other sign that they ever existed. He turned his head back to his left fist, which still held Milton's hanging body.

As Michael examined the damage to Milton's face, he exhaled one deep breath and blurted two words. "What happened?"

Then with a bewildered look in his scrunched eyebrows, Michael found his molecules ripping apart as he and Solar Flare teleported back to the transport room in Hero City. A group of students stood waiting for their return, each with the same expression of shock and horror from witnessing Michael's actions. After easing Milton's unconscious body down to the ground, Michael turned to his classmates who all backed up out of fear.

He didn't know what to say. No explanation existed to justify how brutal and ferocious he had been in that battle. The last time he experienced such primal rage was in his fight with Mr. All-American. This worried Michael that when embracing his identity as Mr. Infiniti, he might also unleash an ugly and infuriated side of his personality that existed outside of his control. This was something he would have to deal with when he had more time to think. However, before he could analyze another thought, Michael heard Professor Malix run into the room, breaking the agonizing silence.

"I couldn't pull him out of there," Professor Malix mumbled to nobody in particular. He looked at Milton's beaten body on the floor and then shifted his gaze to Michael with shock in his wavering eyes. "Melvin's program wouldn't kick in. It prevented me from teleporting either of them out of there—I don't know what happened." At this moment, Michael only wanted to escape the judgmental eyes staring at him, so he sped out of the room without speaking a word.

After flying out of the building's front entrance, he continued down the street toward the dormitories where he hoped to hide from the world. But as he passed the Trifecta Headquarters, he had a vision of Mastermind standing three blocks down the street, just before his wristband jolted a burning sensation up through his arm and into the birthmark on his chest. His mind grew dizzy, his sight blurring as he drifted toward unconsciousness, causing his body to crash into the street below where he rolled to a violent stop.

Michael looked up at the arrogant grin in Mastermind's round, plump cheeks. Just before dozing off into an involuntary slumber, he heard a distant voice whispering to him—a voice which he could have sworn belonged to his brother.

"You're not ready yet."

24. Losing Control

Mr. Mental

February 11th

Mr. Mental strolled down the halls of Mastermind's headquarters toward his dark office. Once there, he planned to upload the most recent data he'd been analyzing. As soon as his office doors closed behind him, the lights went dark and the shadow's green eyes once again glowed from the corner.

Mr. Mental sat down at his desk to activate the virtual computer screen in front of him, but he did not turn to face his visitor. "The Chicago mission was a success," he commented.

"He failed to kill his target," the shadow's voice echoed through the room. "And you couldn't maintain your hold over his mind to accomplish what we needed. I wouldn't call that a success."

Mr. Mental spread out his fingers and pressed them together, pulling them close to his face as he planned out his next words. After releasing a long sigh, he responded, "Indeed, he did show more resistance than we previously thought, but when the time comes, our preparations will pay off. He proved that he can wield his new weapon with expertise, and I successfully infused the necessary memory to resurrect his full power. The hallucinations have already begun. I'd call that a successful mission."

"If you say so," the shadow replied while Mr. Mental rubbed the temples on each side of his head. "Just remember, our future relies on your plan and the precise execution of the final steps. You can't afford to fail."

Swerving around in his chair, Mr. Mental screamed, "Nobody doubts my mind!" His eyes bulged behind his shades, but the shadow had disappeared from the room. The lights activated overhead, revealing the intense veins that protruded from Mr. Mental's forehead. He inhaled a deep breath and brushed his hands down the front of his suit to calm his nerves. After turning back to his computer screen, he mumbled to himself, "I will prove I am the superior mind in this world. And when this is all over, Mastermind will curse the day that she underestimated me."

25. Missing Puzzle Pieces

Michael

March 11th

Just a few hours after the mysterious force knocked Michael unconscious, he woke up in the medical bay, a place he was becoming all too familiar with. After a day of observation, the doctors allowed him to leave, but the Elders certainly kept a close watch on him now—especially Eliki. Over the next few weeks, Michael could have sworn that she was spying on him, watching him every moment she could.

Although Solar Flare still remained in the medical bay, nobody spoke a word of Michael's fight with him. Perhaps because the Elders instructed them not to, but more likely because everyone feared the power that Mr. Infiniti displayed. Yet the person who lived in greatest fear was Michael. His mind constantly worried, shifting from his haunting nightmares and daydreams to his brother's missing body to the escaped Mr. Mental and Fireball.

Over six months had passed since the two villains escaped, yet they made no visible attempts to re-enter the world. Some Trifecta members foolishly believed this meant the world was safe, but Michael knew better. If such powerful enemies were lingering in silence, that could only mean that they were planning something big. But more worrisome to Michael was Mastermind's inactivity. If she truly did have Alex's body, Michael couldn't stop wondering what she was planning to do.

Another day of classes came to an end, so Michael headed back toward his dorm room. As his mind buzzed,

Archer rolled up behind him on his motor-bike. "So what time do you wanna eat today?" he asked Michael, who didn't respond.

His mind stayed preoccupied with so many questions that Archer couldn't even register in his brain. Just then Sabrina and Allison ran up behind Michael, blurting something he didn't understand but still startled him back into the real world.

"Whoa, sorry I didn't mean to shock you," Allison apologized upon seeing Michael nearly jump out of his black dress shoes while his breathing grew more rapid.

Michael shook his head back and forth as he rubbed his temples with his middle and forefingers. He squinted his eyes and scrunched his forehead like he was in agony from an intense migraine. While he tried to sooth his aching head, a ghostly voice called out to him, but identifying the speaker proved difficult.

"Was it another daydream?" Archer asked in a concerned voice, quite unusual for his comical personality.

"No, it wasn't a dream this time," Michael answered. "It was something else—something I can't put my finger on."

Allison and Sabrina gazed at Michael with bewildered eyes. He had discussed his recent dreams and hallucinations with Archer and Stone, but he didn't want to announce to the world that his mind was constantly in a state of chaos. "I thought your nightmares ended months ago?" Sabrina asked in a rhetorical tone.

"They did stop for a short time, but ever since my encounter with Mastermind and Mr. Mental, new ones have manifested their way into my brain," Michael explained. "And worse, they're escalating, no longer contained to my dreams. I've started hallucinating while I'm awake."

"Hallucinating what?" Allison inquired.

Michael glanced around at the dozens of people walking down the streets and sidewalks, which reminded him of Malix's warning about prying ears. "Let's head back to the dorms, so I can explain in a more private setting." Allison and Sabrina nodded in agreement without saying a word, while Archer chose to break the serious tone of the conversation.

"I'll meet you there slowpokes," he chuckled as the engine of his motor-bike roared just before taking off toward the dorms. But when Archer turned right at the next block, Michael's eyes widened in shock upon seeing a shadow-covered figure standing at the street corner. His cloaked face pointed straight at Michael while he stood motionless, like he was analyzing the young student.

A white cargo truck hovered by with a Trifecta logo on the side, and after the vehicle passed, Michael found the figure had disappeared. He stopped walking and turned to Sabrina on his left. "Did you see someone there?" he asked, pointing at the street corner.

But Sabrina only shook her head as she responded, "No, why? Who did you see?" However, Michael didn't answer her—because he could have sworn that the face cloaked by that hood belonged to his brother. *Could this be another hallucination?* he wondered. *But how would Alex have found his way into Hero City?* Sabrina tapped Michael on the arm to get a response from him, which broke his shocked expression.

"I just thought I saw someone standing up there," Michael responded, playing the whole incident off as nothing to worry about. But he did worry, and both Allison and Sabrina's stares showed their concern at seeing Michael's tightened forehead and disconcerting, pale complexion.

"Come on, we should hurry to catch up to Archer," Allison suggested, hoping to alter Michael's train of thought. "Otherwise he'll never stop bragging about how much he beat us by."

"Yeah," Michael agreed in a despondent and lifeless tone. No matter how hard he tried, he couldn't stop thinking about his brother.

Back in the seclusion of his dorm room, Michael planned to divulge the details of his recent dreams, even some parts that he hadn't told Archer about. Using the advanced technology on his wristband, he held out his arm to scan for any hidden bugs in his room. "All results negative," the computer's voice announced, so Michael felt safe in conversing with his friends.

"My dreams have gotten more and more intense as the year's progressed," Michael explained. "But only over the last few weeks have I started seeing parts of my nightmare while I'm awake. In the most recent ones, I've experienced flashing images of Mr. Mental watching me with an arrogant smirk."

"Does he say anything?" Allison questioned as she leaned forward in Michael's computer chair. The overhead light beamed down and gleamed off of her inquisitive irises.

"No, he doesn't say anything," Michael answered. "He just stands there smiling. The last time he was directly behind Professor Eliki during one of her seminars, but nobody else noticed him. I feel like I'm losing my mind."

"Tell them more about the nightmares," Archer recommended, despite the fact that Michael hated reliving such horrors by discussing them.

After taking a deep breath, Michael started by describing the original parts of his dream, explaining how Mastermind comes to taunt him with the proclamation that she has his brother, followed by the ominous computer screen. But then he disclosed the newest and most disturbing part of his dream.

"After the computer fades away, Mr. Mental appears with my brother. Both are dressed in pinstriped business suits with dark collared shirts and red ties. They each wear fedoras on their heads and large shades that cover most of their face, but I can still recognize them."

"What do they do?" Sabrina asked as she also leaned forward in her seat, her mind completely mesmerized by Michael's re-telling of his dream.

"Mr. Mental just places his hand on my brother's shoulder and says, 'The time is almost upon us. You must ready yourself, Mr. Infiniti.'" Michael tried to imitate Mr. Mental's deep, smug voice as he revealed this statement. "And then they both smirk and chuckle under their breath while their chests bounce in and out without saying another word."

"Is that the end of the dream?" Allison asked, a puzzled look in her contemplative eyes. Sabrina bit the end of her thumb as she also tried to make some sense of such a bizarre nightmare.

"There is one last part," Michael confessed. This was the detail that he hadn't shared with anyone, not even Stone or Malix. "As my brother and Mr. Mental drift backwards into darkness, a pair of giant eyes form above them, and a familiar voice echoes through the dark abyss."

"Whose voice?" Archer interrupted with a surprised leap from his bed. "You didn't mention this part."

"The same voice that has spoken to me over my headset," Michael announced, which elicited three slight gasps from his friends.

"Are you sure it's him?" Allison asked, her eyes bulging from surprise.

Nodding his head, Michael bit his lip before continuing. "He has given the same warning each time. 'You must fully prepare Mr. Infiniti to defeat Mastermind, or risk losing your brother to her forever.' This was shocking because I hadn't heard anything from him for months, but the day after this first dream, I started hearing brief whispers from him again. He speaks to me in short pieces, almost like a ghost who is trapped and trying to contact someone in the physical world. But I heard him most clearly during my battle with Solar Flare. I think he might be the one who pushed me to the brink of killing Milton."

All three of Michael's friends sat silent, their brains so vexed that they couldn't string together a sentence. Michael, on the other hand, had a disturbing speculation that deduced the significance of these events, yet he refused to accept his own conclusion.

"Anyway, that's where my nightmare loops back to the beginning with Mastermind." Michael exhaled as he contemplated how to explain the next part of his story. "Even worse—I've started having flashes of her attacking me while I'm awake. Just yesterday, I was walking down Main Street, and I viewed an incredibly realistic image of her descending toward me from the sky. But just before her fists hit me, the image dissolved like the wisps of an apparition."

"Is it possible she did something to you that's causing these hallucinations?" Sabrina asked.

Shaking his head back and forth, Michael responded, "I doubt it. It wouldn't make sense for her to train me to defeat her. And when she attacked me in Africa, her missiles seemed to only affect my body, not my mind." Michael sighed, his sunken face a clear sign of the burden weighing on him.

Archer and Sabrina were speechless, unable to formulate a response, but Allison knew just what to say to brighten his spirits. "What can we do to help?" she inquired.

"Yeah, what are friends for, if not to provide help and make comments about your bad hair," Archer joked, rubbing his palm over Michael's shaggy brown locks.

Michael smiled at this display of friendship. He felt lucky to have such a great circle of allies who would do anything for him. "There might be something," he answered, but he wasn't sure if he was ready to share his theory with others. After a moment of hesitation, he decided that if his friends could show such faith in him, he should return the favor, so he laid out his idea. "If we can find my brother's body, that might answer all of the riddles since my arrival here in Hero City. Somehow, I have a feeling that every looming secret can be answered with his discovery."

While Archer nodded in agreement, Sabrina asked, "So how do we find him?"

This was a valid question. As Michael narrowed his gaze, he thought through his dilemma for a few moments before an idea dawned upon him. Malix and Stone both suspected that Alex was hidden somewhere within the city, and after Michael's vision just a few minutes earlier, he started to believe this theory.

"I think I know someone who can help," Michael mumbled, just loud enough so that his friends could hear him. "I'm going to go see him, but I need you three to do something for me in the meantime."

"What do you want us to do?" Allison asked.

"Go to the Hall of Archives," Michael instructed. "I need some information that might help in our search."

"Why don't we just use Melvin to do a database search?" Archer questioned. "That'll be a lot quicker and more accurate." Michael wasn't surprised that his tech savvy roommate would look to Melvin to make his task easier, so he elaborated.

"The information I need has most likely been deleted from the server's database, but hopefully the hard copy of this file is still in tact. You'll have to sneak into the restricted archives to retrieve the data, and then meet me back here in two hours."

"And what file should we retrieve?" Sabrina asked.

"I think I know who engineered my brother's resurrection and many of the events that have followed. Find everything you can on a villain called The Magician."

And with that last instruction, Michael zoomed out of the room to find some answers of his own. For he had a gut feeling that Malix withheld a key piece of information he would need to find his brother.

Michael stood at the bottom of the steps to Malix's castle, and he pulled out the coin-sized contact device Stone gave to him. After pressing the smooth surface with his thumb, a 6-inch tall, 3-dimensional image of Stone popped out and spoke the words, "Go on in," before fading back into the tiny piece of metal.

The door at the top of the stairs popped open, so Michael sprinted up the stone stairway and through the main entrance. He noticed dozens of cameras bolted against the walls and ceiling; they turned and watched him as he hustled down the hallway toward the building's computer room. After scanning his palm against the identification plate next to the fortress door, Michael barged into the room, his mind intent on exacting the truth from Malix, who was sitting in his computer chair.

But Michael's determined train of thought wavered when he saw Malix had a visitor. Molly turned her head from one of the computer screens and smiled at the sight of Michael. "Hey!" she exclaimed. "I feel like I haven't seen you in forever." Her heels clicked off of the tile floor as she rushed over to give Michael a hug. He stood with a bewildered look of shock in his eyes and half-open mouth.

"Well, I guess this is as good a time as any to reveal the third member of our group," Malix sighed. "After Aldridge gave his life for our cause, we recruited Blue Moon here to take his place. She brings many of the same great qualities he did, including a superior knowledge of history. And I assume that's why you are here?" Malix expressed this last statement in a matter-of-fact tone as if he could read Michael's thoughts.

Still, Michael remained in shock at discovering Molly held yet another secret, so he took a moment to respond. After shaking the dumbfounded expression from his face, he looked over to Malix and tried to understand what he said. "Wh– what?" he stumbled to blurt out.

The professor stood up from his chair before taking a few steps toward Michael. "You came for information about the data reel, no?" he grinned.

How did he know? Michael questioned to himself, but his thoughts must have been transparent on his face because Malix explained without a word from Michael.

"No, I'm not reading your thoughts, I just know how your mind works. And I figured you would eventually put the pieces together, considering your friends are headed toward the Hall of Archives." Professor Malix pointed to one of the screens at the top right corner of the wall behind him, which displayed video footage of Archer, Allison and Sabrina trying to enter the back entrance to the Hall of Archives. "But they won't find what you need."

"You knew all this time," Michael interrupted with a barking growl, activating the blue energy around his fists.

"I know many things," Malix chuckled to lighten the mood. "But we only reveal what we think you are capable of handling. Many things in your life, you will need to discover for yourself. I was wondering how long it would take for you to recognize the importance of the nightmare that showed you the death of Mr. All-American."

"So you agree, it was no coincidence that someone showed me how he died," Michael surmised. "I thought it was because they wanted me to see his life end, but now I realize there was a crucial piece of information that I overlooked. That shadow mentioned the data reel that Mr. All-American was trying to steal. And this mystery man took it instead. Someone wanted me to know that. So tell me, what was on that reel?" Michael's voice grew more determined, almost to the point of hostility.

"Neither Stone nor I ever discovered what was on the reel," Malix explained. "We only knew that it contained data so confidential that the Elders never uploaded the information to the city's main database. The reel itself was kept locked away in a secret location until we discovered that Mr. All-American was looking for it. Only Professor Aldridge and one other soul had knowledge of its location. Even Auto was kept in the dark, much to his disliking."

"Did Professor Aldridge know what was on the reel?" Michael inquired.

"Yes, but he coveted this information more than anything, so before his untimely death, he only shared his knowledge with that one other soul that I mentioned—his most trusted confidant," Malix elaborated.

"Well then we have to find him," Michael blurted in an urgent tone. "Who is he?"

"She—is me," Molly interrupted. Michael turned his head toward her, a hurt and distrustful look in his tightened cheeks.

"How could you keep that from me?" Michael exhaled, his watering eyes on the verge of breaking into tears. "We're supposed to be friends."

The room's only door opened, and Stone entered to jump into their conversation. "I'm afraid I instructed her not to tell you." While the door closed behind him, the giant brute stepped over to join the group's conversation. "As Professor Malix stated a moment ago, there are some things that you have to discover for yourself, and neither of us believed you were ready for this information."

"What information?" Michael demanded, his chin vibrating from left to right with rage. "What have you been keeping from me?" Malix looked to Stone, who gave him a solemn nod. Then the professor turned his head to Molly and also nodded, granting her permission to reveal what they had been hiding.

"Michael, I know you are mad that we kept this hidden, but you have to understand," Molly began explaining. "All three of us care about you, and we know you have so many burdens already weighing on you every day. Problems that we can't even comprehend. We didn't want to alarm you without due cause." Michael froze, his heart fearful of what she might say next. Mostly because Molly was right . . . He did feel burdened every day, and perhaps he couldn't take much more. But he'd reached the point of no return now, so he wanted—no, he needed to hear the rest.

"I never viewed the information on the data reel myself," Molly continued. "But Professor Aldridge trusted me with the knowledge of its contents. The data reel was created by the Trifecta's most brilliant scientist. He included top-secret information on all of his most powerful and prominent experiments from his time working for the Trifecta."

Molly paused to lick her lips as she prepared her next sentence. "He was the head scientist who designed the Infinity-Omega project. His formula and procedure were the reason the experiment succeeded. If Mastermind does have the reel, she could decipher the encrypted information, which includes details on how they infused the power into Omega and Mr. Infinity's body." As she paused one final time, Molly exhaled through her nose to reveal the most shocking part. "The reel also tells of the only way to destroy both Mr. Infinity and Omega."

Michael's head started to tingle, as if a dozen needles were pricking his forehead and cheeks while his stomach felt like throwing up from this last bit of information. "In other words—" Michael exhaled but paused before completing his sentence, allowing Stone to jump in and finish the thought for him.

"Yes, it could tell her how to kill you." Stone kept his usual grim expression, but both Malix and Molly looked at Michael with painful eyes. They each appeared guilty for having to pile this new pain on his shoulders.

While Stone showed little compassion for Michael's situation, Professor Malix placed his right hand on his student's shoulder to comfort him. "I realize this is tough for you to hear," he acknowledged. "But there is more, and I'm afraid this news won't be good either."

"He can handle it," Stone grunted through his tough scowl, a sign of his confidence in Michael's strength of character.

"The reel contains in-depth details about Mr. Infinity's creation, which means Mastermind not only knows how to kill you, but possibly also how to control you," Molly disclosed. "In your dream, you said she claims she will control you. That could be possible if she interprets the data correctly."

Michael nodded his head, fighting to hold back an urge to cry from such a horrible revelation. "How do you even know that Mastermind is the one who has the reel?"

Molly paused before answering him. She bit her lower lip so hard she almost pierced her skin. "When her forces infiltrated the city to release Mr. Mental and Fireball, she dismantled parts of our shield while forging a similar one to protect her helicopter. The only place she could have found that information was on the data reel."

"Why?" Michael asked, his disconcertion subsiding with each syllable from Molly's harmonious voice.

"The same scientist who headed the Infinity-Omega project was also an integral designer of Hero City's shield. When Professor Aldridge hid the reel, he told me the information could also be used to break through our protective barrier. Mastermind's invasion at the beginning of the school year was proof that she has possession of the reel."

As he took in a deep breath, Michael shuffled all of this information through his head, piecing each of the new bits with what he already knew. "So what can I do from here?" he asked of his three friends.

"You must sharpen your mind," Malix instructed. "All of these events revolve around you, not us. You are a brilliant detective, but even the greatest sleuths can be blinded by the clues that are most personal to them. Only you can decide how to interpret this information and how to prepare for future events."

Michael looked back at Malix with a puzzled expression, squinting his right eye and lifting his left eyebrow—even though he knew exactly what the professor meant. All of the clues pointed to one answer—one eventuality—but Michael couldn't come to grips. Perhaps his personal relationship in this plot was clouding his judgment.

He kept hoping he was missing something, but now he feared more than ever that he already had the most crucial piece of information.

"At this time, we have pressing business to take care of, so we'll have to ask you to leave," Stone announced while Molly and Malix gazed down toward the floor out of shame.

"So there's nothing else?" Michael inquired, suspicious of their coy reactions to Stone's dismissal.

"No," Stone snorted before either of his compatriots could answer. "Now get out of here before I throw you out." Michael narrowed his eyes on Stone, now even more skeptical that they knew something else. But Stone's intimidating stare told Michael he wasn't going to elicit any more information here, so he turned back toward the building's front entrance, hoping to meet up with his friends to see if they found anything.

Without another word, Michael stumbled his way back down the main hall toward the large double doors. But after walking halfway, he heard a beautiful voice echoing from behind him.

"Michael, wait!" Blue Moon called out to him. He turned and saw her marching toward him, her heels clicking through the corridor at a methodical rate. When she caught up to him, she tried to force her usual smile into her cheeks. But her conscience seemed to get the best of her because all she could muster was a fake smirk that caused her chin to shake like a shivering child.

Although he wanted to say many things, Michael couldn't find a single word to express what he was feeling. Lucky for him, Molly broke the tension. "I wanted to tell you how sorry I am that you had to learn all of that information."

Michael opened his mouth, ready to scream, releasing all of his frustration on Molly, but then he saw a tear in the corner of her left eye. "There is so much I've wanted to tell you, but I don't want to hurt you. You've handled so much pain since joining us. I just—" She tried to finish her sentence but found no more words, so she reached out and pulled Michael close to her. Wrapping her arms around him, Molly squeezed him as if she was afraid to let go. Her red lips were close to his ear as she whispered, "I just wanted to say that I'm sorry."

And with that last apology, Molly released Michael, turned her body, and power-walked her way back toward the computer room. As she hustled away from him, he observed her wiping another tear from her left eye.

26. Final Plans

Mr. Mental

March 25th

A single, oval shaped light illuminated the conference room deep within Mastermind's lair. She sat in the chair closest to the exit with Titanon standing on guard behind her like the faithful lapdog that he was. On the opposite side of the circular table, Fireball and Mr. Mental sat next to each other, leaning back in their plush leather chairs. Both villains were clearly unhappy to be at the meeting, their arms crossed in front of their chests with sneering scowls in their scrunched noses and squinting eyes. They wore their intimidating, black pinstripe suits with their red shades shielding their eyes.

"We've recruited all of the players, retrieved the technology you requested, and I personally supplied you with imperative information you needed for your plan," Mr. Mental scoffed from across the table. "Now I expect you to hold up your end of our bargain and deliver the rest of the details for the invasion."

"You can expect all you like," Mastermind chuckled, "but in the end, I'm in charge here, not you."

"You should think about the future," Mr. Mental suggested. "After the invasion, our bargain will be complete, and you will no longer be in charge here."

"So I'd stay on our good side if I was you," Fireball advised, uncrossing his arms to place his palms flat against the table as he leaned forward.

"Well, that's the difference between you and me," Mastermind smiled. "Your feeble minds contemplate the future, while mine makes the future."

Mr. Mental slammed both of his hands on the table but still kept a cool demeanor as he inched his torso toward Mastermind. "Don't think you can bully us with your overconfidence, Katelyn. You aren't dealing with the same pushovers you're used to like that dolt standing behind you." He lifted his head, pointing his nose to Titanon, who opened his mouth to object against these demeaning remarks. But then he apparently thought better of that decision, resealing his lips before taking a heavy gulp that pushed out on his throat.

Mastermind squinted her eyes, tightening her gaze on the two insolent villains, like a mother scolding her bratty, disobedient children. "Watch your tone, Patrick," Mastermind sneered as she relaxed her posture. Her smooth, round cheeks appeared unconcerned with anything Mr. Mental or Fireball could say or do, a small detail that annoyed, even slightly enraged, Mr. Mental.

Sitting up from her chair, Mastermind ordered her trained monkey to exit. "I'd like to have a word alone with you," she insisted to Mr. Mental. Fireball looked to him, unwilling to leave unless Mr. Mental agreed. The super genius turned to his head left and gave Fireball a reassuring nod, signaling his brother to leave him alone with Mastermind.

Before Fireball stood up, Mr. Mental forced a short, telepathic explanation into his comrade's mind. *Perhaps this will give me the opportunity to discover the final ulterior motive she has hidden from my mind.* Fireball slowly closed his eyes and pushed back his chair. He sidled his way around the edge of the table and followed Titanon out through the sliding glass doors that automatically shut behind them, leaving the two evil geniuses alone to a battle of wits.

"Enough petty squabbling," Mastermind jeered. "Let's get down to business."

"If that's what you want," Mr. Mental grinned, aware that this was his best chance to extract the missing information he needed to decipher Mastermind's full intentions behind her plan.

"That's what I want," Mastermind replied, her confidence beaming in an arrogant smirk.

"Then let's get started."

"Very well, are all of the pieces assembled and ready per my instructions?" Mastermind asked.

"Yes, but—" Mr. Mental began to object in an attempt to keep their dialogue running until he obtained the details he wanted.

Before he could complete his thought, Mastermind instructed, "Good, then get Sharp Shot's army outfitted with the new equipment and order her to lead them in the full frontal assault. She will take The Magician and The Wolfman with her to lead Beta team in an all-out attack designed to draw the Trifecta's forces away from the heart of the city. This will give our team the opportunity to slip behind their defenses and obtain the packages we need."

"Then you plan to infiltrate the city with us?" Mr. Mental asked, a suspicion he had since the day he was liberated from the city's prison. "The original plan called for you to monitor both teams from your floating base in the sky."

"Change of plans," Mastermind explained with a smug smirk in her left cheek. "I will lead Alpha team in the extraction of our newest weapon. And you and Fireball will assist me in the infiltration of the Trifecta Headquarters." Just as Mr. Mental anticipated. She wanted something else inside the city, something well-guarded that she couldn't obtain without their help.

"What about Mr. Infiniti?" Mr. Mental asked, fully aware that he would play a key role in both his and her plan. He was the unsuspecting pawn in their game, but both mental giants were struggling to take control of the Limitless Hero.

Mastermind placed her hands on the glass table and pushed herself up from her chair. "I've already made the necessary preparations for him," she smiled, turning her back on Mr. Mental. "Just make sure you follow the instructions I gave you exactly as I laid them out. Or are they too complicated for you?"

Mr. Mental growled under his breath before grunting, "No, I think I can handle that."

"Good, see that you do," Mastermind commanded. She flipped her cape over her right shoulder and strolled through the sliding door of the conference room.

As soon as the doors closed, Mr. Mental snorted, "Arrogant witch!" Out of frustration, he smacked his left hand on the conference table and plopped his chin into his right palm while resting his right elbow on the glass surface.

"Patience," a voice echoed from behind Mr. Mental's chair.

"I can't stand taking orders from that halfwit for another day," Mr. Mental grumbled. His left hand tapped his fingers against the glass table while he kept his chin nestled in the cup of his right hand. He didn't turn to face the cloaked figure who was hiding in the dark shadows behind him.

"I understand your frustration, brother, but you must remain vigilant," the shadow's booming voice echoed through the room like a god instructing his subject.

"She's plotting something else," Mr. Mental answered to the shadow. "From the very start, she knew she was going to lead our team into Hero City."

"Your analysis is correct. Her agreement to help me was self-serving from the beginning, but I anticipated her treachery even before approaching her. She thinks the secondary objective of this invasion sits beyond our gaze, but she is mistaken. Her vision is the one that is blinded. Our assault on Hero City will fulfill two of our Master's goals; however, Mastermind could not fully comprehend the ramifications of her cooperation in retrieving both weapons from within the city's defenses. Your revenge will come when she realizes her doom."

"You know what else she desires from within the city?" Mr. Mental asked, a surprised, high pitch in his tone.

"Yes, a once significant item has recently regained importance in our world, a turn of events that has eluded the Trifecta. Their Elders currently sit on two of the most powerful weapons on the planet, yet they remain unaware. Think back to the data that you've been analyzing."

Mr. Mental's eyes lit up in a yellow glow as a realization dawned on him. "Alpha," he blurted.

"Ineed. Now you see. She will meet her demise. So prepare the troops as she instructed, and await my signal once you are inside the building's defenses. I'll take care of the rest."

"Understood," Mr. Mental agreed, pushing his chair back as he stood up from the table. He turned to face the mysterious shadow but found only darkness remained.

A wide grin lifted Mr. Mental's cheeks as he spoke to himself, "The battle is approaching. He is ready."

27. Loose Cannon

Michael

April 7th, 4:45 PM

"Hurry, they posted our teams for next year!" Allison shouted back to Michael and Archer as they exited their history class, data books in hand. Archer's eyes lit up, and he sprinted ahead to catch up with Allison while every other second-year student rushed behind him. They all wanted to reach the main entrance to the Hall of Heroes, so they could discover who would join their squad the following year.

Michael, on the other hand, waited behind, less excited to discover his results. His battle with Solar Flare would be the most prominent basis for the Elders' decision, a bout he wished he could wipe from his memory. Taking the shortest steps he could, Michael headed toward the building's atrium to discover his fate.

But as he entered the main corridor, something strange happened. Michael experienced a mysterious moment between him and the staff in the middle of the room—the one with the A on top—the same one that Malix featured in the hallway of his castle. While dozens of students jumped up and down with joy, their screaming voices echoing through the hall, Michael felt dizzy, and he heard a voice drawing him toward the staff. The hissing screech captivated his mind, pulling him in like the hypnotic call of the Sirens.

When Michael reached the glass case, he noticed the glaring overhead light shining off of the red A on top of the staff, and the voice grew clearer. "They are coming," the man's voice hissed. "You must ready yourself—they are coming."

As Michael stared at this monument with a dead expression in his frozen cheeks, he tried to analyze the message, but his mind could only repeat the same words over and over. "They are coming. I must ready myself."

He repeated these two sentences nearly a dozen times until Allison finally shook him from his trance. "Hey, did you hear what I said?" she shouted into Michael's ear. "You and I were placed on the same team."

Throwing his head left and right, in an attempt to shake his mind clear, Michael regained his senses and responded to Allison in a despondent tone. "That's great. I'm glad I'll get to work with you."

Allison's face scrunched into a puzzled expression from Michael's disinterested reply. Unfortunately, she couldn't comprehend the complications that he had to deal with at this moment. Brushing his hands down his suit jacket, Michael composed himself and compiled an appropriate response so as not to alarm Allison that something was wrong. "Yeah, I mean that *is* really exciting." He struggled to lift his cheeks into a fake smile. "I'll go check out the board right now." As Michael slipped away from her grip, Allison stared at him like his body and soul had transformed into someone she didn't recognize. Her eyes squinted in on his face and then the back of his head while she exhaled a disconcerted sigh.

When Michael reached the back wall of the atrium, he found 2-foot by 3-foot mugshots of all 30 students projected into 3-dimensional holograms. All of the students' profiles provided detailed information about them with their pictures grouped next to their new squad members for the following year. Michael located his profile toward the top right, accompanied by Allison, Archer, and Max Force. *Strange that the Elders didn't pair me up with Sabrina*, Michael thought. They did complement each other rather well, after all. But at least he had three of his other close friends in his group.

Then as Michael used his shades to zoom in on the personal evaluation information in his profile, he grew dizzy at what he read:

"Mr. Infiniti shows dangerous signs of aggression when provoked or enraged, and his development should be handled with caution. He cares more for his own well-being than the welfare of his teammates, which is why he is not recommended for a leadership role on this team. Max Force or Archer would be better suited for such designation. Although we do believe that he is prepared for his third year of training, we recommend that his field leaders keep a watchful eye on his actions and decisions in battle."

Michael's heart beat faster as the whole room spun out of control. He couldn't believe what the Elders had written about him and then posted on this wall for their entire organization to see. Their analysis made him seem like a crazy stick of dynamite that could explode and destroy their world at the slightest provocation.

"Looks like the Elders have your number," Solar Flare jeered from behind Michael's shoulder.

He turned to face the loud mouth who had only recently recovered and returned from the medical bay. Although he sustained incredible damage, the Trifecta's advanced healing technology rehabilitated him close to 100 percent health in miraculous time.

Solar Flare's shrill voice reignited the fire that Michael felt in his heart during their battle. "You just never let up, do you?" Michael growled through clenched teeth as he gripped Milton by the collar of his suit jacket.

Solar Flare's right hand burst into flames, and he snarled back at Michael, "I'll never let up until the world sees you for what I know you are—weak." Just as the tension looked close to the point of explosion, Allison jumped in between the two nemeses, pushing her tiny arms to her side to separate them.

"Whoa there, let's all just calm down," she urged. "We don't need the two of you to end up expelled for destroying this building—along with everyone inside." Michael and Milton stared each other down, their eyes unwavering while a fire burned deep within each of their irises.

Sabrina and Archer helped Allison run interference, each of them taking hold of Michael's arms to drag him away. He realized he was displacing his anger onto Milton when his true fury stemmed from the Elders' assessment—although Michael had a hunch that Eliki was mostly responsible for their harsh report. Scrunching his forehead, Michael determined to track down the Trifecta leaders to confront them regarding their analysis of his apparently erratic psyche.

After Michael pulled himself free from Archer and Sabrina, he took off toward the Hall of Heroes' main entrance. "Wait, where are you going?" Allison called out, her short legs hopelessly trying to catch up to the much faster Michael.

"Let him go," Archer called to her. Then he turned to Sabrina and commented, "We have to let him work this out on his own."

Because Michael was in no mood to defend his decision to his friends, he continued on out to the streets where he boomed his way toward the Trifecta Headquarters, leaving Allison behind to worry about what he might do.

As Michael blazed through the air over the streets of Hero City, he felt a massive headache pressuring the temples on the side of his head. The strain on his mind built to an almost unbearable peak, but Michael's fury kept him focused. After landing at the bottom of the stairs below the Headquarters' entrance, he fell prey to another vision. Mastermind stood at the top of the stairs with a confident smile in her right cheek.

"After all of this time, you still haven't learned a thing," she mocked from her pedestal. "At the end of this day, both you and your brother will belong to me. And there's nothing you can do to stop me." Then she let out a short cackle that dissipated along with her body.

Michael shook his head, but Mastermind's words only increased his anger, goading him into a solid state of determination.

If she thinks she's going to claim me as her slave, she'll be sorely surprised, Michael thought. After a year of training and preparation, and with the addition of his new wristband, he felt confident that he had the tools to defeat her.

As he took one step up the stone stairway, Melvin interrupted his ascent. "Mr. Infiniti, you are being summoned by the Elders," he reported. Michael froze mid-step, wondering if they preemptively called for his arrival because they saw him coming.

"I'm heading up to see them right now," Michael responded through gritted teeth. "Tell them I'll be there in a second." He began sprinting up the stairs toward the large glass doors, his eyes locked straight ahead.

"You misunderstand," Melvin interrupted his gait again. "The Elders request your presence in the War Room."

Freezing in his place, Michael grew perplexed. He'd never set foot in the War Room. No low-ranking student had. So he paused and asked Melvin to repeat his message. "Can you say that again?"

"The Elders are in need of your presence in the War Room," Melvin responded. "They've requested that you report there immediately." Michael felt conflicted. He did want to confront the Elders, but he feared why they might request a meeting with him in the War Room.

In the end, Michael's rage overruled his more cautious side, so he dashed off down the street toward the War Room. This was a smaller building that lay only a block east of the Hall of Heroes. The eight-story structure was covered in brown bricks with an enormous statue of Auto erected on the roof. The sculpture must have been 5 times larger than life, but then so was the Mr. Infinity statue in front of the Hall of Heroes.

When Michael landed at the entrance of the building, the front doors automatically opened for him, so he walked inside. Although the main atrium's reinforced glass ceilings stood eight stories overhead, the area was significantly smaller than Michael would have expected. He didn't know how to reach the main room of the building, so he opened his mouth to ask Melvin for directions; however, Melvin beat him to the punch.

"Follow the lights in the floor," the robotic super-computer instructed. And as he finished his sentence, the glass tiles in the floor began glowing with a golden light that outlined a path, directing Michael toward the center of the building. After running ahead 20 feet, the lights turned right, leading him into an elevator. But all of this felt too easy to Michael. If he didn't know better, he would have sworn someone was leading him into a trap.

Once the elevator doors closed in on each other, the compartment sped Michael up to the fourth floor before dropping him off at the center of the building. He exited into a 30-foot-long hallway and ran toward a reinforced door at the far end. The circular entrance was shiny and must have been at least three feet thick, which separated Michael from the main chamber of the War Room. When he stopped outside, the entrance locks disengaged, and the heavy, silver port swung open like the entrance to a bank vault.

As Michael stepped in, he found the Elders standing in front of a round, golden table measuring at least 8 feet in diameter. All four of Michael's superiors turned their heads with perplexed expressions.

"How did you get in here!" Eliki screamed so loudly that she startled Malix, Scylla and Auto. "What are you doing here?" Her enraged tone only escalated from there. "This is a restricted area, and second-year students are banned from entering—" She might have gone on, but her rant was cut short by a siren that blared through the room—a siren warning of an imminent attack on the city.

28. Battle Facade

Mr. Mental

April 7th, 5:00 PM

"Sharp Shot, engage the enemy," Mastermind commanded through her headset. Mr. Mental stood next to Fireball in Mastermind's observation ship, which hovered a thousand feet above the battlegrounds with both mental giants ready to oversee the attack on the Trifecta shield. For the moment, Mr. Mental linked his own mind with Sharp Shot's, allowing him to see, hear and experience everything she did. There were many variables in this part of his plan, so he needed to keep a close eye on the most important players every step of the way.

Sharp Shot grinned at the opportunity to finally attack. She carried a high-powered assault rifle with a two foot long barrel and a magnifying scope on the top. Her two pistols lay waiting in her hip holsters, and jutting over her right shoulder was the handle to a samurai sword, which she only used in the event that she ran out of ammunition.

While standing at the top of a hill nearly a mile east of the invisible shield, she stared down over the open field and the single road that led to Hero City. The setting sun beamed through the invisible barrier as Sharp Shot zoomed in on the point where the road eventually converged with the city's main entrance.

"Let's go," she instructed of Jonathan Breck and The Magician, who each stood a few feet behind her. Breck licked his lips before nodding to her from his frozen position while The Magician closed his eyes to calm himself. Backing up the three villains were roughly 20,000 armed men and women, dressed in black and red combat suits. Sharp Shot pressed a button on her left glove and ordered her generals to march forward.

"Jonathan, you lead our army toward the city wall," Sharp Shot commanded. "The Magician and I will remain here where we can monitor the movements of their forces and aid you from afar."

"Ha, how noble of you both," Breck sneered in a sarcastic tone. But he did as he was told, this being his best chance to draw out Mr. Infiniti so The Wolfman could break his spine. As the troops marched on, Sharp Shot's magnified eye piece allowed her to zoom in beyond the invisible barrier that protected the city. She observed at least fifty heroes emerging from a dozen different building entrances like water seeping from a cracked container. Soon they would rush out even faster as if the water had broken the cracks wide open. An alarm must have sounded within the city wall, but the invisible barrier muffled all noise to those looking in.

Sharp Shot placed her right fingers on her headset to give the first attack order. "General Zadine, fire all cannons." The hundred tanks rolling their way forward halted in their tracks, and a mechanism opened up underneath the belly of each beast. Three hooks emerged from the opening and shot down into the ground, attaching all three hooks 15 feet below Earth's surface to create an anchor for each tank.

A few seconds later, all one hundred tank cannons simultaneously blasted a single-shot energy ray that tore through the air before impacting against the city's impenetrable shield. The intense recoil would have pushed the heavy tanks back, but their anchors kept them firmly in place. Although an intense wave of fire and smoke rose from the protective shield, the explosions impressed no effect on the forcefield, a fact that Sharp Shot and Mastermind were well aware of. Her forces were there to draw out as many heroes as possible. Both women knew that breaking through the barrier with force was futile, but the Elders couldn't risk that.

"Fire again," Sharp Shot ordered over her headset. After recharging, the tanks rip-fired another explosive blast of energy that crashed into the city's exterior wall. "That should be enough to draw out some of their best heroes," Sharp Shot commented to The Magician, who remained eerily quiet while she did all of the commanding.

But Sharp Shot was correct; a small hole opened at the base of the city's shield, allowing 15 heroes to emerge from within. They sprinted forward, heading straight toward Sharp Shot's forces who marched within half a mile of the invisible shield—but the Elders didn't care for them to draw any closer.

Dozens of auto-turrets sprang up from beneath the ground and started firing stun rays in a 180-degree arc. Despite their heavy armor, Sharp Shot's forces toppled over like ants being burned by a fire.

"Breck, get in there and take out those turrets!" she shouted over her communicator, hoping he could draw most of their fire.

"No," he sassed back to her. "That's a waste of my skills. I want the heroes."

"You'll have plenty of time to engage them once you've taken out those turrets," she explained. "Follow the plan as Mr. Mental discussed with us, or my forces won't last more than a few minutes out there, which won't give Alpha team nearly enough time."

"Take them out yourself!" Breck barked back at her before ripping the communicator out of his ear, which began sprouting brown patches of hair. As Breck sprinted toward the growing group of heroes, his human half transformed into the beast that lay within. While his limbs and chest expanded first, his nose nose took shape second, extending out into a long, fearsome snout. More intensified laser blasts from the turrets whizzed by him, some ripping right through his flesh, but each hit only made him angrier and stronger. By the time he passed the turrets, his bone-plated armor had emerged from the skin on his arms and torso; only the devilish horns remained dormant within his body.

The first two heroes on the scene paused when they observed a hairy beast bounding his way toward them on all four limbs—like an African lion chasing a gazelle. After bursting off the ground, The Wolfman brought his weight crashing down on the pair of heroes. He took two swiping slashes with his right and left claws, which ripped one of the heroes to shreds while the other rolled to the side, using his hands to push himself back up on his feet.

Sharp Shot's cheeks trembled with anger. "That insolent little—" she began growling but couldn't finish her thought because her mind grew too frustrated with anger. She needed to redirect her attention to her forces that were falling like dominoes. "Magician," she called to her comrade standing behind her.

"Yes," he immediately responded like an ideal soldier ready to take orders. This must have been why Mastermind assigned him to this detail. She could have easily anticipated that The Wolfman would be uncontrollable once his rage and lust for blood took over.

"Can you use a spell to dismantle some of those turrets?" Sharp Shot asked.

"My telekinesis spell can take out a few per minute," he answered. "But that will take some time—time that your soldiers don't have. Can't the tanks take them out?"

"Ughhhh, not unless we want the explosion to wipe out half of our forces in the process," Sharp Shot pouted, stamping her right heel against the ground. "Focus your efforts on the turrets starting on the left. I'll take out the other ones on the right. Gogogo," she ordered, pulling the butt of her her assault rifle up to her right shoulder. Her right trigger finger pulled back twice, firing two golfball-sized bullets. The metal projectiles soared through the air and then broke into a dozen smaller pieces, each one targeting the Trifecta defenses. Three seconds after these smaller bullets impacted against the turrets, they exploded into rising, cylindrical flames.

Meanwhile, a small army of Trifecta defense droids stormed out onto the battlefield, but they posed little threat to The Wolfman, who was already having his way with the overmatched group of heroes attempting to oppose him—that is until Stone arrived. The savage beast already managed to maim at least a dozen valiant members of the Trifecta, but Stone would be another story.

"Ahahaha," The Wolfman snickered through his raspy voice. His pointy devil horns slid through his skull, amplifying his rage and strength for his imminent battle. "The great Stone," he howled across the 50 meters that separated them. "I was wondering when the Elders would send someone worthy of my talents."

"Here I am," Stone shouted across the battlefield, raising his hands out to his side. "Let's see if I can break those horns off your head."

The Wolfman barked twice before charging forward. He needed only three powerful, bounding leaps to reach his enemy. As his heavy body crashed down on Stone's rough exterior, he took one diagonal swipe across Stone's shoulder and chest. But to The Wolfman's dismay, his claws barely left a scratch over Stone's rock hard shell.

Mr. Mental pulled his mind back from peering through Sharp Shot's eyes, so he could monitor all of the action from Mastermind's observation ship where the three villains still hovered a thousand feet above the battleground. Turning to Mastermind with a sly smile, he gloated, "It seems that the battle isn't going as planned. Sharp Shot's forces will be depleted within minutes, which will leave the city full of heroes, preventing our stealth infiltration of the city streets. I could have told you that she wouldn't be able to command The Wolfman."

"You presume too much," Mastermind responded. "Watch what happens next."

Sure enough, Sharp Shot's specialized bullets, combined with The Magician's telekinetic powers, provided enough force to take out a large portion of the Trifecta turrets. Mastermind had taken time to upgrade Sharp Shot's rifle with the anticipation that she would need to destroy the turrets. And while Sharp Shot's forces continued charging closer to the city shield, a dozen more heroes emerged from within the city's safe confines.

"Surge forward!" Sharp Shot ordered over her communication link while she and The Magician remained safely at the rear of their forces. They both assisted the mindless drones who fired their bullets at the far more powerful super humans while still keeping their distance from any real danger.

As Sharp Shot's soldiers battled with the heroes of the Trifecta, the fight between The Wolfman and Stone raged on. "Owwooooooo," The Wolfman howled as dusk began to pass, darkening the sky above. "You're growing tired," he gloated to Stone. "But the more I fight, the stronger I get. And your old age has only made you weak."

Stone wasn't in the mood for banter, so he let two more right jabs do the talking for him. The first punch smashed up against The Wolfman's cheek, leaving a temporary bruise, but the second fist slammed into the beast's teeth, shattering at least a dozen of his snarling canine fangs.

"Owoooooo!" The Wolfman cried from the pain. A handful of yellow bits of teeth lay scattered across the ground. And although The Wolfman's healing powers would regenerate new teeth, Stone gave his enemy no time to recover; he delivered a whopping uppercut to the monster's jaw, which sent the demon soaring 20 feet above the ground. Pushing his heavy boots off of the grass and dirt, Stone rushed toward the falling body of The Wolfman. Then before the animal could crash into the earth below, Stone twirled forward with his right leg, smashing his black boot into his enemy's rib cage.

"Stone is crushing The Wolfman," Sharp Shot commented to The Magician. Her quivering lip revealed her dying confidence. "And the Trifecta's heroes are getting closer to us. We won't last much longer out here. We'd better order a retreat."

"Have faith," The Magician responded, raising his right palm out to point his fingers at one of the approaching Trifecta members. He blasted a purple beam of light that lifted the hero off the ground, propelling him 100 feet up into the sky before he would fall to his doom. "Mr. Mental wouldn't send us into a battle that he thought we couldn't win. Just wait. The Wolfman is building steam, and soon, his rage will grow unstoppable."

Sharp Shot fired two high-powered bullets that tore through a Trifecta vehicle's tires before she responded, "If you say so. But I'm not giving him much more time before I order my troops to fall back."

"Then I suggest we join the battle up closer," The Magician answered. He extended his arms out to his sides with his palms facing up, levitating his body five feet above the ground. "Are you coming?" His dark eyes looked back upon Sharp Shot, whose forehead scrunched with concern.

"That's not what Mastermind instructed when we went over the plan," Sharp Shot objected. "We shouldn't deviate from her instructions, or this whole scheme might fall apart."

"I sense fear," The Magician gloated. "Perhaps you are not as brave as you seem." The powerful sorcerer hovered down toward the battlefield with a crimson, protective bubble surrounding his body.

As The Magician joined the battle, The Wolfman's rage continued to grow with each punishing blow he sustained from Stone. His horns grew to their full length of 12 inches, and his broad shoulders rose nearly 8 feet above the ground. Even Stone's tank-sized physique appeared insignificant next to the brooding body of The Wolfman.

"No more playing around," The Wolfman growled through his clenched fangs. "Stand aside and send out Mr.

Infiniti, so I can snap him in two." The beast's blood-red eyes glared at Stone, whose rock hard chest pumped in and out. While The Wolfman grew stronger, fatigue started to wear on Stone.

"Infinity is dead," Stone lied as he tried to catch his breath. "He was killed in the Big Boom. Didn't you know?"

"Hahahaha," The Wolfman cackled in a deep voice that sounded like the crunching of leaves under a boot. "You think me a fool? I know of your new recruit, and I am going to exact my revenge upon him for the sins of his predecessor."

"Not while I'm still standing." Stone's breathing increased, and his muscles weakened while his joints began freezing up.

"I'll take care of that now." The Wolfman crouched low to the ground on all four paws and then leapt in the air. His heavy body dropped down onto his prey, and he kicked his hind legs into Stone's chest with enough force to send the hero's sturdy body crashing into the earth beneath his feet. As Stone's shoulders and torso forged a ten foot wide crater in the ground, The Wolfman slashed his right and then left hand across his body, slicing a thin X-shaped scar into Stone's rock hard exterior.

"I have to thank you," The Wolfman grumbled with his enormous palms pinning Stone's shoulders against the hard earth. "I needed a good fight to build my rage before facing off against Mr. Infiniti. Now call him out here to your aid." The devilish beast increased the pressure on Stone's left arm, crushing the muscles beneath his sturdy shell. But Stone wasn't done yet, retaliating with a double uppercut to The Wolfman's chest, which broke his pinning hold on the hero.

"I won't call to him, no matter what you do," Stone shouted in an exasperation of pain. "You'll just have to kill me." Before The Wolfman could strike back, Stone hit him with a right hook, then two left hooks and finished with a charged, double-fisted uppercut that launched his enemy out of the crater in the ground.

"The battle is in full swing," Mr. Mental observed. "Most of the city is empty, and the south end is weak. What are we waiting for?" He turned to Mastermind and glared upon her with an eager lust for blood in his bright eyes.

"Patience," Mastermind replied, ignoring Mr. Mental's angst while she intensified her gaze on the virtual battlefield projecting from the table below her hands. "Mr. Infiniti still lies within the city, and I wouldn't recommend moving on our target while their champion has a chance of interfering."

"I'm surprised at you Kate," Mr. Mental scoffed his disgust for her lack of aggression. "I thought you feared no one. Why should you worry about a second-year student?"

Mastermind sneered at Mr. Mental, holding back an obvious urge to snap at him. Despite Mr. Mental's attempt to rattle her confidence, she refused to abandon her strategy. He grew worried that he was too close to showing his hand—and for his plan to work, Mastermind could not discover that he wanted her to face off against Mr. Infiniti.

"At this stage in the game, we can't take any chances," Mastermind responded in a calm tone. "I would think you and your comrades would agree with that." She looked to Fireball, who remained all too quiet during this spat. "My plan will work, I assure you, but only if we infiltrate the city at the right moment. So we will move in on my command. Got it?"

"As you wish," Mr. Mental grumbled, followed by a glance over to his brother with a confident grin in his right cheek.

Back on the ground, The Wolfman found himself on his back with Stone using his hard, gritty knuckles to pummel the beast's hairy face. The heroic giant smashed The Wolfman twice in the snout, dislocating his jaw from the rest of his skull. But the monster retaliated by tucking his knees up against his chest before extending his legs upward, launching Stone through the air.

The Wolfman stood up from the ground, the lower half of his jaw hanging from the top half at an awkward, slanted angle. He lifted both hands and squeezed his chin between his palms before snapping the lower half of his mouth back into place. An eerie crunch echoed 100 feet across the battlefield to Stone's ears where the rest of his body remained sprawled across the ground. Needing only one leap, The Wolfman bounded from his spot to land on Stone's motionless body. Leaning back, he opened his healed jaw as wide as possible before snapping down like a crocodile at Stone's face.

Fortunately, the heroic brute awakened just in time and caught The Wolfman's snout before the razor sharp teeth could reach him. He needed every last bit of strength in his rock hard fingers to hold back the snarling fangs as they crept closer to his eyeballs. A green acidic drool dripped from The Wolfman's mouth and splattered across Stone's cheeks, sizzling a searing mark into his gray exoskeleton. The pointed yellow teeth closed in on Stone, his strength fading fast, but before The Wolfman could sink his chompers into his weakening prey, his eyes widened in surprise as a sudden jolt sent him flying through the air.

"Get away from him!" Blue Moon ordered from her position 20 yards behind Stone. She spread her long legs apart with her white boots planted firmly against the ground. While extending both of her fists out from her torso, a blue light glimmered around her clenched fingers. "Back off or I'll fire again," she warned, the intensified light expanding into a royal blue ball of energy.

"Ahahaha," The Wolfman snorted through his long snout. "How many of you must I kill before Mr. Infiniti finally comes out to face me? Don't worry dear. You have a pretty face, so I'll make quick work of you." The malicious monster took two powerful leaps toward Blue Moon, but as his body pounced down toward her, she unleashed a burst of blue and gold energy particles that hit him in the chest like a battering ram, sending him sailing nearly a hundred yards. His howling expanded across the battlefield, instilling shivers down every man and woman's spine.

But before The Wolfman hit the ground, Sharp Shot came to his aid, using the pistol in her right hand to fire two bullets toward Blue Moon's chest. However, she found disappointment when Blue Moon dissolved the bullets into dust with her golden laser shield.

"Sharp Shot," Blue Moon called out to her. "I've heard you're quite the markswoman."

"Blue Moon," Sharp Shot laughed in a high-pitched, amused tone. "You've put an annoying wrench in some of my recent plans. My men often speak of your ferocity in battle— and your natural beauty." The deadly assassin holstered her pistols and removed the long rifle from over her shoulder. "Unfortunately for you, I'm greater on both accounts."

"We'll see," Blue Moon bantered back at Sharp Shot, lifting her right hand in front of her to blast two short beams of light, which forced Sharp Shot to dodge left before rolling across the ground. After landing on one knee with her rifle aimed at Blue Moon, she pressed a red button on the side and pulled the trigger to fire a single, focused, red laser stream. The needle-thin beam cut right through Blue Moon's energy shield and knocked her back twenty feet.

"Ahhhhhh," she screamed in agony, her piercing voice hitting an incredibly high pitch as she collapsed to the ground. Even though the powerful laser slipped past her defenses, Blue Moon's shield still provided enough cushion to save her from death.

"You should have chosen your allies more wisely," Sharp Shot gloated while Blue Moon lay nearly passed out on the ground. She remained just conscious enough to keep her eyes locked on the prowling predator drawing closer. "My friends gave me the technology I needed to pierce your energy shield. What have your friends done for you?"

"How about this?" Mr. Infiniti called from behind Molly's helpless body, firing a white laser from his clenched right fist. The impact of the beam caught Sharp Shot off guard, launching her back a hundred feet into her own crowd of soldiers. While she disappeared into a sea of infantry, Mr. Infiniti rushed straight to Blue Moon's side and placed his right hand on her left shoulder.

"Molly, are you okay?" he asked, a trembling bounce in his frantic eyes.

Blue Moon exhaled, nodding in response. "I'll be fine." She took hold of Michael's hand. "But this doesn't make any sense. There's no logic behind this attack, and Mastermind is anything but illogical. There's something else going on that we aren't meant to see until it's too late. You've got to stop her."

Unfortunately, before Michael could pause to think for even a second, he heard someone growling his name like a barbarian. "Mr. Infinitiiiiii!" The Wolfman bellowed with his arms branched out on each side of his torso and his foot long fingers extended from his hands.

"Just as I planned," Mastermind smirked. "He should keep Mr. Infiniti busy while we raid their city. Let's move gentlemen. Our prize awaits."

29. Battle Response

Michael

April 7th, 5:05 PM

The blaring siren echoed through the War Room as the 20-foot-wide circular table projected a virtual head of Melvin who warned the Trifecta leaders of the imminent danger that lurked outside their city. "Elders, I must beg your attention," he announced to the room. It appears that an army is preparing to storm the city."

"What?!" Auto rushed to the virtual table and pressed a square, green button on the touch screen. "Give me an overhead shot of the city outskirts," he commanded of Melvin. The large circular table transformed the virtual map in less than a second, showing the Elders a realistic view of the city from their satellite in the sky.

"Now zoom out and redirect to the point of attack," Eliki instructed. The map reshaped again, moving the virtual landscape to the area of the city where Sharp Shot's soldiers and tanks were advancing. "There must be at least 20,000 well-equipped soldiers out there," Eliki remarked.

"Why didn't Melvin warn us of their approach earlier?" Scylla asked.

"They must have an advanced cloaking device," Eliki answered. "I told both of you not to underestimate Mastermind."

"Is the shield still up?" Auto asked.

Professor Malix rolled his chair over to the nearest computer console and tapped a few buttons on the touch screen controls. "Yeah, it's still operational. Our manual precautions must have paid off. I guess Mastermind couldn't bring that down this time."

"She's got hundreds of mega-tanks, but there aren't enough tanks in the world that could break through our city's barrier," Eliki explained.

All three Elders adopted concerned looks in their scrunched foreheads. "How could Mastermind have amassed such an army?" Scylla inquired.

"She's been recruiting these past few months," Malix explained. "I'd bet she absorbed Sharp Shot into her ranks, most likely for her extensive resources."

"Prepare the defense turrets," Auto commanded. "Are the new drones ready for battle?"

Malix pushed himself back from the computer console and slid over to the glowing, holographic monitor a few feet behind him. After pulling his hands apart to expand the virtual screen, he double-tapped a glowing orange circle in the top left corner. "A few are operational, but we still don't have clearance to use them in battle," he answered Auto.

"Uuuugh," Auto grunted, squeezing both fists while tightening the muscles in his face. "Deploy our standard drones then," he instructed. "And why aren't those auto-turrets up yet?"

Malix turned around in his chair and slid himself back to the first computer console. "I've activated them," he answered. "And the basic defense drones are moving toward that end of the city, but that won't be enough to stop so many soldiers."

"He's right," Eliki agreed. "The robots will keep Mr. Mental at bay, but Mastermind still has Fireball, Sharp Shot and most likely a few other super humans out there."

"I say we allow them to continue their attack on the city shield," Scylla suggested. "They can't break through, so we should let them destroy themselves trying."

"Negative," Melvin interrupted from the overhead speakers. "I detect an energy surge similar to the one from the breakout last fall."

"That makes sense," Eliki added, throwing her hands out in front of her chest to point at the virtual battlefield. "Mastermind wouldn't attack our city without a plan to penetrate our defenses." The longer this discussion lagged on, the more animated Eliki's gesticulations became.

Michael stood silent, almost unnoticed throughout this conversation. He placed his right thumb and forefinger over his lips, pondering the veracity of each Elder's words. His instincts told him that someone was lying, but for what purpose, he wasn't sure. In any case, he knew what Eliki would suggest next.

"We need to deploy our forces," she proclaimed. "That's our best chance of snuffing out her troops to put an end to her plotting right here and now. We have the home field advantage, so I suggest we take this opportunity to recapture Mr. Mental and Fireball along with any other super humans she's collected."

"Don't underestimate Mr. Mental and Fireball," Auto interjected. "They won't go down easy. Melvin, can you identify any other super humans on the battlefield?"

All five heroes in the room remained quiet while Melvin scanned the area outside the city. As his satellite cameras searched through the thousands of faces, the holographic screens in the War Room began flashing white light, like dozens of cameras, as they flipped through thousands of criminal mugshots.

After a minute of searching, he compiled three photos on the screen. The first was of The Magician, accompanied by a picture from his youth, possibly taken when he was only fifteen. And the second image depicted Sharp Shot with her long, brown hair pulled back in a pony tail while her telescopic, left eye protruded out two inches. But the third screen caught the attention of every hero in the room.

"The Wolfman," Scylla muttered, his mouth dropping to the ground.

"He completely fell off the grid after the Big Boom," Eliki recalled aloud. "Nobody knew if he survived the explosion of that day."

"I'd hoped he simply died, but apparently he just crawled into a hole, waiting for the right time to emerge," Auto added, intensifying his gaze on the virtual picture of a man with a wolf's head that had horns emerging from the top.

"This will complicate things," Malix proclaimed, moving his fingers across the keyboard as fast as the feet of a frantic tap dancer. "The teleporter is still down, and most of our strongest members are out around the world on other missions. Let me check the database for which of our most powerful heroes are available." He touched the virtual console in front of his waist and expanded the controls by swirling his hands 360 degrees into a circle.

The largest screen in front of him brought up three hero profiles, including Stone. Malix exhaled his disappointment and rubbed his forehead with his right thumb and pointer finger. "Very few of our members will survive an attack by The Wolfman once he reaches his berserker level. We'll need someone else to assist in the fight."

At the same time, Auto and Scylla glanced at Mr. Infiniti, who turned his head from one Elder to the other, confused why they were looking to him.

"No way," Eliki interrupted their thought. "He's too inexperienced. He wouldn't last more than a minute against The Wolfman's unique mixture of raw rage and brute force."

"We don't have a choice," Scylla cried as he dashed over to the virtual battlefield where he pointed to Sharp Shot's soldiers. "They've already taken out most of our turrets, and Mastermind's forces are advancing. If they get that many soldiers past the city's protective barrier, who knows what irreparable damage they'll do?"

"No," Eliki shook her head in disagreement. "Mastermind wouldn't arrange such an elaborate attack without some higher goal than causing damage and destruction to the city."

"Then what do you propose is her ultimate goal?" Scylla inquired of his comrade.

"I'm not sure—but I can guarantee that she's hoping to get more from this attack than simple revenge. Any ideas?" Eliki asked of Auto, whose hand was resting over his mouth, his eyes deep in thought.

Turning his head to Malix, Auto asked, "Was there any more information she might need from the data archives?"

Professor Malix shook his head and responded, "None that I'm aware of." Auto exhaled, his mind clearly stumped to find a logical solution.

Just then, Michael interrupted the conversation. "What if it's not something that she's here for, but someone?" He looked over to Malix, who was throwing a threatening stare in his direction, signaling Michael to shut up now, but the conscientious teen couldn't stand idly by while heroes died to protect him.

"What do you mean?" Scylla asked. "Who would she be here for—another prisoner?"

"In a matter of speaking," Michael answered, taking a heavy gulp before giving Professor Malix a slow, but sorrowful glance of regret. "She's haunted my dreams, telling me she has my brother under her control. I think she's here to collect him."

Auto moved over and placed his hand on Michael's right shoulder. "Why didn't you tell us about this sooner?" he questioned, a hint of anger in the undertone of his voice.

"I was worried what the dream might signify," Michael explained. "She told me that she would own me and my brother. So she's either here for me, or she came for my brother, and I'm inclined to believe it's the latter."

"But your brother isn't here," Eliki interjected. "If he was, I think we would know—unless you've been keeping that from us as well."

"I'm not sure where Alex is, but I'm telling you that's what Mastermind wants most, so why else would she be here other than to collect us?" Michael's eyes narrowed and he exhaled through his nose, revealing the earnest nature of his words. He thought back to the hallucinations of his brother standing along the streets, and he grew more certain that Alex resided somewhere in Hero City.

"What makes you so sure she's here to collect your brother and not you?" Scylla asked. He and Eliki did most of the interrogation at this point while Auto and Professor Malix remained ominously quiet.

"If Mastermind was after me, I don't feel she would use an all-out attack. Her approach would be more subtle, like it was when she attacked me in Africa. But more than that, my dream indicated she already has control of Alex. She only needed to collect him, and once she accomplished that, she planned to come after me second."

"There's no use fighting over this here," Scylla hissed. "Our defenses are dwindling, and without our best heroes, Mastermind will storm the city within minutes. We need Mr. Infiniti out there."

"I agree," Malix jumped in, ending his silence. "The Wolfman is currently tearing apart our other heroes, and our small militia of robots can only keep Mastermind's soldiers at bay for so long. I've already called for all of our level four and five heroes to enter the battlefield, but like I said, most of them are too far away to return in time."

"What if we send out our new robo-prototypes?" Auto suggested. "Their advanced circuitry and adaptability might be enough to push back Mastermind's forces."

"That's possible, but even they won't last long against The Wolfman," Malix explained. "And even more important, we don't have permission to use them outside the city. The public would explode in outrage if they found out we used equipment that they hadn't approved."

"Hmmm, unfortunately you are correct," Auto agreed in a disgruntled tone. "It seems that sending in Mr. Infiniti is our only viable option."

Eliki closed her eyes and shook her head in disagreement, but she didn't say a word. Meanwhile, Scylla moved over to the closest virtual screen and used both of his hands to flip the monitor counterclockwise by 90 degrees. He tapped two virtual buttons, which projected a 3-dimensional image of The Wolfman, along with facts and statistics about the monster.

"I'm uploading all pertinent information about The Wolfman to your shades," Scylla explained. "Search through the information quickly while you head toward the battlefield. It might save your life."

"We'll keep in contact with you," Malix added. "While you're out there, we will do our best to monitor Mastermind's forces and update you if something arises. I agree that there's something more going on here than a simple attack, so keep your eyes open when you're out there."

Michael nodded his accord with a slight tremble in his cheeks. Neither Malix nor the Elders could fault him for showing fear. This would be his first real field mission, a task never asked of any other first or second-year student, and with his luck, he had to face one of the most ferocious enemies ever.

Malix grabbed Michael by the shoulders and looked into his young friend's eyes. "Michael, I have confidence in you," he assured. "You are a phenomenal hero with the strength and intellect to defeat The Wolfman. Use your superior intelligence to your advantage. Despite his appearance of invincibility, he does have weaknesses."

"Like what?" Michael asked.

"That I don't know, but you're the master detective. I'm sure you'll figure it out. Just remember, be confident."

"Got it," Michael nodded as he triple-tapped the screen on his wristband and then slid his finger forward. The fabric and gear of his battle suit emerged from the armband, replacing the expensive pinstripe suit he was wearing.

Just before Michael dashed out of the War Room and toward the city limits, Auto gave one final word of advice. "Michael, The Wolfman gets stronger with each punch he sustains, so find a weakness and defeat him as quickly as possible."

"Will do," Michael responded in an undaunted voice. "I won't fail you," he assured them before zooming off past the building's exit and out onto the city streets. He took to the air, soaring his way over the top of the closest building to reach Main Street where he boomed his way east toward the city's shield.

As Michael approached the impenetrable barrier, he felt his head grow dizzy while his sight blurred. His body began lowering back down toward the ground, but the voice in his head had his full attention.

"This is what Mastermind wants," the mysterious force hissed through his communication link. Michael grew more dizzy, and he looked up to view Omega standing in the distance, his body surrounded by raging flames. Another hallucination just like the ones Michael had suffered during the past few weeks—but this was almost identical to the one that ended his battle with Solar Flare. "You're falling right into her hand."

After landing on the ground, Michael grabbed his head in an attempt to cure his dizziness. "She's waiting for you to leave the city," the voice elaborated. "You scare her more than you know."

"Who are you?" Michael cried up into the sky, still clasping his head between his hands. He feared who might truly be pulling the strings in this battle. If he misperceived Mastermind's motives, this voice could be the true puppet master.

"My identity is an insignificant detail," the voice answered. "I've helped you thus far, but from here on you must make your own decisions. I can only give you one last piece of advice. Find Mastermind's true objective, or all will be lost."

The street lamp in front of Michael's face stopped spinning as his sight returned to normal. "I appreciate your help, but I have to know who you are," he shouted up into the air. However, the response he received was from someone else.

"Michael, what are you doing? Why have you stopped?" Auto called over his earpiece. "Stone is almost down, and Blue Moon is attempting to take on The Wolfman without backup. You have to help her."

This mention of Blue Moon generated a look of panic in Michael's face. Gazing toward the end of the street, he eyed the city's gateway in the shield and took off through the air. "I'm on my way," he replied with a new determination in his voice. "Open the shield's entrance now," he ordered Melvin. A small hole formed at the base of the shield, allowing him to blast his way through the opening, ready to crush anyone who laid a finger on Molly. But what Michael failed to realize was his emotions blinded him from the true danger lurking in the shadows.

30. Infiltration

Mr. Mental

April 7th, 5:20

While Mr. Infiniti rushed out to the battlefield, Mastermind, Mr. Mental and Fireball stepped up to the opposite side of the shield's perimeter. "So now comes the time for you to reveal how you plan to get past their greatest security system," Mr. Mental smiled. He and Fireball stood behind Mastermind, who was nearly on top of the impenetrable shield. She wore her battle suit with her large shades over her eyes, ready to transform into helmet form should the she face danger. Meanwhile, Mr. Mental and Fireball each dressed in their formal pinstripe suits with their fedoras, an odd decision for such a dangerous mission, but Fireball trusted his comrade's judgment.

"Unfortunately, no device can penetrate this barrier," Mastermind explained. "They've made the necessary adjustments since we stormed the city for your breakout, but we won't need to crack open the shield this time." Fireball squinted at her with a confused expression, but Mr. Mental just smiled.

"How are we going to get inside then," Fireball questioned.

"I have a man on the inside," Mastermind smirked. "Well, not exactly a man." And as she finished this statement, a 5 foot wide hole opened in the shield, revealing what Mr. Mental suspected from day one. Professor Eliki waited for them on the other side of the barrier, a concerned stare in her eyes and tight cheeks.

"Hurry sister, I can only create a small opening for a short time; the shield will close shortly, and I must return to the War Room soon, or Malix and Scylla will surely grow suspicious," she explained. Fireball's eyes widened in shock, but Mr. Mental could only continue smiling as his prediction came to fruition. He knew Eliki was feeding Mastermind information from inside the Trifecta, but even the Elders remained blind to Mr. Mental's hidden agenda, which would work to his advantage.

Mastermind strode forward past the barrier and into the city streets. Her heels clicked against the pavement like a marching pair of hooves. Without uttering a word to her sister, she sped toward the Trifecta Headquarters.

Mr. Mental followed, but Fireball snagged the sleeve of his suit jacket to grab his attention. "Won't their super smart computer alert them we've entered the city?" he asked.

"No need to worry brother," Mr. Mental answered. "He won't interfere with our mission. Now head to the Hall of Heroes. You know what you need to do." After a confirming nod, Fireball broke away from the distracted Mastermind while Mr. Mental continued a few steps behind her. He had already prepared Fireball for a secondary mission.

Eliki's absence might have drawn attention to her betrayal, so she hurried back to the War Room as Mastermind reached the Trifecta Headquarters. "Is he inside?" Mr. Mental inquired.

"Yes, he's waiting for us," Mastermind replied with a cocky grin. "Right where I left him the day of your breakout."

"Good, then let's go wake him up," Mr. Mental smiled while holding his left hand out in front of him. "Lead the way."

After hovering her way up above the stairs to the main entrance, Mastermind lifted her right fist and fired an expanding piece of metal that smashed the fortified glass doors. Subtlety was no longer necessary at this point. Even if the Trifecta's forces weren't tied up in a massive battle, they couldn't stop Mastermind from completing her scheme, a fact that Mr. Mental was well aware of. All proceeded according to plan, so long as Sharp Shot was holding up her part.

31. Acceleration

Michael

April 7th, 5:20

Michael exited the city to find The Wolfman had already worn down Stone, but his enormous, hairy body also lay dazed on the ground. The immediate danger was Sharp Shot, who had knocked Molly onto her back. As the magnificent markswoman closed in, she pointed her high-powered rifle right at Molly's head. Michael's shades lit up and his eyes widened at the thought of losing Molly, so he flew right toward the prowling villain.

"What have your friends done for you?" Sharp Shot cackled, completely blind to Mr. Infiniti, who accelerated directly behind Molly. His fists radiated a pure white light as he pointed them out in front of his body.

"How about this?" he called to the overconfident Sharp Shot while firing a white laser from his clenched fist. The impact of the beam caught Sharp Shot off guard, launching her back a hundred feet into her own crowd of soldiers. While she disappeared into a sea of infantry, Mr. Infiniti rushed straight to Blue Moon's side and placed his right hand on her left shoulder.

"Molly, are you okay?" he asked, a trembling bounce in his frantic eyes.

Blue Moon exhaled, nodding in response. "I'll be okay." She took hold of Michael's hand. "But this doesn't make any sense. There's no logic behind this attack, and Mastermind is anything but illogical. There's something else going on that we aren't meant to see until it's too late. You've got to stop her."

Unfortunately, before Michael could pause to think for even a second, he heard someone growling his name like a barbarian. "Mr. Infinitiiiii!" The Wolfman bellowed with his arms branched out on each side of his torso and his foot long fingers extended from his hands.

Michael jerked his head left to catch his first view of The Wolfman up close and personal. The 9-foot tall bruiser's chest rose and fell while his lungs expanded and contracted faster than an exhausted marathoner. As his yellow fangs snarled, they grew with his devious smile. "I've been waiting 16 years for my rematch with you," he growled. "And now I'm going to break you in half!" the beast howled, charging forward on all four limbs before pouncing his way toward Michael's body.

As over a thousand pounds of muscle tackled Michael to the ground, he barely managed to lift his hands to hold back The Wolfman's snapping snout. The monster dug his long nails into Michael's battle suit, but he failed to pierce his way through to Michael's skin. Still, the hold he had on the armor kept Michael pinned to the ground while The Wolfman squeezed his prey like a water bottle. Although Michael's gloves restrained The Wolfman's jaws, his body couldn't take much more damage. So in a desperate attempt, he ignited the blue energy around his fists, which reverberated up through The Wolfman's snarling face like a current of electricity.

"Nothing will stop me," the monster grunted through Mr. Infiniti's energized hands as he tightened his vice grip on his enemy's spine.

"Eat this!" Michael screamed back, thrusting both hands forward while firing a potent, charged blast of blue energy into The Wolfman's mouth. The concussive beam surged up through his throat, catapulting his body through the air.

"Arghhh," The Wolman cried before his flailing body hit the ground with a loud thud. A couple of Sharp Shot's forces fired their weapons at Mr. Infiniti, but their bullets couldn't puncture his armor, and nothing was going to distract him from his mission to defeat The Wolfman. Remembering what Professor Malix told him, Michael realized he needed to finish this fight within the next minute because his foe only grew more powerful by the second.

After lifting his body from the ground, The Wolfman threw his arms to his side and howled in a fit of rage. His horns grew slightly longer, curving a few inches at the top as he charged toward Mr. Infiniti, who stood in a crouched stance, ready for an imminent pouncing attack. The Wolfman took two final bounds forward, but instead of leaping on top of Michael, he lowered his body close to the ground before lifting the hero up over his head.

Michael's eyes widened behind his shades as The Wolfman wrapped his enormous hands around Michael's legs and torso. After raising the hero's body over his head like a barbell, The Wolfman flexed his biceps, which began snapping Mr. Infiniti's vertebrae.

"Your predecessor broke my spine in half," The Wolfman snarled. "Now let me return the favor to you." As the monster's overpowering strength grew closer to ripping his enemy in two, Michael wriggled his muscles back and forth like a snake in a futile attempt to free himself. He felt two of his vertebrae crack as they disconnected from each other like two lego pieces being pulled apart. The pain was immeasurable, too much for Michael to bear, so his consciousness started to fade to black.

But as his fluttering eyes began closing, a bellowing shriek woke him from near death, just before his body dropped to the ground. The Wolfman toppled over on his face, the fur on his back burning in red flames that raged up through the air. Using both paws, the monster reached over his shoulders to scratch at his burning back while he whimpered in pain.

Michael glanced up at the cause of his enemy's agony. Standing with his bow pointed at The Wolfman, Michael's loyal friend Archer extended his left leg forward and pulled back on his bow string like a Greek warrior ready to fire another arrow through his enemy's heart.

"I got your back Mikey," he called over to his friend. The arrow he stuck in The Wolfman's back finally stopped burning, allowing the brute to roll over, smothering the remaining flames. But before The Wolfman could stand up, Archer launched another arrow that stuck into the ground on the right side of the villain's body.

Meanwhile, the wristband on Michael's arm surged an electric current through his blood, which activated the healing energy in his core. A hot, white power flowed through Michael's body, reconnecting his vertebrae before fusing a new, metallic substance through the bones in his back—a substance that would prove unbreakable in the future.

After five seconds of writhing on the ground, Mr. Infiniti felt his spine had fully healed, so he pushed himself up onto his feet, his rage burning bright at his reverberating core. He relished the scene of The Wolfman covering his ears from the pain of Archer's second arrow. Michael deduced that the arrow projected a high-pitched, sonic frequency that only The Wolfman could hear. Still, realizing this would only keep the beast at bay for a short moment, Michael devised a plan to remove his enemy from the battlefield.

After cracking the arrow in half, The Wolfman snapped his head at Archer. Blinded by his fury, he temporarily forgot about Mr. Infiniti, charging instead toward his new enemy who reached over his shoulder to draw another arrow. Placing two new projectiles against his bow string, he pulled back his arm to fire. Once he released the arrows, he dove right, fully aware that the explosives wouldn't stop the charging berserker.

But before The Wolfman could leap onto his prey, Mr. Infiniti gripped him by the hide behind his neck as he flew toward the sky, dragging the ferocious beast with him. The

Wolfman looked up at the hero's determined face as Mr. Infiniti carried him hundreds of feet above the ground. "You think I'm afraid to fall?" he called up to Michael. "Nothing can kill me!" he screamed over the howling wind caused by their acceleration.

"Maybe not, but it will take you a while to return to the battlefield after this," Michael responded. He gripped The Wolfman with his other hand and began twirling his body in a circle like an Olympic hammer thrower. After spinning himself four full times, he released The Wolfman, sending the villain sailing through the air, heading east for at least a thousand miles. "Have a nice trip," Mr. Infiniti scowled before lowering his body back down to the battlefield.

After a moment of descending toward the ground, Michael located Archer who was waiting for him. "Thanks man," Michael nodded to to his friend as he planted his feet on the ground. "Is Molly okay?"

As he fired an arrow that emitted green gas through a dwindling crowd of soldiers, Archer answered, "She's fine. A med-bot carried her back into the city. Most of their soldiers are starting to retreat, but—"

"Blue Archer!" Sharp Shot shouted with a single pistol aimed at him. "I was hoping you'd show your face here. Now I'm going to make it as ugly as your father made mine." She zoomed her mechanical eye in on Archer and fired two rapid shots. The defenseless hero didn't even have enough time to close his eyes before the bullets traveled the 200 feet separating him and Sharp Shot. But he was in luck because he happened to have a friend with lightning quick reflexes.

Michael sped his way in front of the bullets, which bounced off of his chest, leaving Sharp Shot infuriated with a menacing glare in her purple, mechanical eye. "You don't scare me," she called out to Michael as she holstered her pistol, never averting her gaze from his determined scowl. He glared across the battlefield with his sunglasses narrowed on Sharp

Shot while his jaw shook from the anger that had mounted inside of him.

Reaching over her shoulder, Sharp Shot pulled out her rifle, and activated a green button on the side before firing two red laser beams. The blasts tore through the air, but Michael formed a blue laser shield before she even pulled the trigger. As the beams collided with his shield, they exploded into a 30 foot wide ball of energy with a gravitational force that jerked Michael forward. "A little piece of technology that my own scientists formed to deal with the likes of you," Sharp Shot laughed at seeing the black energy ball lifting Michael and Archer's body from the ground like a vacuum sucking up dirt.

Utilizing his advanced instincts and quick reflexes, Michael grabbed Archer and began flying away from the gravitational pull. "What is this thing?" Archer called to Michael over the sound of screaming bodies being sucked into the ball of energy where they disintegrated into nothing.

"I don't know," Michael responded. But he was going to find out. "Melvin, analyze this phenomenon," he commanded through his shades.

"Sharp Shot has utilized a force called graviton," Melvin explained. "Similar to a black hole, the energy at the core of this force will pull in and destroy solid matter."

"How do I stop it?" Michael asked.

"Your armband contains a polarity chip that can counteract the effects, neutralizing the gravitational pull."

"Got it." Michael lifted his left wrist up two inches from his mouth and ordered, "Bring up polarity chip." Then after aiming his left fist at the growing energy ball, he fired the micro-chip from the top of his mechanical arm band. The moment the projectile hit the ball of energy, the gravitational force died, allowing Michael to drop back down to the ground.

"I've got more prepared for you," Sharp Shot yelled, lifting her rifle back up toward Michael. But before she could fire this time, he knocked her out with a concussive blast from his right fist, which collapsed her body to the paved street below her feet.

"Maybe another time," Michael gloated with a smirk.

"Mr. Infiniti?" Melvin called over his headset, which was odd because Melvin rarely initiated contact with Trifecta members while they engaged in battle.

"Yes?" Michael answered through the comm. link on his shades.

"I felt I should inform you that there has been a break-in at the Hall of Heroes."

Michael looked back toward the shield and realized the true motive behind Mastermind's attack. While she lured him away from the city, she planned to infiltrate the Hall of Heroes. Without saying a word to Archer, Mr. Infiniti zoomed toward the skyscrapers behind him, passing his way through the small opening in the shield.

At the top of the hill outside the heart of the battle, The Magician stood watching before he lifted his right wrist to his mouth and reported, "He's at full power, and he's on his way . . . All according to your plan."

32. Resurrection

Mr. Mental

April 7th, 5:25

Mr. Mental followed Mastermind through the Headquarters lobby. Neither of them hesitated to over-think their approach at this point. Their goal appeared within sight, and both villains grew more determined to see that they came out on top.

"The main console is located at the back right quadrant" Mastermind announced. "Where is Fireball?" she asked, only now realizing that he had slipped away.

Pointing back to the front entrance, Mr. Mental made up a transparent lie. "He's guarding our exit, making sure Mr. Infiniti doesn't interfere with our escape." Mastermind looked at Mr. Mental with a smile of disbelief. She clearly knew he had an ulterior agenda, yet she didn't seem concerned. With her prize so close, she most likely figured Mr. Mental could do nothing to stop her—and that was what Mr. Mental counted on—Mastermind's overconfidence.

"Very well," Mastermind responded. "Come, we should hurry then before their champion can stop us." Her jet boots hovered through the air, carrying her body down the second hallway on the right hand side of the lobby. She moved so swiftly that Mr. Mental's hover shoe technology had trouble keeping up with her quick pace. Had he worn his battle suit, he could have flown alongside her, but he wanted to wear his formal suit for such a momentous occasion.

Most of the halls and corridors in the building were decoys to prevent intruders from finding the central core, but with Eliki's information, Mastermind navigated her way straight through to her destination.

In less than two minutes, the two competing geniuses arrived at the heavily armored doors that protected the Trifecta's central operating room, the housing place of Melvin, their super computer system.

"Open," Mastermind ordered, which activated the advanced locking mechanism, forcing the grinding gears to slide the two doors apart. Once they fully split open, Mr. Mental gazed into the modest 1,000 square foot room with a metallic, 10-foot wide cylindrical tube in the center. The walls were lined with dozens of virtual monitors that displayed video feed from around the city. But only one of the screens was blinking—the one that was following Mr. Infiniti, which drew Mastermind's attention from the task at hand.

Mr. Mental also viewed the video footage, taking a mental note of Mr. Infiniti's position. The satellite camera showed the hero standing next to The Blue Archer before darting back into the city. As Mastermind hurried over to the enormous tube, Mr. Mental received a message from The Magician via the communication link in his shades.

"Excellent," he muttered in response to his comrade's information. Mastermind snapped her head back to give Mr. Mental a suspicious glare.

"Is there something you would like to share with me?" she asked. But Mr. Mental was aware that Mastermind already knew of his deception. She just didn't care—and in the end, her arrogance would be her undoing.

"I suggest we hurry," Mr. Mental responded. "Mr. Infiniti has returned to the city, which means he'll likely be here soon, so get on with the procedure." Mastermind squinted her brown eyes into a glare meant to intimidate Mr. Mental, but he still kept the same superior smirk in his left cheek. "Are you sure the download will have worked?"

"Ha, I deciphered the reel's information with absolute precision," Mastermind gloated. "I am 100 percent sure that the process is complete. My plan will come to fruition, you'll see." She ended this sentence with a sly tone that would have made any other villain nervous, but Mr. Mental remained confident he had outwitted her.

A control panel with a touch screen rested next to the metal tube. Mastermind pressed her right pointer finger against the surface and then began moving her fingers up and down the screen faster than the legs of a scurrying spider. The panel beeped with each tap, and after nearly a minute of inputting codes, the extraction was ready. Now the final step required her to upload a slim, metal disk into the central computer. Reaching into her belt, she pulled out a red rectangle and inserted the disk before stepping back from the tube. As the center cracked open like a walnut, the seal released a white gas from the interior.

Once the doors completely opened, a familiar face exited the tube.

Alex Fleming, Michael Fleming's brother, stepped down from the container's platform, a lifeless expression in his face. Both Mastermind and Mr. Mental stood motionless, wary of how Alex might react after being stuck in a stasis tube for nearly a year. But he showed no signs of fatigue or anger, just a stone cold determination as his eyes bounced between his two liberators.

"How are you feeling?" Mr. Mental inquired, taking one step forward but no more than that.

Alex inhaled a deep breath through his nose, adjusting to the renewal of all of his senses. While exhaling, he answered the question with a single word. "Strong."

"Excellent," Mastermind commented. "Now we must be going before the Trifecta's full forces return to the city."

"Members of our organization don't run in fear," Mr. Mental replied in a snide tone. "I suggest you get that into your inferior brain. But then you won't be around much longer for that lesson to matter."

Mastermind dropped her chin, opening her mouth like a fish to give Mr. Mental a fake look of shock; meanwhile, Alex remained silent. "You mean you won't allow me to continue leading your band of overconfident egomaniacs?" The sarcasm in Mastermind's voice only angered Mr. Mental further.

"You insolent little," he began. "The time for your demise is upon us."

"I don't think so," Mastermind chuckled. "The data in the reel showed me how to access his technological side. So long as my unrivaled mind is running, he is under my control. So my devoted slave, grab Mr. Mental."

Alex turned his glaring eyes onto Mr. Mental and lifted his right hand to grip his suit collar with newly strengthened fingers. "Did you really think I would unleash his power without a plan to control him? He is now my new most paramount and omnipotent weapon. And with his resurrection complete, I no longer have any use for you."

"Treacherous witch!" Mr. Mental shouted.

"You knew who you were dealing with," she laughed. "But you made the most dangerous mistake any of my opponents can make. You believed yourself more intelligent than me. Only now before your death do you realize, my genius cannot be rivaled." Mastermind reached in and grabbed hold of Mr. Mental's face with her right hand. She squeezed his cheeks between her thumb and fingers before pushing his head back. "Kill him," she ordered Omega, who cocked back his left hand to punch Mr. Mental in the face.

"Wait!" Mr. Mental called out to Mastermind. He anticipated this duplicitous move on her part, but he needed to stall her a few more moments while his comrades prepped his own secret weapon.

"I have nothing left to say to you," Mastermind scoffed, continuing her walk toward the room's exit. "Besides, I have no time for you. My other prizes await."

Turning to her new slave, Mastermind commanded, "Finish him and meet me at The Hall of Heroes." After issuing this last order, she left the room with a blazing confidence in her eyes that showed she now held the world in the palm of her hand.

33. Battle of the Mind

Michael

April 7th, 5:35

Michael slowed his flying body to a hover as he approached the main entrance to the Hall of Heroes. He observed the large statue of the original Mr. Infinity while cautiously lowering his boots down to the base of the steps. A strange atmosphere surrounded the building's giant glass doors with an ominous shroud of darkness covering the entire area as if the sun had been blotted from this small region.

After taking one step forward, the shade collapsed down over a single silhouette at the top of stairs. This was the same dark figure who Michael had now encountered on multiple occasions without ever discerning his identity—the same man who killed Mr. All-American. "Who are you?" Michael barked up at the cloaked figure.

"Who am I?" the man called down to him. "You mean you still haven't figured it out?"

The surrounding shroud of darkness dissolved from the figure, and he dropped the hood on his cloak behind his shoulders, revealing his true identity. Michael froze in shock at the sight of Light-bender, Omega's third enforcer. He stood dressed in a black suit and a long overcoat that was lined with green glowing stripes along the border and the side of his arms. The majority of his face remained covered by a single-lens goggle visor that wrapped around his head. Just above his cocky smirk, his goggles glowed in and out with a menacing green light.

"You?" Michael squinted in disbelief. "No, that's not possible."

"You of all people should know that anything is possible," Light-bender commented, taking a few methodical steps forward. "I've been monitoring your activity for the past few years now," he elaborated. "Nobody ever looks closely at the shadows. My ability to bend and refract light waves allowed me to follow you without the slightest notice from you or your allies."

While Light-bender spoke, Michael couldn't wipe the perturbed expression from his face, his whole body frozen in place as a revelation dawned upon him.

"You're the mysterious voice, the one who helped me defeat Mr. All-American—the one who guided me to discover my powers. But why?"

Light-bender stopped advancing to answer Michael's question. "All this time, I gave you so much credit as a master sleuth, but you are more blind than I thought. Every action you took was by design. And now you must help us complete the third phase of our plan."

"Why would I help you with anything?" Michael jeered, squeezing his fingers into a fist.

"As I said, every action you took was by design, which is how we know you will complete phase three, just as we know what you will do after that. Your whole future is mapped out. I tried to warn you long ago, but you failed to heed my words of caution."

Michael's eyes widened. "My induction day, the day I received my name. You were the one in the locker room."

"Hmmm, maybe your detective skills aren't so inept, after all." Immense anger welled in Michael's chest, so he couldn't formulate a response to this insult.

"In any case, I've come to warn you again," Light-bender announced. "Dark days are approaching. Strength of body will not save you. Only strength of *mind* and *soul* can prevail."

"I'll show you strength!" Michael huffed, launching two blue laser blasts at Light-bender. But both beams dissipated instantly after only firing ten feet from Michael's fist.

"Ha, you try to use a light-based attack against the Master of Light," the villain laughed in a cocky tone. "If you bring that weak crap against Mastermind, she will tear you apart. Only the full power of Mr. Infiniti will stand a chance against her. You must ready yourself."

Michael stopped breathing for a moment. "Those words," he mumbled. "They're the same ones that have haunted me in my nightmares." Then he spoke louder toward Light-bender. "You created the computer in my dream. But why?"

"All of your questions will be answered in time, but right now you have a bigger problem heading your way." Light-bender jerked his head toward the approaching danger, prompting Michael to turn and face Mastermind as she hovered her way over the streets. "If you want your brother to regain autonomy of his body, you'll need the full power of Infiniti to defeat her. Otherwise, he'll remain her slave forever, and you with him." With those last words, Light-bender beamed himself up through the air and out of sight, leaving Michael alone to face one of his greatest foes—Mastermind.

"Mr. Infiniti!" the femme fatale called out, never breaking stride as she marched forward. "I guess The Wolfman didn't keep you busy for as long as I predicted. No matter, I can still defeat you, even without your brother here to enforce my will."

Michael's eyes narrowed behind his shades, realizing Light-bender was right. She had taken control of Alex somehow, and he needed to stop her. But Michael also worried, *Why would Light-bender, one of the world's greatest villains, want me to succeed?* However, this thought was short-lived, replaced by a growing sense of fury.

"Where is he?" Michael cried back to Mastermind, who was now less than 100 feet away. He ignited his fists in an intimidating blue laser that rotated around his fingers with a reverberating tone that hummed down the city block.

"Your brother? He's taking care of the bothersome Mr. Mental right now, but he should be along shortly to dispose of Fireball and Light-bender." Michael stood still, his mind unable to piece all of the betrayals together.

"You look confused," Mastermind laughed. "If only you had a stronger mind, you might have stood a chance. But you played your part perfectly, and now the time has come for me to enslave you, as well." By this point in her speech, Mastermind stood only 20 feet from Michael, which was as close as he intended to let her reach.

Raising his right hand, Michael unleashed a continuous laser stream toward his enemy, but Mastermind came prepared. She lifted her left forearm to form an indestructible, metallic alloy shield that refracted the laser back onto Michael. After disengaging his attack, he dove to his right to avoid being hit by the blowback.

"Didn't you learn your lesson in our last encounter?" Mastermind gloated. "Those mini-missiles I hit you with. They weren't just for show. They left behind a poison in your blood stream. Every time you used your powers this year, you only made yourself more susceptible to my technology. I extensively studied *all* of your powers, and I know *all* of your weaknesses. My plan outwitted you, Mr. Mental, and Auto. Now your brother is mine, and soon you will be too. What a momentous day for the world."

Michael kneeled on the paved street, his right knuckles propping him up in a crouched position. He heard a gentle whisper in the wind from a voice he identified as Light-bender's. "Remember, embrace Mr. Infiniti."

As he pushed himself up from the ground, Michael sensed the core in his chest had started to expand, surging intense power through his body. But even more important for Michael, he felt he was seeing the world from a different perspective, like parts of his surroundings fell under a microscope. His confidence escalated to new heights, and for the first time in months, his vision became clear enough to see—Mr. Infiniti was always a part of his being. He spent most of his life trying to run from that persona, afraid that embracing his powers, or rather embracing Mr. Infiniti, would erase his past. But such logic was folly.

As Mr. Infiniti stood tall, the birthmark on his chest began glowing with a bright light. "Unfortunately for you, there's more to me than my powers and abilities," he called back to Mastermind.

"Please," Mastermind laughed. "You are a one-dimensional character with a feeble mind that cannot comprehend what the world needs. At least your brother aspired to be more than a police drone who can be wound up and aimed in the direction of the Trifecta's enemies." As she chuckled to herself, Mastermind thrusted her right fist forward, launching two thin wires from the top of her wrist. The long metal snakes landed on the cement and expanded before slithering their way across the street.

Mr. Infiniti took a step backward but then recalled that he had nothing to fear. Using his strength and wisdom, he knew he could defeat Mastermind. The first of her mechanical snakes began wrapping his metallic body around Mr. Infiniti's armored boots before squeezing his legs together. As Mr. Infiniti bent down to rip himself free of the constrictor, the second snake leapt from the ground to bind around his torso. Each of the mechanical wires possessed the strength to rip a tank in half, but Mr. Infiniti's body proved more resilient than Mastermind anticipated. Mr. Mental and Light-bender's precautions had given Michael new strength that Mastermind did not calculate into her equations.

Using all of the strength in his muscles, Mr. Infiniti snapped both metallic ropes into a hundred thin shards of steel that hurled through the air. As the metal shrapnel flew toward Mastermind, she technopathically activated a magnetic force to repel them in all directions. Her mouth dropped an inch from surprise at seeing Mr. Infiniti's unexpected strength. "That's not possible," she muttered to herself with a fearful doubt in her voice.

With his enhanced hearing, Mr. Infiniti detected the growing dismay in each word she spoke before he responded, "The world is a chaotic place where anything is possible. I may not be able to match your incredible intelligence. But there is so much more to life than simple information. Perhaps your focus on facts and equations has made you lose sight of the power imagination can have."

Regaining her composure, Mastermind sneered, lifting the right side of her lips just enough to show half of her front teeth. She raised her left wrist up in front of her chest and began pressing a few buttons on the control screen. "I understand the importance of imagination. That is how I was able to imagine and mastermind such a brilliant plan to enslave your brother, the most powerful weapon on this planet. But my intelligence is what allowed me to enact such a plan. He is the superior mega-human because you lack the brains to accurately execute what you can imagine. But your brother excels in both categories. Now, let's see how you do against my transfiguring orbs." As she finished her last sentence, she threw out her left hand, releasing six floating spheres the size of cue balls.

Using the information database in his shades, Mr. Infiniti analyzed his new enemies as they whizzed toward him. The visor on his sunglasses placed a square with identifying arrows around each sphere. "More of your tricks," Mr. Infiniti smirked.

"Imagine your way out of this one," the witch hollered back. Each floating orb started glowing and then launched a focused orange laser beam at Mr. Infiniti. But he threw up the wristband on his left arm, which automatically adjusted his laser shield to deflect each of the attacks. Mastermind removed her dark sunglasses, revealing her eyes, which widened in disbelief. "Impossible," she muttered again, placing her right hand to her right temple. "I designed that trap just for you," she called out to Mr. Infiniti.

"Your technology won't supply you with an advantage this time," he shouted back, no longer content with playing defense. After waiting all year to find his brother, Mr. Infiniti recognized this was his best chance to force some answers out of Mastermind. Closing his eyes, he calmed his mind and accessed the power in his core, amplified by the circuits in his armband, just as he had practiced over the past few months. As if projecting an astral version of himself, his thoughts extended to the hovering orbs, and after reaching their core, he pulled the plug. All six spheres dropped to the ground where they bounced a few times like marbles before rolling to a stop.

Mastermind stood dumbfounded, her eyes just slightly bouncing up and down while gazing forward. Her superior mind couldn't comprehend where Mr. Infiniti discovered such an unpredictable power, so she had to change tactics. "No matter, my ace in the hole is only a short distance away. If you won't be controlled, I'll just have to command him to dispose of you."

"No, I'm not backing off now," Mr. Infiniti shouted like a barbarian as he dashed through the air, flying forward twenty feet before spearing Mastermind to the ground. Her shades crashed against the pavement and bounced away, revealing the fear in her trembling brown eyes. Mr. Infiniti placed his hands around each side of her skull with his thumbs pressing just below her eye sockets. "Tell me where my brother is," he shouted. "What did you do with him?"

Speaking through quivering lips, Mastermind felt compelled to answer. "Trust me when I tell you, you won't want to know. I can see now that your powers extend far beyond the comprehensive, yet you still don't stand a chance against him."

This answer increased Mr. Infiniti's fury as his wristband began humming, allowing him to probe deeper into her mind, a power he'd never wielded before. As he navigated his way through Mastermind's brain, he found thousands of technological components implanted throughout, but the most important were three main chips planted at the base of the cerebellum, cerebrum, and brain stem. This was how Mastermind enhanced her already supreme intelligence, and Mr. Infiniti deduced that this also gave her the ability to mentally control her technology. Curiously, Michael recognized these advanced microchips because the circuits running through his own wristband were almost identical to them.

Mr. Infiniti tightened his grip on Mastermind's face, pressing his fingertips into her skull as he delved deeper into her subconscious, searching for the location of his lost brother. Each of the microchips in her brain resisted him at first, but after a boost from his armband, he gained control of all three.

"You have her where you want her," he heard a voice whisper to him. "Now you must destroy the chips if you ever wish to see me alive."

"Alex?" Michael muttered as he turned his head, temporarily breaking his concentration, which freed Mastermind from his hold. She scrambled back on her hands and feet, gasping for a breath of air as if she might never breathe again.

"Alex, are you there?" Michael called out, but he received no response. "Another trick, huh?" he bellowed at Mastermind. "Well it was your last." Reaching out with his right hand, he grabbed hold of her left boot and reeled her back in. Her mind remained dazed as some of the circuitry in her brain had already fried like a frayed wire.

"No more—please," Mastermind pleaded, but Michael felt his logic and reasoning fading with the escalation of his temper. Each of his nightmares with Mastermind had festered a fuming rage that just now boiled over, replacing what remained of Michael with a more primal Mr. Infiniti.

After re-establishing his grip on Mastermind's face, Mr. Infiniti once again plugged himself into her brain. Discovering the three chips during this trip took far less time. In mere seconds, Mr. Infiniti had complete control over the core technological parts that enhanced her mind. Mastermind's eyes fluttered before rolling back into her head as her body convulsed.

"Now send a surge through her brain," Alex's mysterious voice hissed into his mind. "End this fight, and liberate me from her control. Kill her!"

Mr. Infiniti closed his eyes but did not relinquish control over Mastermind's brain this time. "No, I can't kill her," he mumbled back. "That's not who I am."

"You must kill her, or I will forever be her slave."

Still, Mr. Infiniti refused to give in to what he knew was wrong. "No, I won't do it," he called back as his control over Mastermind began to slip again. Her eyes rolled back to their correct position, and she regained partial awareness of her surroundings.

"Where is my brother?" Mr. Infiniti shouted in her face, small specks of spit splashing across her cheeks like shotgun spray.

Mastermind coughed as she struggled to speak. "He's on his way, and when he arrives, he will kill you."

"Liar!" Mr. Infiniti shrieked, re-engaging his full connection into her mind, hoping to find the location where she hid his brother's body. But this time when he delved into her skull, someone else took the wheel, steering him away from the cerebrum part of her brain where he wanted to go. "What's happening?" Mr. Infiniti asked. "What are you doing?"

Unfortunately, both Mastermind's body and mind entered a state of seizure, preventing her from responding. The wristband on Mr. Infiniti's left arm started humming and vibrating, but he couldn't disengage his connection with Mastermind. They were linked together while someone else took control. An electrical energy surged from the wristband, traveling through Mr. Infiniti's left fist and into Mastermind's head. As the electricity transferred from his left hand to his right, every bit of energy focused on the chip at the cerebrum of Mastermind's brain.

Mr. Infiniti tried to pull back his arms, but he was too late. The electrical surge fried the circuitry in Mastermind's treacherous brain, leaving her in a catatonic state. And unbeknownst to Mr. Infiniti, this surge also released Alex from her hold.

"Nooooo," Mr. Infiniti cried. "You're not getting off that easy. What did you do with my brother? Where is heeee?" A violent tremble shook through Mr. Infiniti's cheeks as he shouted, but Mastermind's brain had fried for good; she'd become physically incapable of ever answering a question again. Yet still Mr. Infiniti received the answer to his question.

"I'm right here," Alex called from behind his brother. Mr. Infiniti recognized his voice, so he jerked his head left with a relieved excitement. But when he looked upon the man standing 100 feet down the street, he was shocked by the face staring back at him.

Mr. Infiniti could only utter one word.

"Omega."

34. The Best Laid Plans

Mr. Mental

April 7th, 5:35

After Mastermind left the Trifecta Headquarters, Omega prepared to destroy Mr. Mental. The mega-human threw his fist forward to smash a crater in Mr. Mental's face, but he found the genius had an ace up his sleeve. Just before the punch landed, Fireball blasted Omega with a bowling ball-sized orb of fire that knocked him across the room. Mr. Mental's body dropped to the floor while Omega crashed into a data screen on the far wall.

"Come, we must go brother," Fireball called to Mr. Mental. "Everything is in place. Now let's move quickly."

"Excellent, she is on her way there now," Mr. Mental laughed. Omega lifted his body from the ground with an angry snarl in his teeth. "I'm sorry about this My Lord," Mr. Mental apologized while pulling four silver marbles from his belt before tossing them up in the air. As they passed over Omega, the orbs projected a green triangular laser prism designed as a powerful trap.

Mr. Mental sprinted toward the exit, pumping his arms and legs as hard as he could. "Hurry, that won't hold him for long," he shouted to Fireball, and so the two villains rushed through the hallway, back out to the streets of Hero City.

But after Mr. Mental burst through the entrance to the Trifecta Headquarters, with Fireball following a few steps behind him, he suddenly felt dizzy. His sight went out of focus and he lost control of his legs, which made standing up incredibly difficult—running altogether impossible. Mr. Mental remained slightly aware of his surroundings, but he realized if he didn't start moving, Omega would soon arrive to crush him. He had carefully calculated every possibility in his plan, but such a daze was unprecedented, so he could not foresee this complication.

"Fireball!" Mr. Mental called out, his sight now fading into blackness. "Help me." However, those were his last words before he passed out into a dream that flashed back 22 years.

"So, you decided to join us," Fireball grinned as Mr. Mental stepped down a ramp that extended from the back of a loading truck. Light-bender stood next to Fireball, his arms crossed over his chest while his green goggles glowed like an emerald in the sun. "I told my brother here that you would."

Although Light-bender looked down his nose with a scrutinizing squint in his eyes, he said nothing. "Nice to meet you," Mr. Mental smiled, extending his hand to shake Light-bender's. Only the ultra-powerful super human didn't reciprocate the friendly greeting, keeping his arms pressed against his chest.

"We've met before," Light-bender sneered. "Yesterday in the warehouse. I thought you said he had a superior mind." He turned his head to Fireball with a skeptical look of doubt on his face.

"Give him time to adjust," Fireball responded, keeping his tone calm but defensive. "Our Master believes in him, so you should too. Or would you prefer to explain to him that you don't trust his judgment?"

"No," Light-bender answered without abandoning his disgruntled tone. "I'll give him some time, but he'd better pan out as our fourth member, or this whole plan will fall apart." The glowing villain gave Mr. Mental one last scowl before marching off toward the shadows of the nearest building where he disappeared into the darkness.

"Don't worry about him," Fireball reassured his new friend. "He's just a bit tense with getting our organization off

the ground. I am glad to see that you decided to join us. We have a lot of work to do, starting with your initiation. Follow me."

Fireball turned to his right and began walking toward the entrance of the run-down building on the left side of the street. The inside was just as dilapidated as the outside, making Mr. Mental nervous that the walls and ceiling might collapse at any moment. As Fireball led the way farther into the center of the building, he further explained the purpose of their organization.

"Light-bender and I have each spent years fighting against the Trifecta. Over that time, he took control of crime on the West Coast while I claimed the East. But thanks to the severity of the Trifecta's newest laws, our forces have disbanded, leaving us no choice but to run and hide. That is until now."

"Why, what's changing now?" Mr. Mental questioned. "I still don't understand how you can possibly expect us to compete with their duo of Omega and Infinity."

"They won't be a problem," Fireball smirked. "We have a secret weapon of our own. One that will turn the tide against the Elders and their proclaimed champion in Mr. Infinity." Fireball lifted a plastic sheet that covered a doorway before he ducked under to enter a new room. "Our organization has one goal—to return balance to the world by any means necessary. And our Master believes that deep down your own personal views align with this goal. That is the first reason why he selected you to join us."

"What was the second?" Mr. Mental asked.

"You have a potential that surpasses even my own. And with our Master's guidance, you will become one of the most powerful forces on this planet, possibly strong enough to even rival the Elders themselves."

Mr. Mental wasn't sure how to respond to this compliment, so he kept his mouth shut, his mind more concerned with how far they were going to travel into this *broken building. "For you to join, you need only promise one thing."*

"And what's that?" Mr. Mental inquired, still a little nervous about his decision to join them.

"Unquestioning loyalty to our Master," Fireball answered. "That is all that he demands of us. Light-bender and I have both put our faith in his wisdom and supreme intelligence. So, before I introduce you to him, are you 100 percent certain that you want to help us return balance to the world, and are you prepared to faithfully follow his plan?"

Mr. Mental froze to think while he bit his lip in deep contemplation. But despite his brief hesitance, he had already made up his mind. No matter what, he had a deep feeling that this was his destiny. "I'm ready," he answered.

"Great, then let's go meet your new leader." Fireball opened a brown door and led Mr. Mental into a small office with a desk and a single window. A man stood on the other side of the room with his eyes focused directly through the grime and dirt on the glass window.

"Master, here is our fourth member as you requested," Fireball announced. The man turned to face his new recruit, and Mr. Mental jumped back a step with a look of shock as he gazed upon Omega's menacing, mechanical eye.

"Welcome to the Four Faces," he announced with an arrogant smirk. "Today is the beginning of your new life."

That was the last moment of Mr. Mental's dream, and when he awoke, he caught sight of Omega's sneering face blazing toward him. After shaking his head free of his daze, Mr. Mental realized Fireball was carrying him over his shoulder while they both retreated away from Omega. "What happened?" Mr. Mental cried.

Fireball dropped his comrade to the ground, allowing Mr. Mental to regain the sensation in his legs. "We're in trouble," Fireball explained. "You said Mr. Infiniti would have killed Mastermind by now, but she still has control over

Omega." Their Lord and Master leapt in the air to tackle them to the ground, but Light-bender blasted him back down into the street.

"Mr. Infiniti is refusing to kill her," Light-bender called down to them from the edge of the nearest rooftop. His body hovered over the street as he lowered himself toward his brethren. "All of that preparation we did, all of your mind probing, yet his will still refuses to do what we require."

"You two engage Omega in battle for as long as possible," Mr. Mental instructed. "Mr. Infiniti's wristband may allow me to tap into his mind one final time. Just keep our Master off of me, so I can focus." After giving this final order, Mr. Mental closed his eyes and calmed his mind to zone in on controlling Mr. Infiniti's will.

35. Battle Supreme

Michael

April 7th, 5:45

Omega, the tall, smirking villain stood 100 feet from Michael's face. His torso was bare with a pair of armored black pants covering his legs. He looked so much like Alex with the same square head topped by short black hair and a muscular physique built like a linebacker. Still, Michael recognized him right away; he was Omega, the same figure who haunted so many nightmares with only a few subtle differences.

"No, it's not possible," Michael cried. "How could this be?"

"Hmmm, hmmm, hmmm," Omega chuckled in a low hum. "It is very possible. In fact, you made it possible." While Michael's face scrunched together, his jaw quivered with shock. "Look before you, for without your help, my resurrection would never have come to pass. You played your part so well. So predictable, just like your predecessor."

"What do you mean?" Michael asked, struggling to wipe the horror from his face.

"All this time, I was pushing you toward this inevitable moment. You made all of the moves that I knew you would, and they worked out perfectly for me. The hunter, Mr. All-American, your nightmares, Mastermind—they were all put in place to bring about *my* resurrection."

Omega extended his arms to his sides, stretching them like a bear awakened from hibernation. He rotated his neck left and then right, cracking his vertebrae so loudly that the echo bounced off all of the buildings on each side of him. "My brothers, reveal yourself to our young, naive fool."

Mr. Mental and Fireball emerged from an alley next to the Hall of Heroes while Light-bender beamed down from the roof of the next building over, landing on the street without making a sound. Omega snapped his fingers and called over to his comrade, "Fireball, my equipment."

Michael couldn't move, his mind frantically trying to sort through all of this shocking information as Fireball obeyed Omega's command.

"It was hidden in the far wing of the technology sector, just as you said," Fireball responded while he walked over toward his newly resurrected leader. Michael watched Fireball dragging a heavy, metal backpack that had four long, mechanical limbs like the legs of a spider. Omega licked his lips, a devious hunger burning in his eyes at the sight of his mechanical hookup.

Though Michael wanted to stop them, he remained in a state of shock, unable to move his legs as these events unfolded.

"Ahhh, how I've longed to reconnect with my weaponry," Omega sighed.

"May I have the honors, my Lord?" Fireball asked, to which Omega nodded in the affirmative before turning his back on his brother. Using both hands, Fireball lifted the heavy pack and placed the flat side against Omega's back. A turning of gears clicked as hundreds of spikes pierced Omega's skin, attaching both the pack and the limbs to his nervous system. For any other being on the planet, this would have caused immeasurable pain, but Omega felt little more than a slight prick. Attaching these mechanical limbs was nearly the final step needed to fully resurrect him.

Only a few pieces remained. Reaching into the belt that wrapped around his waist, Omega pulled out a single cylindrical tube of metal with a red, glass lens. He gripped the device like a fork in his left hand before stabbing the end into his right pupil. After replacing his brown eye, the glass circle started glowing in a menacing, crimson light. Lifting his head, Omega revealed his terrifying face. While he shrugged his shoulders, the metal pieces that hooked into his arms made a slight grinding noise like an engine that hasn't been started in years. "Now I truly am All-powerful."

"I will stop you!" Michael shouted, taking two antagonizing steps toward his nemesis. His daze was wearing off, replaced by the growing rage in his heart.

"Ahahaha," Omega cackled, shaking his head back and forth with the devious grin of a shark. "You are a fool. Your actions these past two years solidified my assumption that you pose no threat to my plans. Too much of your time is spent trying to catch up with what has already happened, rather than looking to the future. Meanwhile, my approach has been proactive. A true genius only looks forward, never backward."

"You may have been a step ahead of me, but—" Michael began to respond.

"No, I'm not a step ahead of you," Omega interrupted in a disgusted tone, his pace of speech increasing with each word. "That would imply that you have some degree of control in this war. But you don't seem to understand. I've already determined how this will end, and you will follow my directions. I told you long ago, if you wouldn't be my ally, then you would be my pawn. All of the moves you've made—and will make—are by *My* design."

As Michael's anger increased, he ignited his right fist with a powerful blue energy before launching one short blast at the goading villain. The single laser cut through the air, but Omega's mechanical upgrade formed a rounded, electrical shield that deflected the attack without requiring him to move a muscle. Off in the distance, the beam of light crashed into a building's exterior, causing dozens of bricks and debris to rain down on the street.

"Pathetic," Omega mocked. "In my exile I discovered new power that you cannot yet comprehend—but more importantly, I found new purpose. You will make this discovery in time, but not until I choose to reveal your blunders."

All of these words were hurtful to Michael's ego, but they didn't deter him from his primary mission. Realizing a full frontal attack was too dangerous against all four members of The Four Faces of Evil, Michael chose to probe Omega for more answers and hopefully stall him long enough to receive backup. "What did you do to my brother?" he shouted, using the most commanding voice he could muster.

At this question, all four villains laughed and laughed while Michael's puzzled look showed his confusion—so Omega enlightened him. "I'm right here," he announced with his arms pointing out to his side, palms facing up to the sky. "I knew your love for me would blind you to the truth of our relationship."

The veracity of this statement stung Michael worse than any pain he'd felt before. Deep down, his mind had known for some time that his brother was in fact Omega, but his heart refused to entertain such a damaging notion. This was the truth that Malix and Stone knew he needed to discover for himself. "I saw my brother die," Michael called back, fighting the tears welling in his eyes. "That hunter killed him."

"Indeed he did, just as Light-bender instructed him to," Omega explained. "His body was just a shell until you released the dark energy from your core. I must thank you. You were instrumental in resurrecting his body, which then allowed Mastermind to prepare him for the download of my persona."

"How could you be my brother?" Michael wept through tears of regret and sorrow. "Alex, how could you do this? Are you in there?"

"You truly are naive," Omega sneered with a tone of disdain. "You must sharpen your mind if you ever hope to compete at my level. In the Big Boom, our bodies were destroyed, but our entities are immortal. While Mr. Infinity's latched on to you, mine was not so lucky. Unfortunately, my technological essence split from my physical form. The physical reached out to your brother Alex, while my other half united with the nearest piece of technology it could find, a primitive cellular phone. Over the years, I managed to upgrade my brain to higher forms of technology until I reached my final destination, the Trifecta."

Michael's eyes widened upon hearing this. A revelation dawned on him and he blurted the name, "Melvin."

"Quite right," Omega nodded.

"Then it was you," Michael spoke his thought aloud. He couldn't shake the disturbed look of horror in his cheeks and wavering eyes. "You were the voice that guided me these past two years. You were the computer screen in my nightmares."

"What a detective," Omega laughed while he clapped his hands to emphasize his sarcastic tone. "Didn't you ever question how simple things were for you? How easily you slipped into the Trifecta Headquarters? How I kept your actions hidden from the Elders? Why you were summoned to the War Room this afternoon? Didn't you wonder why a mysterious voice was guiding you through your most difficult trials? Just like a pawn, you are blind to the logic around you. You wouldn't have lasted more than a few days here if Light-bender and I hadn't helped you overcome the obstacles you faced."

Michael exhaled through his nose, his fury growing with each arrogant word that leaked from Omega's lips. His boasting made him seem so confident that his victory was already assured, and his comment about Michael being his pawn only increased the hero's rage. Everything Omega did up to this point was chosen with careful intentions. He knew how Michael would react to every move he made, which brought doubt into Michael's mind. *What if I really am Omega's piece to control?* he questioned.

Having foolishly overlooked his brother's role in this game, Michael diminished his own ability to counter Omega's plan. As his heart sank, he felt a desire to just lie down and die. But just before his confidence dropped to rock bottom, he remembered what he was fighting to preserve. Archer, and Allison, and Molly—and even Stone popped into his head. Refusing to fail his friends, Michael refocused his determination to stop Omega right there before he could do more damage.

"I am going to defeat you," Michael proclaimed, taking one intimidating step toward his enemy.

Omega could only smile, amused by Michael's misplaced self-confidence. "You have grown so much since I first engineered your arrival here, but still, you do not yet have the power to compete with me." After releasing a few chuckles, he turned his back on Michael.

"I guess we'll find out," Michael murmured, taking off toward Omega. The clapping of his boots against the pavement echoed through the street until he lifted himself off the ground, bulleting his whole body toward the overconfident Omega.

Mr. Mental and company did nothing, aware that Omega could handle himself. The villain's smile grew, his eyes peering over his shoulder as he sensed the imminent attack. Just before Michael crashed into the armored plating on Omega's back, the overpowering villain flung his technologically enhanced arm around, landing a left hook across Michael's right cheek. A cracking noise, like a shattering piece of hard candy, resonated through the entire city, and Michael's eyes shook from the vibration rattling around his face.

"Ahahaha," Omega laughed. "You really do amuse me, brother. Watching your efforts over the past two years has been quite entertaining. I've enjoyed observing the futility of your attempts to save this world. You see, I know the real you, the soul that lies deep within you—even if you still deny it. You can only fool yourself for so long. For in time, I will reveal your true destiny."

Although Michael wanted to fire back with a smart quip, Omega's powerful punch had broken his jaw. The cracked bones quickly began gluing back together, but Omega wasn't waiting for him to regain his strength. Instead, he widened his right mechanical eye and unleashed a focused red blast of energy that knocked Michael to the ground, pinning him against the cement while frying his skin like a sizzling steak.

"You and I are the same," Omega shouted over the reverberating sound of his beaming eye. This was the final antagonizing remark that unleashed a beast within Mr. Infiniti. The core inside his chest expanded, releasing a potent burst of energy that allowed him to roll out from under the laser beam.

Pushing his way back up from the ground, he roared in a deep, lion-like voice, "I'm nothing like you. You are pure evil, and I am a hero." With that retort, Mr. Infiniti launched both fists forward, unleashing two 5-inch thick blue lasers that shot Omega up in the air like a bullet. His soaring body crashed through the brick wall and reinforced metal exterior that protected the Hall of Heroes. Exhaling a sigh of relief, Mr. Infiniti felt his jaw had healed back to 100 percent, while the bubbling burns on his back stopped sizzling. Using his wristband, he activated the repairs to his dark blue battle suit and his tattered cape.

Then while preparing for Omega to come flying out in a fury, Mr. Infiniti activated the cloaking device in his wristband. Keeping his eyes focused on the hole in the wall, he remained perfectly still, creating a cloak of invisibility, an advantage that he hoped to use against Omega. Thirty seconds of suspenseful agony passed before Mr. Infiniti felt the pavement rumbling beneath his feet. As the thundering in the ground vibrated through his legs, he glanced down at the cement stairs under his boots. But while his attention focused on the thundering ground in front of him, Omega exploded out from beneath the stairs behind him, grabbing Mr. Infiniti's cape as he soared up toward the sky.

The shock of this attack left Mr. Infiniti's mind scrambling to recover. He hadn't expected Omega to attack from beneath the ground, nor did he think Omega could find him while he used the wristband to cloak himself.

"Fool," Omega shouted down to Mr. Infiniti, who struggled to free himself from the devilish anti-hero's hold. As if Omega had read Mr. Infiniti's mind, he screamed over the swirling wind, "That wristband is *my* technology. You can't use *my* technology against me. In fact, I think I'll retrieve my weapon from you now." While still clutching Mr. Infiniti's cape with his right fist, he extended his left forearm straight out from his body. Mr. Infiniti's wristband wobbled up and down before splitting apart, relinquishing his hold on the device. In a quick flash, the wristband flew up through the air and attached to Omega's outstretched arm, completing his technological armor.

Although these events dumbfounded Mr. Infiniti, he realized he needed to fight back. He fumbled to reach up and release the golden clasp on his cape, but Omega flipped him up a few feet before he could succeed. As Mr. Infiniti's body flailed through the air, his head grew disoriented, and his vision shook back and forth like someone was fumbling a camera lens. Just then Omega thrust both of his fists down, slamming his enemy back into the pavement below.

Mr. Infiniti smashed into the street with a cracking sound as chunks of concrete launched in all directions like a splash of water. He felt his right arm snap in several different places while at least three tendons tore in his right knee, generating a loud tearing sound like a ripping piece of velcro. While his head spun like a run-away carrousel, he had to focus to fight an urge to throw up. Omega could have eased himself back down to ground level, but instead he dropped his body at 150 miles per hour, crashing the heel of his boots into Mr. Infiniti's gut. The impact squeezed the air from his lungs while also rocketing vomit from his stomach.

After reaching down, Omega lifted a defeated Michael Fleming off the ground before dragging him back up above the crater in the street. "So utterly foolish," Omega reiterated.

"You and I are the same—you just don't know it yet." He dropped Michael's body onto the stairs at the bottom of the Hall of Heroes.

Michael stared up at the oversized statue of the original Mr. Infinity while his healing powers tried to decide where to start working. The pain running through his body left him disoriented with just enough strength to hear Omega's last few words. "You may think you're a hero—." The evil overlord paused for a second to place his right boot on Michael's neck, pressing all of his weight down upon him. "But you'll learn in time, this is not a hero's story."

Those were the last few words Michael heard before Omega pressed his leg down harder, causing Michael to pass out. Turning his body toward the outskirts of the city, Omega began walking away, leaving the defeated hero lying unconscious on the cement stairs.

"Shouldn't we finish him now?" Fireball asked in an eager tone, his eyes burning for action.

"Are you questioning my decision, Jason?" Omega sneered over his shoulder as he pressed a few buttons on his newly acquired wristband. The technological circuits flashed a red light from his left forearm causing his bulky armor to liquify before submerging into the veins beneath his skin. In place of his battle gear, a finely woven, pinstripe suit formed to clothe him.

"No my Lord, I was mistaken to speak out of turn," Fireball immediately responded, lowering his eyes toward the sidewalk out of fear.

Now dressed in his dark business suit, Omega stopped to look up at the statue of Mr. Infinity. He scrunched his left eye at the stone sculpture, scrutinizing the words printed below his feet. Then he mumbled, "Salvation indeed," before speaking louder. "His time will come. We must wait until his power and fame have risen to their greatest heights. Only then will I tear him down." As Omega finished his last sentence, he ignited a red light in his right, mechanical eye. The radiance expanded into an energy beam that sliced the statue in half before generating an explosion that shattered pieces of limestone like shrapnel in all directions.

Mr. Mental and Fireball smirked at this action, but Light-bender kept his serious, straight-forward stare. He carried a long black bag over his back, which extended above his right shoulder like a samurai sword. The three villains followed behind Omega who led his resurrected Four Faces toward the western sunset. As they approached the city limits, Omega pushed back his suit cuff and activated a switch on his armband, which initiated a series of explosions that razed the buildings behind him, just the first step in his plan to topple the Trifecta.

"This is just the beginning," he grinned.

36. New Genesis

Mr. Mental

April 7th, 10:05 PM

"Welcome back to your castle, My Lord," Mr. Mental announced as if he was a museum tour guide. His hands pointed up toward a large stone structure that stood over 200 feet tall on the edge of a cliff that rose a few hundred feet above a large body of water. The castle's arched double doors waited on the other side of a long, brick bridge that connected the cliff to the mainland. "I updated all aspects of the exterior and interior to your specifications," Mr. Mental elaborated.

Omega paused at the edge of the bridge, his eyes analyzing every aspect of his former residence. The grey stone bricks formed a wide base with a dozen turrets raised hundreds of feet toward the sky, topped off by red, conical roofs with pointy spires jutting upward. "You installed all of the defensive upgrades I designed?" Omega inquired.

"Yes," Mr. Mental answered. "Exactly as the data drive instructed."

A smile curled up in Omega's right cheek. "Excellent. You did well, my brother. Now, let's take a look inside."

While Omega led Fireball, Light-bender and Mr. Mental across the bridge, a small jet appeared through the clouds overhead. Mr. Mental's eyes lit up, radiating a yellow light through his shades as he made mental contact with the pilot. The jet plane entered a hover mode, allowing the aircraft to descend into the castle's hangar entrance at the base of the cliff.

As the four villains approached the 30 foot tall entrance, Omega needed only to lift his left hand, and the arched doors split open for them to enter. The technological suit that hooked into his nervous system granted him mental communication and control over nearly any piece of technology. After passing through the entrance, Omega relished the lavish entry hall with a stone staircase on his left and right, illuminated by an intricate gold chandelier hanging from the 200 foot tall ceiling.

Pointing his hands to his sides, Omega lifted himself from the floor, rotating his body counterclockwise like a floating ballerina as he soaked in the magnificent architecture around him. While he lowered his body back down to the other side of the hall, his brothers walked across the brilliant brick floor, following their leader into the dark elevator doorway on the far wall. After the elevator doors closed in on each other, the shaft dropped hundreds of feet at an alarming rate before slowing to a stop.

When the doors parted, Omega exhaled at the sight of his refurbished war room. He stepped out of the elevator and reveled in awe as his mechanical eye scanned and downloaded all of the technology lining the walls of the magnificent oval chamber. Dozens of virtually projected computer screens covered the stone surfaces on the left and right side. And at the base of these monitors, varying touchscreen control consoles blinked red and yellow lights like an air traffic control tower. These command consoles linked directly to a built-in virtual projector on the round marble table at the center of the room.

Omega's attention shifted to the wooden door on the opposite side of the room as the hatch popped open. Sharp Shot and The Magician walked through, revealing the hangar behind them, which was filled with at least ten different advanced transport ships.

"Ah, you found your way," Mr. Mental smiled. "Sharp Shot, let me introduce you to our leader, the All-Powerful Omega."

"It's a pleasure," Sharp Shot assured him as she navigated her way around the table to shake his hand. He looked her up and down, analyzing all of her attributes before turning his attention to The Magician, who remained at the other end of the table, his hands resting on a chair in front of him. "I'm glad to see that you chose to rejoin us, my friend." The Magician grunted through his nose before answering.

"I'm here solely because of a deal between Mr. Mental and myself," he huffed. "Believe me when I say I take no pleasure in working for you again."

Despite The Magician's insolence, Omega showed his amusement with a light chuckle. "No matter the reason, we are happy to have your allegiance—though disgruntled it may be." Moving closer to the table, Omega took a seat in the largest chair that hovered two feet off the ground. "Please sit," he instructed. "All of you take a seat."

Mr. Mental sat on the opposite side of the table with Fireball resting directly to his right. Light-bender took his place next to Omega while The Magician sat two seats to the left of him. Sharp Shot looked at each of the chairs, contemplating which one she should take. Mr. Mental scanned her mind, and he understood her worry that a position at the table would forever signify her status in their organization. He could have telepathically helped her, but he wanted to let her forge her own path.

After a moment of thought, she chose the spot next to her mentor, Mr. Mental. "Wonderful, you found a new protégé," Omega laughed. "But we still have six empty seats left to fill. Where are Titanon and The Wolfman?"

"I instructed Titanon to hold down Mastermind's fortress until we can pillage all of her resources," Mr. Mental explained. "I only wish that she could have lived long enough to realize he was actually working for us. But I can only guess where The Wolfman is at this time."

"Leaving four remaining seats," Omega commented. "I have one saved for our spy within the Trifecta. She will rejoin us by this time next year."

"And what of Mastermind's mole within Hero City?" Mr. Mental inquired. "Eliki could pose a threat if we don't recruit her into our ranks."

"Ha, she won't be a problem," Omega smirked. "Before I finished downloading my mind from Melvin, I left behind some damaging evidence for the Elders to find. They will soon discover that Professor Eliki is the one who fed Mastermind all of her inside information, which will provide them with a stressful headache for some time."

"Excellent, then shall we begin moving forward with phase four of your plan?" Mr. Mental asked.

Omega nodded and then turned to Light-bender. "Did you procure the Alpha Staff?" he asked of his enforcer.

"I did," Light-bender responded, retrieving the long bag he had carried out of Hero City. He unzipped the duffle bag and removed a long staff with an A at the top, the same one that once stood on display in the center of the Hall of Heroes. "Just as you planned, the virus you planted in their defense systems allowed me to remove the staff from the plasma protected case. And with the destruction of their city, they won't notice it's missing until it's too late."

"Then we split our forces from here," Omega announced. "Mr. Mental, you take Fireball, Sharp Shot, and Titanon to begin construction of the tower." The super genius gave a single nod of agreement. "Light-bender and The Magician will accompany me as I track down The Wolfman and a few other super humans whom I located by using the Trifecta's satellites."

"What of Mr. Infiniti and the remaining Trifecta forces?" Fireball asked as he played with a tiny flame that he kinetically rotated around his outstretched fingers. Then after extinguishing the fire in the palm of his hand, he finished his thought. "They will surely oppose us from moving forward."

"We will let our spy handle Mr. Infiniti for the time being," Omega explained. "And the Trifecta won't pose a problem. The damage to their city and central computer system will keep them busy for the next few months. Sharp Shot, we'll need the bulk of your resources to initiate the construction of our tower. Mr. Mental will lead the project."

"I understand," Sharp Shot acknowledged, nodding her head once.

"Good, then lady and gentlemen, the time has come to go on the offensive," Omega elaborated. "From this point on, our power only accelerates."

37. Just The Beginning

Michael

April 10th

When Michael woke up, he discovered he was lying on a cot underneath the cover of a large tent. Two empty green cots stood on his right with three occupied ones on his left, but before he could squint to identify the occupants, a startling voice grabbed his attention.

"I'm glad to see you made it," Stone grunted as he stepped up from behind Michael, who could only smile at the sincerity in his mentor's voice. "You seem to have a knack for surviving the most severe encounters with death."

"I guess so," Michael responded. "Where are we?" He rubbed the top of his head while squinting to recover all of his senses.

"As Omega exited our city, he set off hundreds of planted explosives that destroyed dozens of our buildings, including the medical sector," Stone explained. "So we had to set up these tents as new residences on the outskirts of the city."

"How long was I out this time?" Michael asked, now rubbing his left hand up and down his right wrist, which was good as new.

"Less than five days," Stone answered. "An amazing feat, considering how much punishment you sustained before Omega brought the Hall of Heroes down on you."

As he flexed his right bicep, Michael grew more astonished at how much stronger he felt—more powerful than ever before. "Then I take it they got away." Sorrow and disappointment filled Michael's voice. He'd never felt so beaten in his life—not just because Omega literally did beat the snot out of him, but because he failed to save and protect the people he came to care so much about.

"They did," Stone huffed through a large breath. "We still don't know much of what happened. The Elders remain in a state of shock while the rest of the organization is in chaos from confusion. Lucky for you, Blue Moon found and saved you from the rubble. Otherwise you might have lain there for days. Meanwhile, dozens of members are still missing in action."

"It's all my fault," Michael blurted, interrupting Stone's train of thought.

Shaking his head, Stone reassured Michael, "You can't blame yourself. We should have seen this coming, but Omega and his lackeys are cunning. They cleverly hid their plans from all of us, even our most intelligent members."

"Don't patronize me!" Michael shouted so loud that he woke the other three injured Trifecta agents lying next to him. "You and I both know that my dreams warned this is where I was headed. He needed me. All this time, I worked so hard to develop my powers—always trying to improve myself, thinking that I was going to make a difference in the world—but instead, I resurrected the greatest evil on the planet. All because I ignored what was right in front of me."

"It wasn't you who—" Stone began to say, but Michael cut him off.

"It was me. I unleashed the dark energy that brought Alex's body back to life. I helped Mr. Mental and Fireball escape. I deactivated Mastermind's control over Omega. I– I——" Michael knew what he wanted to say next but he was afraid to admit. Finally he released his true feeling. "I failed."

Stone said nothing, unable to even look into Michael's eyes, perhaps because he felt almost as guilty as his protégé. Michael wanted to say something, but no more words existed—none that could describe how he was feeling. Finally, after what felt like hours of painful contemplation, Stone broke the silence.

"Don't be so hard on yourself," he said. "There is more going on here than either of us realized, and more than we realize now."

"What do you mean?"

But before Stone could answer, Auto stepped through the thin cloth opening to the tent with Scylla standing on his right. "I'll take it from here," he instructed in a stern voice. "You are dismissed." Stone took one last concerned look at Michael, then gave Auto a distrustful scowl, and finally exited the tent.

"Your friends are waiting for you outside, but we have much to discuss before you can reunite with them," Auto explained to Michael. "Can you stand?"

Bending both of his knees, Michael internally analyzed the physical state of his whole body. "I actually feel stronger than ever. I know that must sound strange but—"

"Not at all," Auto interrupted. "We expected as much. Now change into this suit and follow us. We have much to discuss with you." Scylla tossed a black suit bag onto the foot of the cot before following Auto out through the opening in the tent. Michael squinted his eyes, wondering what Auto wanted to discuss.

Reaching down with his left hand, he grabbed the bag, which drew his attention to the missing wristband on his naked left forearm; this recalled to his mind the moment when Omega stole the weapon right off of his arm. He'd been too naive and foolish to realize that the wristband was manipulating him all of that time. Without question, he accepted the gift from Jacque, unaware that Omega was the one, true owner of the power that lay within. So many blunders led Michael to this point, but with a determined squint in his eyes, he vowed to avenge all of the damage that he caused.

After inhaling a deep breath of sorrow, Michael suited up the old-fashioned way. Inside the bag, he found a navy blue suit with a black collared shirt and dark blue tie. Within a few minutes, Michael finished dressing and met with Auto outside the tent. When he walked out, he couldn't believe his eyes. Somewhere around fifty blue, red and green tents faced the site where the great Hero City once stood. Like a shroud of evil, a cloud of dust still pervaded the area where dozens of magnificent buildings had collapsed.

"Follow us," Auto ordered, leading the way down the long aisle of tents. Hundreds of Trifecta members stood outside the other cloth canopies, and they all fixated their eyes on Michael. By now, they undoubtedly knew that Omega was the cause of their destruction, but Michael wondered if they also knew he was the one responsible for Omega's return.

Auto led Michael all the way to the end of the line of tents where the crumbled pieces of the city began. Hundreds of bricks and steel beams littered the city streets, so Auto and Scylla lifted their bodies off the ground into a hover mode. Michael followed their lead, flying a few feet behind them. As they moved closer to the center of the city, Michael noticed which building they were heading toward, one of the few that remained untouched. The Trifecta Headquarters didn't have a single brick out of place, and the stone steps outside the entrance appeared clean and smooth.

"Why are we here?" Michael asked, suspicious of the Elders' motives and their sullen mood. But what he hadn't asked himself until now was, *Why wasn't Professor Eliki with them?*

"There is information inside," Auto answered, pushing his way through the main entrance. From there on, he and Scylla had to labor to move some of the heavier doors before they could pass through. Apparently the city lost all power after the explosions, but the lights still worked, most likely from an emergency generator.

The Elders stopped somewhere deep within the building. Here Michael observed a tall, silver door with a large spindle lock on the left side like the handle to a bank vault.

After Scylla turned the handle counter-clockwise, he pushed open the heavy door. Inside the room, a single white light shone down on the body of Professor Eliki. She hung from two shackles that wrapped around her fists while her feet were cemented to the floor.

Eliki's head drooped toward the ground, but she lifted her eyes when she heard approaching footsteps. "So, the golden boy survived his encounter with Omega," she coughed. "Maybe I really did underestimate you."

Michael's eyes widened in shock, his mind confused as to why the Elders were detaining their fellow member. "Professor Eliki," he blurted. "Why do you have her strung up?"

"She was the leak in our organization," Scylla explained. "Without her help, Mastermind could never have stormed our city with such ease, and Omega would not have been resurrected." He stopped speaking to give Eliki a glare of disgust. "You treacherous harpy."

"No, I just played the best strategic option," Eliki retorted. "You've put your faith in the wrong place, and that is why your city and organization both lie in ruin. The Four Faces is on the rise, Omega is ten steps ahead of you, and your savior is doomed to fail."

Eliki had always been cold toward Michael, but now she wasn't holding anything back. Narrowing his eyebrows, Michael took a deep breath as he clenched his teeth. "Why are we here?" he asked of Auto.

"Eliki has something she wishes to discuss with you," Auto clarified. "We promised her 2 minutes alone with you in exchange for all of Mastermind's documents. So here he is."

She turned her head toward Auto with a ferocious sneer in her right cheek. "I believe our deal was that you and Scylla would leave me *alone* with him." Auto shot her a scrutinizing glare before agreeing to step out of the room. As he passed Michael, he placed his arm on the teen's shoulder and whispered into his ear, "Don't trust anything that she says."

Once Scylla and Auto exited, the door sealed shut behind Michael, leaving him alone with Eliki. After calming her demeanor, she turned to Michael to speak. "This is just the beginning," the fallen professor proclaimed. "You have no idea the plans that Omega has already laid out for this world. When you defeated Mastermind, you destroyed all hope for the human race." Michael exhaled a deep breath through his nose as his anger welled. He prepared to damn her and her words, but her next question caught his attention.

"Do you remember the test you took on your first day of my class, the one that analyzed your personality and potential in battle?" she inquired with a sneer in her left cheek. Although he wanted to, Michael didn't respond, possibly because he'd grown too infuriated to form a sentence, but more likely because he feared that Eliki might have shared these dangerous thoughts with the other two Elders. "Didn't you find it odd that I never revealed the results of that test?" Eliki paused for effect to let Michael's brain ponder this.

"It was because of your results," Eliki elaborated. "They showed me two possible statistical outcomes for the people of earth. Either Omega will destroy them—or you will. You can only give two mega-humans so many chances to destroy the planet before they will succeed. Mastermind's plan was the only chance to stop the two of you from completely annihilating our world. And now you've doomed us all."

Though Michael should have grown more enraged, instead his anger subsided, replaced by guilt. For deep down, he worried that she was right. Omega did tell him he would be the villain of this story. But still Michael fought these dark thoughts from his mind, holding hope that he could change the path Omega had sent him out on. He would have to be the master of his own destiny—not Omega.

"At this point, you have only one chance to alter your destiny," Eliki elaborated, a sincerity in her voice that gained Michael's close attention for the next few seconds. "Place your trust in Blue Moon. She is the one variable that can set his plan awry. Only she can liberate you from Omega's control. Here, take this." Using her tongue, Eliki reached deep into her mouth to unhook something stuck to the back of her jaw, and she spit out a small piece of plastic half the size of a tooth. "When you are ready, review the information in this data drive, and remember—Blue Moon is your only hope."

Michael bent down to pick up the data drive just as the door behind him opened again, allowing the Elders to enter and end Michael's conversation with Eliki. "Mr. Infiniti, you are dismissed," Auto instructed. "Head back to the tents where you may reunite with your friends."

"You're not coming with me?" Michael asked.

"No, we have more questions to ask of this traitor," Auto answered. Nodding his head, Michael exited the room and headed back toward the main entrance.

After leaving the Headquarters, Michael took a moment to survey the damage to Hero City with a more analytical eye. Lifting himself up in the air, he ascended 100 feet above the Headquarters, taking close notice of the buildings that Omega had spared. Hundreds of workers in green, blue, and red jumpsuits scurried up and down the streets like trained, robotic drone determined to remove the most prominent debris spread across the city.

Omega chose to completely demolish six specific buildings, a seemingly random act to others, but Michael now realized that Omega did nothing at random. After taking a mental picture of the city, memorizing the specific location of the six buildings, Michael lowered his body back down to the street where Archer, Allison and Sabrina stood waiting for him.

Before Michael could set his feet on the pavement, Allison and Sabrina rushed over to squeeze him with a tight bear hug. "Michael, I'm so happy you're okay," Allison cried in her loud, raspy voice. She kissed him on the cheek, which made his own cheeks blush.

"Yeah, when the explosions erupted in the city, we worried that the worst had happened to you," Archer added, revealing true concern for his best friend before reverting to his playful demeanor with a sarcastic joke. "We thought you were wound so tightly that you finally exploded."

Michael scrunched his nose as if he'd just bitten into a lemon before he responded, "Ha-ha, you are just too hilarious."

"Come on, you know I'm just kidding," Archer laughed. "So tell us what happened when you faced off against Omega."

Michael sighed. His encounter with his brother, the most powerful and evil villain of all time, was an experience he never wanted to look back on. But with Omega's rising power, Michael understood he would have to retell and analyze every moment. Still, he wasn't quite ready to start recounting the tale just yet, so he changed the subject.

"Another time," he exhaled, shaking his head. "I'm still pretty exhausted. Right now, I just want to rest and enjoy some time with my best friends." They each gave him an understanding smile right as the most soothing voice interrupted them.

"I hope that includes me," Molly called out from 20 feet behind Michael. He turned to face her, a beaming smile in his cheeks as his heart jumped two feet. After running over to Molly, he threw his arms around her. She reciprocated the hug, pulling his head close to her shoulder, allowing her stream of tears to run down his cheeks.

"I'm so glad to see that you are okay," she whispered to Michael, squeezing him so hard that he thought she might never let go.

"After Omega knocked me unconscious, I worried I would never see any of you again," Michael admitted, his face turning red as a raspberry. Molly stepped back and smiled while everyone else rushed over to join them. After Allison threw her left arm around Michael's waist, she and Sabrina pulled him back toward the city outskirts. They could relax for a moment in the temporary tents before returning to help with the reconstruction of Hero City.

Although Michael realized he would have to face great adversity in the coming days, he temporarily managed to push that to the back of his mind.

While he and his friends walked ahead, smiles all around, Molly waited behind for a moment. Placing her right hand to the communication link in her ear, she announced to the listener on the other side. "Don't worry, I'll keep a close eye on him. He will stay on course." And after making that single reassuring statement, she hovered through the air to catch up with Mr. Infiniti, whose powers were only beginning to accelerate.

Michael Fleming and Mr. Mental will return in Book Three, *The Trifecta: Acceleration*. To learn more about J.P. Brewner and his upcoming projects, visit his website jpbrewner.com or follow him on twitter @jp_brewner.

Thank you.